SHADE'S FIRST RULE

DIVINE APOSTASY BOOK 1

A. F. KAY

Shade's First Rule, Divine Apostasy Book 1 by A. F. Kay

afkauthor.com

Copyright © 2019 by A. F. Kay

Published by Black Pyramid Press, LLC

blackpyramidpress.com

Editing by coraljenrette.com/editing-services

Cover by coverquill.com

For Nicole, who never stopped believing.
Love you to the sea and back.

CHAPTER 1

*T*oday, Ruwen would finally die for the first time.

He stepped out of his home and into the predawn light, alone. Almost a year had passed since his parents had disappeared, but this morning, their absence was especially hard to ignore. Ascendancy was the biggest event of his life, and they should have been here.

His revival would take at least a week, and he wondered if they'd be back when he woke up. He knew better though and pushed the thoughts away. This day was too important to wallow in self-pity or false hope.

Not wanting to waste any more time, Ruwen strode down the packed stone road toward the city's center and Uru's Temple. The smell of baking bread made his mouth water and his stomach rumble, but he was too nervous to eat breakfast. If he puked during his ceremony, he didn't want to make a mess.

A cool breeze from the mountains west of town made Ruwen's skin prickle, and he rubbed his arms to warm them. He focused on the top right portion of his vision, just above his map, and read the temperature: forty-eight degrees. He thought about going back and getting a jacket, but he'd worn his best clothes, and the only coat that fit had frayed hems. Today he would rather look presentable than be comfortable.

He superimposed the map over his vision and placed a marker on the temple. The walk would take twenty minutes at this pace. He blinked the map away and veered to the opposite side of the street to avoid two laborers unloading wood from a wagon. They both had scarves around their necks, gloves on their hands, and long-sleeved shirts. It didn't seem cold enough for scarves, but maybe they'd worked through the chilly night.

The three of them were the only people on the street at this early hour, and the larger of the two Workers gave him a curious stare. The man's eyes looked too big, and Ruwen quickly glanced away. He didn't bother to bring up the man's Profile. Worker Profiles never had anything interesting in them. Their days were filled with mundane tasks, not spells or fighting or exciting discoveries.

Most people ended up as Workers, but not Ruwen. He'd been blessed with brains, and today his life would finally turn around. Today he would start gaining the skills he needed to find his parents and clear their name.

He tripped as the packed stone of the road transitioned into flagstone. He refocused his attention and saw the name Center Road hovering in the air. The road ran down the middle of town. Whoever had named the streets here in Deepwell had no imagination. He dismissed the name with a thought and turned left.

He couldn't wait to get rid of his student interface. Sixteen years with the same basic information and no way to customize what it showed him. Ascension would give him his Class-specific interface, which he could change to his heart's content. That alone was worth dying for.

He mumbled a quick prayer to Uru in case the goddess thought him ungrateful. The information and abilities she provided her people were truly blessings. He shook his head. Of all days, today was not the day to upset the protector of his town. The priests said she watched over all the townsfolk and knew their capabilities and strengths. She blessed them with their Class choices.

And he knew what Class he'd get. He had known as soon as his attributes settled down after the surge of puberty. Now that his body had stopped changing so much, he was ready for Ascendancy. Death, after today, would very rarely be permanent. Ruwen looked to make sure his path remained clear and then focused on the round icon in the upper left-hand part of his vision to bring up his Profile.

Name: Ruwen Starfield
Race: Human
Age: 16
Class: Not Ascended
Strength: 10
Stamina: 10
Dexterity: 10
Intelligence: 16
Wisdom: 10
Charisma: 12

He couldn't wait to see what his other stats were once he received his Class. Ruwen rubbed his hands together. He would make a terrible Fighter, but his natural intelligence made him a sure candidate for a Mage. School had come easily to him, and he had finished the required education three years early. His teachers had given Ruwen over to Tremine, the head librarian, who had let Ruwen spend his days reading.

A blinking arrow pulsed on his map and he turned right. The Temple of Uru came into view. The building had been made of granite from quarries in the nearby mountains. Bits of mica in the stone caused the temple to sparkle in the early morning light. Only three stories high, it didn't seem that majestic, but Ruwen knew the temple was constructed in a depression, and most of it remained hidden underground.

A Guardian stood at each of the four corners. They were identical oblong spheres like an egg had been stretched. Priests ceremoniously cleaned them every month, and the Guardians would gleam white for a few days until the blowing dirt colored them brown again. They were made from terium, the same metal the townspeople mined from the nearby mountains, and were nearly indestructible. The Guardians hovered a few feet off the ground and were completely still and silent.

The Guardians protected the area from attackers and had come to life twice in Ruwen's lifetime: once when a band of Fighters approached the town and refused to turn back, and once when some Keld tried to burrow into the city. Ruwen hadn't seen the battles, but the stories all agreed the attackers had been turned into ash. He had researched the Guardians in the library and had decided they were some sort of high-level golems made by a Grand Master Summoner.

Three adults and a teenager exited the temple, and Ruwen stopped when he recognized them. He looked for somewhere to hide, but there were no options in the middle of the street.

Ruwen stared, paralyzed, and his interface mistook his focus as a request for name and Class information.

The tallest adult had grey hair and wore a white robe with a blue circle stitched on the chest. Basic information appeared above his head:

Name: *High Priest Fusil*
Class: *Order*
Sub Class: *Priest*
Specialization: *Administration*
Class Rank: *Adept*

The other adult male, dressed in a fine grey robe with blue fringe read:

Name: *Luim Strongspell*
Class: *Mage*
Sub Class: *Elemental*
Specialization: *Cold*
Class Rank: *Acolyte*

The only woman wore a light blue dress with a grey vest. She had a ring on every finger, each with a small glass bulb. Even from here Ruwen could see the movement in the glass. He read her information:

Name: *Annul Strongspell*
Class: *Merchant*
Sub Class: *Crafter*
Specialization: *Glass*
Class Rank: *Journeyman*

And finally the smirking teenager, who stared directly at Ruwen. His tailored pants and shirt were dark grey, and he wore a blue scarf that hung loosely around his neck. Ruwen gasped as he read:

Name: *Slib Strongspell*
Class: *Mage*
Sub Class: *-----*
Specialization: *-----*
Class Rank: *Novice*

A Mage! How could that be? Slib was one of the dumbest kids he knew. Why would the goddess make him a Mage? It didn't make sense. Slib's family had a shop where they sold glass figurines with magically trapped ice storms inside them. It was a status symbol to own one of the Strongspell's figurines.

The two men shook hands and laughed while Annul looked pleased. Slib strode toward Ruwen, and he forced himself to stay put. Slib was shorter than Ruwen but had to weigh at least a hundred pounds more. Ruwen wished he could see Slib's attributes, but until he received his Class interface, all he knew was what he could see with his own eyes. It appeared to Ruwen like Slib must have at least a sixteen Constitution. His Strength had to be above average as well since he had felt Slib's punches on more than one occasion.

Slib's bullying had started when Ruwen was singled out for being smarter and then separated from the rest of the students. Slib wasn't the only one who had bullied Ruwen the past three years, but he was the worst.

"Hey, Rock Head," Slib said.

Rock Head? Even his insults were stupid. Ruwen didn't think Slib would hit him in front of adults, but there was no reason to risk it, so Ruwen kept his mouth shut. Slib didn't matter today. In a few minutes, Ruwen would be a Mage as well. Then he could put the bully in his place during their Mage training. That made Ruwen smile.

"What's so funny?" Slib asked.

Ruwen couldn't help himself. "Your future."

Slib took a quick step forward, but Ruwen stood his ground.

"Oh yeah? If you didn't notice I'm a Mage now, you traitor piece of trash," Slib said.

Ruwen frowned and tried to let the insult go. Slib wanted to get a reaction out of him, which had been a lot easier this past year with all the rumors surrounding his parents.

Ruwen leaned forward and whispered. "You probably have the Mana of a maggot. I'll be an Apprentice Rune Mage before you learn to light a candle."

So much for letting the insult go. Ruwen needed to work harder on keeping his mouth shut.

"You piece of —" Slib started.

"Slib!" Annul called.

Slib turned around.

"Let's go get you settled at the Mage Academy," Annul said.

"Coming, Mom," Slib said.

Slib turned back to him. "I'll find you later, Book Brain."

Was Book Brain even an insult? Again, he wondered how the goddess could have allowed this to happen. Slib gave him a toothy grin and then rejoined his parents. After a moment, the three of them walked away and disappeared behind the temple. The high priest looked at him and scowled.

"Come here, boy," High Priest Fusil said.

Ruwen didn't like the priest's tone or that he called him boy when the man could easily see his name. His stomach turned. Something wasn't right. Ruwen jogged to the man, gave a small bow, and crossed his arms in an x over his chest.

"May Uru's light shine on you," Ruwen said and then stood up straight.

The priest narrowed his eyes. "Have your parents contacted you?"

Ruwen took a step backward. He had expected the priest to return the blessing, not to bring up his parents. The priest didn't sound worried about them either. The tone was more accusatory as if Ruwen were hiding them.

"No, I haven't seen them for a year," Ruwen said.

The priest's expression made it clear he didn't believe Ruwen.

"Let's get this over with," Fusil said.

The priest turned and walked through the open door of the temple. Ruwen glanced at the Guardians and then followed, leaving the door open behind him. Inside, large shakers illuminated six statues, three along each wall. They faced the rear of the temple and the large statue of Uru that stood there. Oak benches lined each side of the room, creating a path down the center that led to an altar in front of Uru's statue.

The priest had already walked halfway down the aisle. Ruwen had read books on the Ascension, and this wasn't what they described. The priest should have taken Ruwen to each statue, explained how the Class benefited the community, and compared that with Ruwen's natural abilities. The statue of your future Class sometimes glowed when Uru decided your destiny. But the priest walked briskly past the six figures.

"Aren't you going to present me to Uru?" Ruwen asked.

The priest didn't stop. "No need. I know what to do with you."

Ruwen relaxed. The priest must have reviewed his school records and his attributes. Why waste time with this ceremony when the choice was obvious.

Ruwen took a moment to study the statues along the west wall. The first was a robed woman, her head thrown back, arms reaching into the sky, a flame in one hand and lightning in the other. Ruwen stood straight, pride filling him. In moments he would die and be revived as this Class, a Mage. He wouldn't be a simple Elemental Mage like Slib's dad. Ruwen wanted to be a Rune or maybe even a Chaos Mage.

The next statue crouched low, a bow in his left hand, his right reaching back for an arrow. Daggers rested on each hip. This was an Observer, the base Class for Shades, Marksman, and Scouts.

The last statue on this side was a bulky man with a pack on his back. His left hand held a pick and his right a handful of wheat. The statue represented the Worker, the most common Class by far. Their lives were filled with mundane tasks that were necessary but dreary.

Ruwen quickly looked to his right. For the Merchant, a man stood with a blacksmith hammer in one hand and a bag of coins in the other. This Class had two main branches, one for Crafters and one for those that made money trading and selling.

Next stood the Fighter, a woman with a long sword in her right hand and a short sword in her left. A shield was strapped to her back. She wore mail and had a determined look on her face. Both of Ruwen's parents had been Fighters.

The last statue was a robed man, his arms crossed over his chest in prayer, his head bowed. The Order Class contained Priests, Judges, and Healers.

Ruwen faced the back wall of the temple as Fusil disappeared through a door behind the altar. Ruwen hurried to follow but took a second to stare at the statue of Uru. The goddess had many forms but was usually depicted as a young woman with kind eyes. Ruwen crossed his arms in respect and then walked through the door.

He immediately began descending a circular granite staircase. Taking the stairs two at a time, he quickly reached the bottom. He followed the priest down the only hallway.

The hallway's floor, ceiling, and walls were made of oak planks, which ended in a doorway with rounded corners. Ruwen stepped into a grey room about twenty feet wide. Chairs lined the walls, and a single closed door was across the room. Since the priest had disappeared, Ruwen assumed he'd left through the far door. Should he follow him? Unsure, he sat on the nearest chair. This was the strangest room he had ever seen. Everything seemed to be made from the same metal, which Ruwen didn't recognize. What an incredible waste. Why would anyone do this? They could make hundreds of swords with the metal in this room. There were no paintings or tapestries on the walls, and the floor didn't have a single rug. It felt like he was floating in the middle of a thundercloud.

The cotton vest he'd worn made it hard to breathe. His growth spurt had made all his clothes too tight. He had tucked his pants into his leather boots to hide their short length. Soon he would be able to afford new clothes. Mages made even more than Merchants.

Instead of shakers, illumination came from a three-inch line that ran along the top of the wall, its glow providing an even light. The far door opened, and a brown-haired priest waved at him to approach. The priest must have had his settings on private since Ruwen couldn't read his name.

Ruwen's stomach turned with anxiety and excitement. It was finally time.

He entered the new room and stopped next to the brown-haired priest. High Priest Fusil and a priestess with short dark hair stood next to the Ascendancy Pool. The rest of the room was empty.

The brown-haired priest handed him a bag. "Strip and put everything in here."

"Take off everything?" Ruwen asked.

"Everything," the priest said.

Ruwen did as he was told and stared at the Ascendancy Pool. Well, it was more like a bathtub. In a minute, they would drown him in that tub. It was a necessary process so Uru could store his exact makeup and assign the Class he would have for the rest of his life. After this, the goddess would keep track of the changes in his body, memories, and experience. But it all had to start from a base template. That's what he would provide now. He took a deep breath and let it out slowly as the brown-haired priest took the bag with Ruwen's things.

The priestess waved Ruwen over and handed him a small cup. Ruwen had a hand over his crotch and one over the small red birthmark over his bellybutton. For a moment, he couldn't decide which would be more embarrassing to uncover. Modesty won, and he revealed his birthmark as he drank the contents. The drink smelled like vanilla but tasted like rotten pears.

He knew the liquid was for the priests' safety. The mind resisted dying, and without something to paralyze the body, it would struggle and fight against his impending death. The adults seemed almost bored, and Ruwen realized that while this was the most significant moment of his life, to them, it was just another day. Many people would go through this same process today.

The priestess grabbed his elbow and steered him toward the tub. "Please get in."

Ruwen studied the water, conscious of the fact that Slib had been in here recently. But the water looked crystal clear. Actually, he didn't even know if it was water. His hands over his crotch, he stepped into the tub. The liquid felt warm. His whole body felt warm. He wavered, and the priestess quickly steadied him.

"Lay on your back," she said.

Ruwen laid back, and the priestess supported him while the brown-haired priest folded out supports from inside the tub. The priestess withdrew her hands, and Ruwen remained floating. The world spun as the high priest came into view.

"You already performed the ceremony?" the priestess asked.

"Yes," the high priest said.

"Did Uru give him a sign?" the priestess asked.

The high priest looked down at Ruwen. "The Worker glowed brightly."

Ruwen tried to shout in protest, but the drink had already taken effect, and he couldn't make his mouth move.

The priestess looked down at him, and her eyes glazed over. She was probably accessing his attributes.

"That's surprising," she said.

"Who are we to know the mind of a goddess," the high priest said.

The priestess nodded and then she and the brown-haired priest disappeared from view. Ruwen tried to scream that the high priest hadn't tested him at all. That Ruwen was meant to be a Mage. How could he find his parents if he didn't have any power? But the medicine had numbed his body, making it impossible to argue or fight.

The high priest's face filled Ruwen's vision. "What your parents did was unforgivable. My son-in-law was in their party. He lost six months of experience, and his revival left him with a limp. You should have run off and joined your parents when you had the chance. I should throw you out of the city without a Class right now. Let you join the Unbound and live a life of misery. But this is better. You can spend the rest of your life using your grand intelligence to stack boxes and carry wood."

It didn't matter what Ruwen thought. Everyone believed his parents had killed their party while transporting a load of terium, worth a fortune, far from town a year ago. His parents' entire group had been reborn in the bowels of this very building. A larger group had been dispatched to recover the terium metal, but when they arrived at the old camp, the terium had disappeared. Since Ruwen's parents were the only ones who didn't die, everyone assumed they had killed their group, taken the terium shipment for themselves, and disappeared.

Ruwen had been abandoned and become an outcast on the same day.

He knew his parents would never do something like that. He didn't know what had happened, but he knew they were good people and not capable of what they were accused of. Murder, especially away from the city where all the experience and memories couldn't be channeled to Uru and would be lost, was grounds for execution.

All he wanted was the power to find his parents, understand what really had happened, and clear their name. Clear *his* name.

Instead, he was going to be a Worker.

For the first time in his life, he didn't want to Ascend. Dying now would seal his fate. He would spend the rest of his life as a powerless Worker, unable to accomplish any of the tasks he needed to perform.

"This is for the pain you caused my family," the high priest said.

The high priest's hands glowed as he began the spell that would assign Ruwen the Class of Worker.

Fusil pushed Ruwen's chest, forcing him into the liquid. He closed his eyes as his head submerged. Ruwen held his breath, even though it was useless. The drug had made him helpless. His mind screamed for air. Unable to resist any longer, he opened his mouth and exhaled for the last time.

His life was over.

CHAPTER 2

The darkness disappeared, and Ruwen stood on a cliff. Brown grass covered his boots, the wind pushed his shirt against his body, and a strange light blue sea crashed into rocks hundreds of feet below. Vertigo swamped Ruwen, and he rocked on his feet. A hand grabbed his arm and steadied him.

"Careful."

A young woman, her red hair in a braid that reached the middle of her back, let go of his arm and smiled up at him. Freckles sprinkled her nose and cheeks. She barely made it to his shoulders.

A tree, thirty-feet tall, stood a stone's throw behind the woman. The limbs were bare, the trunk twisted, and it leaned away from the ocean. The brown grass stretched to the horizon. He focused back on the young woman.

"Where are we?"

"Home," she said.

This was certainly not home. Stone Harbor, on the coast of the Frigid Sea, took two days to reach from Deepwell, and the sea was a much darker blue than this.

"I don't think so," Ruwen said.

The woman's smile faded as she looked back at the ocean.

"Am I dead?" he asked.

"Yes. No. You are in-between."

Ruwen remembered the high priest, his spell, and the Worker Class Ruwen would be when he returned. He thought of his lost parents and how he wouldn't have the power to find them now.

"It would be better to stay dead," Ruwen whispered.

The young woman didn't respond.

They stood in silence for a while. The sound of the waves crashing into the cliff face warred with the wind that howled around them. Ruwen's curiosity got the better of him.

"Who are you?" he asked.

The woman faced him. "You don't have time for that answer, but we might have enough for this question. What do you desire, Ruwen Starfield?"

That was an easy question. "I want to be a Mage. Rune or maybe Fire."

"Always Fire. Destruction and chaos. Your kind definitely has a type," she said in a sad voice.

A knot formed in Ruwen's stomach. Had he gone crazy? Was he talking to a creation of his mind? Is this what happened when a person died? Had he lost his sanity?

"What do you *want*?" she repeated.

Ruwen wanted a lot of things. Respect, safety, his parents back.

His throat tightened. The years of bullying had been hard, but not as hard as the uncertainty surrounding his parents.

"The truth," he whispered.

The woman nodded. "Do you know the strongest part of a tree?"

This was not the follow-up question he'd expected.

"The trunk?" he guessed.

The woman frowned, and Ruwen's heart beat faster. He snapped his fingers.

"The root," he said.

"Yes, the root is the foundation for the entire tree."

She paused and then said, "I have a final question."

He nodded, surer than ever that this woman was a figment of his dying mind.

She pointed to the water below. "Could you swim in a sea of lies if it brought you to the shore of truth?"

Ruwen pondered her question. Was she trying to trick him? Should he say no? That one should never lie. But he knew he would. If it helped him find his parents, he would lie. He would do much more than lie.

"Yes."

Her smile returned, and she took a step closer. Ruwen could smell cinnamon and roses. She placed her hands on his shoulders.

"I hope you're a good swimmer," she said.

Then, with impossible strength, she picked him up and threw him off the cliff. Ruwen screamed as he plummeted toward the ocean.

* * *

"HEY!" a voice said, followed quickly by, "Stop screaming!"

A moment later, his cheek started to burn. Someone shook him, and he realized he'd stopped falling. He closed his mouth and opened his eyes. He was on his back, a blanket over his naked body. The ceiling looked like the same grey metal he'd seen before. A blonde teenage girl looked down at him. She had brown eyes, and her features were distinct but not sharp. He hadn't expected to wake up to a pretty girl. The name Hamma floated above her head.

"Uru's crack, you scared me," Hamma said. "Who wakes up from their revival, screaming?"

Ruwen tried to talk, but his throat felt dry. He cleared it and tried again. "Sorry."

"Nobody does, that's who," Hamma said, ignoring Ruwen's apology.

Ruwen raised an arm to try and apologize again, but Hamma kept talking.

"And how did you materialize so fast? You're not on the priority list."

Ruwen didn't know what that meant, so he stayed quiet.

Hamma narrowed her eyes, but after a moment she shook her head. "I shouldn't have slapped you. Please don't tell Brother Yull."

Ruwen had no idea who Brother Yull was. "Okay."

He grimaced as pain throbbed through his head. It felt like someone had shredded his mind with ice crystals.

"The headache is from the new interface," Hamma said. "You shouldn't have that the next time you revive. I'm going to check the other revival baths. I'll be back in a little bit. You should start going through your displays. This first time always takes awhile. Oh, and welcome back."

Hamma disappeared, and her words brought back the moments before he was drowned and the high priest's decision for Ruwen's Class. His stomach twisted in misery. He closed his eyes, but it only made it worse. His interface had changed, and every part of it was pulsing a soft gold color.

He couldn't bear to look at his Profile, so he started with his map in the upper right-hand corner. As soon as he focused on it, the map filled his vision. Instead of just the town, which was all he'd had access to his whole life, the map included the surrounding area as well.

Ruwen pulled his focus back, and a larger area appeared. He could see the mountain range now, and small markers for mines. Large square areas surrounded the city, each with the name of the crop being grown there. He drew back again, and most of the markers disappeared. His town, Deepwell, was just a small house in the middle of the map. The capital, Stone Harbor, was visible to the east right next to the Frigid Sea.

A rough circle surrounded Deepwell, Stone Harbor, and the mountains. The area inside the shape was colored green. Uru's Blessing was superimposed on the colored area. He knew this was the area where his experience and memories could be transferred to Uru with a simple prayer.

He pulled back again a few times until the green circle was barely visible. From his studies, he knew the world was vast, but seeing it on his map made him feel tiny. There were a few other areas with green shapes. They must be the other locations where Uru was present, and he could transfer his current state.

The entire continent lay in front of his eyes. Most countries were named after their deity, and Ruwen could see over twenty capitals scattered over the map. The people ruled in Uru's lands, but Ruwen knew most countries had some sort of theocracy and a few had monarchies. Mountain ranges ran down the east and west coasts and the Sea of Tears, a vast inland sea, sat like a scar between them. The north was filled with forests and tundra, and the south eventually gave way to desert.

He closed the map with a thought and focused on the first of three golden squares that pulsed just below his map. He mentally touched the first one. A sound like a chime being struck filled his mind, and the quest text appeared.

Ting!
You have received the quest...
Work is its Own Reward
As a Worker, you are the hands of Uru. Travel to the Workers' Lodge and speak with Crew Chief Bliz to understand your options.

Reward: Clothes of the Novice Worker
Reward: 200 experience
Reward: 50 copper
Accept or Decline

Ruwen had avoided looking at his Profile because part of him hoped that the high priest had been playing some sort of joke. That he really was a Mage. But this quest proved his new reality. His life would be horrible. He accepted the quest and a yellow triangle appeared on his map. Probably the location of Crew Chief Bliz.

He selected the next glowing square, and new text appeared.

Ting!
You have received the quest...
If at First You Don't Succeed
As a Novice, your capabilities are unfamiliar. Travel with your fellow Novices and learn the strengths and weaknesses of your Class. Speak with Pit Boss Durn at the Workers' Lodge to begin.
Reward: Level 1 Worker Spell
Reward: Level 1 Worker Ability
Reward: 300 experience
Reward: 10 silver
Accept or Decline

Great, he could learn a spell for sweeping or for cleaning windows. Ruwen mentally punched *Accept*, and the quest disappeared. Two little triangles overlapped on his map now.

Ruwen selected the last glowing square, and the quest text appeared.

Ting!
You have received Uru's quest...

The Strongest Part of a Tree

Whether it is a tree, a building, or a nation, the foundation is critical for long term stability. The strongest foundations are hidden from sight. Goddess Uru has taken an interest in you and offered you a second Class.

Beware: *Friends and foes alike will resent this blessing and strive to permanently remove you from the world. Secrecy is your only safety.*

Beware: *This Class obligates you to perform quests for the Goddess Uru, failure of which will result in serious consequences.*

Beware: *The strength of this Class comes at a high cost.*

Reward: *Root Class (Hidden)*

Accept or Decline

Ruwen stared at the text. Had his dream been real? It must have been. The quest's name came right from his conversation with the young woman. Ruwen shivered. That meant the woman must have been Uru. Ruwen had thought only the Order Class could talk to the goddess. He focused on the three warnings. The last one bothered him the most. What was the high cost?

He knew there were other Classes than the six Uru provide her people. There were other gods and goddess, and each had their own Classes. Most were the same, however, and while Ruwen wasn't an expert, he didn't remember ever reading about one called Root. Probably some Class that made trees grow faster or some other useless ability. It didn't matter though. He already knew he'd accept it because there was a chance this Class might help him and offset the handicap of being a Worker.

Ruwen chose *Accept* and felt his entire body flush. Another quest icon immediately appeared below his map. This one, however, was a blue circle and not the previous gold square. He opened it.

Ting!
You have received Uru's quest...
The Search for Truth (Part 1)
Truth is hard to find, and it is rarely close to home. Find a way to leave Deepwell's protection area in the next 30 days to begin your search.
Reward: *Spell, Uru's Touch*
Reward: *750 experience*
Penalty: *Permanently lose 1 from every attribute*
Accept or Decline

Ruwen hesitated. Permanently losing a point in every attribute would be catastrophic for him. He was average in four of his attributes, and dropping from ten to nine in them would penalize him. And what was Uru's Touch? He'd never heard of that spell. Not that he knew all the spells, but if it was powerful, wouldn't he have read about it? But he had just accepted Uru's Hidden Class. Should he risk telling her no on the first quest she gave him? He slowly chose *Accept*.

No new quests appeared, so he moved down to the small figure in the bottom right of his vision and mentally touched it. The figure enlarged to fill his vision. There wasn't much to look at. Every slot on his body was empty, not surprising since he was naked, and the Inventory grid under the body was greyed out. He remembered that the basic outline would change as you specialized in your Class. He knew that Observers who specialized in a Sniper subclass would gain a quiver. The Worker's template wouldn't change regardless of the specialization. They didn't get anything interesting enough to warrant it. It didn't look like his Hidden Class gave him any extra slots.

He closed the Inventory page and focused on the bottom left corner of his vision until his log appeared. He scrolled to the top and compared the first timestamp to the current time and calculated he'd been awake less than ten minutes. He ignored the timestamps and just read the text.

Materialization Sequence: Begin...
Initial Revive: True
Queue Priority: Critical
Resource Utilization: 93.34%
Materialization Sequence: ...Complete
Total Elapsed Time: 327.17 seconds
Synchronization Gap: 3.46 seconds
Scanning...
Scanning Complete
Anomalies: True (Memory Substrate Contaminated)
Revival: Halted
Anomaly Alert Notification...
Notification Override
Anomalies => False
Revival: Restarted
Anomalies: False
Imprinting...
Imprinting Complete
Revival: Successful
You are being attacked!
50% defense reduction (Prone)
You have received a blow to the head
You have taken 5 damage
You are being attacked!
50% defense reduction (Prone)
You have received a blow to the head
Critical Strike!
You have taken 20 damage (5 base+(5*3)critical)
You have been stunned!
You have been healed for 32 Health! (Minor Heal)
Accessing Map...

Ruwen stopped reading the log and closed it. Had Uru been the one to override the anomaly? And his revival time didn't make any sense. The rich could afford to be revived faster, but he'd expected his to take over a week. Instead, it had taken just over five minutes.

And no wonder Hamma had felt bad. She had struck him. Twice! He noticed the 3.46 second gap between the last time his memories had been taken by Uru and the time of his death. Not a big deal since the memory was probably of water filling his lungs and his hatred of the high priest.

The three second time gap was nothing compared to the high priest's son-in-law, who had lost six months of experience and memories. That meant he had been gone from Deepwell a dangerous amount of time. Ruwen's parents had only been gone a month when the incident happened. What had the high priest's son-in-law been doing the previous five months before Ruwen's parents joined him?

"You fall asleep?" Hamma asked.

Ruwen opened his eyes to find the blonde priestess standing over him.

"Just dizzy from the concussion," he said.

Hamma gasped and her eyes glazed as she inspected him. A moment later she glared at him. "You don't have a concussion."

Ruwen smiled. "Not anymore. You're stronger than you look."

Ruwen inspected her. Her settings must have been public, because he received more information than he expected.

Name: *Hamma Blakrock*
Class: *Order*
Sub Class: -----
Specialization: -----
Class Rank: *Novice*
Level: *6*

Health: 120
Mana: 235
Energy: 240

Not being able to see her attributes was disappointing, but he knew in time when his Perception skill increased enough, they would be visible to him.

She gave a small laugh. "Who would have guessed I'd have to invest in Strength as a priest. But moving bodies around is heavy work."

Ruwen's cheeks burned again, but this time from embarrassment. He was naked under this blanket and if Hamma moved bodies...

"You look like an apple. Relax, I see naked people every day. I don't even notice anymore," she said.

That didn't make him feel any better.

"How are you feeling? Is the headache gone?" Hamma asked.

"Yes, it's more of dull ache now."

"How does your stomach feel?"

"Empty. And I'm kind of thirsty."

"Okay, if you don't puke in the next ten minutes, I'll give you some food and water. Then you'll be on your way. Are there people waiting for you up top? Parents or a girlfriend?"

Ruwen's cheeks went from hot to on fire.

Hamma laughed again, the sound light. "Oh, Ruwen, you are too easy."

Hamma left the room, and Ruwen shook his head. Girls always made him uncomfortable, and Hamma seemed to enjoy making it worse. He'd certainly never met a priestess like her before.

Staring at the ceiling, he decided he'd avoided his Profile long enough. With a sigh of resignation, he focused on the small tree icon in the upper left corner of his vision. Text overlaid the grey ceiling. A small upside-down triangle sat next to his name, and he selected it. The text expanded, providing detailed information on his stats. If he was going to face this, he wanted to see it all.

General
Name: *Ruwen Starfield*
Race: *Human*
Age: *16*
Class: *Worker*
Hidden Class: *Root*
Level: *1*
Class Rank: *Novice*
Deaths: *1*
Deity: *Goddess Uru*
Experience: *0/1000*

Pools
Health: *100/100 (Stamina*10)*
Mana: *160/160 (Intelligence*10)*
Energy: *200/200 (((Strength+Stamina+Dexterity)/3)*20)*

Attributes
Strength: *10*
Stamina: *10*
Dexterity: *10*
Intelligence: *16*
Wisdom: *10*
Charisma: *12*

Ratings
Knowledge: *35*
Armor Class: *0 (Armor+(Dexterity/10)+Shield)*
Encumbrance: *0 (Pounds)*
Max Encumbrance: *150 (Strength*15)*

Critical Chance %: 2.00% (1+(Dexterity/10))/100
Power Strike %: 2.00% (Strength/5)/100
Haste %: 2.00% (Dexterity/5)/100
Dodge %: 4.00% (2+(Dexterity/5)-(Encumbrance/100))/100
Persuasion %: 4.70% ((Charisma+Knowledge)/10)/100
Resilience %: 4.00% ((Wisdom+Stamina)/5))/100
Endurance %: 2.00% ((Strength+Stamina)/10)/100
Cleverness %: 37.60% (((Intelligence+Wisdom)/10)+Knowledge)/100
Perception %: 2.60% ((Dexterity+Intelligence)/10)/100

Resistances
Elemental Resistance %: 6.00% (2%+Resilience %)
Poison Resistance %: 6.00% (2%+Resilience %)
Acid Resistance %: 6.00% (2%+Resilience %)
Mind Resistance %: 6.00% (2%+Resilience %)
Order Resistance %: 6.00% (2%+Resilience %)
Chaos Resistance %: 2.00% (-2%+Resilience %)
Disease Resistance %: 6.00% (2%+Resilience %)
Light Resistance %: 6.00% (2%+Resilience %)
Dark Resistance %: 2.00% (-2%+Resilience %)

Regeneration
Health Regeneration per second: 0.20 (Base% (0.2)*Health)
Mana Regeneration per second: 0.40 (Base% (0.25)*Mana)
Energy Regeneration per second: 2.00 (Base% (1.0)*Energy)

There were three other tabs: Abilities, Spells, and Skills. But they were all empty. He returned to his Profile and studied it. What was this Hidden Class? It didn't seem to give him anything of value. His attributes were unchanged, and there were no spells or abilities associated with it. His hopes fell. Maybe this Hidden Class wasn't going to help him after all.

His Knowledge Rating seemed really high. Probably from all the time spent in the library. Especially this last year. It didn't seem to do much for him other than his Cleverness Rating. But who cared about being clever? Cleverness wasn't going to give him the power he needed to get his parents back.

Ruwen closed his Profile and stared at the grey ceiling. Grey, just like his future. This was the worst day of his life.

CHAPTER 3

*H*amma reentered the room. "You look miserable."

"I've had better days," said Ruwen.

"Really? People are usually a lot happier after being revived. Maybe it's because yours went so quick. Fastest I've ever seen. Not that I've been here as long as Brother Yull, but –"

Ruwen interrupted her. "What's normal?"

"It's rude to interrupt."

Ruwen's face flushed.

Hamma leaned down, and he smelled lavender. For a moment, Ruwen thought she was going to kiss him. His face felt so hot he hoped she didn't feel it. Hamma pulled something under his bed and then jerked his bed into a chair.

Hamma shook her head but didn't tease him about the color of his cheeks this time. Ruwen's blanket slid down his chest and pooled around his waist. He pulled it back up to cover the red birthmark over his bellybutton. The roughly circular-shaped birthmark was only the size of a fingernail, but its bright red appearance made it look like some sort of terrible tattoo, and it made him self-conscious. In fact, it seemed a little smaller.

Maybe Uru fixed blemishes where she could as you were being reformed.

His recovery room was narrow with a row of about thirty beds along one side. Ruwen sat in the first bed, closest to a half-closed door. The door had the same strange rounded corners as the other doors he'd seen here in the temple's basement.

"Okay, I need to verify you're in the correct body. Sometimes the templates get mixed up." Hamma's eyes glazed over, and she mumbled while she read what her interface showed her. "Yep, you look correct: 5 feet 2 inches tall, grey hair, pink eyes, buck teeth, no eyebrows –"

Ruwen leaned forward his heart thudding. He was 6 feet tall, had black hair, light blue eyes, and his teeth and eyebrows were fine. Oh, Uru help him, had they put him in the wrong body?

Ruwen held out his hands and shook them. "No, no, there must be a mistake. I –"

Hamma grinned and slapped his leg. "I'm kidding. It's impossible to get put in the wrong body."

"You were joking?" Ruwen asked as his heartbeat slowed.

"I'm surrounded by priests all day, and it gets pretty boring. I have to make my own entertainment."

Ruwen leaned back. "That's really mean."

"Or really funny, depending on your perspective. You should've seen your face."

Hamma disappeared into the other room and returned with a glass of water.

Ruwen drank the entire thing without taking a breath and handed the glass back.

"Thanks," he said.

Hamma nodded. "You are welcome, child of Uru," she said in a gentle voice. "May her light give you peace."

Ruwen stared, mouth open. Her voice and demeanor were the opposite of how she'd been acting.

29

Hamma stared at him with an innocent face and then laughed.

"That's how they expect us to talk," she said. "It's so stupid."

Ruwen could see more of her now. She wore a white robe with the blue circle marking her a priestess. She had the lean build of a runner.

"A week," she said.

"What?"

"Earlier you asked about normal revival times. You took just over five minutes. I didn't know that was possible. That little cow patty from this morning paid a lot of money to be on the priority list, and he still took three days to bake."

Ruwen knew who she meant.

"Bake?" he asked.

"Sorry," she deepened her voice to sound like a know-it-all teacher. "The proper term is revival. It consists of the assembly of a new body from base components, the imprinting of memories and abilities on that body, and a final check to make sure no anomalies are detected."

In her normal voice, she continued. "It's easier to just say baking. But Brother Yull hates that term. Not proper and all that."

Ruwen remembered the anomaly messages in his log. "What causes an anomaly?"

"Lots of stuff. The revival baths might not have all the resources they need, or something is wrong with the information Uru has, or –"

"What does memory substrate contaminated mean?"

Hamma put her hands on her hips.

"Sorry," he said.

She stared at him for a couple more seconds and then relaxed. "Well, that means there are already memories in the new body. Before the imprinting of the old memories. That error isn't possible because you're still in the revival bath. There isn't any way to make memories." She narrowed her eyes. "How do you know about that error? You shouldn't—"

"Sister Hamma!" a male voice shouted from the other room.

Hamma clenched her hands and whispered, "If one more person interrupts me today..." She turned to the half-open door and yelled back. "I'm in the recovery room Brother Yull."

"There is a new Worker in the queue, Ruwen Starfield. Fusil wants him paused," Brother Yull yelled.

Hamma's eyes grew wide, and she stared at Ruwen. She faced the door again.

"Why?" she yelled.

"It is not your place to question, Sister. Do as you're told," Brother Yull responded.

Hamma's hands clenched again. It made Ruwen angry that Fusil was still trying to hurt him. The high priest had already ruined his life. Why make things worse? Hamma turned and stared at him for a few seconds, but Ruwen couldn't read her expression.

"Sister?" Brother Yull yelled.

Hamma stood up straight and faced the door again. "Yes, Brother. I'll pause his revival bath...regardless of its current state." Hamma paused a moment and then shouted. "For how long?"

Brother Yull's voice was faint like he had already started to leave. "Until you're told differently, Sister."

Hamma stared at the door for a few seconds and then faced Ruwen. "Uru's armpits, I hate those guys."

Ruwen winced. It made him uncomfortable that a priestess talked like this.

"Whose bed did you pee in?" Hamma asked.

"I didn't do anything. Fusil never even presented me to Uru. He just marched me down to the tank and drowned me."

Hamma's eyes widened. "Fusil did your ceremony? He usually only does the rich and important ones."

"Well, he thinks my parents hurt his family and he –"

Ruwen stopped talking when Hamma snapped her fingers.

"Now I know why you sounded familiar. I had just started down here when Fusil's son-in-law came out of a revival tank. His foot hadn't formed right, and it gave him a limp. They discussed killing him again so his body could be built correctly, but he didn't want to lose any more attribute points. Plus, Fusil and his son-in-law were in a hurry to get back to where he'd died. Some sort of important cargo. Wow, I haven't thought about that day in a while. People were running around like crazy. All our revival baths were full. There were people in the queue that had to wait a week to revive. The only time that's happened. Must have been over thirty people. The whole party revived except for two. Both named Starfield."

Ruwen looked down. He couldn't escape his name or the automatic guilt everyone placed on him. It was quiet, and after a few seconds, he glanced back up. Hamma looked at him, but not in an accusatory way, more like curiosity.

"Now I understand the special attention," Hamma said.

"Fusil acts like I had something to do with it. Like I'm part of whatever happened."

Hamma looked lost in thought, but after a few seconds, Ruwen's curiosity got the best of him.

"Why didn't you tell Yull I was already out?"

"I'm tired of those sanctimonious, controlling, fart sniffers." Hamma paused a few moments. "On my Ascendancy Day, the Order statue glowed so brightly it hurt my eyes. For the life of me, I can't figure out why Uru put me here. The last Class I thought I'd get was Order. I'm not exactly a rule follower."

"Yeah, I get that."

"What's that supposed to mean?"

Ruwen held up his hands. "It means thanks. Those guys have it out for me for something I didn't do. For something I don't think my parents did. They've taken everything from me. It's good to get back at them in a small way."

Hamma relaxed and then smiled. "It does feel good."

Hamma reached behind Ruwen and brought out the sack with his clothes.

"Get dressed while I give you the speech. Then I'll sneak you out of here."

Ruwen waited for her to turn around, but she didn't.

"I've already seen everything you've got, Starfield. I'm the one that pulled you from the revival tank, remember?"

Once again, blood rushed to his face.

"Oh, that color just never gets old," Hamma said. "It's adorable how shy you are."

"Well, I don't spend a lot of time around people."

"You don't say."

"No really, I'm usually in the library…"

Ruwen let the sentence trail off when he realized she was being sarcastic. Hamma giggled and then turned around. Ruwen slid off the table and started to dress.

Tring!
You have discovered a blessing from Uru…
Name: *Cotton Underwear*
Armor Class: *0*
Quality: *Common*
Durability: *3 of 8*
Weight: *0.12 lbs.*
Effect: *Support.*
Description: *Not meant for protection.*

Ruwen closed the item notification and focused on the small star icon next to his log. A page appeared with his preferences, which must have reset when he revived. He changed the threshold for item notifications from Common to Uncommon.

He didn't need a description of his entire outfit. He began dressing again.

Hamma began her talk. "Okay, if you paid attention in school you know this is your only free revive. After this, you permanently lose a point from every attribute. Killing stuff or questing will get you more experience than crafting, but it's a lot more dangerous. Leveling up will get you four attribute points, but dying removes six. You do the math. If you suck, it won't be long until your attributes are below average, and you'll get debuffs. That's when the accidents start happening. Bad Dexterity and you trip and fall down some stairs. Dead. Bad Constitution and you get sick. Dead. Bad Strength –"

"I get it. Don't die. Especially at my current level where everything is already close to below average."

"Not *everything*," Hamma said.

Ruwen gasped.

"I can almost feel the heat hitting my back from your blush, Starfield," Hamma said. "I was talking about your Intelligence, you idiot. You really have a dirty mind. We're in a temple. Please try and purify your thoughts."

Ruwen heard the playfulness in her tone but couldn't tell if she was telling the truth. She really knew how to keep him off balance. Maybe he wasn't as smart as he thought. Or maybe Hamma was just that clever.

"I knew what you meant," Ruwen said weakly.

Hamma laughed. "Right, don't die. That is a good plan. My advice is to pick up a craft or a profession you like and level that way. Crafting experience will be slow since you aren't a Merchant Class, but it'll be safe. Where do you live?"

The last question caught him off guard. "South-side. By Aspen Park."

"Oh, nice area. Maybe I misjudged you. I usually don't like rich boys."

"We're not rich. Smallest house on the farthest edge. My

parents moved there for the schools. Wanted to give me a chance. They did a lot of adventuring to pay for it."

Ruwen hung his head. "And look what it got them," he said quietly. "They're gone, maybe in danger, and their son is a Worker. I'm a complete failure."

Hamma turned and brought Ruwen's head up with a finger. "Listen, dummy, life is what you make of it. Feeling sorry for yourself is a recipe for misery. You got screwed by the high priest. The only way he wins is if you're unhappy. So, don't let him win."

Ruwen swallowed hard and then nodded. Her brown eyes had flecks of gold, like tiny suns, and her intensity melted his sadness. His chest warmed, and he gave a small smile.

"Thanks. Yeah, I won't," Ruwen said.

"Now, make your Inspection private. We're trying to get you out of here unnoticed."

Ruwen opened his preferences and set Inspection to private. His name wouldn't appear over his head, and only basic information would be visible to inspection. A person would need a decent Perception skill to get information about him now.

Hamma frowned as she looked him up and down. "One second."

She strode through the half-open door and returned a minute later with a robe.

"Put this on," Hamma said.

Ruwen took the white robe and held it out in front of him. "Can't we get in trouble for this?

Hamma shrugged. "Maybe."

"Why are you helping me?"

"Because it will cause Yull and Fusil heartburn. That's enough for me."

"Maybe this will make it worse. I wonder if I should just go out the normal way."

Hamma held up two fingers. "Two things. One, you overthink. Two, why, after everything Fusil has done, would you want to give him a chance to do more?"

"You are very wise," Ruwen said.

Hamma's cheeks turned pink. "Thanks, it is my base attribute, after all."

They both laughed, and Ruwen pulled the robe over his head.

Shing!
You have learned a new skill!
Skill: *Disguise*
Level: *1*
Effect: *Anyone observing you has a 1% reduction to their Perception.*

His first skill! Despite the situation, he grinned and read the notification three times. This definitely wasn't what he expected his first skill to be, but it didn't matter. After sixteen years, his progress was finally being measured. He closed the notification and focused back on his surroundings.

Hamma peeked through the half-open door and then entered the next room. Ruwen followed and stepped into what must have been the revival room. Three rows of five rectangular tubs were spaced evenly in the room. He looked down at one as he passed and was shocked to see the lid was clear and a half-formed body lay in the bubbling yellow liquid. It looked like a dumpling in a chicken broth. He covered his mouth, thankful that his stomach was empty.

He looked away from the tank and found Hamma had almost made it to the door on the left wall. He strode toward her, eyes straight ahead and away from the tubs. It made him nauseous that not even an hour ago he'd been a dumpling. Hamma waited at the door.

"That is really gross," Ruwen said.

"I know, but you get used to it. Well, kind of. I still can't eat soup. And that isn't nearly as bad as the tub they put the dead ones in."

"Wait. I thought the priests performed some sort of ceremony and then, I don't know, vaporized the bodies."

"That would be really wasteful. All the base components to make a new body are there in a dead one. Recycle and reuse, my friend."

"What!"

Hamma covered his mouth with her hand, which smelled like cedar and ammonia. "Keep quiet, you moron. Are you trying to get caught?"

She quickly pulled her hand away as her cheeks turned pink.

Ruwen rubbed his arms. "I'm a bunch of dead people?"

"People are always made from other people and plants and animals and rocks and fish and minerals. The temple breaks all those things down and stores the resources. I thought you were smart."

"I am smart. School never gave us the details," Ruwen said, a bit defensively. "I just never realized how directly it all happened. I have this weird feeling like I'm not me anymore. That the real me is still dead in that tank upstairs, and I'm just a piece of soggy bread."

Hamma's face lost its anger. "Your body *is* just a piece of soggy bread. What makes you Ruwen is here," she said and touched his forehead.

Ruwen closed his eyes and tried to relax. A moment later, she flicked him between the eyes. He stepped back and rubbed the stinging away.

"So, quit being a baby and move your soggy butt," Hamma said, opening the door.

They walked down a short grey tunnel made of the same strange metal he had seen before. It ended at a ladder that rose through a hole in the ceiling.

Hamma pointed up. "I'll go first. Follow close behind. We're climbing through all five levels. If there are people on one of the floors, ignore them. Just keep climbing. Oh, and I'm wearing shorts, so don't think you're getting a free look."

Ruwen's eyes felt like they might burst from his head. He stepped back, shaking his hands. His mouth moved but didn't make any sounds.

Hamma winked and then started climbing. He took a few deep breaths and wiped his hands on the robe. He looked straight ahead and followed her. He thought he heard Hamma laugh.

It didn't take them long to climb the five levels. Ruwen heard voices on the last two levels but didn't stop or look around. When the ladder ended, he followed Hamma down a hallway, and a middle-aged priest walked toward them.

"Her Blessings, Sister," the priest said as he approached.

"Blessings, Brother," Hamma responded.

"Her Blessings, Brother," the priest said as he passed.

Ruwen looked at the floor. His heart beat so quickly he reached up and pushed on his chest. His throat felt dry, and his legs suddenly seemed to weigh a thousand pounds.

"Blessings," he croaked.

Ruwen paused, sure he had given himself away, and the priest would grab him. But the priest kept walking. Hamma grabbed his hand, pulling it from his chest, and dragged him forward. He heard a small gasp from her at the same moment a notification appeared in his vision.

Shing!
You have learned a new skill!
Skill: *Deception*
Level: *1*
Effect: *Increases your Persuasion by 1%.*

He closed the notification, happy to have gained another

skill so quickly. Hamma released his hand, and in moments they were up the stone stairs and out of the small building that covered the stairwell. Ruwen could see the back of the temple fifty feet away.

"Thank you," he said.

Her eyes were wide, and her skin seemed to glow in the sunlight. "I had fun. And I earned a couple of new skills."

"Me too. How do I return your robe?"

She waved her hand. "Keep it. It was one of Yull's."

He stood there, frustrated there were no pockets for him to stick his hands in. He shuffled his feet and looked down. He had enjoyed being around Hamma and wanted to see her again, but it felt like he had forgotten how to form words.

"Listen, I really did have fun. Have you heard of the Screaming Rabbit?" Hamma asked.

Ruwen shook his head.

"It's a tea shop on North-Side just west of the arena. I spend a lot of my free time there. Come by if you'd like to hang out."

Her eyes glazed over for a moment. She must have gotten a notification.

"Three new skills in a single morning. That, Mr. Starfield, is a good start. See you later."

Before he could say anything, she strode back to the small building over the stairs. He watched her for a few seconds wondering what skills she had gotten. Then he brought up his map, searched for the Screaming Rabbit, and labeled it. Then he zoomed back until the two gold quest triangles appeared. He marked them as his destination and started walking. As horrible as this day had been, it hadn't been a total loss.

CHAPTER 4

*R*uwen squinted as he walked east toward the rising sun. The temple sat in the center of the city, and so the walk to the Worker's Lodge wouldn't take too long. He had removed the robe once he'd cleared the temple grounds. Since he didn't have a Dimensional Bag yet, his Inventory wasn't accessible. He didn't want to chance upsetting Uru by throwing away her priest's robe, though, so he rolled it up and carried it under his arm. Getting swallowed by a sinkhole or being hit by a falling tree were probably accidents, but he figured it was better to be safe than sorry when it came to the gods.

The city had woken up, and there were far more people about than that morning. The crowds slowed his pace, but he didn't mind. He spent the time inspecting everyone around him and enjoying the new capabilities of his interface. Almost everyone was some type of low-level Worker. Ruwen saw a few Merchants and two Fighters wearing the city's Order Enforcement tabard. The dark blue tabard had a white circle in the middle with a white sword laying on top. No one gave him a second glance.

The smell of food filled the air, and his stomach rumbled.

But he didn't have any coins on him, so he ignored it as best he could. Ruwen noticed that some of the merchants he passed had a golden light surrounding them. He assumed these were people who would give him quests if he stopped and asked.

As he moved eastward, the buildings transitioned from stone to wood and the houses off the main street turned into multi-story apartments. The flagstones in the road here showed heavy use with many of the stones chipped and worn. People here moved with purpose, and Ruwen's pace sped up.

Ten minutes later, a large round building came into view. It sat in the middle of the road like a boulder in a stream, and the crowd flowed around it. Large white blocks made up the first thirty feet of the building, and planked oak created an arched roof. Hundreds of Workers milled around, most in small groups. Laughter and shouts came from everywhere, and Ruwen could feel the energy around him. For the first time, he started to see Workers higher than Novice. He weaved through the groups and entered the Lodge through the open double doors.

The noise, trapped by the roof, made the inside of the building incredibly loud. Ruwen had spent most of the last three years in the library, and the sound here felt like an assault on his ears. Men and women stood on stone blocks that were spaced evenly around the outer wall. There were large boards next to each with what looked like job postings. Workers clumped in front of the boards. Every person on a block glowed yellow and would provide him a quest if approached. How was he supposed to find his quest if everyone here already glowed?

At the center of the building, a square stone pillar rose, each side twenty feet long to support the ceiling. A closed iron-banded door stood at the bottom of the pillar. A line of tables created a barrier in front of the support, and a single man sat behind them, near the door. He had the same golden color as those along the walls, but his pulsed like a slow heartbeat.

Ruwen inspected him.

Name: *Crew Chief Bliz*
Class: *Worker*
Sub Class: *Collector*
Specialization: *Mining*
Class Rank: *Disciple*
Level: *51*
Health: *870*
Mana: *170*
Energy: *1,273*

Ruwen walked up, placed the rolled-up robe on the table, and crossed his arms over his chest. "Uru's blessings, Crew Chief Bliz. My name is Ruwen Starfield."

His growth spurt had put him just over six feet tall, but when the crew chief stood, Ruwen had to look up. The man's hair, a mixture of grey and black, had been cut short and stood up straight like the bristles of a brush. His skin appeared tanned by years in the sun. Bliz held out his arm, and Ruwen extended his as well. The crew chief grabbed his forearm just under his elbow, and Ruwen copied the gesture. The older man's grip was firm but not painful. Ruwen could see the bulges of powerful muscles under the man's shirt, and he knew this man could literally break him in two without a sweat.

"Well met, Ruwen Starfield," Bliz said.

Ruwen cleared his throat as the man let go of his arm. "Well met, Crew Chief Bliz."

"I only got the notification of your Class assignment this morning. I didn't expect you for another week."

Ruwen bit his lip. How did he explain his morning? His rapid revival would only cause more questions, but he didn't want to lie. He decided on a half-truth. "I think some of those priests don't like following the process."

Bliz laughed. "Isn't that the truth. Well, I'm glad you're here. I've been excited to meet you."

A notification appeared.

Ting!
You have completed the Quest – Work is its Own Reward.
You have received 200 experience.
You have received 50 copper.

"Do you have a Sub-Class in mind yet? It will help us with your gear and training if we know what your intentions are," Bliz said.

Ruwen had spent years planning his Sub-Class and Specialization path in the Mage tree, not the Worker one. He didn't even remember what options were available for Workers. He had never expected to be in this situation.

"Not really," Ruwen said.

"Uru never sends me the smart ones. How did you end up here?"

"Just lucky, I guess."

Bad luck, he thought.

Bliz narrowed his eyes. "You need to get better at hiding your emotions. You'll lose your paycheck playing Crowns and Swords."

Ruwen knew better than to play cards for money, but he kept his mouth shut. He obviously wasn't hiding his disappointment very well, and he didn't want to upset Bliz.

"You a reader?" Bliz asked. "Not the ones with pictures, mind you."

"Yeah, I read a lot."

"You like working with your hands? Do you carve or sculpt or anything like that?"

"No."

"Nobody likes to be told what to do, but could you tolerate some rich fart bossing you around if it paid well?"

Ruwen thought about Slib and him telling Ruwen to clean his room or muck out the stables or…

"Definitely not," Ruwen said.

"Do you mind being by yourself?"

"I usually prefer it."

"Last question. Have you ever thought about leaving Deepwell? Or is the risk too great?"

Ruwen thought about the quest Uru had given him. He needed to leave to find his parents, and Uru's quest would force him to go in the next thirty days.

"I want to leave," Ruwen said.

Bliz thumped the table with his hand. "Well, that settles it. You're a boy after my own heart. You sound like a Collector to me."

That triggered an old memory from a book about the basics of each Class.

"Aren't Collectors just farmworkers?" Ruwen asked and immediately regretted it.

But Bliz didn't seem offended. "That is what people think. As if all we do is harvest wheat or apples. But we can also mine or find herbs or skin animals."

"What are the other options?"

"We don't fall into many buckets. The only other two are Laborer and Household. You didn't sound like a good fit for either."

Collector didn't sound that great either, but it was still better than the alternatives.

"And I don't have to decide for sure until level ten?" he asked.

"Right, declaring your intent just helps us focus your gear, ability, and spell choices. Are you in?"

A notification appeared.

Ting!
You have received the quest...
Tools of the Trade
Crew Chief Bliz thinks you are special and has spent extra time to determine the Sub-Class you should focus on. Laborers are generalists and useful for any job. They can stack boxes, dig holes, or carry lumber. The Household Sub-Class is most comfortable working for a family or business and generally works inside. Collectors tend to work outside and away from the city. They can plant and sow crops, harvest fruit, or collect resources not found in the city. Crew Chief Bliz believes you would be happiest as a Collector. Declaring your Sub-Class intent will allow the Workers' Lodge to focus your training, spells, and abilities.
Reward: *Mentorship in your chosen path.*
Reward: *Specialized equipment*
Laborer or Household or Collector or Decline

Ruwen felt sick. All these choices were terrible. He selected *Collector,* and the notification disappeared.

"Good choice," Bliz said.

Bliz looked Ruwen up and down and then walked to the iron-bound door, opened it, and disappeared inside the central pillar.

Another notification appeared.

Ting!
You have received the quest...
Does This Taste Funny to You? (Part 1)
The world is a dangerous place, and a Collector seeks out valuable and unsafe resources in it. Without proper information, these items will kill you or be rendered useless. Successful Collectors know the most crucial resource is knowledge. Speak with Librarian Tremine.
Reward: *Collector Novice Manual (part 1)*
Reward: *200 experience*

Accept or Decline

Ruwen gasped, and his stomach turned. Tremine had been in charge of his schooling for the last three years and had acted as his father for the last one. The man had put so much time and effort into his education, Ruwen was terrified the librarian would be disappointed in him. None of this was Ruwen's fault, but what if Tremine didn't understand or believe that?

He reluctantly accepted the quest, and the notification disappeared. He knew he would eventually have to face his friend, but it was too painful to think about right now.

The door remained open, and Ruwen looked inside. Shelves lined the inside of the pillar, and they contained stacks of clothes and equipment. Bliz returned a minute later and made four piles: the first of clothes and a small bag, the second a pair of hard leather boots, the third an oddly shaped silver baton, and the fourth looked like a black wristband that matched the one Bliz wore.

"These are your Novice uniforms and quest money," Bliz said, pointing to the first pile.

All the clothes were the same dirty brown color. There were three pairs of pants, two pairs of shorts, three long-sleeved shirts, and three short-sleeved ones. Next to the clothes was a belt, a pair of gloves, and a wide-brimmed hat. A far cry from the Mage robes Ruwen had expected to wear today. He ran his hands over everything, but no new notifications appeared. They were all common.

"Now for your specialized gear. If you change your focus to a new Sub-Class, you'll need to trade these in for new items. Understand?"

Ruwen nodded.

Bliz moved to the next pile and handed Ruwen a pair of hard leather boots.

"Our high Constitution and Strength make us heavy. The

extra weight can cause problems. When you're planting seeds in freshly tilled soil, for instance."

Tring!
You have discovered a blessing from Uru...
Name: *Feather Boots of Grasping*
Armor Class: *5*
Quality: *Uncommon*
Durability: *20 of 20*
Weight: *4.00 lbs.*
Effect: *Reduces force of each step by 20%.*
Effect: *Increases friction against any surface by 10%.*
Restriction: *Worker*
Description: *Not as popular as Feather Boots of Massage but more durable.*

Ruwen stared at the boots in his hand. They were the first magical thing he had ever owned, and he smiled in spite of his mood.

Bliz took the boots and placed them back on the table. He moved to the next item and picked up the knobby cylinder. He pulled on one of the bumps and a pick head emerged that was much too large to fit in the baton. He folded it back into place and then unfolded a hammer. On and on it went: ax, crowbar, flint, spoon, fork, knife, a long thin rod, and finally a spade. Ruwen stood speechless, amazed by the magical baton.

"It attaches like this," Bliz said.

The man grabbed the belt from the clothes pile and pointed to squares that were spaced evenly around the leather. He brought the belt near a similar square on the top of the baton and Ruwen heard a click. Bliz briefly pulled on the baton and belt, but they remained together.

"You have to twist the baton to separate them," Bliz said and then rotated the baton up. It came away with another click.

"Workers have the least problems with storage so you might wonder why this would be useful," Bliz said. "Trust me when I tell you this will become the second most valuable thing you own."

He held out the rod, and Ruwen took it.

Tring!
You have discovered a blessing from Uru...
Name: *Baton of a Thousand Uses*
Damage: *1-4*
Quality: *Uncommon*
Durability: *50 of 50*
Weight: *12.00 lbs.*
Effect: *Produces useful tools.*
Restriction: *Worker*
Description: *Not quite a thousand. Cup not included.*

It had a nice weight to it, and Ruwen spent a minute pulling on different protrusions to see what would come out.

"Amazing," he said.

Bliz moved to the final pile. "This last item is different in that it has additional requirements."

Ruwen replaced the Baton and moved in front of the crew chief. Bliz held up his left arm, and Ruwen got a close look at the thin black wristband. He couldn't tell what it was made from, but it fit snugly around the big man's wrist. Bliz reached up with his right hand, grabbed the wristband, and pulled.

Bliz spread his arms wide, and the wristband stretched, leaving a blackness behind it. The blackness hid everything behind it. Bliz moved his arms back together, and the dark hole shrunk. The crew chief touched the wristband to the table, and it stuck there as he backed away, creating an opening large enough to crawl through. After a moment, he quickly walked back to the table and released the wristband. He turned so

Ruwen could see that the darkness only existed between the edges of the wristband. His wrist looked like it had been sliced in half, but there was no blood.

Ruwen had spent little time studying Workers. That's why he didn't know about their multi-tool. But Ruwen recognized this wristband now. He knew a song that featured one.

"It's the Death's Grip from the Farmer's Ballad," Ruwen said.

Bliz laughed and pressed the wristband closed. "Yes, it's in that song, but it's really called a Void Band."

"It kills him," Ruwen said. "Nine times!"

"It's just a song. And the farmer wasn't very bright."

Ruwen looked around at the hundreds of people in the Lodge. He couldn't see a single person with a Void Band. Bliz pulled a Dimensional Bag from his back pocket and placed it next to the Void Band. Ruwen's parents both had similar Dimensional Bags. Everyone had something like them.

Bliz pointed to the bag. "A Worker's Bag. Access to your personal storage. A ten by ten grid of containers you can fill with whatever fits through the bag's opening. 75% weight reduction. Only you can access it. If you lose the bag, you've lost your things, but the bag will appear on your map if you're near it. Nothing living will go in it. There is no danger in using it. It is only available to Workers. Non-Worker Bags are ten by five, have a smaller opening, and only have a 50% weight reduction. Otherwise, they are the same."

The Worker Bags had twice the storage of standard Dimensional Bags or Belts, and it explained why Workers had value. Ruwen had met a few Workers in the library, but he hadn't talked to them. The truth was he had assumed they were too dumb to waste time on. That made him feel even worse. What if those Workers had fallen prey to the same unfairness he had? Why had he judged people based on their Class?

Bliz snapped his fingers, and Ruwen refocused.

"Sorry, I was thinking about how I've never seen a Worker with anything but a bag."

"As I told you before, Uru doesn't send me many smart ones."

Ruwen didn't know about that. An Inventory Bag that could kill you didn't sound like an intelligent idea.

Bliz pointed to the band. "Access to your personal storage. A twenty-five by forty grid of containers you can fill with whatever fits through the band's opening, which you can make as wide and long as you wish. 100% weight reduction. Only you can access it. It is soulbound and will materialize like the rest of your body during your revival. Living things will go in the bag. There is significant danger in using it. Not every Worker gets this choice, as your base Intelligence must be quite high."

"Wait, I know how Inventory Bags work. They're portals to an alternate space. Everyone knows living things can't survive there," Ruwen said.

Bliz grabbed his band and pulled. When he let go, the band stayed open. He reached inside, his hand and wrist disappearing. When he removed his hand, he held a palm-sized wooden cube. One side of the cube was made of glass, and he could see a bright red snake. In a heartbeat, it had coiled its body and struck the glass. Ruwen jerked backward, his pulse doubling in an instant. He hated snakes.

Bliz put the cube back in the band, and Ruwen thought he saw the big man grimace.

"Why in Uru's name do you have a snake in there?" Ruwen asked.

"That snake is not from around here, and its venom has a lot of uses. It's too valuable to just leave laying around. Certain types of people will pay good money to keep things like that in a safe place. Pay enough that a man can stop adventuring and spend some time with his family."

"But how is that possible? That alone seems like a reason everyone would take the band."

"Well, now we've come to the cost. I've died five times since my Ascendancy Day."

Ruwen winced. That meant Bliz had permanently lost five points from every attribute. Thirty points, gone!

Bliz continued. "Three of those times were because of this Void Band. And when you die, anything living in your Inventory dies as well."

"But how can your Void Band kill you?"

"Opening it takes Energy. The bigger the opening, the more it needs. Anything living in your Inventory will constantly drain your Energy. If your Energy refresh can't keep up, you're dead. Plants you'll barely notice, this snake is a small strain, a dog would probably completely drain me in under a minute."

Ruwen looked at the three bars under his Profile icon.

Health: 100/100
Mana: 160/160
Energy: 200/200

Bliz still had the Void Band activated, and the opening looked about two hands wide and a hand long.

"How much is it taking to keep that open?" Ruwen asked.

"About three per second. You don't want to just stand around with it open, which is another reason you've probably never seen it."

"And the snake?"

"Four per second even when the bag is closed."

Ruwen had never cared about Energy since it wasn't valued much by Mages, but he still knew the calculation. Without anything to speed the refresh up, everyone regenerated 1% of their total a second. That meant he could handle a constant drain of two Energy per second. The opening Bliz had created would kill him in a few minutes. He began to see how dangerous the band could be.

"The problem is everyone thinks they're smarter than they are. How hard can it be to watch your bar and not let it get to zero?"

Ruwen had been thinking the same thing.

"The first time I died because a rancher paid me to move some bales of hay. I made an opening large enough to fit the bale. I planned to use my right hand to pull the hay into the hole. I lacked the strength, so I cast *Strong Back* to give me the extra strength I needed. You'll learn shortly how that spell channels energy to power it. Ten per second to be precise. I woke up in the basement of the temple."

Ruwen didn't know what to say. He didn't think he would make a mistake like that.

"And the other times?"

"I've made my point. Although I'll give you one more warning. If you ever get curious what is on the other side of that black hole, regardless of what the description says, don't stick your head in to look. It kills you, and the view isn't worth it. Whoever wrote that description is evil. Trading your life for five strange symbols is a poor trade. Hypothetically."

Ruwen's eyes widened, and then he laughed. Bliz pressed the band back against his wrist and chuckled.

"Let's keep that one between us," Bliz said.

Ruwen wiped his eyes and nodded.

"You mentioned you wanted to leave Deepwell. I'll just add that Workers with a band are highly prized as they can carry the entire group's supplies and cargo. You will never have a problem finding someone to travel with."

The Void Band gave him ten times the amount of storage as a standard Worker Bag. But the one-hundred slots in the Worker Bag seemed like it would be just fine. How much stuff did a person need to keep anyway? The fact that his Inventory could kill him seemed like an unnecessary risk to take just for storage. The ability to store living things was powerful, but also incredibly expensive, energy-wise. It would probably be a long time before he could even keep a caterpillar. The weight reduction was incredible, but again, if he didn't carry much, the 75% reduction of the Worker Bag would be sufficient.

He had to admit he was a bit absent-minded and he lost things a lot. But Dimensional Bags appeared on the map from miles away, which made them pretty easy to find. Dying outside the city was riskier as it might take a while to find your body. If someone looted your things before you returned, you might not recover your bag.

Death away from the city had consequences, and it tied back to what Bliz had just told him about adventuring. He needed to leave Deepwell if he wanted to find his parents and owning this band seemed like a sure ticket out. That alone made it worth having.

"I'll take the band," Ruwen said.

"I need to ask if you're sure. Once you put it on and bind it, the band will never come off."

"Never? What if I snag it on something and it breaks?"

"The fabric is part of another plane. It's indestructible."

"What if someone cuts my arm off?"

"That is an excellent question. As soon as the band isn't connected to your thoughts, the portal vanishes. The band becomes nothing more than decoration."

"And to get the portal back?"

"You have to die. Revival will create the connection again."

Ruwen spent another moment letting this new information sink in. It didn't change anything.

"I still want it."

"Wise choice."

Bliz picked up the band. "Usually you put it on the wrist of your non-dominant hand. That way, you can use your dominant hand to fetch things and shape the portal."

Ruwen had done everything with both hands until he was ambidextrous. It was a necessary skill for advanced spell casting, and he wanted to be ahead of the learning curve. Another vast amount of wasted time. It didn't matter, but he held up his left wrist, and Bliz slipped it over his hand. The band's material felt like a cross between leather and silk.

Tring!
You have discovered a blessing from Uru...
Name: *Void Band*
Quality: *Rare*
Durability: *Indestructible*
Weight: *0.12 lbs.*
Effect: *100% weight reduction.*
Effect: *Flexible opening.*
Effect: *Enhanced storage.*
Effect: *No type limitations.*
Restriction: *Worker*
Restriction: *Base (Level 1) Intelligence 15 or greater*
Restriction: *Energy-dependent*
Restriction: *Soulbound*
Description: *The view inside is worth dying for.*

Another smaller notification appeared over the item description. It had red borders and couldn't be minimized.

Warning!
The Void Band requires full integration to function.
Warning!
This binding cannot be undone.
Do you wish to permanently bind to the Void Band?
Yes or No

Ruwen chose *Yes*, and the notification disappeared. The Void Band grew cold against his wrist, and it shrunk to fit snugly against his skin. Ruwen rubbed the back of his head, trying to warm the area above his neck that had become intensely cold. After a moment, it passed.

"Open your Inventory," Bliz said.

Ruwen focused on the lower right corner, and his Inventory appeared. His shirt, pants, and boot slots were filled, their background white to signify the items were common. His left wrist slot had a small image of the Void Band, and the background was colored yellow. Just below the equipment display, his coin totals were displayed. The copper, silver, gold, platinum, and terium were all zero. Below the coins, the inventory grid began, and it was no longer greyed out.

"Now open your band and stow your uniforms and tool," Bliz said.

As soon as Ruwen touched the band with his right hand, it seemed to stick to his fingers. As he pulled his hand away, the Void Band came as well, trailing inky blackness. His whole body flushed as he felt it remove Energy from his body. Ruwen had made a portal about three feet long.

Bliz pushed back on Ruwen's hand, making the hole smaller until it was only the size of a hand.

"Look at your log," Bliz said.

Ruwen opened his log, which overlaid the open Inventory.

Void Band Active!
Void Band has consumed 1 Energy
Void Band has consumed 3 Energy
Void Band has consumed 7 Energy
Void Band has consumed 12 Energy
Void Band has consumed 1 Energy
Void Band has consumed 1 Energy

As he watched, the last message kept repeating. He closed his log.

"This is about a one," Bliz said. "Do you see how fast you can spend it?"

Ruwen nodded. Maybe this wasn't as easy as he'd thought.

"Letting go is just like the baton. Rotate your hand forty-five degrees, and it will detach," Bliz said.

Ruwen angled his hand upward, and it came away without a sound. The Void Band's edge stayed put. He moved his left hand around, and the hand-sized patch of blackness followed.

"Now add your things and watch your Inventory," Bliz said.

Ruwen retrieved the rolled-up priest's robe from the table and dropped it into the blackness. It disappeared without a sound and appeared in the first grid of his Inventory. He made the portal a little larger and then grabbed his uniforms and stuffed them through. The items that were identical stacked in the same grid and a small number indicated how many were there. He took the bag of coins and emptied it into the opening, and his coin display showed 50 copper. He dropped the empty coin purse in as well. In a few moments, Ruwen placed all his things in the Void Band and then closed it.

"Parts of your uniform probably stacked together. All your pants, for instance. That was only because they are identical right now. Once something changes, like their durability, they will require their own grid container," Bliz said.

Ruwen nodded and closed his Inventory.

"One last thing. You have options when it comes to removing items from your Inventory. For normal bags, you just stick your hand in and think about what you want. That works on your band, too. But, probably because a lot of what we carry is big and heavy, the band will allow things to drop out of it. This is very dangerous."

"What do you mean drop?"

Bliz opened his Void Band again and pointed to what Ruwen thought of as the bottom of the hole.

"There is no top or bottom. You put your things in the top, but you could have just as easily stuffed them up through the bottom here. What I'm saying is the band doesn't care which side you put things in or take things out. When you want to remove something, it will come out the side your free hand is on. That means you can do things like this..."

Bliz held his free hand under the open Void Band, and a small sack dropped out. Bliz caught the bag and then tossed it up into the underside of the band's black opening. The bag disappeared.

"I can see how that might be useful. But you said it was dangerous," Ruwen said.

"If you want to remove an item, your band will create an opening big enough for that item and bring it to the surface. If your free hand is under your Void Band, then gravity takes over, and it will fall out. There are two dangers in what I just described. First, you can crush yourself if you don't pay attention. Second, if your Energy is low, and you try and remove something too big, you could deplete all your Energy and kill yourself. Think about that. Depending on what is in your bag, you are a thought away from killing yourself."

Ruwen's mouth dropped open, and he held up his left arm. "That would have been good to know *before* I was soulbound to it!"

"That is why you need to have some brains to have one. Otherwise, people would kill themselves constantly. Yes, it is dangerous, but it is also powerful. The story I told you earlier with the rancher and the bales provides another example. Once I got those bales into my band, removing them was simple. I just walked to the new location, put my hand under the band, and thought about retrieving them. They fell right out into their new location."

"I'm a little scared now about a stray thought causing a thousand-pound rock or something to fall out of my Void Band and kill me. Maybe I'll only carry feathers."

Bliz laughed. "Don't worry about it. You have to put real mental effort into retrieving an item. A stray thought or an intense dream are not going to be enough. There are some other things you can do, but I'll wait to show you those. Better you get the basics down. Why don't you try it?"

Ruwen didn't feel much better, but it was too late now. He held his left arm just out from his chest and then placed his right hand under the band. He thought about what he had in his Inventory that was small. Probably the littlest thing was the copper he'd earned from Bliz's quest.

He concentrated on the copper in his bag. A coin dropped into his hand, immediately followed by the other forty-nine. Coins bounced off his hand and struck the ground. Bliz laughed, and Ruwen dropped to his knees and scrambled to gather his coins. He glanced around, but no one seemed to have noticed.

"Oh, by the way, if you have more than one in your bag you need to think about the quantity you want," Bliz said.

Ruwen looked up at the grinning crew chief. "Again, you are a little late with important details."

"Better a few coins than say a thousand horseshoes. That took longer than a few seconds to pick up. Hypothetically."

Ruwen stared up at Bliz. "Seriously?"

Bliz laughed again and then knelt down to help pick up the coins. "I'm not aware of any limit on stacks, and it's hard to remember how much of something you have unless you look first. It is better to just always think in quantities of one regardless of how many you think you have."

"That is good advice."

"Also, instead of showing off for a pretty girl and having stuff drop into your hand, you could just reach in and grab things like everyone else. Although picking up that many horse-shoes takes a lot of time. Time you could spend getting to know that pretty girl. Maybe even eventually marry her. Hypothetically."

"Really?" Ruwen asked.

Bliz winked and handed Ruwen his coins, which Ruwen dropped into his band. They both stood.

"You'll need your spells next. Big D is on the other side of this pillar," Bliz said.

"Thanks for all the stuff," Ruwen said.

"My pleasure, young man. Out of the tens of thousands of workers in Deepwell, fewer than 20 have a band. We meet at the Dizzy Judge every night for a drink after work. You're one of us now and are welcome there."

Bliz held out his arm, and Ruwen gripped it.

"We are the hands of Uru," Bliz said. "When she wants something done, she relies on us."

Ruwen nodded to acknowledge Bliz's earnestness. As unusual as the Void Band seemed to be, he still felt like the least smelly turd in a pile of poop.

CHAPTER 5

*R*uwen moved around the pillar to find Pit Boss Durn. Bliz had called the pit boss Big D, and he wondered how large a person had to be for Bliz to think they were big. As Ruwen walked, he opened his map and searched for the Dizzy Judge. Surprisingly, the bar was only a block away from the library, and he marked it. The taste of alcohol turned his stomach, but going to the bar would still be useful. He might learn some tricks listening to their conversations. He wavered on his feet, and he realized he hadn't eaten anything today. Now that he had some coins, he would fix that. But first, he needed to talk to Durn.

On the opposite side of the pillar, Ruwen found a woman sitting in a chair, her feet barely touching the ground. Her black hair had been pulled into a bun, but a few strands had escaped and been trapped behind the woman's ear. She pulsed with gold light. Big D was not big.

As if feeling his stare, Pit Boss Durn looked up and directly at him. Her gaze flicked down to his wrist, and her eyes widened. She turned to the man beside her and whispered. The man turned and sprinted away. Big D faced Ruwen again and waved at him to approach.

Ruwen glanced at the twenty people waiting their turn, but none of them seemed to care he was cutting the line. In fact, they all looked scared.

Ruwen inspected her.

Name: *Pit Boss Durn*
Class: *Worker*
Sub Class: *Laborer*
Specialization: *Planning*
Class Rank: *Adept*
Level: *73*
Health: *1,090*
Mana: *200*
Energy: *1,547*

He swallowed hard and shuffled forward. About four feet away, he stopped and crossed his arms over his chest. "Uru's blessings, Pit Boss Durn. My name is Ruwen Starfield."

"Uru's freckled butt, your timing is perfect," Durn said.

Ruwen dropped his arms as a notification appeared.

Ting!
You have completed the Quest – If at First You Don't Succeed.
You have received 300 experience.
You have received 10 silver.

Ruwen dismissed the notification and glanced up at Durn.

"That's weird. You should have leveled," Durn said.

He opened his Profile and glanced at his experience, but it showed 500/1000.

"From that noose around your wrist you've obviously done

Bliz's quest, and I just saw you complete mine. Did you not do the quest at the temple?"

She must have seen his look of confusion. "The quest the priests give you after they pull you from the tub. They tell you how important they are and that regular contributions to the temple are critical. That those resources are the only thing that guarantees your revival. The blackmail one."

He must have missed that quest when he was sneaking out.

"I haven't gotten around to that one yet," he said.

A notification appeared, and he closed it quickly.

Shing!
You have advanced a skill!
Skill: *Deception*
Level: *2*
Effect: *Increases your Persuasion by 2%.*

Durn narrowed her eyes. "Well, that puts a rock in your boot. You'll start a level behind all the others tomorrow. That isn't a good beginning, Ruwen Starfield. Do you like doing things the hard way?"

"I'm just trying to get through this. I really have no idea what I'm doing."

"That is the first honest thing you've said to me."

Durn laughed and jumped off her chair. She only came up to his chest, but he realized why they called her Big D. There was a force to her personality, like a wave that pushed on you. He found himself smiling back at her.

"Bliz will be unbearable now. You're the first band in over a decade, and he'll be strutting around here like a peacock for the next month. That bunch is already irritating, and the last thing we need is more of them."

"As I said, this morning has been kind of a mess."

She extended her arm, and he clasped it.

"Kidding aside, this is a good day for the Lodge. Well met, Ruwen Starfield."

"Well met…" he hesitated, not sure what to call her.

"Just call me Big D, everyone else does."

"Well met, Big D."

She let go of his arm. "In general, I think you Black Bands are a lazy lot. Running around the world instead of doing honest work. But I have to admit you're nice to have around when there are heavy things to carry."

"You mentioned something about starting a level behind."

"Right, you need to be back here tomorrow morning by seven bells. I'll take you and the rest of the tadpoles to the warehouse to gear up for your Class orientation. We'll meet up with the other Classes at the West Gate and then head out."

"The other Classes?"

"The city council thinks they can solve the Class strife issues by making all the new additions learn about each other for a week in the wilderness. Forced fun as we say."

Panic welled up in Ruwen. Many of his old classmates would have gone through Ascendancy lately. He knew Slib had. The last thing he wanted was a week stuck with them where there was nowhere to hide. The teasing and bullying would be unbearable.

"Do I have to go?" Ruwen asked.

"Workers are required to go. Usually, only a fraction of the other Classes have to go."

Ruwen relaxed. If only a few had to go, there was no way Slib would be one of them. His parents would make sure he was protected from such obligations. But, it didn't make sense that all Workers were forced to go.

"All the Workers? That isn't fair. If the Council's purpose is to reduce fighting between Classes, shouldn't everyone have to go?"

"Workers are required because someone has to carry all the

heavy items. But, even at 75% weight reduction, there are never enough Workers to carry all the other Classes' gear. Hiring a Worker bound to a Void Band with its extra storage and 100% weight reduction would cost more than the Council wants to pay. That's why not everyone has to go." Durn smiled. "Usually."

A sick feeling hit Ruwen. He looked down at the black band around his wrist.

Durn looked up at him, her blue eyes twinkling. "Yep, not only do you have to go, but you're the most important person on the trip. For the first time since this crazy idea was conceived, every single Ascendant from the last two months, from every Class, will have to go. It will be an epic disaster. The Council will be forced to address the Class strife with real solutions, not camping trips. All thanks to you and a choice you made a few minutes ago."

If Ruwen's stomach hadn't been empty, he would have vomited.

"This is going to be so much fun," Durn said.

Ruwen didn't share Durn's enthusiasm. Tomorrow, everyone impacted by this would know why, know his name, and then have an entire week in the wilderness to demonstrate how unhappy they were. Now, bullying was the least of his worries. People might actually harm him. After all, if the guy with all the supplies died, they would be forced to go back home.

"I can see you're not thrilled," Durn said. "You're probably smart enough to have worked out some of the dangers."

"There seem to be a few."

"I'll have a plan ready by tomorrow. I know kicking this hornet's nest puts you in danger. Your safety will be my highest priority. Do you believe me?"

Oddly, despite his anxiety, he did. He wished his Perception was high enough to see her Charisma.

"I'm doing this for the good of the Lodge. Workers are too

often treated like servants or slaves. All we want is to be treated like everyone else. It isn't personal."

"I feel like I'm being used. That I'm just a tool."

"You are, son. You're a hammer. Now stop thinking about it. You're going to be fine. Let's get your Spell and Ability chosen, and you can be on your way."

Ruwen followed Big D to the central pillar. She placed her right hand on the stone, and a narrow rectangle about two feet wide popped out. She pulled on the edge, and a drawer slid out. Flat square stones were placed in neat rows in the drawer. Designs had been etched into the face of each rock. His heart thumped.

These were runestones. He had seriously considered specializing in Rune magic. Had spent countless nights, in fact, agonizing over which specialization in the Mage tree he would take. He pushed those memories aside. Even if it wasn't what he'd imagined, he was about to actually get magic. He would finally be able to use his Mana.

"I don't know how much school you remember. I'm going to give you the same talk I give all the tadpoles."

Ruwen nodded, staring at all the stones in the drawer.

"Level one magic is simple so it can be trapped by Rune Mages in these stones. Normally you would be level two, and I would give you an extra two spells and another ability. Since you aren't, we can only give you one of each today."

His heart sank. The choices he'd made today kept coming back to hurt him. He had waited sixteen years for magic, and now he'd only get one spell.

"I understand," he said.

"Normally I don't care what you tadpoles choose. Eventually, it doesn't matter anyway. But for you, I'm making a suggestion. About half our spells are powered by channeling Energy, the other half consume Mana. Your band is going to make your

Energy a precious resource. I think you should avoid the Energy spells for now."

"That makes sense."

"There are some useful spells, but there is one that I believe is doubly appropriate for you. I have never given it to a tadpole on their first day because no one ever had the Mana pool for it. But you do. Secondly, its effect plays into your greatest need in the coming days: Energy Regeneration."

That all made sense but Ruwen wanted to look for himself. He loved studying spells; how much they cost, what they did, and when he would take them. On odd levels, you received one spell, while even levels gave you two.

"I believe you, Big D. Is there a list I could look at? I would like to at least know what is available for later."

"Of course."

She opened another drawer in the wall that was filled with papers. She withdrew an oversized sheet that had designs on it that matched the ones on the stones. A brief description appeared next to each spell. He ignored the Energy spells and didn't bother reading the casting times or Mana costs. He just skimmed their effects.

Spell: *Mend Tool*
Effect: *Temporarily bind broken objects together.*

Spell: *Sick Day*
Effect: *Increase all resistances by 10%.*

Spell: *Numb*
Effect: *Decrease sensations by 10%.*

Spell: *Second Wind*
Effect: *Reduce food, water, and sleep requirements by 10%.*

Spell: *Grasp Crate*
Effect: *Increase the roughness of your hands by 10%.*

Spell: *Campfire*
Effect: *Create small magical campfire. Adds 5% to Energy, Mana, and Health Regeneration to all within 3 yards.*

What a disappointing list. Big D probably wanted Ruwen to learn *Campfire*. It would definitely help him the most, and so he looked at its cost.

Cost: *150 Mana*
Type: *Area of Effect*
Casting Time: *5 seconds*
Recovery: *30 minutes*
Duration: *1 hour*

No wonder not many people took *Campfire*. You needed an Intelligence of fifteen to even have the Mana to cast it, and you could only do it once every thirty minutes.

He flipped the sheet over and scanned the available level one abilities. These didn't cost Mana or Energy and were active all the time or could be turned on and off with a thought. Most of them looked useless. But one jumped out at him immediately.

Ability: *Hey You*
Type: *Self*
Effect: *Understand basic commands and terms in any language.*

"Does *Hey You* work for written words as well?" Ruwen asked.

Big D tilted her head. "Yes, but that ability is more useful if you travel or come in contact with foreigners. Don't you think

Owl Eyes or *Sing* would benefit you more right now? The Haste percent increase on *Sing* is small, but it adds up."

Other abilities probably made more sense from a practical standpoint. But Ruwen had seen a glimmer of hope in this otherwise terrible day. High-level Mages had a spell to translate foreign texts, and he had intended to do that once he was a Mage. There was an entire section in the library with books in languages he couldn't read. This ability, if he kept leveling it up, might actually allow him to understand those books.

"That's true, but I think I'd like to start with *Hey You*," he said.

Big D shrugged. "I've already stuck my nose into your business more than is proper. If that is the first ability you want, then it is yours."

She returned the sheet to the drawer. Then she reached into the drawer with the runestones and withdrew two. She held up a stone with a red triangle etched on it.

"This is *Campfire*. In a few levels, the spells get more complicated, and you'll need to use books to study, but for now, press the runestone to your forehead. It should unlock the path to this spell in your mind. You know it has worked when the color fades from the stone. Simply picture this symbol in your mind and push it to the spot in the world you wish it to exist. It helps some people to trace the symbol in the air. If this were a normal spell, I'd have you try it right now. But the last thing we need in here is a fire. You should probably be near water until you master it. Sometimes the flames don't appear where you'd expect."

Ruwen took the smooth stone from her and ran his thumb over the etched red triangle reverently. He opened his band and carefully placed the stone into his inventory.

Big D held up the second stone. It had what looked like an ear in the middle of a blue circle.

"Abilities are different. You need to take this to any statue of the Goddess Uru and press it against your chest. Ask for her blessing, and your ability will be unlocked. The higher-level abilities require elaborate ceremonies. When the color fades, you know it worked."

Ruwen carefully took this stone as well. He traced the blue circle and then placed it in his Inventory. While things hadn't gone as he'd imagined, Ruwen was grateful for the help and power he'd just been given.

"Thank you, Big D. I've waited a long time for this day."

She placed a hand on his shoulder. "I can tell you're disappointed, son. But life has taught me a valuable lesson. Never confuse power with size or silence for acceptance. Everyone underestimates us, dismisses us, and takes us for granted. If you open your eyes, you will see the truth. Change is coming. In fact, it just arrived."

Big D laughed and then held out her arm and Ruwen took it.

"Well met, Ruwen Starfield. Uru has truly blessed the Lodge today."

Ruwen didn't know what Big D had planned and that worried him, but feeling wanted and validated made his chest warm. He had never given Workers a second thought and had in fact been one of the people Big D had just described. But now that he'd been forced into their world, he could see that he'd been wrong.

"Well met, Big D."

She let go of his arm. "See you back here tomorrow morning at seven. Please don't burn the city down tonight."

CHAPTER 6

*R*uwen exited the Lodge on the north side and
crossed the busy street that circled the large building. He glanced at the time above his map and was shocked to
see it was almost eleven. A headache had formed, and his
stomach felt like he'd swallowed an acrobat. Food carts lined the
road each with a painting or chalkboard detailing their options.
The city provided food for everyone, but it was basic and bland.
Street vendors were common all over the city, but Ruwen rarely
went. His family never had a lot of extra money.

He walked slowly, studying the pictures, his hand clutching
his stomach. He opened his band and reached into the top, not
wanting to risk the bottom until he had more practice. He
removed three coppers and bought a small loaf of bread with
pieces of grilled fish stuffed inside.

As he ate his sandwich, he caught sight of the two Workers
he'd seen that morning. He knew it was them because they both
still wore their scarves. Odd now that it was warmer. Maybe it
was some sort of fashion thing. They were probably finished
unloading the wood from this morning and here at the Lodge to

find more work. He felt terrible for dismissing them this morning. Now he was one of them.

With his stomach finally quiet, Ruwen walked toward the library. Later today, he would force himself to face Librarian Tremine and complete his quest, but first, he would go to the park next to the library. The park had a statue of Uru he could use to activate his ability runestone, and there was also a stream. He could learn and practice his *Campfire* spell there. The long cooldown of the spell made him sad. He could finally cast a spell and use his Mana, but the only spell he knew had a thirty-minute cooldown.

As Ruwen walked, he brought up his Profile again. The tabs for Abilities and Spells were still blank. He would fix that as soon as he reached the park. The Skills tab had both his *Disguise* level one and *Deception* level two listed. He grinned at seeing the two entries. He cycled back to his Profile and frowned. The description next to Hidden Class, Root, looked a little different. It almost appeared like it could be selected. He focused on it.

Another display appeared. One Ruwen had never seen in any of the books he'd studied. He strode to the side of the road where he could stand out of the flow of traffic. The display looked like a bigger version of the tree icon he used to access his Profile. The large tree filling his vision had six branches, each forked from the central trunk and ended in one of the six Class symbols.

The only branch with any color was the first one, a deep brown, and it ended in a pair of clasped hands. Hands were the symbol of the Worker. The next branch ended in a brain, and when he focused on it, the entire branch turned the black of the Mage Class. A notification appeared.

Root Class: Access to any Branch
Warning: Choice is permanently bound to current body!
Do you wish to assign Root to Mage?

Yes or No

Ruwen stared at the notification. He read it three more times and then carefully selected *No*. His mind had gone numb. Hope had surged in him, but he wanted to make sure he understood what was happening. He had never read or heard of anything like what he was seeing. He didn't want to make a mistake.

He focused on the next branch, which ended in a pair of eyes. The green color matched that of the Observer. Ruwen received the same notification as before. But this time he could assign Root to Observer.

The next branch turned white and ended in the Order Class's heart symbol. The Fighter's symbol was a body with a shield for a head and swords for arms, all the color blue. The last was a mouth, the Merchant Class, the whole branch red. Each gave him the same notification. Only the assignment of his Root Class differed.

It appeared to Ruwen like he could choose to be any Class. He closed his eyes and took ten deep breaths to try and calm himself. He had experienced so much disappointment today he wanted to be sure. He couldn't bear if this were some mistake because his revival happened too quickly or some other stupid reason.

He accessed his log and went back to when he had accepted the quest that had unlocked this class. He reread the log entries:

Ting!
You have received Uru's quest...
The Strongest Part of a Tree
Whether it is a tree, a building, or a nation, the foundation is critical for long term stability. The strongest foundations are hidden from sight. Goddess Uru has taken an interest in you and offered you a second Class.

Beware: *Friends and foes alike will resent this blessing and strive to permanently remove you from the world. Secrecy is your only safety.*
Beware: *This Class obligates you to perform quests for the Goddess Uru, failure of which will result in serious consequences.*
Beware: *The strength of this Class comes at a high cost.*
Reward: *Root Class (Hidden)*
Accept or Decline

He closed the log. What did "the strength of this Class comes at a high cost" mean exactly? And being permanently killed for having this seemed extreme. If he could choose a second Class, though, then there was only one choice. It is what he would've chosen this morning if he'd had the chance.

He studied the tree one last time and noticed what looked to be symbols below the roots. They were faint, and Ruwen couldn't make them out. He tried selecting them, but nothing happened.

Ruwen focused on the Mage branch, and the notification appeared. This time he chose *Yes*. He held still, not sure what to expect. His heart beat loudly in his ears, but nothing dramatic happened. The only thing that seemed to have changed was now two branches were colored: the brown of the Worker and the black of the Mage.

He closed the Root popup, and just his Profile remained open. The only thing that had changed here was his Hidden Class now had a descriptor: Root (Mage).

Did that mean he was a Mage now? If it did, how was he going to get spells? The quest text clearly warned against letting anyone know. He needed more information. Ruwen eased back into the flow of people and headed toward the park. But this time he set a brisk pace.

By the time he reached the park, he had figured out an initial plan. As much as he wanted to start researching what his Hidden Class meant, he needed to take care of a more practical problem. How was he going to learn Mage spells if he wasn't part of the Mage Guild? He hoped the library might have some resources, but he couldn't count on it. The only thing he could think of was learning by mimicking what he observed. Starting tomorrow, he would be around Mages, and he might be able to watch them practice.

The problem was he didn't know if that was viable. He decided not to use the runestones Big D had given him. Instead, he would try to learn them from just their symbols. If he could learn his Worker ones that way, he might be able to learn his Mage spells the same way. Assuming he really was a Mage.

The park was ringed by large maple trees, and he quickly moved toward the stream and the shrine that sat near it. The priests said Uru liked to be near water, so it made sense they had built it there. The statue of Uru was only a couple feet high and sat on a pedestal. The entire thing barely came to his shoulders. The statue had been carved from white marble, but the elements and dirt had turned it brown. It didn't look much like the young woman he'd seen during his Ascendancy.

He walked to the stream, opened his inventory, and removed the priest's robe. Kneeling on the bank, he soaked the robe in the stream and then returned to the statue. He spent the next few minutes cleaning the marble figure. It felt fitting to use the priest's robe. He repeated the process a few times until Uru gleamed white again. He rinsed the dirt out of the robe as best he could and then placed it back in his band.

There were no benches or chairs, so he just sat cross-legged on the ground. He had a lot of questions for the goddess, but they would have to wait until the next time he saw her. Which would probably be when he died again. Since that wouldn't be for a very long time, he hoped, he would just have to live with not knowing.

He heard the distant laughter of children as they played in the park, but pine trees grew in a large ring around the shrine, and he couldn't see them. The smell of the pines mingled with the heavy scent of the soil. A handful of aspen trees stood like guardians directly around the shrine, and three large maple trees scattered the afternoon light. A breeze rustled the maple branches above him, and for the first time that day, he relaxed. The gurgling stream behind him sounded like a lullaby. Yes, this had been a great place to put a shrine.

He opened his Void Band and removed the runestones. He quickly closed the band to preserve his Energy. Placing the stones on the ground in front of him, he leaned down and studied them.

Since he was sitting in front of Uru, he decided to try the ability runestone first. He picked up the small stone and ran his thumb over the blue circle and etched ear. His heartbeat raced. Sitting up straight, he lifted the runestone into the air like an offering to the statue.

"Thank you for this blessing, Uru. May the words I hear with it make me a better servant."

Then he closed his eyes and pictured himself pressing the stone to his chest while keeping it in his outstretched hands.

Nothing happened. He opened one eye and looked at the runestone. The blue circle around the etched ear remained. He rubbed the stone with his thumb as he thought about what to do. Maybe it was more than just pushing it against his chest but what that represented.

He closed his eyes again and pictured himself pressing the stone against his chest. But this time, he imagined the symbol floating off the runestone and entering his body.

His skin prickled and a sharp pain erupted in his mind. But in a heartbeat, it disappeared, and only the echo of the pain remained. He looked down at the runestone, and his shoulders slumped. The rune had kept its color. It hadn't worked.

A notification appeared.

Ping!
You have learned the Ability Hey You (Worker Level 1)
Ability: *Hey You*
Level: *1*
Class: *Worker*
Effect: *Understand basic commands and terms in any language.*
Type: *Self*

So, it looked like he had learned the ability. He hadn't actually used the runestone, so it made sense that it remained active. Here in the park, though, there was no way to test it for sure. He would probably have to go to the Trading Hall and see if he could find some foreigners. Or he could ask Tremine at the library. The head librarian knew a lot of languages. Ruwen wasn't looking forward to how disappointed Tremine would be that Ruwen had Ascended to a Worker.

His feeling mixed, he placed the runestone back on the ground and picked up the *Campfire* runestone. The red triangle seemed like a warning.

Lifting the stone toward Uru, he repeated his thanks.

"Thank you for this blessing, Uru. May those that warm themselves around this fire serve your needs."

It was much easier to be humble when you had just met the goddess responsible for your power.

Using his newfound process, he closed his eyes and imagined the red triangle floating off the stone and entering his forehead. He pictured his mind splitting open, the red triangle entering, and his mind closing around it like a trap.

His mind erupted in flames, the inside of his skull burning hot, but before he could even move, the sensation disappeared. Looking down at the runestone, he confirmed the lines of the triangle were still red. Just like the ability stone, it had kept its power. A new notification appeared.

Bing!
You have learned the Spell Campfire (Worker Level 1)
Spell: *Campfire*
Level: *1*
Class: *Worker*
Effect: *Create small magical campfire. Adds 5% to Energy, Mana, and Health Regeneration to all within 3 yards.*
Cost: *150 Mana*
Type: *Area of Effect*
Casting Time: *5 seconds*
Recovery: *30 minutes*
Duration: *1 hour*

He closed the notification. *Campfire* was something he could test.

He placed the two runestones back in his Inventory. The ground was covered in dead leaves, pine needles, and small branches. Standing up, he cleared a six-foot area with his foot in front of the statue. Big D had told him to be cautious, and he didn't want to burn the entire park down.

Stepping back, he stared at the brown circle he'd made. Big D had said to picture the symbol of *Campfire* in his mind and push it to where he wanted it to appear. Taking a deep breath, he filled his mind with the red triangle and then imagined it in the middle of the circle he'd cleared. But nothing happened.

He rubbed his temples. Had he done something wrong? Was he following Big D's directions? He thought back to what she'd said. She had also mentioned he might need to trace the symbol in the air until he got used to using it. He didn't want to do that, though. Mages that had to speak or use gestures to use their magic were considered inferior. Workers probably didn't care, but he didn't want to be a weak anything.

He tried visualizing the triangle again and pushing it into the world, but nothing happened. What was he missing? Pushing it into the world must be more than just visualizing it somewhere. Maybe he needed to add something from himself?

There were very few books on the actual process of using magic. It seemed that, for most people, it happened at an intuitive level, and they couldn't explain it. That had bothered him as he liked to understand how everything worked. He remembered reading a book that had talked about the connection between the caster and their magic. It had been a religious book and focused on how that connection symbolized our connection with Uru. It had been a terribly dry read, but maybe the author had given him a clue.

This time, when he visualized the triangle, he imagined a thread connecting back to his forehead. He felt part of himself flowing down the connection. After a few seconds, power surged down the link, leaving a cold emptiness in his mind. The red triangle on the ground flared brightly.

The number one hundred fifty flashed on his Mana bar, and it pulsed an angry red. A small square depicting a falling figure appeared under his status bars as the world spun, and he fell to the ground. A two briefly appeared over his Health bar. Ruwen focused on the small square and saw it was a Vertigo debuff, which caused his Dexterity, Intelligence, and Wisdom to be halved.

A notification filled his vision.

Critical Alert! Mana pool below 10%!

He dismissed it and opened his log.

You have cast Campfire (Worker Level 1) for 150 Mana.
Critical Alert! Mana pool below 10%!
You have Vertigo!
You have struck the ground!
You have taken 2 damage

Laying on the ground and too dizzy to move, he noticed a small square campfire at the top his vision and smiled at his first buff. Ruwen focused on the real fire he'd created, and his smile turned into a grin. He had finally cast a spell. He had used magic! His whole body felt warm, and he realized it wasn't only from his success. Every second, his log was being updated.

You have regained 8 Mana [(0.25% * 160) + (5% * 160)]
You have regained 5 Health [(0.20% * 100) + (5% * 100)]
You have regained 12 Energy [(1% * 200) + (5% * 200)]

He closed his log, opened his Preferences, and set all notifications to *Minimize*. At first, everything appearing in front of him had been interesting, but it had become distracting. Now, most prompts or notifications would stay out of his field of view until he wanted to read them.

The Vertigo debuff disappeared, and he pushed himself to a sitting position. It pleased him how fast his Mana bar refilled while sitting by the fire. The fire gave off warmth but no smoke, and he could faintly hear crackling and smell burning wood. He stretched out his hands, and the closer they got to the flames, the hotter it got. It really did look and feel like a real fire.

Magic was easy! He closed his eyes and mentally flipped through the hundreds of books he'd read on Mages. He found the book he wanted: a memoir of a Fire Mage that included his time at the Mage Academy. The first part of the book had lengthy descriptions of how lonely it was at the Mage Academy, but it had also contained drawings of the spells the Mage had learned. Ruwen found the sketch the Mage had made of his first spell: *Fireball*.

Not surprisingly, the symbol looked like a burning circle. Ruwen let the sketch fill his mind. His whole body flushed, and it felt like a thousand bees were stinging him at the same time.

Then it was gone. A dull yellow rectangle pulsed in the lower corner of his vision. He selected it, and a notification appeared.

Bing!
You have learned the Spell Fireball (Mage Level 1)

This was so easy! He was going to be the greatest Mage in history. He studied the details of the spell.

Spell: *Fireball*
Level: *1*
Class: *Mage*
Range: *Line of Sight*
Damage: *48-64*
Effect: *Creates a ball of flame at the caster's focus. Explodes on impact.*
Cost: *50 Mana*
Type: *Area of Effect (15 feet)*
Casting Time: *3 seconds*
Recovery: *5 seconds*

He closed the notification. Now there was only one thing left to do. Something he had waited his entire life for. His skin prickled with excitement.

Standing, Ruwen carefully looked around. There was no one in sight. He wiped his hands on his pants and stared at the stream. He must be really talented for all of this to come so easy. Maybe it was better he didn't go to the Academy. They would only slow his progress down. Hope blossomed inside him, and he grinned. Things were going to be just fine.

Ruwen stared at the stream about thirty feet away. He just had to try the *Fireball* spell. It would make him an official Mage. He focused on the middle of the stream, not wanting to risk lighting anything on fire. He pictured the flaming circle and pushed it toward the water. He felt the pull of Mana from his body, but it wasn't nearly as bad as when he'd cast *Campfire*.

A branch snapped to his left, and Ruwen glanced that way. A squirrel leaped from the broken limb to a nearby tree. Movement caught his attention, and Ruwen saw a man mostly hidden by the trunk of the maple tree. He was looking at the squirrel above him, and his neck was covered in a scarf. Ruwen gasped in recognition. It was one of the two men he'd seen that morning on his way to the temple and then again while he'd eaten his sandwich near the Lodge. Was he following Ruwen?

Ruwen opened his mouth to confront the man when the three second casting time of *Fireball* finished. In a whoosh, his Mana separated from him, and it felt like someone had flicked him on the forehead. Ruwen locked eyes with the scarfed man just as the *Fireball* materialized in front of him and exploded.

An immediate second explosion occurred, and a sphere of flame expanded outward, incinerating everything. The expanding heatwave threw Ruwen to the ground, and a one flashed on his Health bar. He stared at the inferno. How could his simple *Fireball* have done that?

"Uru help me, what have I done?" Ruwen whispered.

The trees, still dry from the winter, welcomed the flames. In moments, the entire area burned. Ruwen heard distant screams as others saw the fire. The man Ruwen had struck had collapsed to the ground, engulfed in flames. In fact, it seemed like the fire burned even hotter around the man. There was no saving him. But Ruwen needed to save himself.

He got up and ran.

CHAPTER 7

*R*uwen stood at the back of the crowd that had gathered to watch the Water Mages funnel the stream onto the last of the flames. There were at least ten Order Enforcement soldiers keeping onlookers away and searching the area for clues. They'd found the remains of the man he'd killed, and there had been what looked like an intense conversation. One of the soldiers had been sent off running. Had the man he'd murdered been important?

Guilt smothered him. He had killed a man. He needed to turn himself in. It had been an accident. They would understand. Except how would he explain the fire? He was a Worker, not a Mage. Uru said it was dangerous to let anyone know about his dual ability.

And how could a level one *Fireball* cause explosions like that? He opened his log and scanned the encounter.

You have cast Fireball (level 1)!
Fireball (level 1) has ignited for 54 damage (AoE).
You have fallen.
50% defense reduction (Prone).

You have taken 1 damage

There was no indication in his logs that he'd attacked the man. But he'd seen the burning body. Indecision whipped his thoughts back and forth. Why had he been so careless? The sound had surprised him, and he'd looked without thinking. Maybe that's what they taught at the Mage Academy. How to stay focused.

That man might have had a family. Ruwen's stomach twisted in pain. What was he going to do? And what about the man's friend? Had he been there as well? What if he'd seen what happened and told the Order Guild? It would go a lot harder on Ruwen if they had to come looking for him. He really should turn himself in. Even if the head priest didn't like him, it would be a judge who listened to his story. This was a public matter, not a spiritual one. Yes, he needed to figure out a plausible excuse for the fire and then turn himself in before it was too late.

The judge would want to know why the man was following Ruwen. He didn't have an explanation for that. In fact, it could have been a coincidence. This was the first time Ruwen had been to that park in months. For all he knew, this Worker might come to say a prayer to Uru every day after work. There was a good chance that Ruwen had not been followed at all. He had just killed an innocent man because of his own arrogance and ignorance. He grabbed his stomach as pain wracked him again.

Worse, even through the guilt, a question surfaced that Ruwen couldn't seem to ignore. If he had killed that man, why had he not gained any experience? The thought of benefiting from this horrible accident made him feel disgusted, but the logical part of him remained curious.

The guard who had run off returned with someone Ruwen recognized, his friend, Head Librarian Tremine. Why would they bring him here? Did they already know it was Ruwen? Had they already figured the whole thing out and summoned the man responsible for Ruwen's care this past year? But it might be because Tremine was a Master Mage, and they'd figured out it was a Mage spell that had caused it.

Ruwen dry heaved, and those around him quickly stepped away. He turned and ran for the only place he ever felt truly at peace: the library basement. He would hide there until he figured out what to do. Guilt and shame tormented him as he ran. He could imagine Tremine's disappointment. Ruwen had believed this would be the greatest day of his life, and instead, it had been horrible. It couldn't possibly get any worse.

The library's stone walls had windows spaced every twenty feet along the two-story structure, which allowed some natural light into the stacks. Tremine had told him librarians tended to hate windows because the sunlight destroyed ink. They were also easy to break, allowing elements and occasionally thieves easy access. Ruwen avoided the double doors at the entrance and circled around to the rear staff entrance. He entered the alley behind the library and walked into the shadows cast by the tall buildings that blocked most of the afternoon light.

Tremine had taken him in shortly after it was apparent his parents weren't coming back. Because of this, he'd been added to the building's access list and could pass through the safeguards around the doors and rooms of the library.

Ruwen grabbed the handle of the staff door when a man stepped into the alley at the far end of the library. The first thing Ruwen noticed was the scarf. The man's friend had come to confront Ruwen.

The man said something to him, but most of it sounded like clicks and barks. Ruwen only understood a few words. "You... kill...darkness...Naktos...pay now."

Then the man brought his hands up to his chest and in a sudden movement pushed them away from his body and at Ruwen.

Dark blue energy shot from the man's outstretched hands and toward Ruwen. The energy struck him, and his hand, still on the door handle, grew burning hot. He looked down to see the blue energy swirling over some sort of film that covered his body and the library. The sound of glass being scraped down a chalkboard coupled with a terrible keening erupted from the library, and the man with the scarf shouted again. What had protected Ruwen from the spell?

Ruwen turned and sprinted back the way he'd come. He needed to make it to the main road where there were people who could help him. Whoever this man was, he clearly wasn't the Worker Ruwen had assumed. That probably meant the man he'd killed wasn't either, and they'd both been following him.

Ruwen made it to the main road and dashed to the front of the library. A spinning white oval eight-feet high appeared on the steps of the library. The library continued to make the awful noise, and everyone nearby covered their ears.

Ruwen realized he'd probably survived before because he'd been touching the library when the man attacked. The magic had triggered the library's safeguards which had protected him as well. He should have run inside the library instead of out into the open.

Standing in the middle of the street, Ruwen started to turn toward the library entrance when the man with the scarf appeared at the opposite side of the library. He quickly found Ruwen and flicked his wrist like he was skipping a stone. Green energy shot toward Ruwen.

The spell had almost reached him when a black hole appeared in front of Ruwen. It swallowed the green light and then disappeared.

The man with the scarf turned toward the library steps and more blue energy shot from him. Ruwen turned as well and saw his friend Tremine exiting the spinning white disc. Another black hole appeared in front of Tremine, like a shield, and the blue energy disappeared.

Without looking at Ruwen, Tremine shouted. "To the library! Run!"

Ruwen couldn't move, though, as the magical battle took his full attention. He had never seen so much magic and the sight overloaded his brain. Tremine slashed the air with his hand, and black energy whipped toward the attacker. The man in the scarf crossed his arms as the spell struck him. The impact threw him backward, but the black energy dissipated, and the man quickly regained his feet. The attacker's scarf had been blown off, and Ruwen's mouth opened in shock.

On each side of the man's neck were gills. The man screamed again, slapped his hands above his head, and a shimmering bubble surrounded him. Tremine cursed and bolts of black energy shot toward the gilled man. Another sound began to drown out the awful noise from the library. A long deep sound, like the earth itself moaned, grew louder, and it seemed to vibrate every particle in Ruwen's body.

"Ruwen, move!" Tremine shouted.

Ruwen forced himself to start jogging toward the library. He'd made it halfway to the double doors when he froze again, still in the street. Flying across the rooftops directly toward them were two oblong Guardians from the Temple. He could see the other two high in the air above the town. The deep vibrating noise emanated from them, and in moments, they stopped over the gilled man.

Twin beams of multicolored light struck the man at the same time. The man was sixty feet away, but the heat from the Guardians' weapons made Ruwen turn away. When the Guardians stopped, he turned back, expecting to see charred remains. But while the stones below the man had vaporized, he was still alive. The man glanced around his bubble, smiled, and then jumped toward Ruwen.

The man flew at least thirty feet. Now that he was closer, much too close for Ruwen's liking, he could see the man's teeth were sharp.

More of the clicking came from the man's mouth, and again Ruwen understood parts of it. "Naktos…root…sleep…"

One of the Guardians smashed into the top of the bubble, breaking the granite flagstones and pushing the man and bubble a few inches into the ground. The man closed his eyes and waved his hands in the most complex movement Ruwen had ever seen. A dark blue portal opened next to the man, but he didn't step through it. One Guardian smashed into the top of the bubble again and then the other shot another beam of energy at the man. Ruwen's face burned, and the smell of his hair melting filled his nostrils. His Health bar dropped as a thirty-five flashed over it.

The man locked eyes with Ruwen and then shot his hand forward. A dark blue rope of energy shot from the man and struck Ruwen in the chest. Coldness wrapped him like a wet blanket. He felt a small tug, and then the energy wrapped around him tighter and he lurched forward to his knees.

Ruwen looked up as Tremine appeared next to him. Fist-sized black orbs spun in a circle over the Master Mage's head like a crown of death. Ruwen had never seen his friend use magic, and now he knew why. Tremine was a Void Mage. It was a type of magic so dangerous few tried to master it and most who tried killed themselves. Ruwen was in awe. This gilled man didn't stand a chance.

Tremine slashed at the cord of blue magic with a knife made of black energy. A high-pitched whine joined the assault on Ruwen's ears, but nothing else happened. Tremine cursed again and faced the attacker.

The Guardians continued their onslaught against the gilled man, and the bubble showed its first cracks. The gilled man pulled on the cord, and Ruwen felt for a moment like he'd separated from his body. He snapped back, and it felt like he'd been pinched over his entire body.

The gilled man shouted something that Ruwen's *Hey You* didn't understand. Tremine shouted back in the same strange clicking language.

Ruwen grinned in excitement. This gilled man was about to get a taste of real power. In a few moments, his bubble would break, and he would be destroyed by Tremine's Void magic. Ruwen would survive, and he'd gotten to see all this rare magic up close.

The gilled man tensed, preparing to tug on the cord of energy he had attached to Ruwen.

Tremine cursed again and then slammed the black void blade through Ruwen's eye and into his brain. The last thing Ruwen saw was the value sixty-five as it flashed over his empty Health bar. Then darkness took him.

CHAPTER 8

*R*uwen stood at the top of the now familiar cliff. The same brown grass covered his boots and waves from the light blue sea crashed into the rocks below. Remembering how far the fall was, he quickly stepped backward.

"Back so soon?" Uru asked.

He turned to find the goddess sitting cross-legged near the cliff. She had taken a few of the longer pieces of grass and was braiding them.

"He killed me," Ruwen said, still shocked.

He rubbed his left eye. The feeling of the blade entering his brain was still fresh in his thoughts and made him shiver.

"He killed me," Ruwen said again.

"You already said that."

"Why would he do that? He was my friend."

"Is. Is your friend. And more."

"Who were those guys?"

"They were not your friends."

He ran his hands through his hair.

"The Guardians came, and the gilled man survived it. How is that possible?" Ruwen asked.

"Naktos has powerful magic."

"Who is Naktos?"

"That is complicated. For now, just know Naktos is someone like me."

"A god? Wait, are you telling me a god wants me dead?"

"I did warn you that your Class is dangerous."

He sat down hard next to her. "Two hours into my new life and a god wants me dead. I'm doomed."

"I will admit they found you quickly." Uru paused for a few moments. "If it weren't for that squirrel, you would already be lost to me."

"You helped me at the park?"

"Of course not, that is against the rules. That squirrel didn't aid in your fight, it was just moving from one tree to another."

It might be true that the squirrel didn't help him fight, but if it hadn't broken that branch, he would've never seen that man. "There are rules?"

Uru gave him an intense look. "Without rules, the world is chaos."

"Well, it kind of feels like chaos right now."

"But whose fault was that? How could they possibly know you were my chosen?"

"Well, I –"

Uru interrupted him. "No need to answer now. Think about it. I had hoped to leave the Hand hidden. But events have outpaced us. I have already contacted two of them. They will help to keep you alive until you can manage on your own."

"The Hand?"

"Special people to aid my Champion. The most vulnerable time for a tree is when the roots are new and shallow. Such a tree is easily uprooted and destroyed. Naktos and others know this as well. The longer you live, the harder you will be to kill."

A thousand questions popped into his head. "I'm your Champion? Others? How many people want to kill me?"

Uru twisted the last braid of grass together, forming a circle. She leaned forward and placed it on his head. The grass felt itchy against his forehead, and the smell of sage made him want to sneeze.

"Assume everyone wants you dead except those marked as your Hand," Uru said.

"What mark? How will I recognize them? I don't have anyone left I can trust. My parents are gone, and the only man I trusted literally just killed me."

Uru stood, and Ruwen did as well. She stepped closer, reached up, and straightened the grass crown.

"It is good that you worry. Thinking is a strength of yours. Although you didn't do a lot of it today. You were careless. You have made things more difficult for yourself, and for me." She stepped closer, and he could feel the heat coming off her body. "However, you can't let your worry and fear paralyze you."

"But who can I trust?"

Uru grabbed his right hand and turned it palm upward. "Now that I have activated the Hand, you will gain a new passive ability. You alone will be able to see my mark on those I have chosen. Not all of them know yet, so care should be taken with those you identify."

Warmth spread from Uru's fingers, and Ruwen's palm grew hot. He looked down to see a tree tattooed on his palm. The same tree that stood behind Uru right now. The bare branches twisted by the harsh sea winds.

Uru closed Ruwen's hand into a fist. "I know you had dreams of your own. And if you live long enough, you can fulfill them. I suggest you don't immediately choose your second branch. Your life will depend on the choices you make."

He'd already chosen Mage as his second branch. Maybe she didn't know that.

"As much as I like hanging out with a goddess, I'm in no hurry to see you again."

Uru smiled, but it was sad. "That is the real danger now. That you will be kept from returning. You are fortunate Tremine recognized the danger. We both are."

He leaned back. "Wait, Tremine *killed* me!"

"Just in time, too," Uru said.

"But he –"

Uru reached up and touched his forehead, and the world went black.

* * *

RUWEN RECOGNIZED the cold metal of the bed against his naked body. A blanket covered him, and he knew if he opened his eyes, he would see the grey ceiling of the temple basement. Part of him wanted to open his eyes just to make sure they worked. He could still feel the sensation of the chaos magic sliding into his eye. But if someone was waiting for him, he didn't want to explain what had happened yet. He didn't even know how to explain it.

He thought about his conversation with Uru. Her Champion? What did that even mean? Was he expected to fight other Champions? Protect her land? He hadn't even known something like that existed. It was too much for him to process, so he pushed all those questions away. He would deal with it later. Instead, he opened his log.

Once again, he compared the first timestamp to his current time and calculated he'd been dead less than 10 minutes. He ignored the timestamps and just read the text.

Materialization Sequence: Begin...
Initial Revive: False
Queue Priority: Critical
Resource Utilization: 99.59%
Materialization Sequence: ...Complete

Total Elapsed Time: 299.73 seconds
Synchronization Gap: 5.89 seconds
Scanning...
Scanning Complete
Anomalies: True (Memory Substrate Contaminated)
Revival: Halted
Anomaly Alert Notification...
Notification Override
Anomalies => False
Revival: Restarted
Anomalies: False
Imprinting...
Imprinting Complete
Revival: Successful

Yellow notifications pulsed in the lower right of his vision, and he opened them. So many warnings appeared that they stacked on top of each other.

Warning!
Your Strength has Decreased. You are now Weak.

Warning!
Your Stamina has Decreased. You are now Sickly.

Warning!
Your Dexterity has Decreased. You are now Clumsy.

Warning!
Your Intelligence has Decreased.

Warning!
Your Wisdom has Decreased. You are now Foolish.

Warning!
Your Charisma has Decreased.

Warning!
Void Band unusable. Minimum Intelligence not met.

Ruwen accepted each notification to dismiss it. Dying permanently dropped each of his attributes by one. He had only been average in four of his six attributes, which meant this death was catastrophic. He needed to level as fast as possible to remove the penalties he'd just incurred.

His Inventory icon, the small outline of a person in the lower-right corner of his vision, had a red glow around the left wrist. Not having access to his Void Band could come in handy tomorrow morning. Big D couldn't drag him out into the wilderness if he couldn't use his band. But that shouldn't be possible, the minimum Intelligence on the Void Band had been fifteen. He should still be able to use it. Something was wrong.

He opened his Profile and scanned the top of it.

Name: Ruwen Starfield
Race: Human
Age: 16
Class: Worker
Hidden Class: Root
Level: 1
Class Rank: Novice
Deaths: 2
Deity: Goddess Uru

Experience: 500/1000

Strength: 09 (08)
Stamina: 09 (08)

Dexterity: 09 *(08)*
Intelligence: 15 *(14)*
Wisdom: 09 *(08)*
Charisma: 11 *(10)*

Knowledge: 35

Health: 80/80 *(Stamina*10)*
Mana: 140/140 *(Intelligence*10)*
Energy: 160/160 (((Strength+Stamina+Dexterity)/3)*20)

"What!" he said.

Why were there two columns for his attributes? The second one showed all his attributes had decreased by two, not one. Had there been some kind of mistake? How did something like this happen? Had he died again since Tremine had stabbed him? But his Profile verified he had only died twice today

"I knew you were awake," Hamma said.

The tabs for Abilities and Spells pulsed yellow but he ignored them for now. Instead, he closed his Profile and opened his eyes. Hamma stood over him.

"Can you read my attributes?" He asked. "Something is wrong."

"I agree something is wrong. You. This has got to be a record for the quickest death after Ascendency. I mean you just left here a –"

His whole body ached, and he felt like puking. He put his hand on her arm. "My attributes. What do you see?"

She pulled her arm away and put her hands on her hips. "I hate being interrupted."

Ruwen closed his eyes. He knew that. She had made a big deal about it earlier. Why didn't he just let her finish speaking? He noticed four red squares under his resource bars. His debuffs. One of which was Foolishness from his penalty to

95

Wisdom. He acted foolish enough on his own and didn't need a debuff making it worse. Did this mean his decisions would be even more terrible? Uru help him.

He opened his eyes again. "I'm sorry, Hamma. My day hasn't gone the best."

"Obviously. Did you want to see me again that badly? You could have just come to the tea shop."

In spite of his day, he smiled. "This seemed faster."

She smiled back. "Well, I guess I could check since you went to all this trouble."

Her eyes glazed for a second, and then she focused on him. "Everything is a nine except your Intelligence and Charisma. They are fifteen and eleven."

Hamma could only see the values in the first column. Even though all Ruwen's stats were based on the second column. Why were there hidden values? It reminded him of Uru and his Hidden Class and the dire warning it had come with. Something about the Class having a high cost. This must have been what Uru meant. Losing six points for every death was enough to keep most people away from danger and adventuring. You had to be desperate or crazy to take that risk. It appeared his Hidden Class cost him twice that penalty.

"Are you okay?" Hamma asked.

"Not really. I just need a minute."

"Okay. I actually have never heard of anyone being resurrected twice in a day. I didn't even think that was possible. Even our priority resurrections take a full day."

"Thanks."

Ruwen closed his eyes and opened his Profile. He selected the pulsing yellow Abilities tab and then read the new ability that had appeared.

Ability: *Uru's Sight*
Level: *1*

Class: Root
Effect: Identify members of Uru's Hand. Caution: These hands will help, but your destiny lies in your own.
Type: Self

This must be the ability Uru had mentioned. He would be able to see a tree mark on the palm of those she had picked to aid him.

He focused on the Spells tab and immediately knew something was wrong. His level one *Fireball* was still listed, but it was now greyed out. He switched to the Profile tab and then on the Root text next to his Class. The picture of the tree appeared, but only the Worker branch had color. The Mage branch was dark again like it had been before he'd chosen to be a caster. Uru had said something about not picking his second branch right away. And then he understood the balance between power and cost in his Hidden Class.

When he died, his Hidden Class reset. It looked like he'd retained what he'd learned, but it wasn't usable unless the proper branch was active. He could literally be whatever he wanted. He was only a death away from having completely different abilities and powers. But to do that, he had to die. And the cost was almost unimaginable: twelve attribute points.

Ruwen had the urge to select Mage again. The desperate need to live his dream was almost too much to bear. Especially if he was forced to pick something else, it meant he would need to die again to become a Mage. That alone almost made him do it. But he wondered if part of that desire was the result of his debuffs. Uru had explicitly told him to wait. There was no harm in waiting a little while. Maybe he would still end up picking the Mage branch.

Hamma and others could only see the standard penalty for death in his attributes. If they could see his true values it would raise questions, which would reveal that he was different. That meant he couldn't use his excuse with Big D tomorrow morning. To her, it would appear that he should be able to use his Void Band. Ruwen didn't want to know what would happen if everyone asked why his band didn't work. He needed to level and fix that issue first.

He opened his eyes.

"Big D said you guys have some sort of talk that gives 500 experience. Do you know what it is?" Ruwen asked.

Hamma's mouth twisted for a moment. "I'm not sure. I think they do that upstairs. Let me look."

Her eyes glazed over, and Ruwen took the opportunity to sit up. It was probably his imagination, but he felt weaker. He thought about the gilled man that had tried to kill him, and then about the man who had actually done it. Tremine had been a second father to him, why would he do that?

A notification pulsed, and he opened it.

Ting!
You have received the quest...
Fill the Tank
Uru wishes the best for her children, but her blessings have a cost. Talk with one of Uru's servants to gain an understanding of the costs associated with your death, and how you can ease the pain and resurrection time of your next death.
Reward: *The knowledge that Uru loves and cares for you.*
Reward: *500 experience*
Accept or Decline

"Did you get it?" Hamma asked.

He accepted the quest and nodded. "Great job. Can you help me complete it?"

"Hmmm, oh, here is the text. Okay, listen. Priests are really important. Most of us drink, and we need lots of money. Pay us, and we will hurry your resurrection along. Don't make regular contributions, and we will let you sit in a tub, or worse, stop you from even starting the revival process. We take raw materials or money. But we prefer money. You know, for the drinking. Also, we are really important, and you should respect us. Oh, Uru's Blessing, my child."

A minimized notification strobed for his attention.

Ting!
You have completed the Quest – Fill the Tank.
You have received 500 experience.
You have received the knowledge that Uru loves and cares for you.

He accepted the notification, and it disappeared.

"Is that what it really said?" Ruwen asked.

Hamma laughed. "Wow, dying really did make you dumber. I might have paraphrased it a little. And skipped some parts. I think the only part that had to be said was the Uru's blessing thing."

"Well, thank you."

"No problem. I didn't know I could do that."

Another notification pulsed in the bottom of his vision and he opened it.

Ding!
Uru's Blessings, Worker! You have reached level 2.
You have gained +1 to Strength!
You have gained +1 to Stamina!
You have 2 unassigned points.
Uru's Blessings, Root! You have reached level 2.
You have 2 unassigned points.
New Spells and Abilities are available to you. Choose wisely.

Ruwen slouched and rubbed his face. He'd hoped that being dual Classed would give him eight points to distribute or even more. Instead, he only got six and two of those were automatically assigned because of his Worker Class. This was terrible news. He had to level twice to just break even with the consequences of one death. It just didn't seem worth it.

Hamma put a finger under his chin and raised his head. "What's wrong?"

He didn't know how to respond to her. The answer was "everything." As she pulled her hand away, a dark mark on her palm caught his eye. He grabbed her hand and turned it upward. The tree from his conversation with Uru covered her palm.

"What's wrong?" she asked, looking from his face to her hand and back to his face.

Maybe she couldn't see it. Uru had warned him that not everyone chosen by her had been told. In fact, she said only two of the five had been activated.

Hamma pulled her hand away. "You're acting odd. I think getting baked that fast has left you a little undercooked."

He didn't want to risk the consequences of revealing what she was before Uru had a chance to talk to her. He had made enough mistakes today. But he'd been staring at her for a few seconds, so he said the first thing that came to mind.

"I'm sorry, your hand felt nice, and I wanted to hold it," Ruwen said.

Her cheeks turned red, and he opened his eyes wide. Why had he said that?

"Well, thanks, I guess," she said.

He felt his own cheeks growing warm.

"Sister Hamma!" Brother Yull yelled.

It sounded like he was far away.

"Yes, Brother Yull?" Hamma yelled back.

"Pause all the baths. We are evacuating. Something activated the Guardians, and we are sealing the temple. Do it now, Sister!" Brother Yull said.

"Right away!" Hamma turned back to me. "Do you know anything about that?"

Ruwen had revived so fast, details of the serious battle were only now reaching the temple. He put on his most innocent expression.

"I knew it," Hamma said. "Your corpse hasn't even arrived yet. We don't have any of your things."

He remembered the terrible heat from the Guardians' weapons and the magic the gilled man had used on him.

"Honestly, I'm not sure there's much left."

"Let's get you another one of Yull's robes and then get out of here," Hamma said. "You've got some explaining to do."

CHAPTER 9

*H*amma left to steal another robe from Yull, and Ruwen focused on the tree in the upper-left-hand part of his vision, opening his Profile. He wanted to get rid of his debuffs. Leveling as a Worker automatically placed points in Strength and Stamina, and with just one additional point in each, he could be rid of two debuffs. If he didn't put any extra points there, then the points already added were wasted since he'd still have the debuffs. Reluctantly, he placed another point in both Strength and Stamina.

He had two remaining points given to him from his Root class. If he wanted to avoid explaining to Big D why he couldn't use his Void Band, he needed to add at least one point to Intelligence. He didn't want to have that conversation, so he added the point.

That left a single point. Ruwen still had the Foolish and Clumsy debuffs. With one point he couldn't be rid of either, so it didn't seem like it was worth adding it there. He hated to admit it, but his Charisma falling two points made him self-conscious. Other than his jealous classmates and the unfair head priest, people tended to like him. He preferred being alone, but when he did venture out, he enjoyed the attention he got.

Now he was just average. Adding a point to Charisma would make him look better, but more importantly, it would help him get aid from people. And if there was ever a time he needed help, it was now. A god wanted him dead. Maybe more than one. Yes, Charisma seemed like the right choice.

As he went to add his final point, the debuffs caught his attention. He hated that the icons were so visible. Was he acting Foolish? He didn't think so, the point in Charisma would definitely help him, and he needed that. But he hesitated. Had he considered everything?

The only other place he could add a point would be his Intelligence. The thought of being dumber made him feel terrible, but in reality, at 15 points, he was already smarter than 99% of everyone he knew. It seemed senseless to add another point.

There were two things he was proud of, and they warred inside his mind: his looks and his smarts. He didn't know what to do. He had already added a point to Intelligence, so it seemed balanced to add one to Charisma as well. But he really couldn't afford to be vain here. He needed to do whatever would give him the best chance at surviving.

It worried him that the Foolish debuff might make him distribute his points wrong. Maybe he should talk to someone before confirming the changes. But who would that be? Even if he was more prone to make bad decisions, there were only three people he trusted to help him. But his parents were missing, and the other had just killed him. Was there another way?

He looked at the details on his Profile. How many things were affected by each attribute? Maybe that would help him decide.

Intelligence directly affected his Mana, Cleverness, and Perception. His Charisma only affected his Persuasion. And Persuasion already had a 2% boost from his Deception skill.

Looking at it this way, it was clear the last point should go into Intelligence.

Reluctantly, he placed his last point into Intelligence and confirmed his choices. Two of the debuffs disappeared along with his nausea and aching muscles. On his Inventory icon, the red around his left wrist disappeared as well. He could use his Void Band again. Now the only debuffs left were Clumsy and Foolish. He looked at the summary of his attributes, ignoring the attributes the public saw and focusing on his actual values.

Class: Worker
Hidden Class: Root
Level: 2
Class Rank: Novice
Deaths: 2
Deity: Goddess Uru

Experience: 0/3000

Strength: 10
Stamina: 10
Dexterity: 08
Intelligence: 16
Wisdom: 08
Charisma: 10

Knowledge: 35

Health: 100/100
Mana: 160/160
Energy: 187/187

What a disaster. He had leveled today, but because the Worker class automatically assigned half of his points, he would have to level another two times just to get back to where he'd started this morning.

"You don't look so good," Hamma said.

He wanted to scream. He knew he should have added that last point to Charisma. He would do that for sure the next time he leveled. Hopefully, Hamma would still be around. He kind of liked her.

He opened his eyes in time to see a robe flying at him. He reached up to snatch it from the air but missed, and it hit him in the face.

"Nice catch," Hamma said.

Damn his Clumsy debuff.

Now that he'd added points to Intelligence his Void Band worked again, and he could've removed a set of Worker clothes. Hamma had already gotten the robe, though, and he didn't want to seem ungrateful. Plus, he didn't want to draw attention to himself as he left, so he quickly put on the priest's robe, and the two of them took the same route they had taken that morning. Other priests joined them, but no one gave them a second look. In minutes, they were outside.

The four Guardians hovered high above the city, and they moved in a slow circle. He flinched when he saw them and thought about going back inside.

"What's wrong? You scared of some oversized eggs?" Hamma asked.

His pride overcame his fear, and he stood up straight. "No, of course not."

Hamma laughed and then strode forward onto Center Street. He followed her and glanced up at the Guardians. He could still feel his skin peeling from their terrible weapons, and he was scared they would swoop down and kill him as soon as they noticed him. In fact, the more he thought about that, the surer he became. He needed to get out of sight.

"Let's get a drink," he said.

Hamma looked at him and then up at the Guardians. "Okay, you have some explaining to do anyway."

The only people left on the street were rushing into buildings, obviously afraid to be caught up in whatever had awakened the Guardians. But every window had faces pressed against the glass looking up at the rotating eggs of death. He followed Hamma through a door.

He stopped to let his eyes adjust to the dim light. There were nearly twenty people in the room, but all of them were at the windows. The center of the room had tables arranged in neat rows. The wall across from him had booths, each with a curtain, and the wall on his right contained a large fireplace but no fire. A long bar took up most of the left wall, and a thin woman waved at them from behind the counter. Her name, Balla, appeared above her head when Ruwen focused on her. Along the top of the wall, in large cursive script, the name of the tavern had been painted.

"The Fainting Goat?" Ruwen asked.

"I come here when Yull gets on my nerves."

"Hamma! You're early today," Balla said.

"Hi, Balla. It's been one of those days," Hamma said.

Balla came out from around the bar, rubbing her hands on her clean apron. She had dark hair with just a hint of grey. Her brown eyes were friendly, and she held out her hand to Ruwen.

"I'm Balla. And you are?" Balla asked.

Ruwen still had his Profile set to private, so he had to tell Balla his name. "Ruwen," he said as he shook her hand.

"Welcome to my place. If you need anything, don't hesitate to ask." She turned to Hamma and pointed at the bar. "You want your usual seat?"

Hamma shook her head. "I think a booth would be better today."

Balla glanced at Ruwen and then smiled at Hamma. "Of course, dear."

Hamma's cheeks turned pink, and she waved her hands, but Balla had already moved toward a booth on the far wall. Balla wiped her apron across the booth's table, but it appeared spotless to Ruwen.

"Here you go. I'll be back with your mint tea. What would you like, young sir?" Balla asked.

Ruwen still felt sick from his resurrection and didn't feel like having anything.

"He'll have some water," Hamma said.

Balla nodded and closed the curtain. Enough light came over the top of the curtain that they could still see, but it grew considerably darker. Hamma grabbed a small jar at the end of the table and poured a shaker into her hands. She gave it a flick, and the shaker burst into light. She dropped it back into the jar and slid it to the wall.

"Okay, spill it. What happened?" Hamma asked.

"I was going to ask the exact same question," a female voice said.

Hamma and Ruwen jerked at the sudden appearance of the woman. She sat next to Hamma and directly across from Ruwen. The woman had a hood pulled over her head that hid her features.

"Who in the void are you?" Hamma asked.

The woman ignored Hamma and pointed at Ruwen. "Open your settings and set your Location to private."

"I already set it to private," Ruwen said.

"Your Profile is but not your Location," the woman said. "The settings are separated in your Ascendant interface. How do you think I found you? Anyone that knows your name can walk to your exact location. And I'm not the only one looking for you."

Ruwen opened his settings and found the woman was right. His Profile was private, but there was a new Location setting, and it was still set to public. He quickly set it to private. He needed to spend some time with his new interface as it had far more options than his student one had offered.

"We need to get moving. They'll be here soon if they aren't already," the woman said.

She set something on the table and flicked it. A spinning disk wandered across the table toward Ruwen. It slowed, wobbled, and then fell over in front of him. It was a ring.

"Put it on," the woman said.

The ring was made of gold and silver strands twisted around each other. He reached out for it.

"Most certainly do not put that on," Hamma said.

"I know, I just want to see what it is," Ruwen said.

"Touching it would be foolish," Hamma said.

She was probably right. But Ruwen's curiosity was too great, and he touched it. He immediately opened the minimized prompt and was excited to see the green text of a fine quality item.

Tring!
You have discovered a blessing from Uru...
Name: *Jaga Wedding Band*
Quality: *Fine*
Durability: *10 of 10*
Weight: *0.12 lbs.*
Effect (Passive): *Enhance Ambient Light by 15%.*
Effect (Active): *Reveal Heart's Desire.*
Restriction: *Active effect requires pair*
Description: *Darkness is no barrier to love. Trust ends with "I do."*

The woman held up her hand. She had a ring on every finger. A ring identical to the one on the table circled her thumb.

"You want to marry me?" Ruwen asked.

Hamma gasped and looked between the two rings.

"Sorry, I'm taken. Put the ring on," the woman said.

Ruwen picked up the ring but didn't put it on. He had never held a piece of magic jewelry before, and this one was of fine quality. It probably cost more than he'd make in a decade of being a Worker. If nothing else, he could sell it to help fund the search for his parents.

"Who. Are. You?" Hamma asked again.

The woman turned to Hamma. "You can call me Ky. How long have you been with him?"

"What? That is none of your business," Hamma said.

Ky tapped her fingers on the table and looked down at her waist. "I know she's not our problem." Ky paused for a few seconds as if listening to someone and then continued. "Carrying two bodies is not feasible. You know that."

"Who are you talking to?" Ruwen asked.

"Are you okay?" Hamma asked as she scooted away from the woman.

Ky reached up, rubbed her temples, and then threw her hood back. Her black hair didn't reach her shoulders, and her eyes were light brown. She was pretty in a severe way, and she looked like she'd missed a lot of meals.

She alternated looking between Ruwen and Hamma as she spoke. "Here's the deal. Usually, the only people who see my face are moments from death." Ky paused and then smiled. "That's true, they are moments from death."

"Is there someone else here?" Ruwen asked.

"Who are you talking to?" Hamma asked.

Ky focused back on Ruwen. "You have complicated my life. And I hate complications. We have got to move before they get here."

"We aren't going anywhere with you," Hamma said. "You're crazy."

"Before who gets here?" Ruwen asked.

Ky looked at Hamma. "Maybe. Probably." Then she looked at

Ruwen. "Do you think those Mages came here unprotected? They obviously wanted you alive. We don't know if that is still the case."

"What Mages?" Hamma asked.

Ky looked down again. "I know you were right. I'm trying to be nice." There was a pause. "Yes, I remember Ishingfal. This will be different."

Hamma faced Ky. "Seriously, that is really creeping me out. I know a healer that might be able to help you."

"I am beyond help, Sister," the woman said. "That is why I'm here. To pay for my sins." The woman tilted her head and narrowed her eyes. "Yes, two I think...no, it's too late for that."

Ruwen and Hamma looked at each other. Hamma's eyes were wide, and Ruwen's stomach turned with anxiety. This woman was clearly crazy.

Ky flicked her wrist twice, and a strip of cloth struck them each in the face. Where had they come from? Ruwen looked at the notification that had appeared.

Tring!
You have discovered a blessing from Uru...
Name: *Scarf of Freshness*
Quality: *Uncommon*
Durability: *5 of 5*
Weight: *0.12 lbs.*
Effect: *Filters out harmful substances.*
Description: *Harmful is subjective, but you'll look fabulous.*

"Wrap that around your nose and mouth," Ky said.

When neither Ruwen or Hamma moved, Ky spoke again. "I'm already tired of both of you. Do me a favor and don't use them. I only promised her I'd try."

Ky wrapped an identical cloth around her nose and mouth and then pulled her hood back over her head.

Ruwen's hands trembled as he wrapped the cloth around his face. After a moment, Hamma did the same. It would be better to humor the crazy woman until they could get away from her.

The curtain opened, and Balla stood there with their drinks on a tray. Before anyone could react, Ky thrust a dagger upward and under Balla's chin. Hamma screamed, and Ruwen gasped. As Balla collapsed, Ky grabbed the tray as it fell and held it in front of Ruwen's face. Two daggers struck the tray and the force of the impacts ripped the tray from Ky's grasp.

Ruwen's heart raced as he realized he'd almost died. Again.

"Get under the table," Ky hissed, as she threw a small ball into the room.

As the sphere arced through the air, he noticed all the people along the windows were on the ground, and a haze filled the room. The ball struck a table and exploded. In moments, the room had filled with smoke. Ky had already disappeared, so Ruwen and Hamma crawled under the table.

His right hand still held the ring Ky had given him, and he quickly slid the ring on his finger so he wouldn't lose it. His hands were wet from the drinks that had been on Balla's tray when Ky had killed her. The strong scent of mint filled the air from Hamma's tea. The scarf must know the smell wasn't harmful, or maybe it wasn't working. He hoped it protected him from whatever had put everyone else in the bar to sleep. At least he hoped they were asleep and not dead.

What was happening? Had Ky really just killed Balla and then casually blocked two daggers aimed at his face? The smoke rolled over them, but the air through the cloth remained clean.

Hamma reached out into the smoke.

"What are you doing?" Ruwen whispered.

"I might be able to save her. I have to try," Hamma sobbed.

He cursed himself for his selfishness and reached out as well. After a few moments, he caught hold of an arm and pulled.

Hamma grabbed on and pulled as well. Balla's body slid into view.

But it wasn't Balla. Ruwen gasped and jerked backward, slamming his head into the bottom of the table. His vision blurred, his Health bar pulsed red as the number twenty flashed, and another debuff appeared next to Clumsy and Foolish. He rubbed the back of his head and looked at his log to understand why his head hurt so bad.

You have received a blow to the head!
Critical Hit! (Clumsy Debuff)
You have taken 20 damage
You have lost 20% of your Health!
You are Dazed

"Are you okay?" Hamma asked.

Wincing at his new headache, he closed his log and watched his Health bar tick upward. The Dazed debuff disappeared, and his vision stabilized.

"I'm fine," Ruwen said.

"Why does Balla have gills on her neck?" Hamma asked.

"I'm not sure. But the thing that attacked me earlier had them as well."

Ky emerged from the smoke and Ruwen and Hamma both screamed.

"You're both hopeless. Are you trying to get killed?" Ky asked.

"You surprised us," Ruwen said.

Ky looked at Hamma. "Set everything to private. We don't want them getting your information, too," Ky said, and then faced Ruwen. "Where is the safest place you can think of?"

"Probably my house," Ruwen said.

Ky stared at him. "You mean the house that literally has your last name attached to it. Are you stupid?"

Ruwen bit his lip. Well, actually he did have some debuffs that weren't helping. But she didn't need to know about those.

Ky turned to Hamma. "What about you, Sister? Do you know somewhere safe?"

Hamma's cheeks turned pink. "I still live with my mom."

"Well that's out, the last thing I want is more baggage," Ky said.

"Hey, don't call my mom baggage. You have a lot of nerve to –" Hamma started.

Ky turned back to Ruwen. "We don't have much time."

He winced as Hamma hissed at Ky's interruption and quickly put a hand on Hamma's arm. "We wouldn't want to endanger your mom."

Hamma nodded.

Where could they go? He really only went to three places: school, home, and the library. The library! It even had some of its own protections. But Tremine would be there, and he had killed Ruwen. Ruwen needed answers about what was happening, though, and would have to face his mentor eventually. Yes, he would head for the library. Ky didn't need to know that, however.

"I appreciate you saving my life. But, to be honest, I don't understand what is happening, and you seem…" he searched for a word other than crazy, "distracted."

"Kid, you have no idea," Ky said. "But that isn't the worst of my problems."

"How about you leave us alone," Hamma said.

"On my dagger, I wish I could. But I can't. You know why?" Ky asked.

Ruwen shook his head.

Ky raised her hand and showed him the small tree on her palm. "Because my biggest problem is you."

CHAPTER 10

*K*y looked at the ceiling and spoke to her invisible friend again. "Yes, I heard it. I'm not deaf." She looked at Ruwen. "Naktos Shadow Blades work in pairs. I killed the apprentice, which means the master is still here. Your best chance of living is if I can kill that other assassin. When I leave, I want you to crawl behind the bar and wait. It's dangerous to stay where they last saw you."

Without waiting for an answer, Ky disappeared. Hamma and Ruwen looked at each other.

"Why did she show you her palm?" Hamma asked.

This wasn't the time to explain Uru's Hands, so he shrugged. "Who knows? She seems a bit off."

"She's crazy. We should run," Hamma said.

"But she saved my life."

Hamma bit her lip and looked down at the dead body. "What if the assassin kills Ky? We'll just be sitting here like two idiots."

"That's true."

Indecision warred in Ruwen's mind. Ky seemed to know what she was doing. Plus, she was one of Uru's Hands. Didn't she deserve some trust? The fact that she kept talking to an invisible person was disconcerting and meant she probably was crazy. But the truth was that if Ky failed, then that assassin was going to get him anyway. He didn't have the skills to protect himself.

"Let's go behind the bar for a few minutes. If she doesn't show up, we'll leave," Ruwen said.

"I thought you were smart," Hamma said in frustration as she crawled along the floor.

Ruwen followed her. His knees grew wet as he crawled through the blood and tea. He had ruined Yull's robe for sure. In less than a minute, they had made it behind the bar. The real Balla lay on the ground, and Hamma quickly crawled to her. Hamma touched Balla's neck and opened the woman's eyes one after the other.

Hamma turned to him. "She's alive. Just unconscious."

"All the people by the window are probably okay, too, then."

"Probably. I feel terrible for coming in here now. Balla is such a nice woman, and I brought this mess to her."

"Well, technically, I did."

Hamma narrowed her eyes, and he cursed himself for speaking.

"Yeah, that's true. This is your fault. What did you do?" she asked.

"Hey, I don't know what is going on!"

"Quiet down, you idiot."

He took a deep breath and then another. "Sorry. This has been the worst day of my life, and it isn't getting any better."

"What happened earlier? How did you end up back in the tub?"

It took him a moment to realize she meant the resurrection bath.

"Well, that is a little complicated."

"How complicated can it be?"

"Hey! It's been a busy morning."

"How did you die? Did you walk in front of a wagon? Choke on a muffin? Fall off a building? Jump in –"

He held up his hands to make her stop.

"Can we talk about this –"

There was a thud from upstairs, and the two of them stopped breathing as they listened for more sounds.

"If that was Ky…" Ruwen didn't finish the thought.

His hands shook with fear.

"We need to get out of here," Hamma said.

"She told us to stay."

"Listen, if that was the assassin, then great. Ky can catch up with us." Hamma swallowed hard. "If that was Ky, then we are sitting here easy prey. Either way, our best option is to run."

That seemed like excellent common sense. Ruwen really couldn't trust his own ideas because of the debuffs. His fear and anxiety swamped him, and he had the urge to get moving.

He stood and moved around the bar. Hamma followed, and they strode toward the door. Halfway there he heard a dull thud from his left. A figure emerged from the large fireplace.

The man's clothes were full of soot, and the gills on his neck opened and closed rapidly. He smiled at them and spoke with the same clicks as the Mage earlier. Again, Ruwen was able to understand pieces of it.

"Protector…trapped," the assassin said and pointed at the ceiling. "Now…die."

Hamma brought her left arm across her chest while her right arm pointed at the assassin. She chanted a quick prayer, and Ruwen's skin prickled. A moment later, there was a loud snap, and a beam of white light shot from Hamma's outstretched hand and directly at the assassin. Before it reached the man, the light struck an invisible barrier, and for a moment, a bubble appeared around him. The assassin laughed and walked toward them.

"That was the best I had," Hamma said.

Ruwen stepped in front of Hamma in case the man threw something.

"They want me, not you. I'll delay him while you run for help."

"I'm not leaving you!"

Ruwen knew he was useless and wouldn't delay the assassin much at all. But he wanted to make sure Hamma was safe.

"You aren't leaving me. You're getting me help. Now go!"

There was a pause, and then he heard Hamma backing away. The assassin's eyes watched her for a moment but then returned to Ruwen. Good, he'd been right. They only wanted him.

Ruwen had nothing to fight with. The only offensive spell he had was *Fireball*, but he no longer had access to it since his Root Class reset when he died. He thought about choosing the Mage branch again so he could use it. But Hamma's higher-level spell had been blocked. Plus, Uru had told him to wait. It looked like he'd be talking to her again soon. This time he would get some answers.

The assassin moved forward, and Ruwen did the only thing he could think of.

"Stop!" he shouted.

To Ruwen's amazement, the man stopped and tilted his head.

The assassin spoke, but Ruwen only understood a few words. "You...words...talk."

Ruwen heard the door open and relaxed a little. Hamma had made it out. At least she wouldn't suffer because of him. Not only had he understood some of the words of this man, but the assassin had also understood him. Earlier today, which felt like an eternity ago, he had taken the Ability *Hey You*. He had hoped it would allow him to read foreign books in the library. But the "understanding" it referenced seemed to extend to his speech. It was only level one, which meant his understanding, and words were the most basic.

"Why kill?" Ruwen asked, touching his chest.

The assassin waved his arm in a circle. "Duty."

Hamma had left the door open, and Ruwen heard the faint hum of a Guardian passing nearby. The Guardians! Why hadn't he thought of that before? All he needed to do was get out the door and get the Guardian's attention. It would do the rest.

He took a small side-step toward the exit. The assassin leaped twenty feet and landed in front of the door.

Ruwen stared at the man in awe and fear. The gilled assassin would kill him. Maybe Hamma would get a Guardian's attention. But he hadn't told her what had happened earlier. She had no idea the Guardians didn't like these guys. Why hadn't he shared what had happened? Probably because that had ended with his closest friend killing him. Who wanted to talk about that? Now, Ruwen was going to die again.

The assassin looked toward the bar. Ruwen turned to look as well but didn't see anything. As he turned back, he saw Ky lower herself into the doorway. She must have climbed down the outside of the building. She moved silently toward the assassin, who was still staring at the bar. Ruwen's eyes widened at Ky's ability. She moved like a shadow toward the man.

The assassin noticed Ruwen's expression and leaped to the side as Ky dove forward with her dagger. Ruwen had alerted the assassin to Ky's presence, and he cringed with guilt.

Her target gone, Ky shifted her momentum into a cartwheel, and in a heartbeat she stood next to Ruwen. The assassin landed near the fireplace and immediately threw a glass ball at Ruwen. Ky flicked her cloak in the air like a shield and the ball shattered against it. Black liquid dripped onto the floor and smoked, but Ky's cloak seemed to be okay.

"Run," Ky said and lowered her cloak.

She flicked a small metal disk and shattered a vial in the assassin's hand. The assassin grimaced, but didn't scream, and used the stone around the fireplace to wipe the brown liquid from his hand. The granite smoked and popped where the liquid touched, but it didn't seem to affect the man's skin.

The assassin gave Ky a small bow and raised his empty hands. Ky grunted and stood up straight. She sheathed her dagger and returned the bow. Then she sprinted at the assassin, and in a blink, they were fighting.

The fighting looked more like a dance. Ky's hand blurred as she aimed for the man's throat. The assassin moved just enough to cause her hand to miss. He reached up and grabbed Ky's elbow, attempting to snap it. Ky did a front flip, pulling the man's arm with her. The man turned in place to uncross his arms, and for a moment, the two assassins stared at each other, their faces a foot apart. Then they began striking and kicking, the blows thrown and blocked faster than Ruwen could follow. He marveled at the deadly beauty of it.

"Run, you moron!" Ky shouted.

He turned and ran out the open door. The sunlight made him wince, but he took a moment to look around. If Hamma was close, he would run to her, but she wasn't visible. Without a second thought, he turned and sprinted toward the library. He could hear the Guardians somewhere above him, but he didn't see them. His white robe smelled like mint and had large blood-stains on it. Thankfully, the streets were still deserted, and no one stopped him.

Nearing the library, he heard voices, so he approached the building from the side opposite his dead body. He really didn't want to see that if it was still there. A large group of Enforcement soldiers stood in a circle around a hole in the ground. The street and buildings had been scorched black, and Ruwen pulled the Scarf of Freshness back over his nose as the burnt smell of melted granite made his nose wrinkle. The Mana unleashed here had fried the air, and it made his eyes water. Tremine stood near the hole in the street along with two Enforcement officers. They seemed deep in conversation.

Ruwen moved another block away from them before crossing the street. He worked his way to the library's staff entrance again. Ruwen reached for the handle and paused. The last time he'd touched this door, he'd been struck by a spell, caused a terrible alarm, and summoned the Guardians. He remembered his skin melting from their weapons and wiped the sweat from his forehead. His hands shook, but if he stood here much longer he would be caught for sure, and the last thing he wanted to do was talk to a bunch of Enforcement officers.

Without giving himself more time to think, Ruwen grabbed the handle, opened the door, and slid inside. To his relief, nothing happened. As soon as he closed the door behind him, the hallway darkened. To Ruwen's surprise, it didn't go completely dark. He could make out the grey outlines of the walls. Was there a light somewhere? Why could he see? Then he remembered the ring Ky had given him. Its passive ability helped you see in the dark. Nice, but it didn't matter. He didn't need light to get around in the library.

Ruwen made his way to the basement. He had spent so much time there, that Tremine had given Ruwen his own room two years ago. Because his parents' jobs took them away for long periods, they approved of this second home. In the last year, he had spent more time here than at the house.

Once in the basement, he moved even faster. His first stop was the bathroom and the shower there. The smell of blood mixed with mint made him nauseous. Taking off Yull's robe, he found the shaker next to the shower and gave it a single flick. Weak light filled the room, and he washed away the past hour. He wondered if Ky was okay and if Hamma had found help in time. Should he look for them? He felt bad for running. He had made a lot of decisions today that made him feel terrible about himself.

Ruwen hadn't stopped to get a towel, so he stood with his

arms out, letting the air dry him. Today should have been the beginning of his journey to greatness. The mightiest Mage to have ever existed. Instead, he felt like crying. He had killed a man, or something like a man, been nearly vaporized by his town's ancient guardians, and had run out on Hamma and Ky. Maybe that was why Tremine had killed him. The librarian must have known how rotten Ruwen was.

Carefully opening his Void Band, he added the Scarf of Freshness and then removed a set of Worker clothes and put them on. He removed the belt next and threaded it through the loops on his pants. Next, he snapped the Baton of a Thousand Uses to his belt on his left side and then pulled on the Feather Boots of Grasping. The hard leather boots were surprisingly soft on the inside.

Ruwen left the bathroom and walked quickly to his room. He had to slow down after just a few steps, as his feet seemed to bounce off the floor. He realized the 20% weight reduction from his new boots made him walk funny. Instead of going to his room, he walked up and down the hallway for the next ten minutes until he felt like his gait appeared more natural.

Entering his bedroom, he quickly looked around with his enhanced sight and then quietly shut the door. The room had once been a storage area, and while the cold granite floor remained, the rest of the room was much more inviting now. A bed sat against the wall across from his door. To the right, he had found two overstuffed reading chairs and placed a small table between them. He walked to the table, removed a shaker from its stand, and gave it two quick shakes. Light filled the room, and he collapsed into his favorite brown chair. Across from his chairs, he had covered the wall with shelves and filled them with hundreds of "borrowed" books.

"Ugh," he said and leaned his head back until it rested on the chair.

For the first time today, he rested. A part of him wanted to sleep. Maybe this was a bad dream, and he needed to wake up and head for his Ascendancy appointment. None of this could be real. He noticed a pulsing yellow in the bottom of his vision and opened the minimized prompts.

The first few were from gaining level two after Hamma's quest. He'd earned another ability and two more spells. The notifications detailed how he could increase the effectiveness of the ones he currently knew or learn new ones. The problem was he didn't know how to learn new abilities or spells. He needed to talk with Tremine and get the book that contained all the Worker details. He almost stuck another point in the ability *Hey You* since the other abilities seemed so useless. But he decided to wait in case there was a good level two ability.

The other prompts notified him of the effects of his passive status items: the ring, scarf, and boots. He closed them all and then opened his Profile. He focused on the Root text, and the hidden page appeared with the other Classes. Why had Uru wanted him to wait? Had he waited long enough? The choice was important, though, since the cost of changing it was horrific. Without a clear direction, he decided to wait a little longer and blinked the display away.

His whole body hurt, like one giant growing pain. He needed to sleep for a few minutes. Then he could make his next decisions with a clear head. He dimmed his interface until it was barely visible, closed his eyes, and let the darkness take him.

CHAPTER 11

A knock on the door woke Ruwen. He jumped out of the chair, adrenaline making his heart race. The shaker's light had faded, but he could still see well thanks to his ring. He brightened his interface and read the time: 5:03 PM. He'd slept for over two hours. The knock came again, a little louder this time. What if the assassin stood on the other side of the door? That was stupid, why would an assassin knock? He walked to the door, unsure of what he should do.

"Hello?" Ruwen asked.

"I want to talk about earlier," Tremine said.

Ruwen's shoulders slumped as he relived the chaos dagger sliding through his eye and into his brain. He shook himself to clear the memory. The last thing he wanted to do was talk about it, and he didn't think he could face his mentor.

"Listen, I know what happened doesn't make sense. Killing you hurt me more than it hurt you."

"I doubt that."

"Please open the door, so I can explain." There was a pause. "I brought poppers."

Ruwen's stomach growled, and he looked down at it in irritation. His mouth watered as thoughts of the wonderful taste filled his mind. His entire body seemed to betray him. Curse Tremine for causing this rebellion.

Well, Ruwen was hungry. He needed to talk to Tremine eventually anyway. Faster than he intended, he unlocked the door and cracked it open. Anger with himself for capitulating so quickly mixed with relief that this conversation would soon be over. Even poppers wouldn't be able to fix the hurt and betrayal he felt.

He walked back to his chair and sat. Tremine closed the door behind him and sat on the chair next to Ruwen. The librarian snapped the shaker a couple of times, and the room brightened. Without saying a word, Tremine started pulling items out of his Portal Bag and setting them on the small table between them: a pitcher of water, a jug of something yellow, two plates and cups, three bowls of sauce, and finally a large bowl of poppers.

The smell of the spiced meat wrapped in fried dough was too much. Ruwen took a plate and grabbed a handful of the poppers. They were still hot, and he shook his hand to cool it. He poured some of the spicy tomato sauce on his plate and started eating.

Tremine's face remained neutral, and after Ruwen began eating, the librarian filled his plate. Ruwen was on his third plate when Tremine broke the silence.

"Naktos's Embrace," Tremine said. "Well, that's what we call it. I'm not positive how their Mages refer to it."

Ruwen wanted to continue giving Tremine the silent treatment, but the truth was Ruwen's curiosity had turned into a fire in his mind. It was foolish to continue to be angry with Tremine when he didn't have all the facts, and he wondered if his Foolish debuff was making this harder. The librarian had been a second father to him and deserved to at least be heard. Plus, Ruwen had been dying to know what Naktos meant since he had heard the gilled man say it. Literally dying.

"He said Naktos to me," Ruwen said.

"You understood him?"

Ruwen set his plate down and went to wipe his hands on his shirt. Tremine cleared his throat and looked at the hand towels on the table. Ruwen's cheeks grew warm, and he grabbed a towel.

Ruwen sighed, and his shoulders slumped. "As you can see, the priest made me a Worker." Anger flared in his chest. "That turd pie didn't even present me to Uru. He just threw me in the tank."

"You give him too much credit. If he made you a Worker, Uru wished it."

"I should have been a Mage!"

"And you still can be."

The words hung in the air between them. Ruwen sat up straight and looked at Tremine for the first time. How could he know about Ruwen's secret Class?

"Uh, that's impossible," he stammered.

Tremine chuckled. "You need to work on your Deception skill."

He had never been a good liar, and Tremine knew him well, which made deception almost impossible. He had to try, though.

"Why would you say that?" Ruwen asked.

Tremine's expression grew thoughtful. "Well, there are three reasons. First, at the park, a fire ignited the methane sack of a low-level follower of Naktos, causing him to explode. From the remains, it appeared the man was a servant. In Naktos culture, only Mages are allowed servants, which meant a Naktos Mage was somewhere in our city. Why would the Naktos risk coming here? And who caused the fire?"

"Those are interesting questions," Ruwen said and quickly took a drink of water.

"Which brings me to my second reason. The Guardians. I can count on one hand the times I've seen one active. Never, in history, have all four activated at the same time. You would have thought the world was ending."

"Yeah, that was scary."

"Interestingly, right before the Guardians awoke, the library alerted me it was under magical attack. It believed the threat so severe it opened a portal to bring me immediately back to protect it."

"Wow, I didn't know it could do that."

"And what do I find when I arrive? You, battling the Naktos Mage. And if this wasn't already beyond belief, the Mage had activated a Karthos Protection Crystal and was channeling Naktos's Embrace on you."

Ruwen rubbed his sweaty palms on his pants. "You mentioned that earlier."

"Yes, we have come full circle."

Ruwen drew a little circle in the air with his finger and then wiped his forehead. "It is really hot in here."

"You have to wonder why a secretive race would use some of the most potent magic on the planet on you. A level –" Tremine paused as he studied Ruwen, "two, now, Worker."

"Seems strange," Ruwen croaked.

"Congratulations on your Ascendancy, by the way. I'm very proud of you."

Ruwen looked down, happy, embarrassed, and sad all at the same time.

"Let me be clear. I would have been proud of you even without this extra burden."

"Thanks," he whispered, not looking up.

"Naktos's Embrace is soul magic. That Mage was seconds away from ripping 'you' out of you."

He looked up at his mentor. "What would that do?"

"For one, you wouldn't resurrect. You would be trapped in a spirit world, and you would be useless to Uru."

"Forever?"

Tremine looked down for a few seconds. "I've never heard of anyone returning. It is terrible magic."

"Oh."

"When I realized we couldn't break through his defenses in time, there was only one option left."

"To kill me."

"I'm sorry."

"You've never told *me* sorry," Ky said from the bed.

Ruwen screamed and threw himself backward.

"He's a jumpy one," Ky said.

Tremine smiled and leaned back in his chair. "Hello, Kysandra. I've told you sorry a hundred times. Have you been here the whole time?"

Ky stuck a popper in her mouth. "I came in with you." She held up another popper. "These are really good. You have to tell me where you bought them."

Ruwen looked from Ky to the bowl next to him and back at Ky. "Did you take those from right in front of us?"

Ky raised her eyebrows and dipped a popper in the sauce bowl she held in her other hand. He looked down at the table and noticed there were only two bowls. When had she taken that?

"Ruwen, meet Kysandra. High Mistress of the Black Pyramid, Keeper of the Silent Blade, Shadow Strider, and," Tremine placed his hands on his chest, "Thief of Hearts."

"Stop, you're making me blush. It's not silent you know," Ky said.

"What isn't?" Ruwen asked.

"The Silent Blade. It's a lie. Why would you lie about something like that? How about calling it 'The Never Shuts Up Blade' or 'Unwelcome Advice Dagger' or –" Ky looked down at her waist. "Your ideas are never useful. Well, yes, you were right that time, but –"

Tremine cleared his throat, and Ky looked up.

"Right, well, the kid and I already met. Seems he's attracted some unwelcome attention," Ky said.

"You've had a busy day," Tremine said.

Ruwen nodded and looked at Ky. "I'm glad you're alive. Is Hamma okay?"

"She's fine. I moved her to a safe house," Ky said.

"Hamma?" Tremine asked.

"A priestess the kid's sweet on," Ky said.

Ruwen sat up straight. "I am not. Why would you...I mean that is ridiculous...she's just..."

Tremine and Ky just stared at him, so he changed the subject.

"The assassin got away?" Ruwen asked.

Ky sighed. "Yeah, he had a blinker and teleported out. I didn't have time to set up my normal barriers."

"The Mage at the library did the same. He was hurt, but he might survive if there was help waiting at his bind point. It's not a good start," Tremine said.

"Start to what?" Ruwen asked.

Ky pointed up. "Her plans."

"I don't know how they discovered Ruwen so quickly," Tremine said.

"Uru had to notify the other deities of her intent to create a new Champion. She said it's in their rules. Naktos must have teams watching all the new Ascendants. Looking for anything suspicious," Ky said.

Tremine snapped his fingers. "Of course. The Ascendancy appointments are posted at the temple. They would only need a couple of teams to watch those going in and out of the temple. The fact that you came out of the temple the same day you entered would already be suspicious and is probably why they followed you. When they saw a Worker casting a Mage spell, they knew for sure."

Ruwen's stomach twisted. "You mean I did this to myself?"

Ky walked over and grabbed another handful of poppers. "Shade's first rule: you only have yourself to blame."

"I assume that's why you're here," Tremine said.

"You know me, nothing better to do," Ky said.

Tremine closed his eyes and sighed. "I'm sorry, Ky. Where were you?"

"The Legion's Vault in Malth. Two months of planning. Was going to hit it tomorrow night," Ky said.

"I'm sorry," Tremine said again.

"Like I told the kid, we only have ourselves to blame."

"Wait," Ruwen said. "Malth is across the entire continent. It's on the other coast."

Ky tilted her head. "Somebody thinks you're important, kid. And she brought me here because of it. I broke Shade's first rule: be seen, never noticed."

"Wait, I thought blaming yourself was the first rule," Ruwen said.

Tremine and Ky ignored him.

"With you here, he'll be safe," Tremine said.

Ky shrugged. "I give him a twenty percent chance of making it. Assuming we can keep him hidden for a while."

"I'm supposed to go on some bonding trip into the forest tomorrow," Ruwen said.

"Not a chance. You'll die for sure," Ky said.

"Fine with me. What do I tell Big D, because she –"

"Big D is organizing this?" Ky asked.

Ruwen nodded.

"You're going then. Durn is far more dangerous than that assassin. That woman can talk you into anything," Ky said.

"But, you just said I'd die for sure if –"

Ky waved her hands. "You'll be okay. Probably. Most likely. Anyway, I'm not messing with Big D's plans, so we're going to train you the hard way."

Tremine groaned, and Ruwen looked at him.

"Is that bad?" Ruwen asked.

Tremine scrunched his face and tried to smile.

"What do you mean train?" Ruwen asked.

"As good as your *Fireball* seems to be, it looks like times are calling for something a little less…explosive. You need to live. Which means you need to learn how to hide. Uru told me you get a reset every time you kick it. So, if you already picked something like Order or Merchant or, I don't know, *Mage*. I'm going to have to kill you. Because your only choice right now is Observer."

Thank Uru he hadn't picked a Class yet, but he winced as Ky blatantly uttered his secret out loud.

Ky saw his reaction and smiled. "Okay, lessons start now. The most important thing an Observer can do is listen. And you're terrible. Trem gave you two reasons why he knows you're different, but he said there were three."

Ruwen looked back at Tremine. The librarian gave Ky a small bow and then faced Ruwen. "Yes, number three. You see, while you've become a servant of Uru today, I've been doing it for over a hundred years."

As Tremine said the last, he opened his palm and showed Ruwen the small tree there.

Ky sighed. "I didn't know about these Hands until a few hours ago when I was volunteered to be one. I should have known." She narrowed her eyes at Tremine. "Was the Nalab job her doing?"

Tremine nodded.

"Kled?"

Tremine nodded again.

"So Uru's been leading you around like a cow, and you spent a couple of decades doing the same to me," Ky said.

"That isn't fair," Tremine said.

"I know," Ky whispered, and then turned to Ruwen. "Kid, now I'm angry. And one of us is going to suffer for it."

Ruwen rubbed the back of his neck and grimaced.

"I'll leave you two to your fun, but first some business," Tremine said.

The librarian opened his bag and removed eight books. Six were the same size and shape and only differed in color. These he stacked together while placing the other two books to the side. One of these was bigger than the others and had a plain brown cover. The last one was half the size and looked very old. Its cover was black, and it had silver writing on it.

Tremine picked up the brown book and handed it to Ruwen. As soon as he touched it, a notification began pulsing in the bottom of his vision, and he opened it.

Ting!
You have completed the Quest – Does This Taste Funny to You
(Part 1).
You have received 200 experience.
You have received Collector Novice Manual (part 1).

The brown book felt heavy, and he fanned the pages. The book was filled with drawings, many in color, all with detailed descriptions. It looked interesting, and he couldn't wait to study it.

Tremine put his hand on the stack of six books. "Here are the textbooks for each Class. They cover the first nine levels of abilities and spells for each respective Class. Most people never need volume two. Obviously, people usually only ever see the textbook for their own Class, so don't be seen with anything other than the Worker one."

The librarian gently placed the black book on top of the stack. "This is one of the few books we have on the god Naktos and his followers. I thought you might want to practice your new-found language skills and learn about the people who want you dead."

"Thank you," Ruwen said, genuinely excited.

Tremine stood, and Ruwen did as well.

"Try not to kill him," Tremine said to Ky.

"You know me," Ky said.

"That's why I mentioned it," Tremine replied.

Ruwen couldn't tell if he was joking or not.

CHAPTER 12

The door closed as Tremine left, and Ruwen placed his books in the Void Band. It was one of the few good things that had happened today.

"If my *Fireball* caused the explosion that killed that servant, why didn't my log show anything about the combat?" Ruwen asked.

"Fighting people is a little different than battling monsters. Your log won't provide information that would unfairly give you an advantage. If your Perception isn't high enough to see things like your enemy's level or combat damage, your log won't show it either. It defers combat information and experience until all the members of the enemy party are killed."

"Oh," he said, not really understanding what Ky meant.

Before he could get clarification, Ky changed the subject.

"What is Big D doing with you tomorrow?"

Ruwen held up his wrist with the Void Band. "I'm the pack-horse for every person that has Ascended in the last two months. Plus all their instructors and whoever else needs to go on this stupid expedition. Big D said everyone was going to be upset, and she seemed happy about that."

"Big D is dangerous. The Council is going to learn that. But that isn't our problem. At least not our immediate one. Tremine said the Naktos tried some type of magic hug on you."

"Embrace."

Ky stared at him.

"Sorry," Ruwen muttered. "Yes, they did, but Tremine stopped it."

Ruwen rubbed his eye.

"Since the assassin threw knives at you in the bar, plan B must be to kill you over and over until you're a vegetable."

If Ky was going to help him survive, she needed to know his weaknesses.

"Making me a vegetable isn't going to take long. My death penalty is twice normal," Ruwen said.

Ky whistled. "That explains the debuffs."

"You can see those?"

"Are you serious? Do you know anything about the Observer Class?"

"Hey, I was meant to be a Mage. I didn't need to know about the other Classes."

"I won't ask how that's working out. And points for leveling?"

"Six in total."

"Ouch."

"Tell me about it."

"How much hand fighting have you learned?"

Ruwen looked down.

"It's a free skill," Ky said.

"I was supposed to be a –"

"Mage. I remember."

Ky stood and waved around the room. "We might as well get started. What is wrong with this room?"

Ruwen looked around. It was on the small side, and it didn't have its own bathroom or kitchen, but he liked its coziness.

Ruwen tried to keep the doubt off his face. "It's small?"

"This is going to be painful," Ky whispered. "There is only one entrance. Which means there is only one exit. It makes my skin crawl just being in here."

"I can see how that's bad."

"Is there a private room nearby with two doors? Or maybe a window?"

Ruwen thought for a moment. "There's a meeting room down the hall that nobody ever uses. It has a door at each end."

"Let's go."

"Now? I was kind of hoping I could rest a little more."

"Are you tired?"

He leaned back in the chair and rubbed his face. "Yes, it's been a long day, and I'd hoped to sleep the rest of it away."

Ky nodded. "You know what I hope?"

Ruwen shook his head.

"I hope the Mage that almost ripped your soul from your body died. I hope the assassin that blinked away decided to go home. I hope your ignorance hasn't alerted any of the other gods who want to burn our country to the ground. I hope –"

Ruwen held up his hands. "Okay, I get it. We need to get started. What do you want to accomplish tonight?"

Ky pursed her lips and looked at the ceiling for a few seconds. "I think level five might give you enough skills to survive this outing."

Ruwen laughed, but when Ky's expression didn't change, he stood and placed a hand on his chest.

"I'm only level two. It's impossible to level three times in a single night."

"True," Ky said. "That's why we're doing things the hard way. Now take me to this room. I have a place I want to show you. I know you'll love it as much as I do."

By the tone in her voice, Ruwen doubted that very much. He

opened the door, entered the hallway, and started for the meeting room.

A question had been nagging him since Ky had first appeared. "How did you find me at the library?"

"I do," Ky said.

"What?"

Ky stopped. "Keep going. When you get to the end of the hallway, open your map, think of me, and say *I do*."

Ruwen did as she instructed. When he said the words, a dot appeared next to his location.

"The ring is how I found you," Ky said as she approached.

He looked at the ring on his finger and realized they hadn't taken a shaker with them for light. But it seemed the rings had other powers than just light enhancement.

"I thought this was just for seeing in the dark," Ruwen said.

"So did the original owners. Let's keep moving."

He started toward the meeting room, and Ky followed.

"The rings are a few hundred years old. They were an engagement gift to the future king and queen of Jaga. Pull up the description."

Ruwen opened his inventory and focused on the ring.

Name: *Jaga Wedding Band*
Quality: *Fine*
Durability: *10 of 10*
Weight: *0.12 lbs.*
Effect (Passive): *Enhance Ambient Light by 15%.*
Effect (Active): *Reveal Heart's Desire.*
Restriction: *Active effect requires pair*
Description: *Darkness is no barrier to love. Trust ends with "I do."*

Ky spoke again. "The lovers thought the rings were just a way for them to sneak through the darkness and meet. Then they discovered the phrase 'I do' allowed them to see where the other person was. It eventually caused the fall of Jaga."

Ruwen had read about Jaga. It had been a prosperous country far to the south. A civil war had been its downfall. Jaga had been divided up by its neighbors and no longer existed.

"How could these rings have done that?" Ruwen asked.

"I'm sure it started innocently enough. Why were you in the stables? Or, what took you so long in the staff quarters? That eventually leads to arguments about being watched, which leads to fights about trust. Eventually, it consumed them both to the point that the country crumbled around them. The description literally warned them."

The ring suddenly felt very heavy on his finger. "These rings are evil."

Ky grabbed his shoulder and turned him around. "This is an important lesson. Things aren't good or bad. The people who use them are. Don't confuse the two."

He nodded. "I get it. But it makes me feel kind of sick wearing something instrumental in the fall of an entire nation."

"Good. There's hope for you."

"Can I take it off?"

"Don't be stupid. Now, show me that room."

A minute later, they entered the room, and Ky walked around the entire perimeter. She opened the far door and disappeared, Ruwen assumed to scout the area for threats. When she returned, she closed both doors and then walked to a tapestry of a woman reading a book.

"Hold this away from the wall," Ky said.

Ruwen dutifully grabbed the bottom of the tapestry and lifted the heavy cloth in the air. Ky pulled a dark rock from her bag. It fit in the palm of her hand and was as thick as a finger. He couldn't tell the exact color because the world looked grey from the Jaga Wedding Band's enhancement. Ky held the rock like a charcoal stick and drew a narrow rectangle just over six foot high. She wrote five strange runes down the center of the rectangle and then put the rock back into her bag. She motioned for him to drop the tapestry.

"Okay, we have to talk about a few things before we proceed. There are some risks to where we are going. First, I have to mark you. If you are not allied with me when we enter, there are safeguards in place that will kill you. Which brings me to the second risk. Where we are going is outside Uru's Blessing, so if you die there, you lose everything you've gained."

"We'd have to travel hundreds of miles before we left the area of her Blessing."

"We are going much further than that."

"That isn't possible."

"Listen, you and Tremine can stay up late and rub books and talk about what is and isn't possible. I'm trying to keep you alive until you can do it for yourself. And that looks like it might be a while."

Ruwen frowned. He didn't like not knowing things, and what Ky was talking about sounded like nonsense.

"One last thing. I've never had anyone with a Void Band in here before. Traveler Bags and Belts work, so I assume yours will, too. But, since I don't know much about the Void Bands, I'm not completely sure."

"What are you worried about?"

"It is kind of a hole within a hole situation. I'm not sure how the universe handles those things. Maybe we should just try it as soon as we enter. Then if you die, I can throw your body back out. Assuming you don't get sucked into some sort of vortex."

Ruwen flinched at the horrible possibilities. "Now I under-stand what you mean by the hard way."

Ky laughed. "We haven't even talked about the hard stuff yet. This is just the first few seconds. Which brings me to my third warning. Time."

"Time?"

"Where we are going, it moves differently."

"How differently?"

"It varies, but it's around four to one."

"What does that mean?"

"For every day that passes there, only six hours pass here."

Ruwen shook his head. "Can we go back to the beginning? Where is there?"

"Not sure, kid. It will be easier to show you the details once we're there. I don't like taking you there. It's a refuge for me, and you can probably tell how fond I am of people."

"Is it safe there?"

"Not even remotely. Also, I should mention if someone erases the door on this side, that pathway between the...let's call them worlds, becomes unstable."

Ruwen took a deep breath. "Let me see if I got this straight. We are going through a portal to a different world. If someone erases the drawing on this wall, we might come out someplace else. We lose our connection with Uru, and if I die there, I won't resurrect or keep any memories or skills I've learned. The place is dangerous. To survive your booby traps, I have to take a mark that will probably cause me issues with law-abiding folk."

"That is a decent summary, Ruwen. I'm glad you were listening. But the mark will probably cause issues with more than just the sheep." Ky looked down at her waist. "I'll be careful. The last few were accidents."

"What is its name?" Ruwen said, pointing to the dagger at Ky's waist.

Ky stared at him as if she were trying to decide something. Then she looked down again. "You are not a king!"

"It's an Elder weapon, isn't it?"

"Smart kid. You've done some reading, then?"

"Some."

"That is a story for another time."

Ruwen knew he wouldn't get anything else out of Ky about

her weapon, so he quit pushing her. "What did your dagger mean about accidents?"

"Oh, it wanted me to tell you the biggest danger is me and your training. But, I'm not the most dangerous thing in that place, and I have someone else in mind for your training. I've worked hard to carve out a place of my own. My cottage on the beach, so to speak."

"Thieves want a cottage on the beach?"

"Oh, kid. I'm no mere Thief. Let's get going. We won't be wasting so much time if we're talking on the other side, and I'm starting to believe you're stalling. Hold out your right hand."

Ruwen slowly raised his hand. He wasn't sure about this. It seemed to be full of danger, and there was no upside other than the time dilation. His heart beat faster, thinking about Ky's dagger. She hadn't wanted to talk about it, but maybe she would later. Sentient weapons were thousands of years old and incredibly rare. No one knew who made them or where they came from. But the weapons were nigh indestructible, and their intelligence made them infinitely more dangerous than a standard weapon. Ruwen had read that some of them could even do magic. He definitely wanted to get a closer look at her blade. Maybe if he went along, she...

His forehead stung, and he focused back on his surroundings. Ky flicked his forehead again, and he stepped away to avoid a third.

"Where do you go when you do that?" Ky asked.

"I was just thinking."

"You do that a lot. And —surprise— it will get you killed. So, stop it."

"Stop thinking?"

"Yes. In my experience, thinkers don't last long. Tremine is the exception."

Ky grabbed his right hand and turned it palm up. She placed her wrist on top of his and locked gazes with him.

"Ruwen Starfield, do you swear upon your eternal soul to keep the secrets of the Black Pyramid and, to the best of your abilities, obey the commands of the High Mistress while in her realm? Furthermore, do you promise to aid any others who carry the mark and do all in your power to help them attain their goals so long as those goals do not conflict with your own? And lastly, if a member of the Pyramid is killed, will you do your utmost to avenge them? Do you, Ruwen Starfield, agree to take this mark freely, and without ill intent?"

A notification appeared in his vision even though he had them set to minimized. It wasn't the standard yellow but a deep red. Instead of print, the notification was in cursive, and his whole body felt tingly.

Thrum!
You have been offered a Soul Oath...
Another Block in the Pyramid
The High Mistress of the Black Pyramid has offered you her mark and a place in her realm.
Reward: *Access to the Black Pyramid*
Warning!
This is a soul binding and bridges death.
Accept or Decline

Ruwen stared at the notification. He hated having to make this decision with so little information. He had no idea what the Black Pyramid was or what it stood for. For all he knew, they could run around killing children. But Ky had been picked by Uru herself, and while he didn't know much about his Class, he knew the goddess wanted to protect him. That is what Ky was here to do, and Ky said she needed the resources of the Black Pyramid to do it. He really didn't have a choice. If he wanted to live instead of being killed until he was a vegetable, he needed to move forward down this path even if it was full of risk.

He selected *Accept*, and his whole body grew ice cold. Ky removed her hand, and he could see a small black pyramid on his wrist. As he watched, it faded away. A notification pulsed and he opened it.

Ping!
You have learned the Ability Black Eye
Ability: *Black Eye*
Level: *1*
Class: *Any*
Effect: *Detect the presence of a member of the Black Pyramid.*
Type: *AoE*

Ky lifted the tapestry. "If you ever need to show your mark, just focus on it, and it will appear. Welcome to the fold, Ruwen." She motioned at the wall. "After you, my young novice."

Ruwen turned sideways to fit through the narrow rectangle Ky had drawn. He pushed forward expecting to hit the wall. Instead, he kept moving, and his left arm and shoulder disappeared into the stone. He stopped, and his heart raced. What was he doing? He had no idea where this place was or how to get back. He needed to —

"On my dagger, I didn't deserve this," Ky said.

Then she shoved Ruwen hard, and he stumbled into darkness.

CHAPTER 13

*R*uwen regained his balance a few feet after exiting the wall. He stood in a large circular room. He doubted he could throw a rock and hit the other side. The ceiling, thirty-feet high, looked rough like a cave while the walls were smooth. A yellow-green light came from the floor, and he knelt and touched the glowing moss that carpeted the entire room.

He stood and turned in a slow circle. The entire room was covered with narrow rectangles like Ky had drawn at the library. Each had different runes down the middle. His feet tangled as he turned, and he fell.

He knew his debuff made him clumsier than normal, but this was ridiculous. Trying to push himself up before Ky could see him, he realized his hands were trapped in the moss. He hadn't been clumsy. The moss had grabbed his boots and tripped him.

His right wrist grew intensely cold, and the Black Pyramid mark briefly appeared. Almost reluctantly, the moss let him go, and he stood.

Ky stepped out of the wall. "Well, it looks like you were sincere."

Standing, he rubbed his wrist to warm it. "What?"

"If you'd been lying about the no ill intent when you took my mark, the Blood Moss would have you mostly digested by now."

"I thought this was just for light. It's a trap?"

"It's both. The most successful things have more than one purpose."

"I feel like it's disappointed. I think it really wanted to eat me."

"Oh, it does. Sift is probably keeping it a little too hungry. I'll talk to him about it."

"What do you feed it?"

"Blood."

Ruwen's stomach turned, and he tried to not step on it, but it filled the entire room. He also realized there wasn't a normal door in the room. Only narrow rectangles, each with runes etched an inch into the stone.

"How do we get out of here?" Ruwen asked.

Ky waved her hand around the room. "We take the right door."

"There are wrong doors?"

"Most of them lead to instant death."

"So, if someone enters through one of your doors, the Blood Moss eats them. If they somehow survive, they'll likely go through a door that will kill them?"

"There are other things in here that might get them before they reach a door."

Ruwen looked around and his mouth went dry. "What happens if someone gets here by accident?"

Ky shrugged.

"That seems really harsh."

"Listen, kid, it's a harsh world, and curiosity always kills you in the end. It's the universe's way of keeping her secrets."

Ruwen raised his eyebrows.

Ky pointed at him. "You and Tremine have the same insatiable curiosity, which is probably why he likes you. But it will get you killed."

"So, stop thinking and don't look at anything interesting," Ruwen said sarcastically.

"Yes. Maybe then you'll survive," Ky said, ignoring his tone. After a pause, she continued. "If you arrived here alone, knowing what you do, with what you have, how would you find a safe door?"

Ting!
You have received the quest...
My Doors are Always Open
The Mistress of the Black Pyramid has asked you to find a safe door. Caution should be exercised, as guessing will most certainly find a painful and unpleasant death.
Reward: *Ciphered Gate Runes*
Accept or Decline

Ruwen accepted the quest and wondered what gate runes were. He thought for a minute, and Ky left him alone. "Okay, I have an idea."

"Show me."

"I'll have to open my Void Band."

"Well, if you explode, at least Sift won't have to feed the lawn."

Ruwen took a few deep breaths and then opened the Band.

"Boom!" Ky yelled.

Ruwen screamed and slammed the Band shut.

Ky laughed for what Ruwen thought was a little too long and then wiped her eyes. "I really needed that."

"Very funny."

"You are really jumpy. Which isn't necessarily a bad thing. You just need to control your reactions better."

"Thanks, I guess."

"Okay, go ahead. I'll be good."

Ruwen stared at Ky, not trusting her to keep her word, as he opened his Void Band. He reached in and thought about the priest robe he'd stashed there. It was still wet from soaking it in the stream to clean the statue of Uru at the park. The dampness wouldn't matter for his plans. He tied the sleeves into a loose knot and then pulled the hood through it, making a sort of bag.

He gently pulled a clump of the Blood Moss, about the size of his hand, from where it met the wall and placed it inside the hood. Walking up to the doorway next to the one he'd entered, he knelt in front of it and gently tossed the hood portion of the robe through the door. Holding the bottom of the robe, he counted to ten and then pulled it back.

The robe returned hard as a rock, and he could feel the coldness coming off it. The cloth immediately steamed in the warm air. After the hood had thawed enough to open, he looked inside. The Blood Moss had turned brittle and collapsed into dust as soon as he touched it.

He dumped out the dust, peeled another section of Blood Moss from the floor, and added it to the hood. Moving one door down, he repeated the process.

After counting to ten, Ruwen pulled the robe back. The white cloth now looked black. What could have caused that? The robe moved, and he realized centipedes covered it. Gasping, he threw himself backward. He hated things with too many legs. Hundreds of centipedes writhed on the fabric, and they crawled onto the Blood Moss and wall.

As the bugs crawled on the Blood Moss, they disappeared, replaced a second later with a red pool, which vanished after another second. Even more frightening, the Blood Moss grew over the cloth. The robe sunk like a ship in a sea of green. In a few seconds it had disappeared, and Ruwen only saw occasional splashes of red in the green tide. The centipedes that made it to the wall sizzled and popped as the walls grew superheated wherever they were touched. The centipedes either stayed on the walls too long and were burnt into black powder, or fell onto the Blood Moss, which consumed them immediately.

"Uru save me," Ruwen said.

"She can't help you here, kid."

"That was horrifying."

"Yeah, that is a bad door to choose."

He tore open the Blood Moss and pulled his robe free. It was spotless. Carefully, he held it away from himself and spun it, making sure no bugs were left. But the Blood Moss had done its work, and the piece in the hood still looked okay and maybe a bit larger than before. Kneeling in front of the next door, he paused.

"I thought I could test the doors with the Blood Moss. If it survived, the door must be safe on the other side. But, I'm not so sure anymore."

"Why is that?"

"Because of the bugs. I've realized the threat could be something less obvious than lava or lightning or whatever. What if it is some sort of noxious gas –"

Ky pointed to a door ten down from him.

"Or bugs too tiny to see –"

Ky pointed to a door across the room.

His voice grew quieter. "Or a thousand-foot cliff —"

She pointed behind him. "Over three thousand feet actually."

"What is wrong with you?" Ruwen whispered.

"Safety first is what I like to say. Well, my safety and the safety of my people."

Ruwen shook his head and placed the robe back in his Void Band, leaving the Blood Moss in the hood. As much as it made his stomach turn, the Blood Moss fascinated him, and he wanted to study it later.

A notification appeared that he'd never seen before. It had a timer, which had already started counting down from ten. Ruwen quickly read the notification.

Notice: A living entity has entered your Void Band. Estimated Energy consumption to sustain life: 0.20 Energy per second. You have ten seconds to make one of the following choices:
Choice 1: *Remove the entity.*
Choice 2: *Select Yes, incur the Energy cost, and sustain the entity's life.*
Choice 3: *Select No and the entity will perish.*

Ruwen focused on his Energy bar, relieved that it only dropped from a one hundred to ninety-nine before returning to one hundred about every five seconds. Bliz had said plants would be an almost unnoticeable drain on his Energy and it appeared the Blood Moss was considered a plant.

He selected *Yes* and then looked at Ky. She either hadn't noticed or didn't care about the Blood Moss.

"This is a good example of you overthinking," Ky said.

Did he overthink, though? He felt like he didn't think enough. If he had spent a little more time thinking about the problem, he would have realized this wouldn't have worked. Then he wouldn't have wasted all this time. In fact, the –

His forehead stung, and he looked at Ky. She was about to flick him in the head again.

"Stop that," Ruwen said and got to his feet.

"Stop thinking, then. The right answers are simple. You complicate everything."

He had never been here before, was only level two, and had almost no skills. Whatever the solution was, it must be related to his recent interactions with Ky. Which had mostly been her appearing and disappearing or making him take soul oaths that would probably end up –

The thought of the soul oath caused Ruwen's brain to feel

cold, and then another idea crashed through his mind. He opened his Abilities tab and reread *Black Eye*.

Ability: Black Eye
Effect: Detect the presence of a member of the Black Pyramid.
Type: AoE

"Detect the presence of a member of the Black Pyramid," Ruwen mumbled.

The ability *Black Eye* allowed him to sense others with the Black Pyramid mark. Even now, he felt a coolness at the base of his hand from being near Ky. She had just talked about the safety of her people and had told him the only way in here was if you had this mark. The doors around him all looked like solid stone, but they allowed people to pass through. While the spell's type was area of effect, it didn't list a radius. If the radius was significant, and the effect passed through the doors, he might find safe doors that way.

He walked around the room, holding his wrist up to each door. Thirty doors down, his wrist grew colder. In all, six of the portals in the room triggered *Black Eye*. He also came across four doors that didn't have any markings at all.

"These six are safe," Ruwen said, pointing to them.

He opened the notification that appeared.

Ting!
You have completed the Quest – My Doors are Always Open.

"Excellent," Ky said and pointed at his feet. "Grab your reward and let's go."

Ruwen looked down and found a brown piece of parchment covered in runes. He picked it up.

Tring!

The Black Pyramid has rewarded you...
Name: *Ciphered Gate Runes*
Quality: *Rare*
Durability: *10 of 10*
Weight: *0.2 lbs.*
Restriction: *Requires Black Pyramid cipher (level 1)*
Restriction: *User must bear the mark of the Black Pyramid*
Description: *A change of scenery is but a door away.*

The information on the parchment was scrambled by the Black Pyramid cipher, and he couldn't read it. Ruwen had hoped his *Hey You* ability might work on the coded text, but it didn't.

"When will I learn the level one cipher?" Ruwen asked.

"Probably in a month or two."

Ruwen's shoulders slumped. What good was loot if you couldn't use it? He opened his Void Band and put the parchment in his inventory.

"I've given Sift too much time. We need to be extra careful now," Ky said.

Ky had said that name earlier when she mentioned feeding the Blood Moss. Ruwen needed to remember to feed his as well.

"Who's Sift?"

"You'll see shortly."

"What do you call this room?"

"Blood Gate."

"How many –"

Ky held up her hand. "Enough questions already. You might be worse than Tremine."

Ky muttered to herself as she walked into one of the doors Ruwen had identified as safe. He decided to save the rest of his questions for later. Pausing, he looked around the room one last time. He memorized the gate runes for the six safe doors as well as the doorway that had brought them here.

What kind of person goes to such lengths to make sure nobody follows them? He felt the Blood Moss move under his feet, and he nearly screamed again. Not wasting any more time, he hurried through the door Ky had already stepped through.

Ruwen emerged from what appeared to be a dead-end hallway. As soon as he exited, the door on the wall dissolved and only blank stone remained. Ky had already started down the tunnel, and he jogged to catch up. The stone walls' shakers were spaced too far apart for comfortable vision. With the enhancement from his ring, though, he could see well enough.

The hallway ended in a vast cavern whose ceiling was lost in darkness. Ky kept them inside the tunnel, and Ruwen studied the stalagmites that covered the cavern's floor. They ranged from tiny slivers to ones so thick he wouldn't be able to reach around them.

"He's here. It's where I would be," Ky said.

"Who?"

Ky turned to Ruwen. "Stay here. I don't want you to accidentally get killed." Ky turned toward the entrance and spoke loudly. "Sift's young and still sloppy."

Without waiting for Ruwen to respond, Ky pulled a small mirror from her bag. She held it between her fingers and eased the tip of the mirror into the cavern. Slowly she turned it back and forth, studying the area above their tunnel. Satisfied, she replaced the mirror, stepped out into the room, and disappeared. Ruwen squinted trying to find her. How had she done that?

He stared intently into the cavern for a minute, but she didn't reappear. Not knowing how long she might be gone, he sat down in the tunnel and brought up his Profile. Selecting the Root Class, he studied the new window that appeared.

Like before, the only branch with any color was the first, a deep brown, which ended in the Worker symbol of clasped hands. The next branch ended in a brain, and when he focused on it, the entire branch turned the black of the Mage Class. Like before, a notification appeared.

Root Class: Access to any Branch
Warning: Choice is permanently bound to body!
Do you wish to assign Root to Mage?
Yes or No

Ruwen wanted with all his heart to select *Yes.* But he knew that Ky would literally kill him. He only had one choice, and there was no reason to torture himself. He carefully selected *No* and then focused on the next branch, which ended in a pair of eyes. After a moment, the prompt reappeared.

Root Class: Access to any Branch
Warning: Choice is permanently bound to body!
Do you wish to assign Root to Observer?
Yes or No

Not giving himself time to think about it, he selected *Yes,* and the Observer branch turned green. He exited the page and went back to his main Profile. As before, his Hidden Class now had a new descriptor: Root (Observer).

He sighed. First, he was stuck with a terrible Class, and now he'd had to give up his dream of being a Mage. He had no plans on ever dying again, so he was probably stuck this way for the rest of his life. His chest tightened, and he took a few deep breaths to keep the depression away.

Reaching into his Void Band, he removed the Worker textbook. Books always made him feel better. He flipped through the first few pages. He'd come back and read them later. Right now, he wanted to see the initial levels of spells and abilities. He had leveled at the library, and he wondered what new things were available.

A section on leveling caught Ruwen's attention. At level two, being an even level, he had gained two spell points instead of one. He could use them to choose a lower-level spell, pick a newly available spell, or increase the level of a spell he already knew. Abilities worked the same way except you always just received one point per level.

He had spent months figuring out precisely what spells he would take as he leveled as a Mage. What a massive waste of time. He skimmed the descriptions and effects of the energy-based spells he'd ignored when he'd talked with Big D earlier that day.

Spell: *Hurry Up*
Level: *1*
Effect: *Adds +2 to Dexterity.*

Spell: *Scrub*
Level: *1*
Effect: *Use Energy to break down and remove stains and odor.*

Spell: *Strong Back*
Level: *2*
Effect: *Adds +2 to Strength.*

Spell: *Sharpen*
Level: *2*
Effect: *Remove a fraction of an object's edge.*

Spell: *Kindling*
Level: *3*
Effect: *Condense the air near your hand into a small blade.*

Spell: *Harden*
Level: *3*

Effect: Increase density.

He moved on to the Mana-based spells to refresh his memory.

Spell: *Mend Tool*
Level: *1*
Effect: *Temporarily bind broken objects together.*

Spell: *Campfire*
Level: *1*
Effect: *Create small magical campfire. Adds 5% to Energy, Mana, and Health Regeneration to all within 3 yards.*

Spell: *Sick Day*
Level: *2*
Effect: *Increase all resistances by 10%.*

Spell: *Numb*
Level: *2*
Effect: *Decrease sensations by 10%.*

Spell: *Second Wind*
Level: *3*
Effect: *Reduce food, water, and sleep requirements by 10%.*

Spell: *Grasp Crate*
Level: *3*
Effect: *Increase the roughness of your hands by 10%.*

Since he already had *Campfire*, he searched until he found the description for the level two version of the spell.

Spell: *Campfire*

Level: 2
Class: Worker
Effect: Create small magical campfire. Adds 7.5% to Energy, Mana, and Health Regeneration to all within 4 yards.
Cost: 160 Mana
Type: Area of Effect
Casting Time: 5 seconds
Recovery: 30 minutes
Duration: 1 hour

Another 2.5% of benefit would make the Spell even more valuable, and the extra yard would help as well. He didn't have a clear idea of what he should do, so he decided to do nothing. He flipped to the Abilities section and scanned them.

Ability: Hey You
Level: 1
Type: Self
Effect: Understand basic commands and terms in any language.

Ability: Owl Eyes
Level: 1
Type: Self
Effect: Magnify ambient light by 10%.

Ability: Sing
Level: 1
Type: AoE
Effect: Increase Haste by 2% and Endurance by 10%.

Ability: Detect Temperature
Level: 2
Type: Self
Effect: The hotter the object, the redder it appears.

Ability: *Glow*
Level: *2*
Type: *Self*
Effect: *Body emits soft light to aid sight in dark areas.*

Ability: *Knots*
Level: *2*
Type: *Object*
Effect: *Movement of secured objects is reduced by 10%.*

Since he already had *Hey You*, he searched until he found the description for the level two version of the ability. He read the description.

Ability: *Hey You*
Level: *2*
Type: *Self*
Effect: *Understand limited commands and terms in any language.*

"I'm not sloppy," a voice whispered.

CHAPTER 14

*R*uwen jumped and dropped his book. It struck the floor with a loud slap. Across from him sat a lean young man. The teenager had short brown hair and brown eyes so light they looked yellow. He was dressed in black cotton pants and a matching long shirt. He had his knees pulled up, and his arms rested on them.

"What?" Ruwen asked.

"Mistress said I was sloppy. I'm not."

It took Ruwen a second to put all the things Ky had said together. "You're Sift."

"And you're noisy," Sift said and then tossed him a small ball.

The grey ball was about an inch wide and had a simple pattern of lines etched on it. It felt damp, but when he looked at his hand, it didn't look wet.

"I'll come back for that," Sift said.

Sift pulled a scarf from his pocket that looked a lot like the Scarf of Freshness Ky had given Ruwen. Sift shoved the scarf in his mouth. He winked at Ruwen, leaped to his feet, and then ran to the entrance of the tunnel. Sift jumped into the air and hung from something above the entrance. Ruwen could only see the bottom half of Sift's body, and then in a blink, Sift had pulled himself up and disappeared from sight. Ruwen picked up his book, stuck it in his Void Band, and walked to the entrance.

Looking up, he didn't see the young man and the wall looked much too smooth to climb. What had Sift grabbed on to?

"So predictable," Ky said, right next to him.

Ruwen yelped in surprise and then shouted. "Will people stop doing that?"

Ky pulled the Elder Dagger from her waist and threw it up the wall in one fluid motion. Sift became visible about twenty feet in the air. He snatched the blade from the air, but the momentum from the weapon pulled him off the wall. As he fell, he thrust his legs out against the wall and flung himself into the cavern. Sift fell in a sharp arc toward the ground. Ruwen expected the sound of snapping bones, but when Sift struck the ground, he rolled, gently set the dagger down, and then sprinted directly at them.

Before Ruwen could react, Ky took three steps forward, and her whole body relaxed. Instead of throwing a punch, Sift tried to sidestep Ky and sweep her feet. Ky moved away from Sift, and the two circled each other.

"Your pride makes you vulnerable," Ky said.

Sift didn't say anything, but his cheeks grew pink.

"You traded surprise for a stranger's validation," Ky said. "Do you really care if he thinks you're sloppy?"

Sift reached forward but not to punch. He grabbed Ky's shirt at the shoulder and tried to pull her off balance. Ky pressed Sift's hand against her body and then turned sideways, twisting Sift's arm in the process. Sift did a cartwheel to keep his arm from breaking and used his free hand to strike at Ky's head. Ky let go of Sift and stepped backward, aiming her own blow at Sift's chest. Ruwen watched in awe as the two exchanged a dozen blows in the span of a few heartbeats. None of the strikes landed, and like before, the fight looked more like a dance than a conflict.

Sift suddenly stopped, stepped back, and bowed to Ky. She paused and then returned his bow.

"You're giving up already?" Ky asked.

Sift remained quiet.

Ky narrowed her eyes. "Why aren't you responding?"

Sift smiled, but his lips didn't part.

There was a soft click from Ruwen's hand, and he looked down at the grey ball. From Ruwen's peripheral vision, he saw Ky leap at him. Before she reached him, the ball hissed, and he smelled the faint scent of burnt almonds. His head spun, and he collapsed. He stared up at the darkness of the cavern and noticed his Health bar had turned red and another debuff had appeared next to his Clumsy and Foolish ones. After a moment, the new debuff disappeared. Opening his log, he read what had happened.

You have been poisoned!
You have taken 92 damage (3,172 damage*0.029(Antidote 97.1% effective))
Critical Alert! Health pool below 10%!
You have Vertigo!
You have struck the ground!
You have taken 2 damage
Critical Alert! Health pool below 10%!

Ky floated into Ruwen's vision, her lower face covered with a Scarf of Freshness.

A heartbeat later Sift appeared behind Ky and lightly touched the back of her neck. Sift's mouth and nose also covered by a scarf.

Sift spoke in a different language, but Ruwen's *Hey You* Ability deciphered one of the words: "Won."

Ky helped Ruwen sit up and leaned him against the cavern wall. She sat next to him and pulled the scarf off her face. Sift sat cross-legged across from them and pulled his scarf down as well.

"You hid the scarf in your mouth?" Ky asked.

Sift nodded.

"How did you give him the antidote?" Ky asked.

"I coated the Hisser with it," Sift said.

"He still might have died."

"He follows your false gods, and his soul is bound to them. His death would be temporary."

"I underestimated your duplicity," Ky said.

"A seed must grow if it wishes to see the sun," Sift said.

Ky reached up and touched the back of her neck. "I thought it would be years before you succeeded."

Sift looked at Ruwen. "Your guest provided a rare opportunity, and your delay allowed me to plan."

Ky looked at Ruwen. "So, this is basically all your fault."

A headache had replaced the vertigo, and it hurt to think. Ruwen didn't understand what they were talking about. "What's my fault?"

"The conversation I'm about to have with Sift's parents," Ky said.

"You will honor our agreement then?" Sift asked.

"Of course, but now is a very complicated time, and I'm not promising –" Ky said.

"Complication is the child of poor planning," Sift said.

"Ugh, you sound just like your father," Ky said.

Sift grinned. "Fish from the same lake –"

"Stop it!" Ky said, and flicked her wrist.

Sift caught the small dagger before it struck his chest and immediately set it on the ground beside him.

Ky stood, and Sift did as well.

"Maybe this is for the best. I need to speak with your parents anyway, and I'll explain to them our agreement. Until then, I need your help." Ky pointed down at Ruwen. "He has wasted his life. Start teaching him the Steps."

"Hey! I haven't wasted my life!" Ruwen said.

Ky ignored him and continued speaking to Sift. "How long since the last sweep?"

"A few weeks," Sift said.

"I need him to level and get some skills. Stay inside and no deeper than level three. Okay?"

Sift pointed back to Ky's Elder Dagger that she'd thrown at him when their fight had begun. "Can I keep him for a bit? I'd like to catch up."

Ky rolled her eyes. "You shouldn't indulge him. Most of what he tells you are lies." Ky turned from Sift to her dagger. She shouted at it. "That isn't true. You lie far more often than me."

Ruwen looked from Ky to Sift. The young man just raised his eyebrows.

"Fine, keep him. But don't believe anything he says." Ky said.

She knelt down next to Ruwen, and a notification pulsed at the bottom of his vision.

"Those are the Pyramid's noncombat quests," Ky said. "The standard Observer quests I can give won't work here, but you might get one or two of these done. Every bit helps. The Addas might have some as well, assuming they find you worthy."

"The Addas?" Ruwen asked.

"My parents, Madda and Padda. They're Step Masters." Sift said.

"Oh," Ruwen said. He had no idea what that meant.

Ky stood. "After talking with them, I'm headed back to Deepwell. I need to get some things in place before we meet Big D and leave town. How much do you know about the Observer Class?"

"I'm not an expert. I planned on being –"

Ky interrupted him. "A Mage. I remember. At level ten,

Observer splits into three sub-classes: Marksman, Shade, and Scout. At level twenty, the Marksman can specialize into Ranged, which focuses on crossbows and bows, or Melee that uses daggers and darts and such. Both are very offensive and won't provide you much protection."

"Okay."

"The Shade divides into two paths at level twenty: Assassin and Thief. While there are some skills in both that would help keep you alive, they take too long to learn."

The thought of assassinating people made his skin prickle. He didn't want to murder anyone.

That wasn't entirely true.

The people that wanted him dead, he would gladly kill first.

"You and your people are all Shades?" Ruwen asked.

"Most of us followed that Class branch. We have a significant number from the last branch as well, Scout. At level twenty, the Scout sub-Class branches into Ranger and Spy. Your Worker Class specialization will likely be Gatherer, and there would be some synergy with Ranger. If your life wasn't in such grave danger, I think that would be a smart choice. But what you really need right now are abilities that help you move around in public unnoticed. That is the realm of the Spy."

"A Spy?"

"That's my advice, but you don't need to make any decisions until level ten. For now, I don't care what spells and abilities you choose before level four. Let's talk through your choices before you pick the level four and five spells and abilities."

Ruwen moved nervously from foot to foot and glanced at Sift. It worried him that they were discussing his dual Classes so openly.

Ky nodded. "Good, you're at least showing some caution. Don't advertise your special nature. If anyone here notices, though, you can trust them to keep it quiet. My people keep bigger secrets than you."

Ky walked away and then stopped and faced Sift. "Two things. Your plan, while risky, was justified by the reward. It showed adaptability and quick thinking. I'm proud of you."

Sift's eyes lit up. "Thank you, Mistress. I would never have succeeded without your training." Sift bowed. "You continue to honor me with your time."

Ky returned the bow. "The second thing is," she pointed at Ruwen, "show him what happened the last time the Blood Moss escaped."

Ky strode away, but her voice floated back to Ruwen. "Shade's first rule: know the risks of what you take."

Then she was gone. So she'd known Ruwen had taken the Blood Moss. It was silly to think he could sneak that by her.

"That's a good rule," Sift said.

"It's the third, first rule, I've heard. Can Shades not count?"

Sift smiled. "So far this week I've been scolded with: caution is wisdom's fruit; fairness only matters to a Judge; eat knowledge, drink sweat, crap luck; be seen, never noticed. They're all the first rule."

"How many are there?"

"I quit counting around a hundred." Sift frowned. "I'm sorry for poisoning you. I would have felt terrible if you'd died."

"Thanks, I'm glad you gave me the antidote. That was a powerful poison."

"I know. But I needed Ky to believe you'd die. Without that distraction, I'd never have won."

"What did you win anyway?"

Sift beamed. "A trip. She promised to take me through the Blood Gate and show me the sea, and snow, and a Step tournament, and –"

Ruwen held up his hands. "Okay, that sounds great."

"It's all I've been thinking about for years."

"You've spent your whole life here?"

"My parents come from the other side, and I was born there,

but all my memories are from here. Rest for a bit. Once more of your Health returns, we'll get started."

Sift ran to the dagger, sat, and crossed his legs. He set the blade on his lap and spoke to it, but Ruwen could only hear Sift's side of the conversation.

"Did you see that?" Sift asked the dagger excitedly.

"I know. And she said she was proud of me."

"I can't wait to go. She said..."

Ruwen quit listening and focused on his notifications.

Ting!
You have completed the Quest – The Search for Truth (Part 1).
You have received 750 experience.
You have received the Spell Uru's Touch.

The quest completion notification surprised him. He opened the quest description to understand what had happened:

Truth is hard to find, and it is rarely close to home. Find a way to leave Deepwell's protection area in the next 30 days to begin your search.

Well, he doubted that is what Uru had in mind when she'd given him the quest, but Ky had said they were far from home, so he guessed it made sense. He closed the notification, and Ky's quests appeared.

Ting! Ting! Ting!
You have received the quest line...
The Black Pyramid (Novice to Initiate)
As a Novice of the Black Pyramid, you have much to learn. Survive these challenges to ascend higher within our ranks.
Reward: *Black Pyramid Rank of Initiate*
Reward: *Private Room in the Black Pyramid*

Accept or Decline

He chose *Accept,* and three black triangles, all stacked nearly on top of each other, appeared below his map. His previous quest indicators had been the golden square of regular quests or the blue circle of Uru's quests. He had never seen the stacked appearance, either.

When he focused on the Black Pyramid quest icon, he didn't get the standard quest text filling his vision. Instead, a drop-down list of quests appeared. Ky had given him a whole set of quests, not just one. Maybe she could do that because this was her area. He would go through them later.

Ruwen closed Ky's quests and was surprised to see another notification appear.

Ting!
You have received Uru's quest...
The Search for Truth (Part 2)
Travel to the Grey Canyon and look for that which has been lost.
Reward: *1,500 experience*
Accept or Decline

Ruwen's breath caught. The Grey Canyon was where his parents and the shipment of terium had disappeared. Why did Uru want him to go there? Was it because she knew he wanted to find his parents? Maybe, but it was more likely she wanted her own questions answered.

He chose *Accept,* and another quest marker appeared under his map. This one had Uru's blue circle for an indicator. Thinking of the goddess reminded him of the spell he'd gotten from completing her first quest. He opened his Profile and then selected the pulsing yellow Spells tab. A new spell had been added, and he focused on it until the description appeared.

Spell: *Uru's Touch*
Level: *1*
Class: *Root*
Effect: *Synchronize your current state with Uru when outside the domain of Uru's Blessing.*
Cost: *200 Health / 200 Mana / 200 Energy*
Type: *Self*
Casting Time: *2 minutes*
Recovery: *1 Week*

He gasped. Everything about this spell shocked him. Synchronizing yourself with Uru outside of her area was impossible. It was one of the first things you learned. It's what made traveling far from home so dangerous. This spell allowed you to do just that. It was incredible.

But the cost! He knew a few advanced spells cost Health and Mana, but he had never seen a spell that used all three pools. It would require a few more levels before he could even cast it. Which took two minutes! Who had that kind of time to cast a spell? Could a person concentrate that long? It seemed the most ludicrous part of the spell until he read the recovery. An entire week! That was seven days longer than even the most complex Rune Mage spells.

Ruwen closed the spell details and looked at Sift. The teenager was wiping tears from his eyes and laughing softly. He noticed Ruwen's attention.

"Io tells the best jokes," Sift said.

"Io?"

"That is what I call him. He follows the old ways like my family. We never speak our true names."

"What? Your name isn't Sift?"

"Of course not. It is what I do, not who I am."

"I've never heard of hiding your name."

"It is old magic. Magic from before your gods. Real magic."

Now he knew Sift was crazy. "You said before that I followed a false god and would be reborn. Does your god not revive you?"

Sift looked horrified. "Why would I want to trap my soul here?"

"So you can live," Ruwen said.

"That's not living. It's a prison."

Until this morning, Ruwen had lived in constant fear that he'd die. He had such big plans for his life, and the thought of not having the safety of Ascension and rebirth made him cringe inside. He wanted to live forever if that was possible. But, his time in school had taught him that no matter how good the argument, there was no convincing the crazy or stupid. He didn't know which one Sift was, but there was no reason to keep discussing this.

Sift stood and placed Io in a sheath strapped to his lower back. "You ready?"

Ruwen pushed himself up and did his best not to groan. It felt like he'd been up for a week. "I guess. What are we doing?"

"We're going to sweep," Sift said. "But first we need to get you some proper clothes."

Sift moved forward, and Ruwen followed. He had hoped that he would learn something useful here. When Ky had told him he needed to get to level five, he'd actually been a little excited about what adventures that might entail. But it turned out all she meant for him to do was sweep her house. He didn't know how much experience Workers got for menial tasks, but it couldn't be much. This was going to be a very long two days here.

"I usually sweep by myself. I have some…skills that make it safer. You'll probably be okay though," Sift said.

Ruwen stopped. "What do you mean safer? I thought we were sweeping."

"We are. And to be honest, I'm glad to have help. I usually don't wait three weeks between cleanings."

"I feel like we are talking past each other. What do you mean, exactly, when you say sweep?"

Sift looked confused. "I mean sweeping through the upper level and removing anything that has made its way up from the deeper levels."

Ruwen's heart beat louder. "And by anything you mean..."

"Bendies, Screamers, Spitters, Sleepies, Clappers –"

Ruwen held up his hands. "I've never heard of any of those things."

"Oh, those are just my names. You might call them something different."

Sift started walking again, and after a moment, Ruwen followed. The names Sift had used conjured up terrible images in Ruwen's mind.

"I could just, you know, sweep. Like with a broom," Ruwen said.

Sift laughed. "You're funny. I like you. But my parents do most of the cleaning. They think fighting is a waste of time and energy."

"Isn't there another way to get experience?"

"My dad once spent two weeks getting seven rocks to balance on each other. He said he experienced the rocks' struggle and pain from being trapped in such rigid forms."

Ruwen shook his head and gave up. Sift was crazy, his family sounded crazy, and Ruwen was crazy for thinking this was the right option. He could have stayed in his room in the library for the rest of his life. It would have been better than this.

"I've made a huge mistake," Ruwen whispered.

"Shade's first rule: you only have yourself to blame," Sift said cheerfully.

Ky had told him and Tremine the same thing. Ruwen hadn't given any thought to what she had given up or how her life had changed because of the choices he'd made. In fact, the more he thought about it, the more he realized how selfish he'd been. To be honest, he was afraid of what the upper levels held. But Ky wanted to keep him alive, and she thought this was the best method, as horrible as it sounded. It would be okay.

Sift's shoulders dropped. "A Shrieker got into the head of my last helper. She didn't survive."

Ruwen's stomach twisted. "I thought you called them Screamers."

"Screamers evolve into Shriekers if they aren't killed, and I haven't been down there for a while."

"So we shouldn't assume Screamers."

"Shade's first rule: assumptions lead to the temple tub."

Ruwen groaned, and Sift smiled.

CHAPTER 15

*T*he hallway ended in a large square room. The floor transitioned into polished granite, and the walls had shakers evenly spaced around the room. Tapestries hung between the lights, and chairs, tables, and couches filled the room. Many of the tables had cards or dice on them, and most had half-filled glasses. The far side of the room had a long wooden bar that took up half its length. Cups and bottles were arranged neatly on shelves but the room, like all the other rooms they had passed, was empty.

"Where is everyone?" Ruwen asked.

"What do you mean?"

"We've been walking for ten minutes, and I haven't seen another person. I thought maybe it was just you and your family here with Ky, but then why have this recreation room?"

Sift stopped and faced him. "You haven't seen a single person?"

The question confused Ruwen. "Have you?"

"We passed four on the way here. There are," Sift glanced around the room, counting, "Seven I can see in here. Which means there are probably triple that number actually in here."

"What?" Ruwen asked and then looked around the room again. "I don't see anyone."

Sift looked concerned. "I understand the hallways. It's like a game with them to move around unnoticed. But few in here are trying very hard to stay hidden. This is where they come to relax."

As Ruwen thought about it, he realized his wrist with the mark had been cool almost the entire time he'd left the cavern. The feeling had been constant, so his mind had just filtered it out.

"Hmm, that isn't good," Sift said. "With a Perception that low, you'll never see the Flickers."

"Flickers?"

"They're kind of like shadows with knives. Maybe Fluffy will have something to help."

Sift moved again, and Ruwen followed. He studied the tables, especially the ones with drinks, but still couldn't see anyone.

"Are they staring at me?" Ruwen asked.

"Not all of them."

They walked past the bar and into another hallway.

"Mistress wanted me to teach you the Steps. I'll start you with Dad's style since you don't have any training. He's a Pull Master, and it's easier to grasp." Sift laughed.

Ruwen stared at him.

"Easier to grasp. Grasp. Okay, never mind. You know less than I thought," Sift said.

"How many kinds of Steps are there?" Ruwen asked.

"Well if you mean styles, there are probably hundreds. If you mean actual moves in my parents' styles, there are one hundred and seventeen in each. Dad's style is soft, and Mom's is hard. But the central truth in both is balance."

"When did you start learning?"

"I've never not been learning." Sift stopped and faced Ruwen.

"For now, let's start with something simple. Thrashers have these," Sift wiggled his fingers and arms, "tendrils, I guess, that shoot out and grab things."

Ruwen's eyes got big, and he took a step backward.

Sift waved his arms. "Don't worry. Usually their prey is small. If they latch on to you," Sift said, grabbing his own arm, "just throw yourself backward."

Sift dropped quickly and did a backward somersault. "It will rip the tendril right out of the Thrasher. You try."

Sift grabbed hold of Ruwen's arm. Ruwen had never done anything like this before. Physical fighting made him uncomfortable, and he'd avoided any activity where he had to wrestle people or hit them. The thought of something whipping some sort of appendage at him and latching on scared him to death. That was definitely something he wanted to know how to escape. Ruwen threw himself backward, pulling Sift along with him. Instead of the graceful backward somersault Sift had performed, Ruwen landed hard on his butt. His momentum forced him back, and he slammed his head into the granite.

His vision swam, and the now familiar Vertigo debuff appeared next to his Clumsy and Foolish ones. His Health bar flashed a four and dropped a fraction. He stood back up and rubbed the back of his head.

"That was, umm, not exactly what we were going for. Do you have some sort of disability?" Sift asked.

Anger tightened Ruwen's chest, but when he looked at Sift, there was no malice or ill intent on his face. He genuinely looked curious.

Ruwen took a deep breath and pushed down his embarrassment. "I have a Clumsy debuff right now, and my Dexterity has never been very high. Honestly, I don't like this kind of thing, so I'm new to it."

Sift nodded and began walking again. "No problem. We'll take it slow. Let's start with your breathing. Until we get to the quartermaster, inhaling and exhaling should each take five seconds. Fill your lungs. Imagine the air powering your body and mind."

Ruwen rarely thought about his breathing. Sometimes when he sat slouched in a chair reading a book, he noticed his breathing was shallow and he'd take some deep breaths. But nothing like this. It felt odd to focus on something that happened naturally. As he walked, he realized how terribly difficult it actually was. His mind rebelled at the activity and continuously wanted to do something else. Ruwen found himself having to spend a lot of mental energy on the simple task.

Sift slowed, and Ruwen focused back on his surroundings. Ten minutes had passed in what felt like a moment, and a small icon at the top of his vision disappeared before he could open it. A notification blinked for his attention, and he opened it.

Shing!
You have learned a new skill!
Skill: *Meditation*
Level: *1*
Effect: *Clear Mind: increase Health, Mana, and Energy Regeneration by 0.5%.*

He did feel better, and the new skill cheered him up. They had stopped at the end of a hallway, and a grey door stood closed in front of them. Sift gave it three quick knocks and then winked at Ruwen.

When no one came, Ruwen glanced up at his clock and saw thirty seconds had gone by.

"Maybe we should knock again," Ruwen said.

"No, that will only make Fluffy grouchy," Sift said.

A small opening appeared in the door at eye height, and a pair of squinting eyes looked at them.

"Who's grouchy?" a gruff voice responded from the other side of the door.

"Hi, Fluffy. It's me," Sift said.

"I can see that. What do you want? And who is the baby?" Fluffy said.

Sift smiled. "This is Ruwen. Mistress just brought him through. He needs the basics and maybe something to help him with sweeping."

"Huh. Her standards are getting lower every year. He looks pathetic. Show me your marks."

Sift held up his wrist, and Ruwen did the same. He concentrated on the mark, and it appeared.

Fluffy grunted, and the window slammed shut. The sound of bolts moving echoed in the hallway.

"He doesn't seem very friendly," Ruwen whispered.

"No, we're lucky. It looks like we caught him in a good mood," Sift said.

Ruwen stood up straight and wondered again how his life had turned so terrible. The door opened, and as soon as Sift and Ruwen entered the room, Fluffy slammed it shut. The quartermaster slid two of the locks into place and then returned to a desk in the far corner. The desk, piled high with papers, almost hid Fluffy from view. He ignored Sift and Ruwen.

Fluffy wore soft leathers and had a green vest lined with a row of pockets. He had no hair on the top of his head but made up for it with a large bushy grey beard. His face had wrinkles from constant frowning, and he twirled a wrapped charcoal stick through his fingers while he read.

Other than the desk, there weren't a lot of furnishings. A standing partition to their left would provide privacy for changing clothes, and to their right, a few chairs sat around an oversized table. The middle of each wall held a door identical to the one they'd entered. They were all closed and locked.

After a minute, Ruwen became upset that Fluffy was ignoring them.

"Why don't you practice your breathing," Sift said.

Ruwen glanced at Sift to see if he'd picked up on Ruwen's frustration. But Sift just smiled.

"Wasted moments make an empty life," Sift said.

"Shade's first rule?"

"No, one of my dad's sayings. It is hard to tell the difference sometimes."

Ruwen concentrated on his breathing again, losing himself in the repetitive task. A moment later, Sift shook him.

"Wow, you really took to that. It's like your mind is getting a rest for the first time," Sift said.

Ruwen blinked a few times and looked at his clock. It hadn't been one minute but five. Sift's comment resonated with him. He spent a ton of time in his head, and his internal thoughts never stopped. Maybe this was the first time in his life he'd given his mind a break. It was like feeding a starving person.

"He's ready for us," Sift said.

They walked over to Fluffy, and the man handed Ruwen a piece of paper. Ruwen scanned it. Fluffy hadn't been ignoring them, he'd been filling out paperwork. Ruwen's name, Class, level, and basic attributes were listed along the top. It only listed his Worker Class, though. As perceptive as Fluffy seemed to be, he hadn't discovered Ruwen's second Class.

"The old lady is losing her mind bringing a Worker in here. What's he going to do, lift our heavy boxes? Is he being trained as a Spy? This is nonsense."

"I'll ask the next time I see her. You know how she likes to explain herself," Sift said.

Fluffy frowned. "Well, there's no need for that. I'm just wondering, that's all. Damn strange sight seeing a Worker in here." He pointed to the bottom of the sheet. "Initial there accepting your standard Novice gear."

Ruwen glanced at the list of items on the bottom half of the page. Most of it was bedding and clothes, but two things caught his eye: a magic ring and dagger. But both had a line through them with a small note: "Minimum Level Not Met."

Ruwen hid his disappointment. He guessed most people that got this far in Ky's organization were much higher level. He took a charcoal pencil from Fluffy's desk and signed his name.

Fluffy took the form back. "Where's he staying?"

"Ah, with me, I guess," Sift said.

"I'll have another bed added to your room," Fluffy said.

Fluffy walked to the door across from his desk and went through it. Ruwen could see it was a huge storage room. Fluffy returned a minute later with a pile of bedding and two sets of shirts, pants, and boots. He held each up to Ruwen, gauging the size, and then went and fetched more of the proper size. In the end, Ruwen got bedding, three shirts and pants, a pair of boots and some sort of soft slipper he'd never seen before. The description called them Scaling Shoes. Everything was black.

"I noticed he didn't get a weapon or ring," Sift said. "Will he get credit for those? Is there any kind of alternative?"

"Of course, I'll credit his account. But my options are limited. The vast majority of our holdings are Class or level restricted. Anything more exotic he can't afford."

Ruwen was frustrated that he hadn't been given the magic items. He could use them, but he couldn't tell Fluffy that. Ky said not to advertise his dual Class. "How much do I have?" Ruwen asked.

"With the credits for the dagger and ring...plus the tokens you get for becoming a novice...you have one hundred and thirteen tokens," Fluffy said.

"Is that a lot?" Ruwen asked.

"Not enough to make a difference downstairs," Sift said. He faced Fluffy. "Remember the girl I brought through a few months back?"

Fluffy raised his hands and mimicked his head exploding. Ruwen's breath caught. Earlier, Sift hadn't provided any details of his helper's death. Now that Ruwen knew his head could explode, he wanted to do this even less.

Sift's face grew sad. "Yeah, that one. I'm still carrying that with me, and I don't want to experience it again."

Fluffy nodded and covered his ears. "I hate those things."

"What's my balance?" Sift asked.

Fluffy searched through his piles and pulled out a bundle of papers that were bound together like a book. He flipped to the back. "One hundred eighty-three thousand nine hundred forty-seven tokens."

"What can we get with that?" Sift asked.

Fluffy looked back and forth between them. "Let me look."

The quartermaster walked to the door behind him, opened three locks with different keys, and then pulled the door open. This door led to a room that looked like a vault.

Ruwen grabbed Sift's shoulder. "You can't do that! That's your money. You shouldn't spend it on me."

Sift smiled. "I'm doing it for myself. I don't want to ever see that again. And to be honest, she had more skills than you. You're going to need an edge."

A minute later, Fluffy returned with a crate under each arm. He walked to the table and set them down. Ruwen and Sift joined him. Fluffy touched the container closest to them.

"These here are useless items. To a Shade that is. But since this is the first time we've had a non-Shade here, I reckon you won't care. They're too valuable to chuck, but they take up my vault space. I have more, but you'll need to come back when you're level ten."

Fluffy carefully removed the items and laid them out in a line on the table.

"I have two suggestions," Sift said.

"Please," Ruwen replied.

"Don't take many daggers. You don't have the knowledge to throw them, which means anything you damage will be close to you. You don't want anything down in the dungeon close to you."

"So one just for emergencies and something to fight with?" Ruwen asked.

"Yes, which brings me to my second point. Avoid anything that requires much strength or skill. Things move a little fast down there."

Ruwen swallowed hard. "Thanks."

He looked over the weapons: three swords, two large axes, and a staff. The staff had been made from a grey wood, and white swirls were etched around it, circling the staff like storm clouds. It was five feet tall and the thickness of two fingers. Ruwen picked it up, and its lightness surprised him.

Tring!
The Black Pyramid has rewarded you...
Name: *Staff of Chimes*
Damage: *6-12*
Area of Effect: *30 feet*
Quality: *Fine*
Durability: *100 of 100*
Weight: *4.2 lbs.*
Effect (Passive): *+1 Intelligence, +1 Wisdom*
Effect: *While in combat the wind chimes of Temple Yulm can be heard, resulting in a 10% chance to distract your opponent for 1 to 3 seconds.*
Restriction: *None*
Description: *The wind never rests. Even if you do.*

Ruwen swung the staff back and forth a couple of times. It had a nice weight to it. Any Class in the Observer tree would want Dexterity on their weapon, not mental attributes, and having the sound of wind chimes giving away your position every time you used it seemed counterproductive to sneaking around. It made sense why this weapon had never been taken by one of Ky's people

Sift nodded. "That's a good choice. You can be effective without a lot of training. Plus, a few Step sequences can incorporate a staff. I'll teach you those first."

Ruwen set the staff to the side and looked through the daggers. Most of them were vicious-looking with serrated edges or spikes for poking out eyes. He had no desire to carry something like that. The last one, though, looked plain. It had a black handle, and the blade was white. Ruwen picked it up.

Tring!
The Black Pyramid has rewarded you...
Name: *Fastidious Blade*
Damage: *4-8*
Quality: *Uncommon*
Durability: *30 of 30*
Weight: *1.20 lbs.*
Effect (Passive): *+1 Dexterity*
Effect: *Contaminants will cause dagger to vibrate until clean.*
Restriction: *None*
Description: *A clean blade is a sharp blade.*

A weapon that cleaned itself. That didn't seem so bad. Why wouldn't an Observer want this? It even had Dexterity on it. He set it next to the staff and then moved to the last pile. A cloak. He couldn't tell if the color was dark grey or maybe a faded black. He picked it up, and the softness of the cloth surprised him.

Tring!
The Black Pyramid has rewarded you...

Name: *Pacifist's Cloak*
AC: *10*
Quality: *Rare*
Durability: *25 of 25*
Weight: *0.12 lbs.*
Effect (Passive): *10% Perception, 10% Detect Traps.*
Effect (Triggered): *Once per day can harden into a 100 hit point shield.*
Restriction: *Weapons of any kind are prohibited*
Description: *Why can't we all just get along?*

The cloak had a short vest connected to it that covered his upper chest and back. He slipped his arms through the holes and then fastened the clasps across his chest. The cloak's weight was barely noticeable. He quickly twisted his body, but the cloak barely moved.

Sift raised an eyebrow. "I don't like cloaks. It's too easy for someone to grab you from behind. But this one is staying close to your body, so the added protection is probably worth the risk." Sift walked over and pulled the collar away from Ruwen's neck. "And the collar isn't connected to the vest, so your staff can still be worn on your back."

A bit of the tightness in his chest disappeared. He had imagined himself in a brilliant red cloak when he joined the Mage Academy. Even though that dream would never come to pass, the cloak made him feel better.

"I like it," Ruwen said.

Fluffy picked up the things Ruwen hadn't chosen and stuck them back in the crate. He carefully laid out the items from the second crate.

Fluffy faced Ruwen. "Between your level and class, I don't have much to show you." Fluffy turned to Sift. "And as generous as your offer is, there are strict rules about how Pyramid equipment is purchased. You'd know them if you ever spent your tokens."

Fluffy raised his hands as Sift protested. "I don't make the rules. But, I'm not heartless." Fluffy turned back to Ruwen. "I have some discretion on what things cost. The cloak, dagger, and staff are useless to the Pyramid. I'm willing to exchange them for the standard equipment you would have been issued. Now these," Fluffy said, patting the other crate, "are usable by the Pyramid but aren't very powerful. All of them are lower than level ten."

Ruwen stared at the crate and the handful of items in it. "How do I earn them?"

"I'm glad you asked. Like I said before, we don't get other classes down here. And many of our items are too valuable to remove from the vault."

Ruwen tilted his head in confusion. "I'm still not seeing how I can help."

Fluffy nodded. "Many of our items were procured violently. Even after normal cleaning, many have stains that just won't come out. In fact, many of the magical items can only be cleaned with other magic."

Ruwen's stomach clenched, and his chest tightened. Of course, Fluffy wanted Ruwen to clean. He was just a Worker, after all. Not good for anything else. Anger pushed its way up from his chest, and he clenched his hands.

"You can really do that?" Sift asked.

Ruwen's anger sputtered at Sift's question. "What?"

"You can remove stains?" Sift asked.

"I guess."

Sift nodded. "That is powerful magic."

Ruwen pressed his lips together. He had really started to like Sift, but now the young man was making fun of him. Ruwen didn't choose this Class. Why did people have to look down at him and make fun of his stupid spells and abilities?

"Shade's first rule: guilt dies with a clean shirt," Sift said.

Confusion warred with Ruwen's anger. "That doesn't even make sense."

Sift brought his right leg up to his left hip and held it there. "Do you see them?"

Dark splotches covered the bottom of his pants. Sift let his leg drop and closed his eyes. "I spend ten minutes every night trying to wash them out. They remind me of Lylan and how I failed her."

"Lylan?" Ruwen asked.

Fluffy made the head exploding motion again, and Ruwen understood.

Sift opened his eyes. "As much as I try and put it behind me, the stains are a reminder. A distraction. Without a clean outside, a clean inside is hopeless."

They were all silent for a few seconds.

"Like I said, your magic is powerful," Sift said.

The last bit of Ruwen's anger disappeared. Sift might be delusional in what he considered powerful magic, but there was no doubt in Ruwen's mind; Sift was sincere.

Ting!
You have received the quest...
Nothing to See Here...
Quartermaster Fluffy has requested your help in cleaning items stored in the Black Pyramid vaults. Magically clean five items to receive your reward. This quest is repeatable.
Reward: *One item from Fluffy's crate of crap*
Accept or Decline

The idea of cleaning made his stomach turn. His parents had kept a clean home, and he had grown up doing chores. So, the cleaning itself wasn't the issue. This was just another reminder of how his life had gone sideways. He hadn't chosen a new spell when he'd turned level two but had planned to increase the level of his magic *Campfire* spell. He supposed taking the *Scrub* spell instead wouldn't be the end of the world. Even if the magic items were low level and probably mostly useless, they would still be better than what he had, which was basically nothing. Logic favored the *Scrub* spell.

Sighing, Ruwen chose *Accept*. He would have to look in his Worker textbook later and see how to learn *Scrub*.

Fluffy put a hand on Sift's shoulder. "Her death wasn't your fault, son. She knew the rules, just like the rest of us."

"Thanks," Sift said.

Fluffy nodded at Ruwen. "Have you been taught the rules?"

"Just the first one," he said.

Fluffy grinned and then laughed. Sift joined him, and their laughter echoed in the room. Ruwen smiled in spite of all the fear and sadness he felt.

Fluffy wiped his eyes. "Well, good. That's the most important one." Then he picked up the two crates and headed for the vault door.

"Change into your Novice gear, and then we'll get going," Sift said. "We should still be able to clear the first level tonight."

CHAPTER 16

*R*uwen saw no one on the way to the first level of the Pyramid's dungeon, although he was pretty sure Sift nodded at someone a few times. Sift still had Io in a sheath on his lower back, but other than that, he had no apparent weapons. Ruwen had changed into the black shirt and pants that Fluffy had given him. They clung to his body, but in a comfortable way that didn't hamper his movement. He had decided to wear his Feather Boots of Grasping and kept the Baton of a Thousand Uses on his left hip. Fluffy had given him a sheath for his dagger, and it rested uncomfortably on his right side. It felt odd having things attached to him.

The lower they went, the rougher the stone walls and ceiling became. Shakers were spaced close enough along the wall that Ruwen could see without squinting. They turned into a smaller tunnel and began working their way through multiple doors. Each door was made of something different. A few he figured out, like the oak and iron doors. But many were strange, and when they came to a door made from what looked like thin cloth, he couldn't keep quiet.

"Fabric? What in Uru's name could this keep out?" Ruwen asked.

Sift closed the door behind them. "Smell it."

He stared at Sift for a few seconds, but the young man seemed serious. Ruwen leaned close to the door and used his hand to waft the scent to him instead of just sticking his nose onto the door. A heartbeat later, Ruwen wrinkled his nose and stood up straight.

Sift noticed how Ruwen had smelled the door. "You've had laboratory training?"

"Some. Just the basics. Nothing fancy like a Merchant or Observer might learn."

"That's good. We make many of our own supplies. So, what did you smell?"

"Pickling acid," Ruwen said.

"Excellent. Any idea why cloth soaked in acid might act as a barrier?"

Ruwen thought for a few seconds and then shook his head. "Nothing comes to mind. Rogue cucumbers?"

Sift smiled. "Misties."

"I've never heard of them."

"They're like a cross between fog and vomit."

"Fog vomit?"

"Yes, but if their fluids become acidic, they quickly break down."

Ruwen thought about that. "So, you use cloth because they'll absorb and mix with the acid quickly, as opposed to wood or some other hard substance."

"Exactly. You're smarter than you look."

Once again, Ruwen cursed himself for not adding another point to Charisma. But Sift's praise made him feel better.

"Thanks," Ruwen said. "So, each of these doors is to keep a specific type of monster out?"

"Yup."

"Why don't they just organize themselves to help each other through the doors?"

Sift chuckled. "Well, if she made them that smart, we'd be in trouble. Half the time they are fighting each other down there, and all I have to do is watch."

Ruwen had noticed none of the doors had locks. Most just had a latch or a slider on both sides. Anything remotely intelligent would be able to pass through all these doors.

"It doesn't seem the safest," Ruwen said.

"Anything that gets through the doors will still have to pass through a tunnel of traps and then the guard room. There are always at least two guards in there, although today I saw four."

"We passed four guards?"

Sift nodded and winced. "You didn't see any of them?"

Ruwen shook his head. "Crap."

They crossed through a couple more doors and then stopped at the top of a wide staircase leading down into darkness. A notification flashed, and Ruwen opened it.

Ting!
You have received the Black Pyramid quest...
Taking out the Trash (Level 1)
Clear the central room and at least two antechambers on the first floor of all vermin.
Reward: *5 Black Pyramid tokens*
Reward: *1,000 experience*
Accept or Decline

"Do you have both quests?" Sift asked.

"I got the Trash one."

"There should be another subquest available. It probably didn't automatically activate because we aren't close enough to the wall of scales to trigger."

Ruwen opened the master quest **The Black Pyramid**

(Novice to Initiate) he'd received from Ky. There were multiple requirements to complete it, one of which was **Clear 10 Levels of the Black Pyramid**. He opened the next requirement, which was **Complete 100 Alchemical Recipes**. A subquest under that was no longer greyed out, and he focused on it.

Ting!
You have received the quest...
Killer Recipes for the Busy Shade
Not every task requires a dagger. A healthy Shade relies on the proper proportions of the Pyramid, with results to die for. Use your mind to discover the appropriate balance.
Restriction: *One attempt per day.*
Reward: *Black Pyramid cipher (Level 1)*
Reward: *Five-Minute Fare to Die For, Volume 1*
Reward: *500 experience*
Accept or Decline

Ruwen accepted the quest. He loved working in the lab at school and had briefly thought about the Merchant Class. But his heart had always belonged to being a Mage. While he could still level up many of the skills associated with Merchants and Crafters, his creations would never be as good and would take longer to make than those with the proper Class. He didn't care, though. Mixing ingredients to create new things excited him, and learning a cipher would be interesting, too. He wondered if this would allow him to read the ciphered parchment from the Blood Gate.

He looked to see if any other quests were available under the requirements, but everything remained greyed out. Well, at least he had two quests. Both had added a black triangle on his map almost directly on top of his current location. It must mean they were below him. Closing the quest window, he nodded at Sift.

"Okay, get ready. Sometimes things make it to the stairs."

Ruwen pulled the staff from the harness on his back. "Is there any light down there?"

"I can trigger some lights, but it will warn them. It makes it a little harder."

In the dungeon, there would be no ambient light for the Jaga Wedding Band to amplify. It would be useless.

"Well, that sucks. But I don't think we have a choice. I can't see much without light. I'll be helpless in the dark."

"Limuno!" Sift said.

The walls began glowing, and the stairwell came into view. Ruwen relaxed a little. He hated the dark.

"Aren't you taking a weapon?" Ruwen asked.

"I am the weapon."

Ruwen raised his eyebrows.

Sift smiled and patted the dagger in the small of his back. "Plus, I have Io for emergencies."

Ruwen moved the staff from one hand to the other, not sure what to do with it. Sift narrowed his eyes and held out a hand. Ruwen gave him the weapon.

"I'll show you some basics, so you're more comfortable."

Ruwen took a few steps backward, and Sift did the same.

"When you attack, step into it, and swing the staff diagonally like this," Sift said.

Sift stepped forward and swung the staff downward, slashing the air. The faint sound of wind chimes filled the room.

"When you block, hold it with both hands and step to the side. Like all fighting, avoidance is better than redirection, which is better than deflection, which is better than absorption."

Sift stepped forward in a lunge and stabbed the staff outward. "Attacking like this is safer, as less of your body is exposed. Look at my feet and stance. You must always keep your balance. Balance is the solution to every problem. Now you try."

Sift handed the staff back to Ruwen and then stepped away.

Ruwen's hands were sweaty. He hated physical activities. But in a few minutes, he would be fighting things that wanted to kill him, and he needed to be as ready as possible. He stepped forward and slashed downward. The staff's weight and momentum made it hard to slow, which Ruwen realized a little too late.

The staff struck the stone floor with a crack, and the vibration of the impact caused the weapon to slip out of his sweaty hands. With a loud clang, the staff fell to the floor, and Ruwen shook his hands to remove the sting of the vibration. His cheeks burned as he knelt to pick up his weapon.

"Well, you get points for enthusiasm," Sift said. "You might want to tell Blapy you're sorry, though. If you get on her bad side, your life here will be a nightmare."

"Blapy?"

"Black Pyramid. I just call her Blapy."

"Wait, are you saying this place is sentient?"

"Yes, aren't all dungeons?"

"No. Out of the thousands of dungeons on my world, there are less than ten that are sentient. They are really, really, really dangerous."

"Well, I've only been in this one."

Sift obviously didn't know what sentient meant. He had spoken earlier about his dad and the feelings a pile of rocks experienced. Ruwen guessed Sift, like his dad, was probably a little crazy. He needed the young man, though, so he played along.

Kneeling again, Ruwen rubbed the small divot he'd caused in the stone. "I'm sorry, Blapy. I'm new to this and still learning. I'll try and be more careful."

Sift nodded with approval. "Try again, but without as much force. You don't have the strength yet to stop your swing or the skills to redirect a blow."

Feeling a little embarrassed, Ruwen swung the staff again, but this time with far less force.

"Better. Now, do another twenty," Sift said.

Sometime after the tenth swing, Ruwen heard chimes, and he smiled. It meant the staff believed it was being wielded and not just swung around. He practiced the lunge for a couple of minutes until Sift nodded. A minimized notification pulsed in the bottom of his vision and he opened it.

Shing!
You have learned a new skill!
Skill: *Staff*
Level: *1*
Effect: *Increase damage by 0.5%.*

His first weapon skill! It made him feel proud. He'd never planned to use his physical skills to protect himself, but a new path had been forced on him, and he was anxious to make up for all the time he'd wasted.

"I'm ready," Ruwen said.

They started down the stairs, which soon curved to the right. A minute later, they stopped at the end of a large rectangular room. It looked similar to the bar he'd walked through above, but this area looked like a war zone. The chairs and couches were mostly broken or destroyed. About every thirty feet along each wall, there were double doors or the remnants of them. In the distance, on the far wall, Ruwen could make out what looked like a bar. Tables dotted the room, and he thought he caught a glimpse of something small scurrying between all the debris.

"This is one of the recreation rooms from back in the old days when people came to test themselves in Blapy," Sift said.

It struck Ruwen that he knew almost nothing about this place. He didn't even know what it looked like outside. His stomach clenched, but he pushed his anxiety down. There would be time to learn all those things. Right now, he needed to focus on staying alive, and hopefully, leveling.

Sift closed his eyes and stood completely still. After a few seconds, Ruwen stepped away from Sift, and took a practice swing with his staff, relieved that he heard the chimes. His hands shook, and his legs felt weak.

Sift put a hand on his shoulder. "Relax, friend." Sift pointed to the two closest doors on the right wall. "Those two antechambers are yours. I'll start on the other side and work my way around."

"You're leaving me?" Ruwen asked.

He hated how weak that made him sound, but he was barely keeping his fear in check.

"If I stay too near you, I'll leach all the experience. Further down that won't matter as much, but up here the monsters just aren't worth enough to share."

"Okay."

"There is nothing too dangerous in here."

"How do you know that?"

"I sifted the energies in here."

"When you closed your eyes?"

"Yeah."

Ruwen didn't know what that meant, but it did make him feel better. Sift was the expert here. Ruwen took a deep breath.

Sift walked toward the doors across from the ones Ruwen would enter. "Remember Shade's first rule."

"Which is?"

"Fear is best heard, not followed."

"What does that mean?"

"Your fear means you aren't stupid. You should be cautious. But, if you follow fear, stay safe your whole life, you will never grow." Sift stopped in front of his doors and faced Ruwen. "And you want to grow, don't you?"

"Yes, very much."

"Good. Then let's get busy."

Sift slid between the half-opened doors and disappeared.

Ruwen faced his doors, which also were ajar. He took another deep breath. People wanted him dead, maybe even a god, too. He needed to get stronger, and the only way to do that quickly was to fight. He swung the staff again, touched the dagger on his right hip, and his baton on the left. His Scarf of Freshness remained wrapped around his neck. He didn't have much, but it would have to do. Before his fear overwhelmed him, he pushed the door open and walked inside.

CHAPTER 17

*R*uwen stopped just inside the door. Pews, most of them broken, lined the room like a freshly plowed field. In the central aisle, a few six-foot-high candle stands had survived the destruction. Their eight-fingered hands were empty now, the candles lost long ago. An altar stood at the far end of the antechamber, fifty feet away, and a statue of Uru leaned against the back wall. Her arms were broken off, and half her face was shattered. Brown webbing covered the walls, and it made the light dimmer. He slowly studied the room and then as much of the ceiling as he could see. The webbing probably meant spiders. He hated spiders.

The room appeared empty, and he relaxed a little. Keeping his back to the wall, he sidestepped to the left. He didn't want anything coming up behind him. When he reached the corner, he stopped again and listened. Nothing. He knelt and tried to look under the pews, but he couldn't see very far because of all the debris.

His heartbeat seemed loud in his ears, and he took a few deep breaths to slow it. The webbing stuck to his arm, and he stepped away from the wall. A new thought struck him: what if they were tiny spiders, and millions of them would swarm his body, consuming him in seconds? His heart thudded again, and he began casting *Campfire*.

The five second cast time felt like an eternity, but then it finally finished, and the room brightened. Ruwen's Mana bar flashed the number one hundred fifty and then dropped to almost empty. The +1 intelligence from the Staff of Chimes had brought his pool up to one hundred seventy, giving him twenty Mana to spare. Not that he had any other spells to cast.

His Mana bar quickly refilled as the magical *Campfire* boosted his Regen rates. With the new light, he studied the webbing, walls, floor, and ceiling. Nothing. He eased forward down the side aisle, passing a couple of the candleholders. They stood about six feet high, and each of the eight fingers of the hand at the top ended in a point. The section of the candle-holder touching the floor looked identical. It was a good design. They didn't have an up or down, you could just place them on the floor and then impale the candles on the side that faced up.

He reached the stone platform that held the altar and care-fully stepped up onto it. A torn red cloth covered the altar, and a candleholder stood on each side. His fire didn't provide much extra light over here, but something about the fabric bothered him. He bent closer and realized the cloth had originally been white. The red coloring that covered most of it looked like a stain. He stood up straight. That cloth had been soaked in blood.

The candleholder on his right bent toward him, the eight fingers spreading wide. Before he could react, it snapped forward, and the eight fingers gripped his head. The pointed ends sunk into his skull and neck, and his Health bar flashed ten as it dropped. Ruwen screamed as a hole opened in the center of the hand, and a fleshy tube emerged, a ring of sharp teeth at its end. The fingers stuck in his head pulled his face toward the ring of teeth.

Ruwen dropped his staff and grabbed the top of the candle

stand, just under the hand. When he pulled though, his hands just slipped down the monster's slick body. A five flashed on his Health bar as it dropped again. He stumbled to the side as something struck him, and a sharp pain erupted on his left side. The other candleholder had attacked him. Ten more Health disappeared. In seconds, he had lost a quarter of his Health and was already down to seventy-five points. Panic overtook him as the writhing tube of teeth inched closer to his face.

He tried again to pull the thing off his face, but its entire body was coated with some sort of oil, and he couldn't grip it. He had dropped his staff, but it probably didn't matter. The weapon was too large to fight something this close. Sift had said not to let things get close to him, and that reminded him of his dagger. Sift had told him to take one just for a time like this.

A five flashed on his Health bar, and then another five. He was down to sixty-five Health, and if those teeth reached his face, it would drop a lot faster. He grabbed the dagger with his right hand and jerked it upward. Frantically, he sawed at the creature's long body.

Nothing happened at first. But then the blade vibrated. The dull sound increased in pitch as the blade started to shake so violently that Ruwen had to hold it with both hands. Warm liquid covered his hands as the teeth in front of his eyes ground against each other. The monster shuddered, and the fingers touching the floor clicked rapidly against the stone.

Ruwen heard a snap and then fell backward as the monster's body separated from the portion holding his head. He landed hard on his butt. The part on his head collapsed forward, and the tube with teeth rested on his cheek. He pulled the thing off his face with his left hand. The dagger, still violently shaking, fell out of his right hand.

The monster on his side dug its teeth into the flesh above his waist, and the sharp pain made him wince. His Health dropped by fifteen, putting him at half Health. Gritting his teeth, Ruwen reached for the blade, which had slowed its vibrations. As soon as Ruwen touched it to the Tube Spider, it ramped up again. In seconds, it had vibrated its way through the shaft of the second one.

Ruwen pulled it off his side, disgusted at the bloody teeth. He looked up in time to see six more of the Tube Spiders coming toward him. Two walked along the ceiling, and the other four bent in the middle, placing their finger-legs on the floor and then flipping themselves forward, like some sort of acrobats.

He stuck the shaking dagger back in its sheath and picked up the staff. If he stayed on the altar, they would swarm him. All he wanted to do was get out of this room. Not giving himself time to overthink it, he moved to the wall on his right. A few steps later, his Health began regenerating faster, and his *Campfire* buff appeared. Too bad he couldn't cast a *Fireball*. He swung his staff back and forth, trying to get rid of the nervous energy filling him. The sound of chimes filled the room, and two of the Tube Spiders stopped as the staff's distraction effect struck them.

This didn't look good, and he didn't know if he was going to survive. Should he yell for Sift? Even if the young man heard him, Ruwen doubted he would make it in time to matter. His quick move to the wall had bought him a little time. In fact, even though the room still crawled with monsters, only one Tube Spider stood between him and the door. If he could kill it quickly and then run, he might make it out.

He dashed forward and swung the staff as hard as he could. A loud snap echoed in the room as his Staff of Chimes shattered the Tube Spider's body. The top part fell to the ground, and as the Tube Spider moved, it dragged the finger-leg head around, and the teeth made a terrible gnashing sound. Clicks filled the room as the other Tube Spiders responded to the sight of their crippled brother.

Ruwen slammed the staff into the head being dragged on the

floor, turned, and pulverized the head that was still walking. In seconds, the area around him was covered in black blood. He stared at the dead Tube Spider, amazed that he'd killed it. Ruwen faced the door now that the way was clear. He tensed to run, but something struck him hard in the back before he could move.

At the top of his vision, a small cloak flashed next to his *Campfire* buff and then disappeared. He stumbled forward and fell to his knees, the staff flying out of his grasp. Another blow struck him in the back, and he fell forward. His fire was a few feet in front of him, and he crawled toward it. One of the Tube Spiders on his back started digging. He could feel its weight and the pressure of the eight-pronged feet but felt no pain, so he pushed himself up and backward. The Tube Spiders struck the pews with a crash, but he didn't turn around to look. Instead, he lurched forward, grabbed his staff, and then placed his back against the wall.

The warmth from the fire felt unpleasant on his sweaty skin, but it had caused the remaining five Tube Spiders to pause. Two still hung from the ceiling across from him, their bodies bent up at an angle, their tube-teeth extended toward him. The other three moved to the right, between him and the door. While he was outnumbered, the staff worked well, and the Tube Spiders were easy to hit because of their length. He swung the staff in front of him and took a small step forward to intimidate them.

One of the Tube Spiders hanging from the ceiling made a clicking noise, and Ruwen looked at it. A wad of webbing struck his face, covering his eyes and nose. He dropped the staff and pulled at the sticky strands. He gasped air through his mouth, his heart beating frantically, and tried to get the mass off his nose and eyes.

The room filled with clicking as the Tube Spiders moved in to finish him off. His efforts to remove the webbing only smeared it further around his face, and his hands were in danger of being stuck. He had dropped his staff and couldn't see to pick it up. The dagger had proved effective against the Tube Spiders, but he didn't want them that close. If all five attacked at once, he would never kill them all before they killed him. That left the Baton of a Thousand Uses.

Twisting the baton off the belt on his left hip, he quickly unfolded the first knob he found. He had no idea what it was, but it extended his reach further than the dagger. Fear flooded his body, and he swung the baton with all his strength.

Immediately he struck a Tube Spider and heard the satisfying sound of its body snapping. Without hesitating, he swung upward and connected with another Tube Spider. Maybe he could do this. Swinging to his left, he didn't hit anything, and the momentum turned his body, making him stumble. A moment later, a Tube Spider struck his right side and threw him to the ground. His Health still hovered at fifty, and the blow brought it down to forty-five.

Unfortunately, he landed face-first in his fire. His Health instantly dropped another ten as he screamed and rolled to the side. A horrible smell, like milk left in the sun, filled his nostrils. His nose was clear! Using his arm, he scraped it down his face, hoping to remove whatever webbing hadn't been burned. His Health dropped another three, and he screamed in pain. His face felt raw, and he worried for a moment about how badly he'd burned himself. Carefully he reached up with his free hand and pulled at the mass over his eyes. The singed webbing dropped away, and he could see again.

The Tube Spider that had attacked him lay in the fire, thrashing and clicking its teeth. It shot a wad of webbing at him, but it struck his shoulder. He pushed himself up and then immediately brought his baton down on the Tube Spider's head. The tool he'd unfolded from his baton while blinded turned out to be a shovel, and he smashed it against the Tube Spider until it stopped moving. Black smoke filled the air, and

Ruwen pulled his Scarf of Freshness over his mouth and nose, worried that the Tube Spiders' airborne remains might harm him.

His Health had dropped all the way to thirty-two, 66% of his total gone in a matter of moments, and he still wasn't finished. The two Tube Spiders he'd hit while blind were still alive and dragging themselves toward him. He stepped forward and swung his shovel down, hitting them over and over until they stopped moving.

Gasping, he stepped back, putting the fire between himself and the remaining two Tube Spiders. They were both on the ground with their fingers spread and their tube-tongues extended. Remembering what had happened last time, Ruwen dodged as both Tube Spiders unleashed more webbing. A wad of webbing grazed his head but didn't do any damage. His staff lay about ten feet away. One of the Tube Spiders was only a few feet from it.

His face throbbed in pain and Tube Spiders had ravaged both sides of his body. The longer he waited, the weaker he'd become. He needed to end this right now. Screaming, he jumped forward, swinging his shovel wildly. Both Tube Spiders backed up, and he recovered his staff. He clipped the baton back to his waist but didn't fold the shovel away. He'd dropped his weapons an embarrassing number of times during this fight, and he wanted the shovel ready to go if he did it again.

For the first time, he actually formulated a plan. He'd spin his staff until the distraction effect triggered and froze one of the Tube Spiders. Then he'd hit it as hard as he could. This wouldn't have worked with six of them, but with only two, he should be able to keep them both in sight.

Ruwen's arms trembled as he swung the staff at nothing, waiting for the chimes to trigger. The Tube Spider in front of him stopped weaving its head, and Ruwen immediately leaped forward, putting all his strength into his attack. This time the

Tube Spider's body snapped and then sheared in two, the pieces twitching.

He turned in time to see the last Tube Spider already airborne as it dived at him. With all his fear, disgust, and pain, Ruwen swung his staff. The Tube Spider's head vaporized in a black cloud of blood. Without hesitating, he smashed the other head. He struck it over and over until his strength failed him. Falling to his knees, he dropped his staff and pulled the scarf off his face.

His whole body trembled from exhaustion and pain. Closing his eyes, he tried to control his breathing and slow his heart. Physical fighting had never been an interest for him, so he was entirely unprepared for his body's reaction. He felt like puking, and his hands still trembled. The future would be full of fights like this, however, and the sooner he learned to deal with it, the better. His chest tightened when he thought about how close he'd come to dying. He could almost hear Hamma's voice scolding him, and, despite his pain and exhaustion, the thought made him happy.

The clatter of coins striking the ground made his breath catch. He looked around for the source. Had he missed one of the Tube Spiders? It had been dumb to not ensure the room was safe before resting. Just another mistake he was thankful hadn't killed him.

But when he looked around, he didn't see any more Tube Spiders. In fact, the ones he'd killed seemed to have disappeared. Using the staff, he pushed himself to his feet. Other than his multiple injuries and the black blood covering his body, there was nothing in the room testifying to his near-death experience.

He reached down and folded the shovel back into the Baton. Both the Baton and the shovel were clean in spite of being used to bludgeon the Tube Spiders. Ruwen on the other hand looked like he'd rolled around in Tube Spider guts. Which actually wasn't far from the truth.

A bag had appeared on top of the altar. It hadn't been there before. What in Uru's name was going on here? He approached the altar carefully and used his staff to push on the bag. The brown container looked like leather and was the size of his head. This could be some sort of trap, and his cloak only gave him a 10% chance of detecting them, which was effectively useless.

"Impressive," Sift said.

Ruwen screamed and dropped his staff. His heart felt like it might explode. Turning around, he watched Sift pick up his weapon.

"It's dangerous to leave things lying around. She'll take them," Sift said, holding out the staff.

"Don't do that!" Ruwen said and jerked the staff out of Sift's hand.

"What?"

"Sneak up on me."

"Oh, I wasn't sneaking."

"Well, whistle or cough or drag your feet or something. Uru help me, I think you took ten years off my life."

"Sorry. And I can't whistle." Sift stuck two fingers in his mouth and blew. Air and spit came out in equal portions.

Ruwen took a step backward. "That wasn't really my point."

Sift tried to whistle again, and even more spit came out. Ruwen held up a hand to stop Sift.

"What is impressive? And who is going to take my stuff?" Ruwen asked.

Sift wiped his hand on his shirt. "Blapy."

"The Black Pyramid? You mentioned that before. But it's just a dungeon."

Sift's eyes got big, and he looked around. He laughed weakly and then whispered. "Just a dungeon? Are you stupid? Blapy is a

Tier One dungeon. Probably more powerful than that but the scale doesn't go any higher. Nobody even knows how deep she goes. You better show some respect, or you'll never leave here alive."

Ruwen's eyes grew large. "We're in a Tier One dungeon?"

"Didn't I say that already?"

There was only one dungeon near Deepwell, a weak Tier Forty, which was good and bad. It meant those that wanted adventure and leveling couldn't use it and had to leave, but it also meant Deepwell didn't have all the problems that accompanied highly trained and deadly people continually passing through.

Ruwen had never even been close to one. When they were young, Ruwen's parents had done some leveling in the mountain dungeon two day's ride from Deepwell, but it didn't challenge them for long. He loved those stories and had planned to go there himself once he'd made it through Mage School.

But now, his first day as a Worker, he was standing in a Tier One dungeon. That meant Blapy could handle parties higher than level one hundred. He thought he might puke.

"I'm sorry, Blapy. I didn't know," Ruwen croaked.

A thought struck him. "Why can't I see any details about the monsters? I didn't know anything was dangerous in here until it attacked me. Then I couldn't tell how much Health they had left."

"Your Perception is too low. Eventually, you'll be able to see things like that. But these creatures have abilities and skills too. So even when your Perception improves, you still might get limited information. Or they might display false attributes to force a mistake from you." Sift said.

"This place is dangerous."

Sift nodded. "Well, let's see what you got. I'm shocked she gave you something for killing such low-level monsters. You must have really impressed her."

Ruwen doubted that. It probably had more to do with the fact that he was so underprepared and untrained that these basic monsters had nearly killed him. It embarrassed him a little actually. For someone like Sift, this room probably took a few seconds to clear. It had required every ounce of Ruwen's strength, plus some luck, to survive.

He placed his staff in the harness on his back, undid the knot on the top of the bag, and dumped it out. A square stack of what looked like the webbing the Tube Spiders had shot at him fell out. Each side of the square was about the length of his hand. He breathed in deeply through his nose at the memory of it covering his face, and then picked it up.

Tring!
The Black Pyramid has rewarded you...
Name: *Rod Spider Webbing*
Quantity: *10*
Quality: *Uncommon*
Durability: *1 of 1*
Weight: *0.10 lbs.*
Effect: *Nullify all bleed effects when placed on wound.*
Effect: *+5 Health per second for 30 seconds.*
Description: *Will adhere to skin. Use alcohol, not fire, to remove.*

Was the description making fun of him falling into the fire?

"That looks like the stuff Bendies shoot out their butt," Sift said.

"Bendies?"

"The long spider things that bend in the middle."

Ruwen held up the bandages. "They're called Rod Spiders."

"Oh, I guess that's a good name, too."

"Wait, how do you not know that?"

Sift shrugged. "My interface is the standard one, remember. I don't get the details you do. Plus, I never take anything, so I don't get the descriptions. I've just made up my own names for everything."

"You never take any loot? Ever?"

Sift shook his head. "Things are a weight on the soul. I try and travel light."

"Wow, I don't know if that's profound or just really dumb."

"It's a game with her now. Blapy keeps offering me more and more valuable things. She thinks she can beat me."

"Okay, I've decided dumb. Also, did you say butt?"

"Yeah, that stuff is disgusting. It shoots right out their butt like some sort of spider diarrhea."

For the first time, he truly understood the possible value of the spell *Scrub*. He wanted to rub his face, but it still throbbed from the burns. Instead, he picked up the item that had been hidden under the webbing, a glass vial the size of his index finger.

Tring!
The Black Pyramid has rewarded you...
Name: *Purified Rod Spider Blood*
Quantity: *10 doses*
Quality: *Uncommon*
Durability: *1 of 1*
Weight: *0.05 lbs.*
Description: *Ingredient in various potions. An excellent hair gel.*

Ruwen ran his free hand through his hair or tried to. His hair had hardened into a tangled mass.

"Blapy is totally poking fun of me in these descriptions," Ruwen said.

"That doesn't surprise me. She loves playing games."

Ruwen opened his Void Band and placed the items away.

"What's that?" Sift asked.

"It's like a Traveler's Bag that I can't lose."

"That would be useful." Sift tapped the Traveler's Belt around his waist. "I lose mine a lot."

Ruwen turned back to the altar. The bag had disappeared.

"That's hard to get used to," Ruwen said.

"Wait till she materializes a Grabber right behind you. Anyway, you don't look so great. Let's get some rest and then finish up here in the morning."

Ruwen sighed, relieved that he'd get a break. He wanted to clean the spider poop and blood off himself, go through his notifications, and then read some of the books Tremine had given him. Sleep didn't sound so bad either.

"That's the best idea I've heard today," Ruwen said.

CHAPTER 18

*R*uwen expected Sift's room to be the size of a closet. Instead, it turned out to be larger than the main floor of Ruwen's house back in Deepwell. Most of it was empty, and Sift explained he practiced his Steps in here, and the extra room made that easier. Their beds were on either side of the door. Sift had a bookshelf that was full of adventure and travel memoirs. He even had one detailing the mountain range next to Deepwell.

Sift sat cross-legged on his bed, Io on his lap, and the two talked softly, although Ruwen could hear only Sift's side of the conversation. Whatever story Io was telling, it made the young man laugh a lot.

The bathroom next to Sift's room had a shower, and Ruwen had spent almost thirty minutes under the water trying to get the blood out of his hair. In the end, he had used his Fastidious Dagger to cut most of the blood out. He had never let his hair get too long, but now it stood up straight on his head. Sift approved and said it would make training easier.

Ruwen placed his dirty clothes in a box outside their door. Sift said they would be clean by the time they woke up. The

Black Pyramid certainly had some perks. He leaned back and rested against the stone wall. He opened his log and skimmed until he found where the two Rod Spiders had attacked him at the altar.

.

.

.

You have been struck by a Rod Spider (Level 1)
You have taken 10 damage
You have taken 5 damage (Bleed)
You have been struck by a Rod Spider (Level 1)
You have taken 10 damage
You have taken 5 damage (Bleed)
You have taken 5 damage (Bleed)
Your Fastidious Dagger has done 4 damage
Your Fastidious Dagger has done 11 damage (+4 vibration)
Your Fastidious Dagger has done 13 damage (+7 vibration)
Your Fastidious Dagger has done 17 damage (+9 vibration)
You have killed a Rod Spider (Level 1)!
You have gained 55 experience!
You have been bitten by a Rod Spider (Level 1)
You have taken 15 damage

.

.

.

The log confirmed what he'd thought. The Fastidious Dagger wanted to remain clean. The longer it stayed dirty, the more violent the vibrations became. He remembered dropping the dagger when it had become too hard to hold. There was one other thing he wanted to check, and he skimmed ahead.

.

.

.

You have been struck by a Rod Spider (Level 1)
Pacifist's Cloak shield has triggered!
You have taken 30 damage (((10 strike)+(5 leap))*2(back attack))
Pacifist's Cloak shield absorbs 30 damage (70 HP remaining)
You have been struck by a Rod Spider (Level 1)
You have taken 36 damage (((15 strike)+(3 leap))*2(back attack))
Pacifist's Cloak shield absorbs 36 damage (34 HP remaining)
You have been bitten by a Rod Spider (Level 1)
You have taken 15 damage
Pacifist's Cloak shield absorbs 15 damage (19 HP remaining)

.

.

.

He stared at the log entries for a few seconds and then closed it. If he hadn't taken that cloak, he'd be dead right now. He had also learned another lesson: don't turn your back on anything that wants to kill you. Those Rod Spiders had doubled their damage because they had attacked him from behind. He needed to be more careful. Now he understood why people didn't adventure or clear dungeons to level. The risk of dying was too high. Unfortunately, he didn't have a choice.

He opened the notifications he'd ignored for the last hour.

Shing!
You have learned a new skill!
Skill: *Dagger*
Level: *1*
Effect: *Increase damage by 0.5%.*

Another weapon skill. Ruwen needed to level these as fast as he could. He opened the next notification.

Shing!
You have advanced a skill!
Skill: *Staff*
Level: *2*
Effect: *Increase damage by 1.0%.*

Closing the notifications, he smiled. He had grown. Made himself stronger. There was a long way to go, but he'd started. He glanced at his Profile, curious how close he was to level three. The two quests he'd completed, along with the eight Rod Spiders, had added one thousand three hundred ninety experience to his total. Level three required three thousand experience, and now he was only six hundred ten experience away. He'd make that tomorrow and would finally be able to get rid of his Foolish and Clumsy debuffs.

He opened his Void Band and removed the Worker textbook Tremine had given him. He still had to allocate his spells and abilities for reaching level two. The deal he made with Fluffy meant Ruwen needed to learn *Scrub*. Since he'd hit an even level, he had four spells, two for each Class, instead of the normal one per Class. Most people never reached level ten, and while he planned to level a lot, learning *Scrub* still felt like a waste. In fact, it made him a little sick. But the cloak he'd received today had already saved his life, so the lesson seemed clear; his gear was critical, and learning this spell would allow him to gear up faster.

He found the page that described *Scrub* and started reading. In moments his upset stomach was replaced by curiosity, and then interest. The spell was channeled like his Void Band and would drain Energy as long as it was in use. But to his surprise, the spell took a lot of knowledge to use.

If you were cleaning a stone floor, removing the organic material would be straight forward. But if the floor consisted of polished oak, scrubbing out organic material would ruin the wood. You couldn't just wave your hand over a stain and make it disappear. The caster needed to understand what made up the stain, the surface it occupied, and how they differed. Tables detailed different substances along with recommended Energy consumption for each.

He set the book in his lap and stared at the ceiling. Once again, he realized how unfair he'd been to Workers. Granted, it wasn't like crystalizing ice shards from the air or melting the armor on a warrior, but it also wasn't as mindless and beneath him as he'd assumed. The complexity of the spell appealed to his mind. And it was dangerous. He looked at the book again and skipped to the last page. Warnings and cautions filled it entirely, but two jumped out at him.

Warning: Scrub can cause severe damage, scarring, and even death.
Warning: Channeling more than 10 Energy per second is highly dangerous.
Caution: Exfoliating before attaining Scrub (Level 3) is highly discouraged.

The warning made him wonder if he could use this to protect himself. He had a terrible habit of dropping his weapons. Having something he could do with just his hands might be useful. The caution made him realize how much control you could eventually attain. The exfoliation footnote in the textbook said to practice taking the skin off of pears before trying to make your employer's face look younger.

Turning back to the beginning of the section, he stared at the image of the brush that represented *Scrub*. Crossing his arms over his chest, he prepared a prayer. He knew you could learn new things outside Uru's area of influence, but he wasn't sure the goddess could hear him in this place. Even if this wasn't what he wanted, it was still magic, and he didn't want to seem ungrateful.

"Thank you for this blessing, Uru. I pray everyone sees your purity through the actions of this spell," Ruwen whispered.

He let his eyes unfocus, and the image seemed to lift off the page. His brain itched as the image vibrated in his mind, and then his whole body grew cold. He opened the new notification.

Bing!
You have learned the spell Scrub (Worker Level 1)
Spell: *Scrub*
Level: *1*
Class: *Worker*
Effect: *Use energy to break down and remove stains and odor.*
Cost: *1-20 Energy per second*
Type: *Self*
Casting Time: *1 second*
Duration: *Channeled*

Closing the notification, he decided *Scrub* deserved some experimentation, and he'd try and do more with it than just clean clothes.

Turning his attention back to the textbook, he found the section on Abilities. He already felt tired and resisted the urge to look over all of them. Until the events in the basement, he'd planned to increase his *Hey You* ability to level two. But now he realized something to help him survive might be more practical. He turned to the detailed description for *Hey You* anyway, just to see what he could look forward to.

It appeared his level one ability gave him the vocabulary of a five-year-old, and level two gave him a firm grasp of the basics. At level three, he would be fluent, and at four, he would understand technical items. The last level, five, would allow him to understand

and communicate on esoteric, arcane, and magical topics. He almost leveled the ability right then, but the memory of the Rod Spider latched to his head and trying to eat his face stopped him.

Reluctantly he turned back to the list of level one and two abilities and looked for anything that might help him. The two most obvious choices were *Glow*, which made his body do just that, and *Owl Eyes*, which magnified ambient light by 10%. Both would allow him to see better. If the lights had suddenly gone out down there, he would have been dead in seconds.

The problem with *Glow* is that it made him a target. In the dark, he would attract everything, and it would make hiding impossible. *Owl Eyes* would add 10% to the 15% the Jaga Wedding Band already gave him. 25% would be a considerable improvement, and as long as there was at least some sort of ambient light, he would be able to see. But there might not be any ambient light down there.

Why did the Worker abilities have to suck so bad? That wasn't fair. They didn't suck as much as they were incredibly practical. The *Knots* ability would be a real boon to anyone working near ships or caravans, and the *Detect Temperature* would make you a fantastic cook. But he wasn't trying to eat anything down in the dungeon, he just wanted to see them. He imagined cooking a Rod Spider over his campfire, and his stomach turned. That was really gross.

He felt a cold pressure in his brain. This always happened when his subconscious had made a connection that his mind hadn't seen yet. He knew from experience not to search for it. Information was the bait that usually revealed the link. He had been thinking about cooking, so he flipped to the detailed description of *Detect Temperature* and read the short passage.

Detect Temperature: *The Worker is sometimes called on to cook items they are unfamiliar with or to unusual specifications. This ability provides a visual indicator of the temperature of the food in relation to* *its surroundings. Higher levels will allow the Worker to gauge the external and internal temperature difference with greater accuracy.*

He thought about the Rod Spiders and the fire he had created. He imagined the cold body being warmed by the fire as it slowly cooked. But the Rod Spiders hadn't been cold when they were alive. Their blood had been warm as it flowed across his hands. The pressure in his head increased and became painful. Ruwen closed the book and let his thoughts lead him to the solution. A picture of a flaming Rod Spider appeared in his mind, burning brightly as it ran around the colder room, and he finally understood what his subconscious had figured out. The pressure in his mind subsided, leaving a dull headache behind.

The ability detected differences in temperature, so even though he had no intention of eating one of the Rod Spiders, this ability should allow him to see the difference in temperature between the creature and the room. And that should work well in the dark. Furniture and anything else that didn't give off heat would still be invisible, but at least it would give him a chance to fight anything attacking him.

The symbol for *Detect Temperature* looked like a pan over a fire, and Ruwen got off his bed and kneeled. He didn't have a statue of Uru, but there was a picture of her at the beginning of the textbook, and he focused on that.

"Uru, thank you for your blessings. I pray this helps me see the work you need me to do," Ruwen whispered.

Just like he'd done with *Hey You*, he imagined the symbol on the book rising and entering his chest. A moment later, he felt a sharp pain in his eyes and immediately rubbed them. He opened the notification.

Ping!
You have learned the Ability Detect Temperature (Worker Level 1)
Ability: *Detect Temperature*

Level: 1
Class: Worker
Effect: The hotter the object, the redder it appears.
Type: Self

He closed the notification and noticed a small eye next to his Profile icon in the top-left of his vision. Focusing on it, the eye turned red, and his vision blurred for a heartbeat. He looked over at Sift and gasped.

CHAPTER 19

"*W*hat?" Sift asked.

"You're really hot."

"Well, thanks. I'm excited to meet some friendly women when Ky takes me to your world. Hopefully, they agree."

Ruwen pushed himself off his knees and sat on the bed. "I mean your temperature."

Sift glowed a dark red, and the things he touched like his pillow or Io, briefly glowed. Ruwen looked at his own hands and realized he glowed as well, but not nearly as much as Sift. The young man looked like a bonfire.

Sift touched his forehead. "I feel fine."

"You mentioned earlier that you...sift, through the energy around you. Does some of it stay?"

"Shade's first rule: curiosity is a hole in the bucket."

"That doesn't make sense."

"Ky says it to me all the time. Usually when I'm asking about what's on the other side of the Blood Gate. She says curiosity is a monster that's never full, so you shouldn't waste time feeding it."

"Well, I kind of can't help myself. Almost everything interests me."

"Me, too. That's why I like Io so much. He never runs out of stories."

Ruwen focused on the eye again near his Profile, and it went from red to black. Sift looked normal now. There wasn't anything visible that gave away the massive amount of energy burning in him.

Sift continued. "Energy is really interesting. Some of it is sticky and hard to get rid of, and some of it feels nice and I don't want to let it go. That is the dangerous stuff Mom yells at me about. I'm still running hot from all the spells Ky hit me with. Shade magic is some of the sticky stuff I mentioned."

"Ky used magic on you? I didn't see anything."

"Well, it wouldn't be much use to a Shade if it was flashy."

Ruwen felt dumb. "That's true. What did she cast?"

"She tried to snare, paralyze, and blind me. She knows better than to try that on me. I think it's just habit."

"Wow, I had no idea all that was happening. She didn't even move her hands or chant or anything."

"That wouldn't –"

"Right, that wouldn't make much sense for a Shade. So, you just absorb it?"

"Yep."

"Do you ever fill up?"

"Yeah. Ky's been helping me find ways to quickly dump the energy I accumulate."

"In the cave, you called Uru a false god. Did your god give you that sifting magic?"

"There are no gods. We are all just souls moving from one journey to the next."

"So you haven't Ascended? What happens if you die?"

"I die."

"But you don't come back."

Sift pointed at his chest. "Not in this form. I will be reborn in another vessel and learn a new lesson until my soul is perfect."

That sounded insane. Ruwen wanted to live as long as possible as himself, not come back after every death as someone different. Ascendancy didn't give you eternal life. Eventually, you grew old, and when you died the body you revived with would reflect that since you were constantly being synched with Uru. An old body dies sooner, and the cycle continued to feed itself until the penalties and cost just didn't make it worth reviving anymore. Even so, it wasn't uncommon for people to live hundreds of years. He had even heard of some people reaching a thousand.

"What about your interface? How did you get your power?" Ruwen asked.

"I have the same interface we're all born with. As far as magic goes, I learned it like everything else. Practice."

Ruwen had heard of people like Sift. They lived outside the protection area. If you caused a lot of trouble before you Ascended a judge might send you out to live with those people. Denying you the chance at Ascension. And if you committed a crime and were found guilty, a judge might decree you to be non-revivable. Then when you died, you were dead for good. All of those options sounded horrible. He couldn't even imagine what it must be like living out in the wild without access to Classes and Specializations and revival.

"You can learn magic without Ascending?" Ruwen asked.

"Of course, how do you think people did it before your gods appeared?"

"I just assumed they'd always been here."

"Shade's first rule: assumptions lead to the temple tub."

"You told me that one already."

"It's an important one. Here's another: shortcuts always have a cost."

"Are you saying I took a shortcut?"

"How many spells did you just learn?"

"A couple," Ruwen said, not bothering to specify one was an ability.

Sift snapped his fingers. "And like that, you are more powerful."

"That's not true. I spent time earning the experience to unlock them."

"A drop in the bucket. But you're missing something bigger. In fact, your choice of words makes me think you suspect it, too."

Ruwen grew defensive, but Sift spoke in a friendly manner, not accusing at all, and Ruwen forced himself to calm down. He liked philosophical discussions and never had them with anyone but Tremine. Knowledge and new perspectives shouldn't be something he feared.

"I don't suspect anything," Ruwen said.

"Why did you use the word unlock, instead of learn?"

Why had he used that word? Probably because of the way it felt when he gained something new. It did feel a bit like a key opening a box in his mind. Plus, he was outside Uru's area of influence, and it hadn't felt like the knowledge had been beamed to him. It had felt like remembering something he already knew.

"You think when I Ascended more than a new interface was put in my head?" Ruwen asked.

Sift tapped his head. "Everything in the universe is already here. Maybe a better way of putting it is some knowledge was placed closer to your consciousness. It makes it easier for you to find."

"Even if that is a shortcut, what you call a cost I consider a benefit. I want to spend hundreds of years becoming the best Mage in history, but a stupid accident might kill me before I'm twenty. The logical thing is to take the second, third, fourth, chance."

"Shade's first rule: nothing should be left to chance."

"I'm really starting to hate these."

Sift laughed. "I hate them, too. But I've never said so many to anyone, and I'm starting to understand why Ky likes saying them to me. Seeing your expression makes it fun."

Ruwen laughed too.

Sift looked down at Io. "That's true." He looked up from the dagger and grew serious. "Io has a good point. Please don't take my comments to mean I think less of you. We have chosen different paths, but that doesn't mean we can't travel together."

"No offense taken. You've given me a lot to think about. Which I like."

Sift nodded and then focused back on the Elder Dagger. Sift had told him some profound things, assuming the young man was correct. If that really was how the gods worked, did that mean he had access to every ability and spell? And what happened if he purposefully or accidentally activated something from another branch? Somehow he doubted the gods would allow a weakness to exist in their system. There was probably some type of terrible consequence. He would ask Uru the next time he saw her. Hopefully, that wouldn't be for a very long time.

Ruwen replaced the Worker textbook in his Void Band and removed the Observer one. This one had a pair of eyes on it, the Observer symbol, and the binding was a dark green. While he had briefly toyed with the idea of becoming a Merchant because his Intelligence would be valued there, he had never considered being an Observer. Too many of their abilities and skills were centered on Dexterity, and he had never been very coordinated. Like Mages, many of them worked alone, but the difference was Observers were usually in very dangerous locations.

Ky had wanted him to take the Scout branch and then specialize in Spying. There were probably good reasons for that, but he planned to study and decide for himself. He agreed with her that the other specialization, Ranger, might provide him more long-term benefit. But he didn't want to sacrifice his future success just to give himself a slightly better chance of surviving now. He had plenty of time to figure it out since he didn't have to commit to the Scout Sub-Class until level ten. And the specialization didn't happen until level twenty. Those levels seemed impossible when viewed from his current one.

His eyes felt heavy, and he considered going to sleep now and learning these Observer spells and abilities later. Sleep would feel so good after today's events. Another debuff appeared next to the two he already had: Exhaustion. A moment later, three more debuffs appeared. He looked at the Exhaustion debuff and saw it lowered all his attributes by one. He was a mess. Five of his six attributes were under ten. He looked at his debuffs: Exhaustion, Sickly, Weak, Clumsy, Ugly, and Foolish.

The six debuffs were a reminder of how meaningless this all was. Ruwen seemed to be getting weaker, and the people aligned against him were already so much stronger. It didn't seem like it was worth the effort to fight back. He stared at the debuffs, their presence a reminder of his failures. A small part of his mind screamed he had succeeded today and that every advantage should be taken.

He started to put the Observer textbook away but stopped. Were the debuffs affecting his judgment? Death came quickly, and he was unprepared for the dungeon. Shouldn't he be doing everything possible to make himself stronger? It would be foolish not to.

Gritting his teeth, he stared at the Foolish debuff. He needed to get rid of that as soon as possible. His whole fight had been full of foolish acts. He'd dropped his weapon multiple times, turned his back on his enemies, and overestimated his chances of escaping. Now the debuff was trying to stop him from improving himself. What if there was no time tomorrow morning? He would enter the dungeon weaker than necessary.

He opened the book again and skimmed the level one and two Observer abilities.

Ability: Freedom
Level: 1
Type: Self
Effect: No penalty for leather armor.

Ability: Rapid Fire
Level: 1
Type: Self
Effect: Launch two projectiles instead of one.

Ability: Keen Senses
Level: 1
Type: Self
Effect: Increase Physical, Magical, and Spiritual senses. Every level increases the effectiveness by 20%.

Ability: Weakness
Level: 2
Type: Self
Effect: Discover a target's weakness. 10% chance per minute of study.

Ability: Pinpoint
Level: 2
Type: Self
Effect: Target a specific location for 200% damage. 400% damage if this location was discovered via Weakness.

Ability: Magnify
Level: 2
Type: Self
Effect: Increase the apparent closeness by 200%.

The *Rapid Fire, Weakness,* and *Pinpoint* were all powerful abilities, but he didn't have any skills for throwing or shooting things. They might be useful later, but for now, he would ignore them. The *Freedom* Ability would be valuable. Any leather armor he wore wouldn't affect his movement. But he didn't have any armor right now, so it seemed like a waste to take it. That left *Keen Senses* and *Magnify*. He read the detailed description for both of them.

Keen Senses: *The Observer is required to be hyper-aware of their surroundings. Success or failure can be decided by the early detection of your target or enemy. This Ability increases all senses by 20% per Ability level and stacks with relevant Skills, Spells, and Effects. In lower Ability levels, the Observer may need to interpret this Ability as it will manifest most often in their emotions.*

Magnify: *The Observer's target is not always nearby. This Ability allows the Observer to decrease the visual distance to the target by 200% per Ability level. A clear view of the target is often necessary to trigger other Abilities, such as Weakness and Pinpoint. For close targets like documents or ingredients, the Ability functions identically, allowing the Observer to detect details or defects not visible to unaided sight.*

Both of these seemed like they could be useful. At least more useful than the others. Ruwen returned to his knees and followed the same process he had with the Worker abilities. Moments later, both abilities were his. A small telescope appeared next to the eye for his *Detect Temperature* ability. Both these abilities could be toggled on and off. *Hey You* and *Keen Senses* were passive and always on.

He could barely stay awake, but he was determined to get through this before tomorrow. Without getting off his knees, he skimmed the basic information for the Energy-based spells available to him. He needed to be careful with these since these spells could kill him with an offhand use while his Void Band was active.

Spell: *Find Trap*
Level: *1*
Effect: *Increase chance of finding traps by 10% per minute.*

Spell: *Sprint*
Level: *1*
Effect: *Increase your top speed by 20%.*

Spell: *Leap*
Level: *2*
Effect: *Increase the distance leaped by 20%.*

Spell: *Climb*
Level: *2*
Effect: *Increase the friction of your skin against any material by 20%.*

Sprint seemed like an easy way to kill himself. Running with his Void Band opened seemed like a terrible idea, but if it was, and then he cast this spell, it might be lights out. Same with the *Climb* spell. He realized these hypothetical situations were probably never going to arise, but in his current state, any more deaths would be catastrophic. *Find Trap* and *Leap* were more one-time things that should be easier to manage. He moved on to the Mana-based spells.

Spell: *Distract*
Level: *1*
Effect: *Create a noise at the location of the Observers focus.*

Spell: *Camouflage*

Level: 1
Effect: *While still, blend into your surroundings with 20% effectiveness.*

Spell: *Bleed*
Level: 2
Effect: *Your next blow will cause the target to bleed for 2 times weapon damage.*

Spell: *Track*
Level: 2
Effect: *Increase the chance of locating your target's trail by 10% per minute.*

These were all useful. But Ruwen didn't think he could sit still long enough for *Camouflage* to work, and he didn't see a real need for *Track* right now. *Distract* might buy him the time he needed to escape, and *Bleed* would be a welcome offensive spell.

He focused on each symbol and said a small prayer to Uru. These spells took longer to learn. It took a couple of minutes, but he cycled through the symbols for *Find Trap*, *Leap*, *Distract*, and *Bleed*. He'd gained four new spells and had finally caught up with his level.

Placing the Observer textbook back in his storage, Ruwen crawled onto his bed. He stared at the row of debuffs again. Ugly? Really? He should have added that last point into Charisma. He was glad Hamma couldn't see him right now. Tomorrow was a new day and, assuming he didn't die, he would fix all these debuffs. The exhaustion took hold of him, and everything faded to black.

CHAPTER 20

*R*uwen woke to Sift tapping his forehead.

"You sleep like you're dead," Sift said.

"Ugh."

Sift laughed and placed Ruwen's clean clothes on his chest.

"Get dressed. We have a full day."

Ruwen wanted to roll over and sleep another couple of hours, but he also wanted to gain some levels. Plus, he didn't think Sift would let him sleep. Ruwen sat up and checked his debuffs. Exhaustion had disappeared, taking Sickly, Weak, and Ugly with it. Today he would get rid of Foolish and Clumsy.

Sift had moved to the center of his room and sat cross-legged. As if he could sense Ruwen's gaze, he spoke up.

"Get dressed and join me," Sift said.

A minute later, Ruwen sat in front of Sift and mirrored his position. Ruwen sighed loudly.

"We're going to meditate for a few minutes and then practice some Steps," Sift said.

"Okay."

Ruwen closed his eyes and remembered what Sift had said last night. He'd told Ruwen to breathe in and out the same amount and to imagine the air powering his body and mind. This morning, however, his interface distracted him. Opening his settings, he minimized the interface to a tiny point in the lower-left part of his vision. Now, when Ruwen looked straight ahead, he couldn't even see the small square. A few heartbeats later, his breathing became more regular.

"Straighten your back," Sift said.

Ruwen opened his eyes, but Sift's eyes were closed. Could he tell Ruwen's posture just by listening to him breathe? Closing his eyes, he sat up straight and immediately noticed the positive change in his breathing.

Just like last night, his mind rebelled at the simple task, but Ruwen stayed focused on his breathing, and his mind cleared. A moment later, Sift spoke.

"Hey, snap out of it," Sift said.

Ruwen pulled himself from the peaceful darkness and opened his eyes. Sift was shaking him.

"Are you okay?" Sift sounded concerned.

Ruwen's body still ached from the beating last night, but his mind felt clear and sharp. The fogginess he'd experienced upon waking had disappeared. In fact, he'd never felt better.

"Yeah, did I do something wrong?" Ruwen asked.

"No, not at all. I just didn't expect you to go so long on your second day."

Ruwen maximized his interface and looked at his clock. Thirty minutes had passed. He opened his notifications, which were blinking for his attention.

Shing!
You have advanced a skill!
Skill: *Meditation*
Level: *2*
Effect: *Clear Mind: increase Health, Mana, and Energy Regeneration by 0.75%.*

Shing!
You have advanced a skill!
Skill: *Meditation*
Level: *3*
Effect: *Clear Mind: increase Health, Mana, and Energy Regeneration by 1.0%.*

He had gone up two levels! The thirty minutes had passed in a blink.

"I'm surprised, too," Ruwen said.

"Wait, you didn't get distracted or have to fight to stay focused that whole time?"

"I did at first."

Sift pursed his lips. "We need to talk to my parents."

"Is something wrong?"

"No, it's good. I think you're better at this than I am. They're experts though, and will make sure everything is okay."

"I doubt I'm better than you at anything."

"Can you whistle?"

Ruwen laughed. "Fine, I doubt I'm better than you at anything important."

"Says the guy that can whistle."

Sift stood, and Ruwen did as well.

"We took longer than I planned for meditation, but I still want to teach you some Steps before we go downstairs," Sift said.

"I'd like that a lot. I kind of struggled last night."

"You're alive, aren't you?"

"Barely."

"Well, barely counts. Give yourself some credit."

Sift waited until Ruwen nodded.

"Okay, this is from Dad's style. It's called Blooming Flower. Slowly punch at my face," Sift said.

Ruwen punched at Sift's face. Sift stepped toward Ruwen

and turned, so his back was to Ruwen. Sift grabbed Ruwen's arm, held it against his chest, and then bent forward. Ruwen was thrown over Sift's shoulder, and Ruwen landed on his back.

Sift helped Ruwen to his feet.

"So if a Bendy, sorry, Rod Spider, tries to eat your face, you can throw them now."

Ruwen practiced with Sift for the next fifteen minutes. Unlike the meditation, this didn't come easily to him. Once Ruwen finally threw Sift successfully twice in a row, Sift ended Ruwen's misery.

"Don't worry. We'll keep practicing, and it will get easier," Sift said.

"I hope so."

Ruwen noticed another notification and checked it.

Shing!
You have learned a new skill!
Skill: *Unarmed Combat*
Level: *1*
Effect: *Increase unarmed damage by 0.50%. Increase chance to deflect or dodge a blow by 0.50%.*

Ruwen closed the notification as satisfaction filled him. He had always dreamed of protecting himself with shields of magical energy. But there was a beauty to the movements Sift had shown Ruwen that he'd never noticed before, and the knowledge that he could defend himself with just his body filled him with pride.

On the way to the dungeon, they stopped at the bar they'd passed through last night. There was a long table with food on it, and Sift walked directly toward it.

Sift took what looked like a pancake, placed a sausage link on one side, poured what smelled like maple syrup on it, and then rolled it up into a tube.

"You have to squeeze the bottom, or the syrup will drip on you. Makes the Thrashers go crazy," Sift said.

Ruwen's eyes got big and Sift laughed.

"I'm joking," Sift said.

He made another one and then gestured at Ruwen to make his own. Sift took a bite of the second one before finishing the first and Ruwen bit his tongue to keep from saying anything. Why would Sift not finish one before starting the next? It was like purposefully hanging a picture at an angle. It made his brain hurt.

Ruwen's stomach rumbled, and he made two of his own but went light on the syrup. He didn't want to get it on his hands and then stick to everything he touched the rest of the day. Although he did have *Scrub* now and could clean his hands whenever he wanted. But the textbook had warned against using it on skin until he'd increased the spell to level three. Better to just go easy on the syrup. He followed Sift to the stairs, both of them eating their breakfast as they walked.

"Lahmuhna," Sift said his mouth full of pancake.

"Lahmuhna!" Sift said louder this time.

Ruwen finally understood what Sift was trying to do.

"Limuno," Ruwen said, and the lights came on.

"Thanths," Sift said.

Ruwen shook his head and smiled.

They descended the stairs, and far too quickly for Ruwen's liking, they stood in the long room again. He peeked into the room he'd cleared last night and found it empty.

Sift looked at the next set of doors. "That's still yours." He pointed at the far door on this side. "I'll start up top and work my way down."

"What about the side you were on last night?"

"I cleaned all those."

"What! You did six rooms in the time I did one?"

"Mine probably had fewer monsters."

Ruwen doubted that. He felt terrible for taking so long while being impressed that Sift could clear so quickly.

Sift strode down the room, and Ruwen shuffled to the closed double doors. Pulling the staff from its harness, he spun it in front of himself until he heard the chimes. He then patted the dagger on his right hip and his baton on the left. Opening his Profile, he focused on his cloak. A timer counted down next to the description of the shield property, and it still had fifteen hours left. He'd hoped that the timer reset at midnight, but it looked like the "once a day" meant a literal day had to pass. He couldn't count on it saving his life again.

He took three deep breaths and pushed the right door open far enough for him to enter. The wood screeched as it scraped across the stones, and he winced at the loud noise.

Sift, who had reached the far end of the room, shouted at him. "If you're not sure they know you're here, I can come back and announce you."

"Very funny. Now you've announced yourself, too, dummy," Ruwen shouted back.

Ruwen grinned at the stricken look on Sift's face.

His amusement fled as he looked at his door. He'd opened it enough to slide through, but not enough to get a good look on what might be around it. The thought of opening the door further and causing that horrible noise made him cringe. Plus, he didn't want to take any more ribbing from Sift.

But, if something was on the other side of the door, it could attack him as soon as he entered, and he didn't have his cloak to protect him. As he stood there trying to decide what to do, a feeling of certainty overcame him that something waited just on the other side of the door.

Was he just being paranoid? Maybe it was just fear. But this felt different. It felt solid like a fact. He opened his Profile and looked at his Abilities tab. The *Keen Senses* ability said it would manifest as feelings at lower levels. That must be why he was convinced something lurked on the other side of the door.

Looking through the spells and abilities he'd recently gained, he made a plan. Staring at his staff, he pictured the symbol for *Bleed*. His mind locked on the image for a full second and then the symbol faded. Twenty-five flashed over his Mana bar, and it dropped to one hundred forty-five. The staff glowed with a red light that continually dripped off the weapon. It felt good to have an offensive spell.

He toggled his *Detect Temperature* ability and then stepped closer to the door. Peering through the opening, he focused on the left wall and a shelf that sat there. He pictured the symbol of *Distraction*. Three things happened almost simultaneously: ten flashed on his Mana bar, a cough sounded from the shelf, and something leaped from behind the door and crashed into the shelf.

Not wanting to waste his opportunity, Ruwen slid into the room and moved away from the entrance and toward the shelf. A round black mass two feet across with a dozen tubular arms had destroyed the shelf. The monster thrashed the wood with four of its arms while the others wriggled at its side. It stood on three of its appendages and bobbed up and down as if it floated on a river. This looked like the Thrasher Sift had described.

Ruwen swung the staff with all his strength and struck the Thrasher right in the middle of its body. The sound of air being expelled was followed by terrible wheezing. The Thrasher staggered to the left and crashed into the wall. It put another two arms down to help keep its balance and weakly shot one of its arms at Ruwen. It struck his chest, and he instinctively jerked backward. The arm ripped off the Thrasher's body, and Ruwen stumbled back a few steps.

The Thrasher glowed red from Ruwen's *Detect Temperature*, and he could even see the blood dripping to the floor. He smiled at his cleverness in realizing he could use this ability for more than cooking. Raising the staff above his head, he brought it down on the Thrasher's body. He did it two more times just to make sure it was dead.

The hair on the back of his neck stood, and he turned to find another Thrasher behind him. He raised his staff to strike, but the Thrasher flicked one of its arms out and struck Ruwen's eye. He screamed, dropped his staff, and gripped the Thrasher's arm, scared the Thrasher might yank it back and rip his eyeball out.

The Thrasher's arm was about the same thickness as Ruwen's wrist, and he didn't feel anything digging into his eye. Holding the appendage against his eye with his right hand, he used his left hand to jerk violently on the Thrasher's arm. He stumbled backward as the arm separated from the monster.

To his horror, the Thrasher's arm didn't release, and the appendage hung off his eye like a wet noodle. Terrified that the monster might strike his other eye, he let go of the Thrasher's arm and prayed it wouldn't pull his eye out. It hung limply from his face as Ruwen knelt and searched for his staff. His left eye had teared up from the force of the strike on the other eye, and everything looked blurry. He prayed he would still be able to see after this was finished.

The Thrasher had paused, and Ruwen stared at it while his hands moved desperately across the ground, searching for his staff. His right hand found it, and he stood quickly, raising the weapon to protect himself. The staff felt slippery, but he couldn't see it due to the three feet of Thrasher arm hanging off his face. Maybe the weapon was coated in blood.

The staff moved, and Ruwen screamed, dropping what he thought was his weapon. But it didn't leave his hand. Instead, it wrapped around it. He brought his arm around so he could see it with his left eye, and he screamed again.

A Giant Centipede four feet long had wrapped itself around his arm. Its small eyes were behind two large pinchers, which clicked together. He hated bugs in general but detested centipedes. He could feel the legs, hundreds of them, wriggling against his skin. The head reared back like it meant to strike him, so Ruwen stretched his arm to get the Giant Centipede as far from his face as he could.

Thoughts raced through his mind as panic threatened to overwhelm him. More than anything, he wanted to kill this horrible monster. He needed to crush its head. Bringing his arm down to the ground in preparation to stomp on it, his heart almost stopped when he saw another Giant Centipede wrapping its body around his leg. Fear paralyzed him.

The Giant Centipede around his legs reared its head and then struck his thigh. The pinchers dug deep into his leg, and he gasped in pain.

Ten flashed on his Health bar as it dropped and then every second two more Health disappeared. An icon flashed next to his debuffs. It looked like a coiled snake. Pain, like liquid fire, moved up his thigh and into his gut, and he realized he'd been poisoned. Ruwen almost collapsed as his legs wobbled.

The Giant Centipede around his leg raised its head to strike again, but Ruwen grabbed it with his left hand. He stood there, hunched over, a Giant Centipede in each hand and a Thrasher appendage hanging from his eye. He puked up his breakfast as the poison reached his stomach, and the sausage burned his nostrils as it came out. His working eye had filled with tears, but he could make out the other Thrasher moving between him and the door. Like a heartbeat, the poison ticked, taking two Health with every beat. In moments, he had lost a quarter of his Health.

He didn't know what to do. If he let go of either Giant Centipede, they would bite him, and he didn't think he would survive another two doses of poison. Reaching for his dagger or the baton was out of the question, as it would bring the Giant Centipede within biting distance of his body. The poison had weakened his leg and core, and he didn't think he could even kick the attacking Thrasher. Not that he had the coordination for that anyway. If he didn't do something soon, one of these three monsters would be the end of him.

Ruwen cast *Distraction* at the far wall, desperate to do something. The Thrasher stopped approaching and slowly rotated. He didn't even know where its eyes were, but it had stopped, and that had bought him a few more seconds to think.

He could cast *Campfire*, but it seemed useless since the Thrasher could easily walk around it. Plus, he probably didn't have the five seconds it would take to cast it. That literally left him a single thing to try: *Scrub.*

If he hadn't been greedy and agreed to Fluffy's deal, he wouldn't have had to take such a useless spell. His other choices hadn't been great, but they couldn't have been worse than a cleaning spell. He only had himself to blame.

The irony didn't escape him. While he had dreamed of fighting monsters like this, it had been with powerful Mage spells. Instead, he would die while cleaning them. He couldn't have made his Worker Class prouder. Sift would find his dead body surrounded by sparkling Giant Centipedes.

He screamed in frustration, and the Thrasher moved toward him again. The poison had stopped taking Health, but the burning and dizziness remained. Resigned to his fate, cursing his Class, he pictured the brush symbol for *Scrub.*

His hands vibrated, and a white glow seeped from his palms. The area he gripped on each Giant Centipede turned from brown to silver. He could see faint traces of pink and blue on the monsters' bodies as the dirt and grime dissolved. How could such disgusting creatures have beautiful scales? A small part of him had hoped the dire warnings in the textbook would have allowed him to use this as a weapon. But the proof was right in front of him. It performed as advertised. It cleaned.

The Thrasher was almost close enough to reach him. Ruwen's time was almost up. A two flashed over his Energy bar every second, but the bar remained full. The two Energy per second he was channeling to *Scrub* was barely more than his 1.9 that he regenerated every second. He could stand here all day cleaning these things. The numbers reminded him what he'd found strange about *Scrub*. Its Energy consumption was variable. In fact, he remembered it went to twenty even though a warning had said to never go past ten.

With a thought, he pushed as much Energy as he could to his hands. His Energy bar dropped in chunks of twenty as his hands vibrated so fast they began to blur. At this rate, he would be out of Energy in less than ten seconds. The white glow, which had been soft before, became blinding. Any part of the Giant Centipedes that touched his hands simply dissolved.

The Giant Centipede in his right hand fell in two pieces to the ground and writhed as it died. The Giant Centipede wrapped around his leg released its grip as its head dropped to the floor. Ruwen reached down to pull the creature off his leg and screamed in pain as his hand neared his leg. A thirty flashed on his Health bar, and Ruwen collapsed as his leg gave out. The shaking in his hands made them impossible to control.

The Thrasher, seeing its opportunity, jumped on him. Instinctively, Ruwen raised his arms and thrust out his hands to shield himself. The Thrasher crashed into Ruwen's body as his hands dissolved a path through the Thrasher's body. The Thrasher convulsed as it died, blood soaking Ruwen's shirt. His Energy bar turned red, and he immediately stopped channeling *Scrub*. He didn't move, the shock of surviving too great.

He stayed like that, staring at the ceiling with his one good eye, a Thrasher half on him like he was putting on a shirt. His mind had gone numb. He never wanted to do anything like this again.

"You're not supposed to wear them," Sift said as he pulled the Thrasher off Ruwen's body.

"Looks like you're going to lose your eye, too," Sift said.

Ruwen didn't react, his mind replaying the horrible events that had almost killed him.

"Hey, I'm joking. You okay?" Sift asked.

Ruwen felt Sift grab the sucker attached to his eye and squeeze. A moment later the appendage came off with a pop. Sift filled his vision. Both eyes still worked.

"You're going to have a black eye from that," Sift said. "You'd think the eye is the worst place to get one of these, but it isn't."

Ruwen's brain started to work a little. Sift helped Ruwen sit up, and he leaned against the wall. For the first time, he could see the whole room. It looked like a library, although most of the books were scattered on the floor.

Ruwen rubbed the eye that had been covered by the sucker and noticed his hand was clean. Really clean.

"What?" Ruwen asked.

"It's the nipple," Sift said.

Ruwen stared at Sift.

"Nevermind, are you okay?" Sift asked.

"No, I'm not."

CHAPTER 21

*S*ift sat down next to Ruwen.

"I honestly thought I was going to die," Ruwen said. "Again."

"Only once has Ky brought someone under level twenty through the Blood Gate. She was level ten," Sift said. He rolled the blood-stained hem of his pants between his fingers. "She didn't last long."

"Are you trying to help? Because you suck at it," Ruwen said.

"My point is, Ky bringing you here means the other options were worse."

Ruwen rubbed his face with his hands. Thoughts of the Giant Centipedes made him shudder. "That's hard to believe."

"I agree. You must be in a real mess back home."

"I am. For reasons I don't even understand."

"Why are you here?"

Why was he here? That was a good question. Because Ky hated him and enjoyed putting him in these miserable situations? No, she had bigger issues than wasting time on a worthless level two Worker. Maybe it was because that stupid high priest had punished him by making him a Worker in the first place. But that rang hollow as well. He'd acted like an idiot and revealed his two-Class ability to the very people looking for it was probably the most accurate answer. Even if that was the catalyst, it wasn't the reason he was here. His goals were basically the same as they were before the madness surrounding his Ascension. He needed to survive long enough to gain the power and skills to find his missing parents.

"I'm here because of my parents," Ruwen said.

"Now that is something I can understand!" Sift said.

Ruwen gave Sift a small smile. Sift was trying hard to cheer him up.

"My parents disappeared a year ago. Their whole party died except for them. They got blamed for killing everyone, and for the fortune in terium that went missing. I've suffered because of it. I want to find them, and I want the truth. But I can't do any of that until I'm stronger."

What Ruwen didn't say was how the constant whispers that his parents had abandoned him for all that money had started to stick to his thoughts.

"I'm sorry," Sift said.

"Thanks."

"But you should find another reason, too. A personal one."

"That is personal. It's my name that got ruined that day, too!"

"Easy, friend. I agree that is powerful motivation, and probably fine for years. But eventually, you're going to need more to power your growth. Something that allows you to push yourself."

"What's yours?"

Sift bit his lip. "I've never told anyone."

Ruwen held up his hands. "I didn't mean to pry."

"No, it's okay. I like you. Even if you have a weird thing with wearing the monsters you kill."

"That was an accident. It was a last resort situation."

"Don't worry, I won't tell...many people."

They both laughed.

After a few seconds of quiet Sift spoke again. "Freedom. That is the prism I see everything through."

"Freedom from here? Your parents?"

Sift nodded. "I want to hear the sound of the sea, taste snow, feel the energy at a Step tournament, and a thousand other things I can't do here. I also might want to get away from my parents."

Ruwen chuckled. "You want to leave your parents, and I want to find mine."

"And yet our paths crossed."

Sift opened his bag, removed a small bar, and handed it to Ruwen. "Eat that. It looks like you lost your breakfast."

"Stupid Giant Centipedes. It's bad enough they have all those legs and pinchers and small dead eyes, but poison too?"

"That's Blapy for you. There are bigger ones below that can fly. I hate those. She is always experimenting with new ways to torture people. How did you kill these?"

Ruwen looked at his leg where the Giant Centipede had bitten him. The wounds had healed, but he could still feel the cold teeth chomping on his leg. A hand-sized hole in his pants reminded him how much damage *Scrub* could do. He could have killed himself if he'd scratched his nose.

"I cleaned them to death," Ruwen said.

"What?"

"Literally, I scrubbed them so hard they fell apart."

"That's a new one."

"I'm so bad at fighting. Before coming in here, I reminded myself not to drop my weapon and not to turn my back on anything. Then, I spent too much time killing the first one, and something got behind me. Then when it attacked me, the first thing I did was drop my weapon. How can I be so bad at this?"

"I'm not going to lie, you are not a natural fighter. And it doesn't help that you have to push yourself here. What you are doing is risky. I trust Ky though, so I know it must be necessary."

"Thanks for your honesty. As much as it hurts."

"That's why we practice. Because nothing has been handed to us. If it makes you feel better, everything past here we'll do together."

"I thought you said the experience loss would be too great."

"These were all level one, and you barely survived. You won't survive level two on your own, so the experience issue is moot."

"That does make me feel better actually."

"Good, now go see if Blapy gave you anything good."

Ruwen pushed himself to his feet, placed his staff in its harness, and looked around. Only a few tables still stood on four legs. On the one closest to him, the familiar brown leather bag had appeared. He walked to the table, opened the bag, and dumped it out.

A centipede, about the size of his pinky, tumbled out of the bag and rolled toward him. He jumped back and grabbed the baton from his waist. Raising it above his head, he prepared to smash the small creature. It lay unmoving on its side, and he slowly lowered his baton. Poking the centipede with the baton didn't cause a reaction, and as he got closer, he realized it wasn't living at all.

"Are you serious?" Ruwen asked.

"What?" Sift said from behind him.

Ruwen carefully picked up the centipede, ready to throw it if it suddenly moved.

Tring!
The Black Pyramid has rewarded you...
Name: *Stuffed Centipede of Solace*
Quality: *Uncommon*
Charges: *5*
Durability: *10 of 10*

Weight: *1.0 lbs.*
Effect: *Cure poison when placed against the lips. 100% effective against level 1 poisons. Effectiveness halves per poison level increase.*
Description: *Gently clean with warm water. Scrubbing will cause damage.*

Ruwen held it up. "She gave me a stuffed centipede."

"It's cute."

"It cures poison, but you have to kiss it."

"Oh, that's evil."

"I think she's really enjoying this," Ruwen said.

"She probably gets bored."

"So, we are some sort of entertainment?"

"Pretty much."

"You never look in the bags?" Ruwen asked.

"She doesn't even put things in bags anymore. When I never opened them, she placed the loot in plain sight."

Ruwen shook his head and looked at the remaining two items on the table. The items closest to him looked like a stack of silver squares about the size of his palm. They reflected the light and rainbows raced across the surface.

Tring!
The Black Pyramid has rewarded you...
Name: *Rock Centipede Scales*
Quantity: *5*
Quality: *Uncommon*
Durability: *50 of 50*
Weight: *5.0 lbs.*
Description: *Alchemy component. Very clean.*

The very clean comment made him wonder if these were actually scales from the ones he'd killed. Blapy had already absorbed them. Probably not, he decided. She was just taking every opportunity to poke fun at him. He put them in his Void Band and then focused on the last reward.

The final items were round, pink, and as wide as his thumb.

Tring!
The Black Pyramid has rewarded you...
Name: *Floating Clasper Sucker*
Quantity: *3*
Quality: *Uncommon*
Durability: *5 of 5*
Weight: *0.10 lbs.*
Description: *The tip of a Clasper limb. Will adhere to any surface. Squeeze to release. Will not improve vision.*

He picked them up and tried to drop them in his Void Band, but the three disks adhered to his hand. With a groan, he attempted to pull them off with his other hand but only succeeded in getting that hand stuck as well.

Ruwen held up his hands, which were stuck together. "Ugh, she is killing me."

"She will definitely try to do that," Sift said. He studied Ruwen's stuck hands. "Those look like the sticky part of a Thrasher arm."

"She calls them Floating Claspers."

Sift, careful to only touch the edges, pinched the disks. The suckers released their hold on Ruwen's hands and fell to the table. Ruwen carefully picked them up by their sides and dropped them in his Void Band.

"Okay, let's go get your first attempt out of the way," Sift said.

"What do you mean?"

"You'll see."

Sift started for the doors, but Ruwen paused and took a good look around the room. There were actually a lot of books still here, but they were scattered all over the floor. He loved books and had spent the last year living in a library, which made the sight painful to look at. It seemed overwhelming to fix, though.

"Hey, if I put some of these books on a shelf, would Blapy leave them? Or is all this carefully staged by her?" Ruwen asked.

Sift turned around. "I don't know."

Ruwen walked to the corner near the door, picked up a few books, and placed them on a shelf. "I want to try something."

After a couple of seconds, Sift came over and helped Ruwen. It took them five minutes, but they cleared a small section around the corner.

"Assuming Blapy allows this change, I'll have to figure out a way to fix the shelves," Ruwen said. "Once I do, I'll get all the books off the floor. Then organize them somehow. I just can't leave them like this."

"You are a strange one. But, I'll help if you want."

"Thanks, that would be great."

The two left the room and started for the far wall. As they got closer, what Ruwen had thought was a bar was actually a wall full of balances. Each scale had items placed on its pans. There had to be a few hundred of them, and almost none of them were balanced. Each had a recipe at its base. The map showed him directly over one of his quest markers, so he opened his quests.

The **Taking out the Trash** quest pulsed yellow now that he'd completed it. He ignored it for now and opened the quest his map indicated he'd arrived at:

Killer Recipes for the Busy Shade

Not every task requires a dagger. A healthy Shade relies on the proper proportions of the Pyramid, with results to die for. Use your mind to discover the appropriate balance.

Restriction: *One attempt per day.*

Reward: *Black Pyramid cipher (Level 1)*

Reward: *Five-Minute Fare to Die For, Volume 1*
Reward: *500 experience*

Ruwen looked at Sift.

"I can't help. All I'll say is this usually takes people a few weeks, so we shouldn't spend all day here. The priority is leveling you," Sift said.

"Okay, can I have a few minutes to study it?"

"Of course."

Sift pulled out Io and walked to the closest intact chair. He sat and placed Io on his lap. Sift laughed at something Io said, and Ruwen turned back to the wall of scales.

The scales varied in size and fanciness, but most were about as large as his head. He strode to the ones directly in front of him and studied them. All three had their own recipes. The first had eight ingredients with six on one plate and two on the other. The scale leaned a little to the six-ingredient side. The next scale was similar but only had three ingredients and leaned to the right. The third had a crossbow bolt on one side and five ingredients on the other. Every recipe was different.

Ruwen stepped back and glanced at the wall. The sheer magnitude of the choices overwhelmed him. He could only choose once per day, so if he guessed, it might be a year before he finished this quest. There had to be a clue in the quest itself. He studied the text again.

Killer Recipes for the Busy Shade

Not every task requires a dagger. A healthy Shade relies on the proper proportions of the Pyramid, with results to die for. Use your mind to discover the appropriate balance.

The first line made him think he should avoid all the scales with weapons. He walked up and down the wall and was disappointed to see that weapons were in very few of the scales. The vast majority just had ingredients.

The second line was the most confusing. It seemed to be saying that the recipe was some sort of poison, but Ruwen had never studied poisons, so he wouldn't recognize a real recipe if he read it. The "healthy" and "pyramid" words were probably a play on the food pyramid everyone learned was necessary for a healthy diet, except the word proportions was used instead of portions. Was that because proportions made more sense in the context of a recipe?

The last line probably just meant he needed to think about it and not blindly pick one. It was interesting that the quest used the word "balance" instead of "scale." Was that on purpose?

He paced back and forth in front of the wall again. A surprisingly large number of scales were out of balance. In fact, there were only thirty in perfect balance, and ten of those had weapons. He studied the twenty without weapons but couldn't see any recipe that he was confident enough to choose.

The more he thought about it, though, the more he was convinced that "balance" was a clue. In frustration, he looked at the ten with weapons. Seven had daggers, one had a crossbow bolt, and two had darts. Why so many daggers? And all on balanced scales.

He felt pressure in his brain as his subconscious made connections that his mind hadn't seen yet. These daggers were important. Only seven daggers on the whole wall and each were on balanced scales. That couldn't be a coincidence. Maybe he had been wrong about weapons being excluded. He reread the quest.

Killer Recipes for the Busy Shade
Not every task requires a dagger. A healthy Shade relies on the proper proportions of the Pyramid, with results to die for. Use your mind to discover the appropriate balance.

The quest might be trying to say that a successful Shade would have to use other methods than just a dagger. That their skills would have to be balanced. In that light, the daggers made sense. Ruwen studied the recipes associated with each of the scales with daggers. Again, they varied wildly.

The quest mentioned "the proper proportions of the Pyramid." But none of the ingredients of the seven scales were piled into the shape of a pyramid. His brain hurt as a headache arced through his forehead. He rubbed his head to ease the pain.

"Are you okay?" Sift asked.

Ruwen walked between the seven scales. "Yes, just give me another minute."

"Sure."

Why the word "proportion"? It seemed out of place. His head felt like it might explode. This was definitely important. What did proportion and pyramid have in common? A burst of light flashed in his mind and then immediate relief as he finally understood: math.

He closed his eyes and remembered his lessons. His memory was almost flawless, and he pictured his advanced math textbook. Mentally flipping pages until he found the section on pyramids, he studied the various calculations associated with them. Two numbers jumped out at him. Numbers that were everywhere in nature and architecture: 22/7 and 196/121. He felt stupid for not recognizing them in the recipes.

He found the correct recipe at the third scale:

1. *Begin with 196 drops of purified water*
2. *Add 22 drops of Spit Viper venom*
3. *Crush Dusk Mold into a fine powder and add 7 pinches to the solution*
4. *Rapidly bring to a boil and then simmer for 121 seconds*
5. *Remove from heat and let cool*

Ruwen reached out and touched the scale. "This is it."

"Hey Sifty, who's your friend?"

Ruwen jumped at the voice and his heart raced. A young girl, maybe seven, sat on a table to his right. She had blonde pigtails tied with black ribbon, and she wore a white dress. Her legs dangled off the table, and she swung them back and forth as she stared at Ruwen. She held a stuffed centipede to her chest. It was a bigger version of the one he'd just received.

"Oh, hi, Blapy. This is Ruwen. He's new," Sift said.

Did Sift just call her Blapy? As in the Black Pyramid Blapy? Was the dungeon able to actually manifest itself as a person? This had to be the aftereffect of the Giant Centipede poison, or maybe a trick Sift was pulling on him. Or maybe something they did to all the new people as some sort of hazing initiation.

"No one has ever gotten it right on the first try," Blapy said to Ruwen. Then she looked over at the dagger on Sift's lap. "I know, Io. It makes me curious about her plans."

Blapy could talk to Io, too? Was Ruwen the only one who couldn't?

"Who knows what Ky's plans are, she –" Sift started.

"No, I mean Uru's," Blapy interrupted.

"Oh," Sift said.

"You know Uru?" Ruwen asked.

"She was always the cleverest of them, and she's trying to drag me into that mess," Blapy said.

"A Tier One dungeon on your side would be a huge advantage," Ruwen said.

Blapy giggled. "I passed that eons ago. The gods themselves adventured here." Blapy looked at the wall. "There is no scale for me."

Ruwen's mouth dropped open. If Blapy could pose a challenge to groups of gods, her power must be beyond comprehension.

"You're more powerful than the gods?" Ruwen asked.

Blapy shrugged. "On this plane I have some advantages they don't. Like you, Kysandra belongs to Uru, and I should have known when Kysandra bonded with me that we were all dancing to Uru's music. You are the first Root Class of any of the gods to enter my halls. Another example of Uru's ability to shape events. You really have to admire that young woman."

"Before yesterday I'd never heard of this Class," Ruwen said.

"Well, that bunch really likes two things: secrets and rules. So many rules. Take how much total magic their followers consume, for example, they put a cap on it. Some gods chose large populations with low magic, and some went with fewer followers that could do powerful magic. Many interesting strategies. The only wild card is every hundred years, each deity can pick a Champion that can multiclass and is outside the normal power restrictions. You are Uru's choice."

"Every hundred years? What if Ruwen is still alive?" Sift asked.

Blapy shook her head. "Roots never last that long. They're too dangerous, and the gods spend vast amounts of energy getting rid of them."

Ruwen's stomach turned. "Setting aside the fact I'm probably going to die soon, are you saying my whole world is just a big game to the gods?"

"That would be a simplistic way of looking at it. Your world is important. If a single entity controlled it, they would have the power to affect the entire universe. The stakes couldn't be higher. Uru has placed her hopes in you."

Ruwen thought he might puke.

"Io tells me you've already been discovered." Blapy raised her eyebrows. "On your first day."

"Why can't I talk to Io?" Ruwen asked.

"Their rules, of course. I remember the day I created Io. An epic treasure for a triumphant Uru when she completed level one hundred thirty-one."

Sift looked at Io. "You belonged to a goddess! Why didn't you tell me those stories?"

Blapy faced Ruwen again. "Well?"

Ruwen shifted his weight from one foot to the other and wiped the sweat off his forehead. As uncomfortable as the truth was, he didn't like lying, so he just admitted it. "Yes, they already found me."

"Well, Ruwen Starfield, I see a portion of the potential Uru sees in you. I hope you don't disappoint her," Blapy said.

Ruwen took a deep breath. "Me, too."

"That won't stop me from trying to kill you, which you are making easy by the way. It's like you want to die," Blapy said.

Ruwen ran a hand through his hair. "I know. I'm a terrible fighter."

"I'll have him up to speed in no time," Sift said.

Blapy turned to Sift. "You haven't ventured very deep lately. I'm beginning to think you don't like me anymore."

"Nothing like that, Blapy. My parents have been trying all these new things to break through my blockage. Thank goodness Ruwen arrived and provided a distraction. Those two are going to kill me."

Blapy laughed mischievously. "They're on the right path." She turned to Ruwen. "I can't wait to see what his parents do with you. Those two serene souls are about to have cognitive dissonance like nothing they've ever experienced. Uru took a great risk in allowing her Champion to bear my mark, and to come here and risk dying. But things are finally moving, and the drama is palpable. I haven't had this much fun in millennia." Blapy jumped off the table, kissed her stuffed centipede, and then stared up at Ruwen. "But that bunch suckered me into playing by their rules. They didn't want me picking favorites. So, you better give me your best, Ruwen Starfield, and even then, I'll still likely kill you."

"I can be your favorite," Sift said. "I don't belong to any of them."

Blapy smiled at Sift. "You might be, except my favorites must know how to whistle."

Blapy giggled and then disappeared. No smoke, bang, or slow fade, she just disappeared in a blink. Two books appeared on the table.

"I knew it. Io, we have to try harder," Sift said.

"You're learning to whistle from something without a mouth?"

Sift picked up Io and pointed him at Ruwen. "Good point. You'll need to teach me."

CHAPTER 22

*R*uwen shook his head, walked over to the table, and looked at the two books. He thought there should be tokens as well, and he checked his notifications to refresh his memory.

Ting!
You have completed the Black Pyramid Quest – Taking out the Trash (Level 1).
You have received 1,000 experience.
You have received 5 Black Pyramid tokens.

It had been the Taking out the Trash quest that had the tokens. Ruwen turned to Sift. "I never received any tokens for the Taking out the Trash quest."

"Blapy automatically updates Fluffy's log with your earnings."

"Oh."

Since he already had them open, he went through the rest of his notifications.

Ding!
Uru's Blessings, Worker! You have reached level 3.
You have gained +1 to Strength!
You have gained +1 to Stamina!
You have 2 unassigned points.
Uru's Blessings, Root! You have reached level 3.
You have 2 unassigned points.
New Spells and Abilities are available to you. Choose wisely.

Ruwen grew excited. He had been in shock after the last fight and missed the fact that he'd leveled up. He immediately opened his Profile.

Strength and Stamina had increased automatically. He immediately added a point to Wisdom and Dexterity and with the +1 modifiers from his dagger and staff it brought him back up to 10. With great satisfaction, he watched the Foolish and Clumsy debuffs disappear. He was finally getting closer to where he'd started at yesterday before his death.

He had two points left to distribute. He could add another point to Dexterity and Wisdom, but he didn't plan on giving up these weapons in the near future, so he wasn't concerned about losing the modifiers. What really bothered him were his looks. Not giving himself time to consider it, he added both points to Charisma. He was being vain, as really only Merchants needed a high Charisma value. But it had bothered him enough that it was worth fixing.

Now he appeared like he had when Hamma had first seen him. But, he was most certainly not doing this because of her. He pushed thoughts of the priestess out of his head. It just made sense to get his attributes back to where they'd started.

At level four, he would add a point to Dexterity and Wisdom and finally be back to his original attributes. Three levels to completely recover from that first death. It hurt his head thinking about it. He opened his last notification.

Ting!
You have completed the Quest – Killer Recipes for the Busy Shade
You have received Black Pyramid cipher (Level 1)
You have received Five-Minute Fare to Die For, Volume 1
You have received 500 experience

He had new abilities and spells to look at, but he wasn't as sure how to distribute those, so he decided to do it later. Opening his Profile tab, he glanced at the major things that had changed since the last time he'd looked. He ignored the attributes the public saw and focused on his actual values.

Level: *3*

Experience: *1130/6000*

Strength: *11*
Stamina: *11*
Dexterity: *10*
Intelligence: *17*
Wisdom: *10*
Charisma: *12*

Health: *110/110*
Mana: *170/170*
Energy: *213/213*

Health Regen: *0.22*
Mana Regen: *0.43*
Energy Regen: *2.13*

The Giant Centipedes and Floating Claspers must have been around sixty experience apiece. Ruwen was almost 20% of the way to level four, and he still had today and tomorrow to get to level five. Maybe this would be possible.

He looked down at the two books, both of which were about the size of his palm. The book on the left was made of paper and had a painted black pyramid on the cover along with a stylized number one. The brown leather book had a title burned into the cover, but Ruwen couldn't read it. Just like in the Blood Gate, his *Hey You* Ability didn't allow him to read ciphered writing.

When he picked up the book containing the cipher, a prompt appeared.

This Black Pyramid cipher will allow the user to read and write text that has been encoded with ciphers up to and including level 1.
Do you wish to learn the Black Pyramid cipher level 1?
Yes or No

He chose *Yes*, and the book in his hand burst into flame. Ruwen jerked his hand back, but he didn't feel any heat and his hand wasn't burned. A cool mist wrapped his brain, and he shivered. In a heartbeat, the sensation disappeared.

Looking down at the brown book, he could now read the title: *Killer Recipes for the Busy Shade.* He picked up the book and opened the notification.

Tring!
The Black Pyramid has rewarded you...
Name: *Manual, Killer Recipes for the Busy Shade*
Quality: *Rare*
Durability: *10 of 10*
Weight: *1.0 lbs.*
Description: *Basic recipes for poisons and potions created from ingredients found in the Black Pyramid. Taste testing not recommended.*

He flipped through the pages. Each recipe had a detailed

description with information on how to find the ingredients, possible substitutes, dangers, uses, storage, and disposal.

"This is really thorough," Ruwen said.

"Shade's first rule: death arrives on an overlooked detail."

Ruwen placed the book in his Void Band. He would study it later when he had the time. His heart beat rapidly as he removed the parchment he'd gotten at the Blood Gate. His curiosity had been killing him ever since he'd gotten it. Paper in hand, he closed his Void Band.

This time when he looked at the text three columns appeared. The first column looked like a list of about thirty capital or large cities, the second had a sequence of gate runes like Ruwen had seen on the stone doors, and the third had a brief description. The descriptions were things like "lower dock warehouse, east slum side" and "high temple, north spire, second subfloor."

A notification blinked and he opened it.

Do you wish to update the map with these Gate Runes?

He chose *Yes* and the parchment in his hands dissolved.

The map pulsed and he opened it, but the only thing visible was the large room they stood in and the eight rooms they'd cleared. He tried zooming outward, but nothing happened. Whatever had just occurred, he couldn't see it. Losing the parchment wasn't ideal, but his memory was good enough to recall everything on the page. He would add the gate runes to his journal later.

"Okay, sorry about that. I'm ready," Ruwen said.

"Io and I have been trying to remember the fastest time for the recipe quest. We think it was six weeks."

"Really? I got lucky. Sometimes I can see patterns in things. My memory helps, too."

"Well, whatever you got going on up there," Sift said and

tapped Ruwen's head, "is pretty impressive. Blapy even showed up."

"She doesn't always come when someone finishes it?"

"Never. I hear her a lot. She likes to walk near me and whistle. But she rarely shows herself."

"Hmm, I don't know if that is good or bad."

"Oh, it's bad. You do not want Blapy's attention."

"Great. Thanks for easing my general level of anxiety."

"Glad to help," Sift said with a smile. "I have my own problems. Io doesn't want to tell me about Uru. It's the first time he hasn't wanted to talk."

"Maybe she made him take a vow of silence or something," Ruwen said.

"Ow!" Sift said.

Ruwen jumped and looked around. "What's wrong?"

"I'm not dumb. Ruwen's just smart," Sift said to Io. Sift looked at Ruwen. "Io says thanks for figuring that out."

Ruwen nodded. "It looks like Io can't talk about it. See if he can answer yes or no questions. Ask him if Uru gave him to Ky."

"Io says yes. And now he's super excited. He can't keep a secret to save his life, and I bet these have been killing him."

"Let's start now. I love learning secrets."

Sift shook his head. "We'll talk to him after we've gotten you to level five. Ky would kill me if she found out we talked to Io instead of focusing on her commands."

"That's true."

Sift walked to the wall and pulled on a scale that had a pile of keys on one plate and opened locks on the other. A small section of the wall opened, revealing a dark tunnel that sloped downward.

Sift walked into the tunnel, and Ruwen followed. As soon as he passed the door, a quest appeared.

Ting!

You have received the Black Pyramid quest...
It's Your Turn to Cook (Level 2)
Collect 3 ingredients that can be used in Killer Recipes for the Busy Shade.
Reward: *10 Black Pyramid tokens*
Reward: *1,000 experience*
Accept or Decline

"Did you get the next quest?" Sift asked.

"Yep," Ruwen said as he chose *Accept.*

"Which one was it? Sometimes Blapy will give you a clue about what's next."

"It's your turn to cook."

"Oh, no."

"Is that bad?"

"Well, there really aren't any good ones."

"The first quest was taking out the trash. This one is cooking. It looks like Blapy has a chore theme going."

"Blapy's humor is much darker than that. I just hope I put extra underwear in my bag."

Ruwen didn't know how to respond to that, so he ignored it. "How do the monsters get through this door?"

Sift closed the door and started down the tunnel. "They don't use it. I'm not sure how they get up here. I don't know if Blapy just creates them there, or if there is this huge network of tunnels and secret doors that only the monsters use."

Ruwen imagined monsters walking to work through service tunnels and shook his head. This whole experience had been unbelievable. "What is the next area like?"

"It's a big open cavern, but Blapy creates different weather inside it. You don't really know what you're going to get until you arrive."

Ruwen noticed it getting darker. "Do the lights not work down here?"

"No. I think the first level has them because it is a waiting area for people. Down here, it's all monsters."

Ruwen turned his *Detect Temperature* on, and Sift turned a light red.

"Just stay close to me until we figure out what the flavor of the day is," Sift said.

"Is it usually just one type of monster?"

"No, more like one type of environment, and the monsters will be native to that environment."

Ruwen pulled his staff off his back and swung it a few times. The temperature increased, and Ruwen wiped the sweat from his forehead. Thankfully, it stopped getting darker, and the ambient light stabilized around dusk. They had been walking downward for almost ten minutes when Sift slowed.

"The tunnel ends at that turn. We'll have about ten feet before it opens into the cavern. Stay close," Sift said.

Ruwen stayed behind Sift as they turned the corner and walked to the tunnel exit. The cavern didn't look like a cavern at all. The ceiling, hundreds of feet above them and obscured by fog, gave him the impression he stood at the bottom of some canyon and not in an underground dungeon. The cavern was devoid of trees or anything living. Boulders and tall red rocks littered the sandy floor, which rose and fell like a stormy sea. There were plenty of places for things to hide. The heat hit Ruwen like a fist, and his *Detect Temperature* made everything red. Sift, cooler than his surroundings, looked blue against all the hot rocks in front of them.

Sift closed his eyes for a few seconds. "Spitters."

"What are those? Are they bad?"

"No worse than anything else. It's just this is my favorite shirt. One second."

Sift took off his shirt. He paused for a moment and then took his pants, socks, and shoes off too. Thankfully, he kept his underwear on. He placed all his clothes, along with a sheathed Io, into his Traveler's Belt.

"Do I need to do that?" Ruwen asked.

The thought of fighting already made him nervous, but having to do it wearing a belt and underwear would make it ten times worse.

Sift bit his lip and stared at Ruwen for a few seconds. "No, it might keep it off your skin. The worst part is –"

Sift leaped to the left as the sound of spitting reached them. A stream of clear liquid arced through the air directly toward them. Sift intercepted it in the air, blocking it with his body, and taking the full brunt of the attack. A few droplets struck Ruwen's arm and a heartbeat later, it ignited.

Ruwen screamed as his skin blistered. An eight flashed on his Health bar as it decreased. He tried to wipe it off, but it just smeared like some sort of burning jelly. A five flashed on his Health bar as his hand burned as well.

Ruwen looked up at Sift and screamed again. Sift stood in front of him, covered in the burning jelly, on fire.

"Are you okay?" Sift asked.

"What! Am I okay? You're on fire!"

Sift looked down at the flames that covered him. "I know. We are fighting a Spitter. That's why I didn't want to ruin my shirt."

"You are on fire!" Ruwen screamed again.

The spitting sounded again, and Ruwen heard more of the gel strike Sift's back.

"I hate how it goes so cold before igniting. It's —" Sift grimaced as his back exploded in flames. "It's like a cold shower. I hate cold showers."

Then he turned and sprinted toward the source of the spitting. Flames trailed him as he ran like some sort of land-bound comet.

What Sift called a Spitter looked more like a six-foot salamander with a black beak for a nose. As Sift neared it, large scaly wings unfolded and snapped downward, sending the creature forty feet to the left. Sift followed, still burning.

While the fire had gone out quickly, Ruwen's arm and hand still burned. How did Sift survive being covered in that stuff? Movement to his right made Ruwen turn. His *Detect Temperature* didn't work well in here because everything was really hot, including the monsters, so he turned it off. He relaxed as he saw what looked like chickens. There were six, about twenty feet from him, and they tilted their heads back and forth. One pecked the ground, and Ruwen sighed in relief. He supposed there had to be normal animals down here too. Probably for the monsters to eat.

As Ruwen turned away, one of the chickens lifted its tail and aimed its butt at him.

"That's not very nice," Ruwen said.

The chicken shot an egg at him. Ruwen stood in shock and at the last moment swung his staff, trying to knock the egg away. His chest filled with pride as he made contact, and then it exploded. He landed hard on his back, the air knocked from his lungs. He rolled onto his stomach and got to his knees, gasping. Once again, he had lost his staff. He looked at the group of chickens and was horrified to see another two aiming at him.

He pushed himself to his feet as two more eggs shot toward him. The lack of air in his lungs made running impossible, but he shuffled away as fast as he could. The two eggs detonated behind him and threw him forward ten feet. His head spun, and the Vertigo debuff appeared under his bars. The entrance to the tunnel was in front of him, and he crawled forward. Just as he entered the tunnel, three more explosions sounded behind him, but the entrance protected him from the shock wave.

The debuff disappeared, and his head cleared. Cursing himself for dropping his staff, he twisted his baton off his belt. He looked at the tube with all its various bumps and indentations and cursed again. Because he hadn't spent any time familiarizing himself with the baton, he had no idea what did what.

An egg exploded in front of the tunnel and rocks peppered him. He realized if those chickens got one in the tunnel, the enclosed space would make the explosion even more powerful. He had actually crawled to the most dangerous place. His breath was back, though, and he pulled on a random bump. A hoe magically unfolded from the rod. It would have to do.

He peered around the corner of the tunnel and saw the chickens wandering around. Thank Uru they weren't too bright. He didn't have a lot of options spell-wise, so he did the same thing he did with the Floating Clasper on the floor above.

Casting *Bleed* on his baton caused his Mana to drop twenty-five points. Peeking around the corner again, he focused on the area just past the chickens and cast *Distract* for another ten Mana.

Ruwen sprinted toward the chickens. Too late, he realized his mistake. The distraction had caused all the chickens to aim their butts at what they thought was a threat, which meant their eyes were all staring directly at him as he left the tunnel. As one, they all turned, aimed their butts, and fired at him.

Ruwen channeled his *Leap* spell and jumped, and jumped again, each leap gaining an extra 20% from his spell. His Energy pool had dropped by twenty in the couple of seconds it had taken, but when the eggs exploded, he was thankfully out of damage range. One more leap and he landed in the middle of the chickens. They scattered as he stopped channeling *Leap*.

Swinging his hoe, he missed the chicken he had aimed for but hit the one next to it. The hoe embedded itself in the chicken's side and Ruwen swung his baton wildly trying to get it off. The chickens ran around in circles.

Reaching up, he pulled the chicken off his hoe and chased the remaining chickens. As long as he kept running at them, they kept moving, and they couldn't set up for a shot. It took him almost ten minutes, but he finally killed them all. Panting, he collapsed to his knees. His arms and legs shook from the constant swinging and running.

He noticed Sift sitting on a boulder, watching him.

"How long have you been sitting there?" Ruwen asked.

"I don't know. Probably five minutes or so."

"And you didn't help?"

"I'm not sure you can be helped."

"Listen, they're faster than they look."

"They only have one, maybe two, eggs in them. You probably weren't in any danger anymore."

Ruwen closed his eyes for a few seconds. "That would have been super helpful to know BEFORE WE CAME IN HERE!"

"Hey, no need to shout. I was going to tell you, but then I wasn't sure you were even trying to kill them."

"I was! They're fast! And you were on fire!"

Sift held up his hands. "Easy. I'm not burning anymore, and look," Sift said, standing, "I even had an extra pair of underwear. Hopefully, that was the only Spitter because this is my last pair."

CHAPTER 23

$\mathcal{R}$uwen laughed, and after a moment, Sift did too. Ruwen let all the fear and embarrassment flow out of him and then stood. Dead chickens surrounded him.

"I really showed them," Ruwen said.

"I'm pretty sure most of them died from confusion or exhaustion."

"Well, you have to work with the tools you've got."

Sift pointed behind Ruwen. "Very wise. Now collect your loot. We haven't even made it fifty feet into the cavern. At this rate, I'll die of old age before we finish."

Ruwen turned around and saw the brown leather bag he expected, but next to it lay a fine mesh shirt made of silver metal.

"Is this yours?" Ruwen asked.

"Yeah, see if you can take it."

Ruwen knelt, touched the shirt, and immediately received a prompt.

This item is soul locked. Interaction may cause serious harm.
Acknowledge

Ruwen quickly removed his hand and acknowledged the prompt.

"Nope," Ruwen said.

"Figures."

Ruwen dumped out his bag and screamed when three eggs bounced around in front of him. He picked one up but didn't receive the notification he expected. They must be common, he realized, so he opened his log.

Tring!
The Black Pyramid has rewarded you...
Name: *Booming Eggs*
Quantity: *3*
Quality: *Common*
Durability: *1 of 1*
Weight: *0.08 lbs.*
Description: *Ingredient in various potions. An explosion of taste in every bite.*

Ruwen carefully placed them in his Void Band. He scrolled up to see the experience he'd received from killing the chickens.

You have killed a Booming Hen (Level 3)!
You have gained 26 (118*(22% level modifier)) experience!
You have missed a Booming Hen (Level 3)
You have missed a Booming Hen (Level 3)
Critical Miss!
You have fallen
50% defense reduction (Prone)
You have been pecked by a Booming Hen (Level 3)
Critical Strike!
You have taken 5 damage (3 base+(2*1 critical))
You have missed a Booming Hen (Level 3)
You have missed a Booming Hen (Level 3)

Alright, maybe Sift did have a point. He scrolled up to see if he'd received any experience for the Spitter.

You have killed a Roasting Lizard (Level 5)!
You have gained 54 (244*(22% level modifier)) experience!

Fifty-four experience wasn't bad for basically doing nothing, but with Sift taking almost 80% of the experience, it was going to take a while to level again. He closed his log and looked at Sift.

"Blapy thinks you're four times better than me," Ruwen said.

Sift frowned. "That's all? Maybe there's a cap to how much she takes."

"Hey! Not all of us can walk around on fire. Please explain that."

Sift shuffled from one foot to the other. "I told you, I sift things."

"So that means you're immune to fire?"

"Yes, well, on these levels. I'm sure there is stuff down below that would overwhelm me. But I can handle all the energy up here."

"You're immune to any form of energy?"

"Pretty much."

"Are you immortal?"

"Don't be dumb. If someone stabs me, I'll bleed out just like you."

"But if they strike you with lightning, you're fine."

"Yes, now you understand."

"How in Uru's name is that possible?"

Sift shrugged. "By being half the person my parents want me to be."

Ruwen had more questions, but he swallowed them because of the depressed look on Sift's face. Instead, he searched the area until he found his staff. Yet another fight in which he'd lost the weapon. He just hoped he gained the skills he needed before his ineptness killed him.

They walked in silence to where Sift had fought, what Ruwen's log called, the Roasting Lizard. The body of the beast had already disappeared. Ruwen's loot bag sat next to Sift's reward, a golden sword that stuck out of the sand like crystalized sunshine. As Ruwen drew near the sword, the hair on his arm stood. He quickly grabbed his bag and returned to Sift. Carefully, Ruwen poured the contents of his bag onto the rocks. A single jar rolled out.

Tring!
The Black Pyramid has rewarded you...
Name: *Fire Mucus*
Quantity: *1 Medium Jar*
Quality: *Uncommon*
Durability: *5 of 5*
Weight: *1.0 lbs.*
Description: *Ingredient in various potions. The secret sauce in the Boomer Omelet.*

Ruwen placed the jar in his Void Band.

"Let's hug the wall as we move," Sift said. "It's too easy to get surprised out here."

They walked back to the wall, and Ruwen let Sift lead. Ruwen wondered how long the *Bleed* spell would last on his staff before expiring, so he took a moment to cast it. He didn't see a countdown anywhere in his vision or in his inventory. Maybe it stayed active until it triggered.

After a minute, Sift slowed, and Ruwen tensed. He looked around for the danger but didn't see anything. His *Detect Temperature* had turned out to be a disappointment when the animals were near the same temperature as their surroundings.

That probably meant it wouldn't work well underwater either. He activated *Magnify* instead and looked around.

He immediately stopped as the sudden closeness of his surroundings confused his brain. It appeared this ability worked best when looking at something specific, not when walking around. No visible scale appeared, and he wondered if he could modify the magnification or if it was stuck at 200%.

After a few seconds of trial and error he learned how to control it. When he activated *Magnify* it automatically started at maximum. If he wanted to decrease the magnification, he had to unfocus his vision and it would decrease. He slowly scanned the room, but he didn't see anything that seemed dangerous or out of place.

Turning off *Magnify*, he saw that Sift had continued walking and was twenty feet in front of him.

"It's a Stabber!" Sift shouted as he dropped to the ground.

Before Ruwen could respond, a small boulder crashed into the wall where Sift had been. Ruwen jerked in surprise and shielded his face from the flying shards of rock. Wondering what had thrown the rock, Ruwen looked out into the field, just in time to see a boulder flying at him. He moved, but it wasn't in time, and the rock struck his right side.

His Health dropped by thirty, and his head swam from the sudden loss of Health. He dove to the ground as another rock smashed into the wall above him. When no more rocks came, he cautiously looked to see if Sift was okay, but his friend was no longer along the wall. Rapid clicking from the middle of the cavern drew Ruwen's attention, and he found Sift, dashing toward one of the tall rock cylinders in the middle of the room.

The shock of the blow wore off, and Ruwen's whole side throbbed in pain. His eyes blurred from the intense pain, and he wiped them clear. Triggering *Magnify*, he focused where Sift was running. Movement drew his attention, and his stomach turned in fear.

The creature Sift had called a Stabber looked like a giant snake with two arms that were shaped like spears. It grabbed a rock with its mouth and tossed it to the side. In a blink, it had spun on its spear arm, and its tail struck the rock, flinging it directly at Sift. Sift jumped fifteen feet in the air, and the boulder passed harmlessly below him.

"No way," Ruwen whispered.

As Sift dropped back to the ground, the Stabber used its spear arms to drive itself forward. The Stabber flew through the air like an arrow. As it neared Sift, it thrust its arm outward and pierced Sift's shoulder. Sift landed hard, and the Stabber pinned him to the ground. Blood covered Sift's side, and rage filled Ruwen's chest. He sprinted toward the Stabber's back. Channeling *Leap*, he jumped.

He realized too late that jumping in this rocky area was a terrible idea, but he had too much momentum now to stop. As he made his final leap toward the Stabber, his foot half-landed on a rock, and he wasn't able to keep his balance. His body rotated sideways as he flew the last few feet through the air, and he worried he might miss the Stabber entirely. Ruwen aimed for the only part of the creature he could reach, the joint where the spear arm connected to the body.

Ruwen's angle was terrible, and with a Strength of only eleven, the Stabber would barely feel his blow. As he swung the staff, he heard the chimes from Temple Yulm. The Stabber heard them too and froze as the *Distraction* effect struck it. As the staff grazed the Stabber's arm, it flashed red as Ruwen's *Bleed* spell activated. Loud clicking hurt his ears as the Stabber regained control of itself and reared back.

Ruwen struck the ground hard and lost another five Health. He rolled over and looked at Sift, who grinned.

"Seriously," Ruwen said, "what's wrong with you?"

Sift pulled a two-foot section of the Stabber's leg out of his shoulder. He must have snapped the leg off after it impaled him.

"That was really gutsy. I'm proud of you. Only fools get in front –"

The Stabber came down and smashed its broken leg into Sift's groin. It tried to strike Ruwen as well, but he had severely damaged the joint and the Stabber's leg dangled uselessly. The Stabber and Ruwen realized this at the same time, and the Stabber slammed its body into Ruwen.

Ruwen lost another twenty-five Health along with his breath as the Stabber rolled off him. He had lost a total of sixty Health in the few seconds the fight had been going. His Health bar flashed yellow letting him know he'd lost over 50% of his total.

Sift leaped forward and landed on the exposed belly of the snake. He raised the broken Stabber leg taken from his shoulder, and slammed it downward, pinning the Stabber to the ground with its own leg.

Gasping, Ruwen rolled onto his stomach and then pushed himself up. He cast *Bleed* again and then brought his staff down onto the Stabber's head. Sift snapped off the Stabber's remaining leg and shoved it through the small black eye of the creature. The Stabber thrashed around for a moment and then stopped as it died. Sift jumped off the monster and cupped his groin.

"They always find a way to hit me here," Sift groaned.

Sift's shoulder had already healed. A wound that bad should have taken a few minutes at least.

"Your shoulder," Ruwen said, pointing at Sift.

Sift still held his groin, half hunched over. "Even after healing, my stomach is in knots for the next hour. Ugh."

"How did you heal so fast?" Ruwen tried again.

"I still have some of the energy from the Spitter."

A thousand questions exploded in Ruwen's mind. "Not only can you absorb the energy, but you can store it and then use it for other things?"

"That's the whole point, isn't it?" Sift asked his face confused.

He winced in pain. "Hey, do you have any magic to make this feel better?" Sift said, pointing at his groin.

"That line might work on Black Pyramid women, but—" Ruwen stopped when Sift's face grew even more confused. "Nevermind. There's one thing I can try."

He thought of the *Campfire* symbol and focused on it for the required five seconds. Crackling flames appeared between them, and Ruwen's Mana bar flashed red. He only had twenty Mana left in his one hundred seventy-point pool.

"Ah, that's nice," Sift said. "The nausea is gone. Thanks, brother!"

CHAPTER 24

*R*uwen watched as the Stabber disappeared into the ground like water into sand. In a couple of heartbeats, it had vanished entirely, and a familiar leather bag appeared along with a small book.

"Bodies melting into the ground is really uncomfortable to watch," Ruwen said as he walked over and knelt by the treasure.

"What is the title of the book?" Sift asked.

"*The Three Minute Whistler. Guaranteed Methods to have you Whistling in Minutes,*" Ruwen read.

"Ugh. IT'S NOT FUNNY BLAPY!" Sift shouted.

Ruwen heard faint giggling but couldn't tell where it originated.

"Are you going to take it?" Ruwen asked.

Sift looked mournfully at the book. "No, because then she'll win."

"It seems this game hurts you more than it does her."

Sift tried to whistle, but mostly spit came out. He half-turned like he was looking over his shoulder. "I am doing it your way, Io. If I pucker my lips anymore, no air comes out."

Ruwen let Sift talk with Io and turned to the bag. He opened it and gently emptied it onto the ground. He didn't trust Blapy enough to actually stick his hand in it, and the eggs had now taught him caution. A ring dropped out and rolled in a little circle. The ring looked mostly white and had red lines running through it like veins. He picked it up.

Tring!
The Black Pyramid has rewarded you...
Name: *Rock Serpent Ring of Health*
Quality: *Uncommon*
Durability: *20 of 20*
Weight: *0.1 lbs.*
Effect (Passive): *+25 Health.*
Description: *The blood of a rock serpent flows through this ring. Let's be honest, it will probably do you as much good as it did the serpent.*

Ruwen shook his head and put the ring on his right hand. The ring shrunk snuggly around his finger. He wondered if the blood came from the Rock Serpent they'd just killed. That thought made him uncomfortable, so he opened his Profile and looked at his attributes.

His Health had expanded to one hundred thirty-five. Not bad. Killing the Rock Serpent had given him almost a hundred experience, and he now sat at one thousand four hundred eighty-six out of six thousand toward the next level. Just a quarter of the way there. He wasn't going to do this quickly by killing things. He really needed more of these quests. They were obviously meant for higher-level people since they gave so much experience. It sucked that Blapy hadn't given him another ingredient. He only needed one more for his quest. Maybe Sift's parents would give him one.

Sift removed Io from the indestructible Traveler's Belt and held the dagger near his face. Sift alternated between talking with Io and trying to whistle.

"Why is whistling so important to you?" Ruwen asked.

Sift put Io away and looked down. "How can I learn hard things, if I can't do simple things?"

"I don't think things work that way."

"Maybe not, but it feels that way."

Sift looked miserable, and Ruwen felt bad for bringing it up.

"If you want to talk, let me know," Ruwen said.

"Thanks, I appreciate that. Let's see if Blapy has anything else on this level."

Instead of going back to the wall, Sift started directly for the far tunnel. Ruwen ran to catch up.

"Aren't we going to use the wall?" Ruwen asked.

Sift looked around. "I don't see anything else. Which means if there is anything left in here, it's underground. You won't be able to hide the vibration of your steps, so we might as well make good time."

Ruwen nodded. They had walked for a few minutes when Ruwen felt the same sensation he'd had when the Floating Clasper was behind the door on level one, and his *Keen Senses* ability had activated. It emanated from above him, and he looked up. Grey fog covered the ceiling and gave the appearance of a cloudy day outside.

"Does anything ever come from up there?" Ruwen asked.

Sift glanced up. "Sometimes. But I didn't sense anything. Although…"

"Although what?"

"Well, this is a big room. And since I can't bring the energy to me, if Blapy created something *after* we arrived, it might take a bit for me to sense it."

"Like, how long?"

"I don't know. Maybe we should pick up the pace."

Ruwen alternated between finding the best path through the rocks and staring up at the clouds. They were about two-thirds of the way to the exit tunnel when he looked up to see a winged creature diving toward them. The body was narrow, like a snake, and it had a long tail that ended in a sharp point.

"Above us!" Ruwen screamed.

Sift looked up. "A Sleeper! Watch its tail! Run!"

Then Sift jumped straight up into the air like he'd been thrown by a giant. Ruwen stood in awe as the young man collided with the Sleeper, and the two spiraled to the ground. Sift turned the Sleeper as they fell, so it struck the ground first.

The creature used its wings to flip itself off its back. Its head looked like a large mouth with teeth. Ruwen couldn't see any eyes. The tail arced back and hovered over its head like a scorpion. Ruwen sighed in relief when Sift stood. He looked ridiculous standing in just his underwear, his hands free of any weapons.

"Run!" Sift said again.

Ruwen wanted nothing more than to get away from this horrible-looking creature. He would probably only get in Sift's way. Clearly, the young man had abilities that made him far more capable than Ruwen. They were supposed to be a team, though. And that meant helping each other. Instead of charging in, Ruwen took a moment to study the creature.

He triggered *Magnify* and carefully looked at the creature's head and tail. There were no eyes that Ruwen could see and detecting vibrations didn't seem likely since it lived up in the clouds. Maybe it used some sort of sound-based mechanism to see? That gave him an idea.

Turning off *Magnify*, he took a second to cast *Bleed* on his staff. He thought about using *Leap* again, but the ground was just too uneven for his level of Dexterity. Without any more thought, he focused to the right of the Sleeper and cast *Distract*. At the last moment, he wondered if he could control the volume of the sound and concentrated on making it loud.

A thunderclap detonated to the right of the Sleeper. Ruwen dropped his staff, fell to his knees, and covered his ears. A debuff flashed under his bars, and he saw what he already knew; he'd been deafened.

Sift hadn't collapsed, but he held his head, and his face twisted in pain. But the Sleeper had taken the worst of it. Blood ran from hundreds of small holes all along its body. Ruwen realized these were its ears, and he'd probably just ruptured all of them. Not wanting to take the chance it would recover, Ruwen picked up his staff and staggered toward the beast. Having learned from his fight with the Rock Serpent, Ruwen struck the creature where the wing met the body. The wing immediately fell against the thing's body as the Sleeper thrashed.

Ruwen turned to run and felt a terrible pain in his back. A moment later, a large spine burst from his chest. He looked down at his own blood covering the brown tail of the beast. His Health bar flashed yellow as he instantly lost fifty-seven Health. The Sleeper flicked its tail, and Ruwen sailed across the room. He struck a large boulder, and another twelve flashed across his Health bar. Dazed, Poisoned, and Bleed debuffs appeared next to his Deafened debuff. His Health bar pulsed a three with every heartbeat.

He knew he should be trying to stop the bleeding or cure his poison, but his brain felt fuzzy, and he couldn't keep his thoughts organized. Pressing his hand against the wound dropped the Bleed damage to two per second. The Dazed debuff scattered his thoughts, and he couldn't do the math, but by the red flashing of his Health bar, it didn't look like he had much time.

Sift appeared in front of him, pulled something from his belt, and tied it around Ruwen's shoulder and over the wound. Then Sift disappeared again. The Bleed debuff vanished, and Ruwen focused on his Health bar until he could see what he had left: Twenty-eight. He hadn't even needed the twenty-five Health from his new ring.

Sift appeared again and picked him up. They walked for a

while and then Sift gently put him back on the ground. Ruwen smelled burning wood and turned to see the *Campfire* he'd cast earlier to help Sift. A minute later Ruwen's head cleared, and he pushed himself up. The Dazed, Poisoned and Deafened debuffs had disappeared, and his Health bar was a third full. He looked down to see Sift's shirt tied around his shoulder.

"This was your favorite shirt," Ruwen said.

"That's okay. I'll get a new one."

Ruwen felt bad for staining Sift's shirt. "I'll clean this for you."

"Don't worry about it. I'm just glad you're okay. I told you to run."

"I know. I'm sorry. But we're a team."

Sift smiled. "True. Speaking of that, how about you warn me before," Sift slammed his hands together, "whatever that was."

"Sorry about that. I'm still figuring out what my stuff does."

"How do you feel?"

"Better."

And he did feel better. With the extra Health Regen from the fire, his Health bar was already half full.

"Can you walk?" Sift asked.

"Sure."

"Okay. Let's collect your loot, and then go get your pass. I'm hungry, and I need to get some new clothes."

Ruwen didn't know what Sift meant by pass, but he didn't bother asking. He'd find out shortly. Pushing himself to his feet, Ruwen untied Sift's shirt and handed the bloody thing back to Sift.

"Sorry," Ruwen said again.

Sift took the shirt and placed it in his belt. "Don't worry about it."

They walked back to where the dead Sleeper lay, but Blapy had already absorbed it.

Ruwen shook his head. "A flying mouth the size of a wagon

with a javelin for a tail and you call it a Sleeper? Your names are terrible."

"That's how I feel when the tail touches me. It's some sort of napping poison."

"Napping poison? Okay, but that's not the first thing that comes to mind when you see it."

Ruwen opened his log and scanned for the entry where the creature had died. He was curious to know its real name, and how much experience he'd gotten for helping kill it.

You have killed a Blind Nightmare (Level 6)!
You have gained 172 (784*(22% level modifier)) experience!

One hundred seventy-two experience was great, but once again, it had almost cost him his life. Trying to get experience this way was like running along a cliff, and he hoped he didn't fall off.

"It's called a Blind Nightmare. Blapy is much better at names than you," Ruwen said.

"I could go with either name."

Ruwen shook his head again.

A shirt that looked precisely like Sift's favorite sat on top of a pile of jewels.

"Ruwen's going to clean mine, so the joke's on you!" Sift shouted.

"Weren't you the one that said be nice to the tier one dungeon?"

Sift raised his eyebrows and then yelled. "But thanks!"

Ruwen laughed and then eased the contents of his leather bag onto the ground. He immediately picked up a set of vials that had been tied together, hoping they were the third ingredient he needed for his quest.

Tring!

The Black Pyramid has rewarded you...
Name: *Blind Nightmare Tears*
Quantity: *10 vials*
Quality: *Uncommon*
Durability: *10 of 10*
Weight: *0.9 lbs.*
Description: *Ingredient in various potions. Even blind, it sheds tears for the hapless.*

Ruwen pumped his fist, excited at completing the quest *It's Your Turn to Cook*, and then scowled when he read the Blind Nightmare Tears description. At least he hadn't dropped his staff this time, and that was progress. The best part was he'd managed to get the three ingredients required to finish the quest. He placed the vials into his Void Band.

The only thing still on the ground was a square piece of paper about the size of his palm. He could see the faint lines of an image on the other side, and he picked it up, unsure if it was part of his loot or just trash.

Tring!
The Black Pyramid has rewarded you...
Name: *Fleeting Tattoo of Dexterity*
Quantity: *1*
Location: *Arm*
Quality: *Uncommon*
Durability: *1 of 1*
Weight: *0.01 lbs.*
Effect: *Dexterity +1.*
Description: *Place on arm to activate effect. Effect valid until tattoo has faded. Scrub to remove earlier.*

Ruwen studied the small ink drawing of a red fox jumping across the rocks in a stream. The artwork looked fantastic.

"I've never heard of tattoos granting effects," Ruwen said.

"It's a Blapy thing. It's one of the reasons she is so popular. She figured out how to do it, and you can only get them here. It is the closest she has ever gotten to winning with me. Not because of the effects, but just because her tattoos are so beautiful. I want to wear them around and show off."

"Are all of them temporary?"

"No, they come in different durations. What did you get?"

"Fleeting."

"That's her lowest type and will last about a month. They go all the way to Soul Bound. That is a nice tattoo for being a Fleeting. It even has color."

Ruwen removed his cloak, staff, harness, and shirt. He took a few seconds to find the exact place he wanted it, and then pressed the tattoo against his upper left arm. Warmth seeped into his skin. When he pulled his hand away, the paper had disappeared, and his upper arm now had the fox tattoo.

"That is really awesome. I thought people only did these for looks," Ruwen said.

"Too late now, but you could have sold that for a small fortune. Merchants have been trying to figure out Blapy's secret for generations."

Ruwen frowned. "I could've used the money. I plan to travel soon, and I'll need funds. Maybe I'll get another."

"It looks good," Sift said wistfully.

"Thanks," Ruwen said as he redressed.

They started for the tunnel exit, and in a few minutes, they arrived. As soon as Ruwen stepped into the tunnel, his wrist turned ice cold. He looked down to see the Black Pyramid mark, but now it had a number two under it.

Sift saw it as well. "Excellent. We'll save a lot of time now."

"What was that?"

"Once you've cleared a level you don't have to do it again if you don't want to. It makes getting home easier too."

Sift pressed his wrist to the wall. "My room."

A smoky rectangle the size of a door appeared.

"That goes to your room?"

"The hallway outside it, actually."

"And to get back here?"

"You have cleared level two and been marked. Next time we will say 'level three,' and a portal will take us to the beginning of level three."

"What about level one? I never felt anything when we started down the tunnel."

"You get that by default."

"Then why did we take the stairs and all the doors?"

"I usually don't. But I didn't want to drop us right into a group of monsters on your first day. Now that level one is cleared, it will stay that way for a couple of weeks. It just fills with monsters because no one is ever down there. It's part of my chores to keep the first level clear."

"Sweeping."

"Exactly."

"Do the portals always work?"

"I was in my underwear, and I wanted to go to the laundry to pick up my clothes, and Blapy put me in the middle of the recreation room."

"Ow."

"Yeah, I think she does that to remind people they are only here because she allows it."

"That is a little scary."

"You don't have things like this on the other side?"

"No. We walk a lot."

"Well, not here. Let's go get some lunch."

Sift walked through the door, and after a moment, Ruwen followed.

CHAPTER 25

*R*uwen stepped into the hallway and bumped into Sift's back. He stepped to the side, wondering what had caused Sift to freeze right in front of the portal. A middle-aged woman stood in front of Sift. Her black hair was pulled into a bun, and her eyes were a light brown, almost yellow, just like Sift's. She wore a loose-fitting shirt and pants that did little to hide her lean muscles.

"Hi, Mom," Sift said.

"Running around in your underwear again?" she asked.

"Spitters on level two." Sift stepped to the side and pushed Ruwen in front of him like a shield. "I was helping Ruwen. Ruwen, this is my mom."

Ruwen crossed his arms over his chest and bowed. "It is an honor to meet you."

Sift's mom turned her focus on Ruwen, but her expression never changed. She reminded Ruwen of a still pond.

"Well met Child of Uru. Her hand sits heavily on you. You can call me Madda."

"We were getting a quick bite to eat before heading back down. Ky needs him leveled," Sift said.

A. F. KAY

"Yes, Ky spoke to us. How fortuitous to run into you. Let's go meet your father, and we can break two bones with one blow," Madda said.

"Can we clean up first?" Sift asked.

"Of course. Meet us in the garden. And walk, no using these lazy portals," Madda said.

"Yes, Mom."

Madda turned and strode down the hallway. "Don't dawdle."

"What does dawdle even mean?" Sift whispered.

"It means she wants us to hurry. That was a saying, right? Not something that is actually going to happen?"

"Be late? Probably, I—"

Ruwen rubbed his face. "No! Break two bones with one blow. Is that a saying or a prediction?"

"Oh, that's just a saying. My parents must want to yell at me about two things."

"Oh, thank Uru."

Sift narrowed his eyes, and Ruwen raised his hands. "Not you getting yelled at. I'm thankful no bones will get broken. Your mom is kind of intense."

"That is one word for her."

They both showered quickly. Sift dumped his dirty clothes in the bin outside the door and then went into his room to dress and put more clothes in his belt. Ruwen changed into new clothes as well. His pants had a massive hole in them where he'd scrubbed the fabric out of existence, and his shirt had a large bloody tear from the Blind Nightmare's tail. Worst of all, his brand new cloak had a large rip in it. Maybe Workers got a sewing ability, and he could fix it. He hoped it didn't ruin the daily one hundred Health point shield. The dungeon sure was rough on clothes.

"Leave all your weapons here. Dad doesn't like them in the garden," Sift said.

"Okay," Ruwen said, placing all his weapons on his bed.

282

"Ky talked to them about our deal," Sift said. "I'm so nervous I could puke."

"What are you nervous about?"

"That after all my work and dreaming and hoping, they'll tell me I can't leave. That I'll never see the ocean or the snow," Sift paused for a few seconds, "or her."

"Her? Who are you talking about?" Another thought occurred to him. "Wait, don't your parents work for Ky? Can't she make them?"

"You can't make Step Masters do anything. Ky relies on them to train her people. And she respects them too much to go against their wishes, especially when it comes to me. I'm on my own."

"Well, I'll help if I can."

Sift looked down.

"What's wrong?" Ruwen asked.

"Please don't take this poorly, you're the reason I even have this chance. But Ky said you're in great danger, and she won't hide that from my parents. They might use you as an excuse to not let me go."

Ruwen's stomach turned. "I'm sorry, Sift."

"It isn't your fault, and it's not fair to even bring it up. I just know my parents are going to use any excuse they can to keep me from being happy."

Ruwen felt bad for Sift. When Ruwen felt bad, Tremine always tried to get him to smile. Even if the librarian had a terrible sense of humor, and told the worst jokes, it did usually raise Ruwen's spirits.

Ruwen lowered his voice to sound more like Sift. "Shade's First Rule: when breaking bones, it's best not to dawdle."

Sift laughed, and the tension in the air broke.

"That's pretty good. I might add that to the suggestion box," Sift said as they walked out the door.

"Ky has a suggestion box?"

"Yes, but I'm pretty sure I'm the only one that uses it."

As they walked to meet Sift's parents, Ruwen opened his notifications.

Ting!
You have completed the Black Pyramid Quest – It's Your Turn to Cook (Level 2).
You have received 1,000 experience.
You have received 10 Black Pyramid tokens.

Eventually, a thousand experience wouldn't mean much, but right now, it made a huge difference. The memory of Sift standing in front of Ruwen engulfed in flames gave the quest name an entirely new meaning. Blapy really did have a dark sense of humor. Ruwen had two more notifications, and he opened them as well.

Shing!
You have advanced a skill!
Skill: *Staff*
Level: *3*
Effect: *Increase damage by 1.5%.*

He actually thought he might level his staff more than once as often as he'd swung it at those chickens. But the extra half percent damage would be welcome. He needed all the help he could get. The last notification was a surprise.

Gong!
You have increased your Knowledge!
Level: *36*
The intelligent know true power is held by knowledge. The wise know knowledge can be dangerous. Greatness is found between them.

Ruwen thought about everything he'd learned since he'd died...the first time. He'd learned spells, abilities, skills, and even ciphers. Whole new worlds had been opened up to him, and a goddess had brought him into a war that he hadn't known was being fought. Not only that, he'd learned some things about himself. Not all of it positive. His biases against Workers especially bothered him. It made him feel bad that it had taken becoming one to open his eyes. But recognizing it was the first step in fixing it. He would be better, and this notification proved it.

He glanced at his Profile. His experience was now two thousand six hundred fifty-eight out of six thousand. Not bad. His tattoo added another point to his Dexterity, which was now eleven. His Knowledge advancing to thirty-six only affected his Persuasion and Cleverness, and his Cleverness was still by far the strongest statistic on his Profile at 38.5%. He didn't know how valuable that was. Everyone thought they were clever.

He closed everything and focused back on his surroundings. It took another ten minutes of walking to reach the garden. Ruwen had expected it to be full of flowers and maybe some trees. Instead, he found gravel paths and pits full of white sand that had been raked in simple designs. They must have been near the outside of the Black Pyramid because shafts filled the ceiling that allowed sunlight into the room. He could see blue sky and the air felt warmer.

The back of the garden held hundreds of rocks in more shapes and colors than Ruwen had ever seen. Most had been stacked or balanced in some fashion. None of it made any sense to Ruwen.

Sift's parents sat cross-legged in the middle of a round circle of white sand. Sift's dad had closely cropped brown hair. His eyes were a light blue, and he had the same clothes and lean physique as his wife. Sift stepped into the sand and sat across from his mother. He turned, grabbed a small rake from the side of the pit, and smoothed the sand where he'd stepped.

Sift looked at Ruwen and then at the spot in the sand across from his dad. Ruwen carefully stepped into the sand but didn't sink very far. It took him a moment to remember his Feather Boots of Grasping reduced the force of his steps by 20%. He sat and mimicked the raking Sift had done.

"Well met, child of Uru. You can call me Padda."

Ruwen crossed his arms over his chest and bowed as best he could while sitting. "Blessings to you and your family, Padda."

"Do you sense it?" Madda asked.

"Yes," Padda said.

Ruwen looked at Sift, but Sift kept his face forward, looking between his parents. Sift looked miserable.

"They have been together less than a day," Madda said.

"Interesting," Padda said.

"Uru's Champion, Ky's promise, the stirring of –"

Padda reached over and put a hand on Madda's leg, interrupting her. "Let's not speak their names here."

Madda patted his hand. "Yes, caution."

Ruwen didn't know what proper etiquette was here, and asking a question might be doing something wrong. But his curiosity was so intense he could feel it in his chest. They were talking about him and Sift, and even if they ignored him, he had to try.

"What do you sense?" Ruwen asked.

To his shock, Madda answered.

"Your energies have intertwined," Madda said.

Sift looked so unhappy Ruwen couldn't help himself. Out of the corner of his mouth, Ruwen whispered. "Get your energy off me."

Sift let out a strangled laugh and looked down for a few seconds to try and stay serious. That made Ruwen laugh, which pushed Sift over the edge. They both laughed and then couldn't stop.

Tears streamed down both their faces, and Ruwen waved his hand, trying to get the word "sorry" out, but his throat had tightened, and the word came out unintelligible. This made Sift laugh even harder. It took them a minute to stop triggering each other into laughter. Ruwen turned his head away from Sift so he couldn't see him.

"I'm sorry. I didn't mean any disrespect," Sift said.

"I apologize as well. I shouldn't have said that. It's my fault," Ruwen said.

Ruwen bit his tongue hard to stop from laughing.

"It is good to hear you laugh again," Padda said.

"That sound is like sunshine on my soul," Madda said.

Sift's parents stared at each other for a few seconds and then Madda nodded. They both faced Sift.

Padda spoke in a soft voice. "You and Kysandra entered into an agreement, which you have won, that earned you the ability to travel through the Blood Gate. Kysandra has explained, as much as she is able, the circumstance she and Ruwen find themselves in. Specifically, she explained it will be highly dangerous. Before we tell you our decision, we want you to know our reasoning."

Sift's shoulders slumped. He knew what was coming.

Madda spoke. "You are very capable, more so compared to those past the Blood Gate, but you are also young. We understand you feel trapped here. With experience, you will recognize it as the refuge it is."

Sift's head dropped until his chin touched his chest. Ruwen's stomach clenched at seeing his friend so despondent. Madda paused, but Sift remained silent. After a few heartbeats, she continued.

"There is also the issue of your meridians. We have not yet

tried everything, and we still have hope. Leaving would delay that process." Madda paused before continuing. "Then there is the danger. We know all too well the carnage and destruction that surrounds the gods. Crossing with Kysandra now means being near Ruwen, and Ruwen has chosen a path where death is a constant companion. You would never be safe."

Sift's parents looked at each other again, and then Padda spoke. "We have thought of nothing else since yesterday. We love you and want to protect you."

Sift stared into the sand.

Madda sighed. "Which is why we've decided to let you go."

Sift's head snapped up. "What?"

"You may leave with Kysandra and Ruwen when they depart if you wish," Padda said.

"But what about all that stuff about death?" Sift asked.

Madda took a deep breath. "It is all true. This is one of the hardest decisions I've ever made, and I've lived long enough to make a lot of them. We love you, but your path is your own. For you to grow, you will need to spread your branches."

Sift dove forward, hugged his mom and then moved to his dad. "Thank you so much. I'll be careful, I promise."

Padda smiled sadly. "Being careful will not be enough. You must listen to Kysandra, both of you, if you wish to survive. Your paths are intertwined."

"Ruwen," Madda said and waited until their eyes locked. "Kysandra did not ask that you be taught the Steps, but her desire was clear. What is your desire?"

That was a good question. Ruwen didn't want to die again, but that sounded a bit selfish. The reality was this wasn't much different than the question Uru had asked him, and recent events had added another desire.

"I desire truth and the ability to protect my friends," Ruwen said.

Padda and Madda looked at each other before facing Ruwen again.

"That is not the answer I expected from a sixteen-year-old," Padda said.

"Two days ago it would've been different. A lot has happened since then," Ruwen said.

Padda and Madda whispered to each other in another language, and Ruwen used the distraction to look over at Sift, who had a huge grin on his face.

"Ruwen?" Padda asked.

Ruwen faced Padda. "Yes?"

"We wish to offer you the mark of our Clan. It will allow you to retain the techniques and skills associated with our Steps," Padda said.

Madda continued. "Our Clan is unique in that our Steps do not focus on offense or defense, but encompass the whole. Those who witness our techniques will not be able to clearly recall them unless they bear our mark."

"We, too, believe in truth," Padda said.

"And we're very invested in you protecting your friends," Madda added looking at Sift.

The chance to learn self defense from masters would be fantastic. It was an incredibly rare opportunity. But he had just discovered a hard lesson about jumping into things without knowing all the consequences.

"Thank you for your generous offer. What will I sacrifice?" Ruwen asked.

"You show your wisdom, Ruwen," Padda said. "For the first few years you will be learning the initial Steps and only be bound to this rule: purposefully harming a Clan member is forbidden unless your life is in danger."

"Once you pass Step thirty, you will need to further bind yourself to the Clan. But that is years away," Madda said.

Padda raised his arm to show his wrist. "Our Clan has ancient enemies who are agents of despair, chaos, and subjugation. Some despise all the Clans for guarding our knowledge. And some wish to test themselves against Clan members. All these and more will be new dangers for you."

Madda displayed her wrist as well. "Most Clans will welcome and aid you. In a world of darkness, they will be islands of light."

"If you wish to join our Clan, hold out your right wrist," Padda said.

The part about new enemies scared Ruwen. He already had so many. But they offered a way for Ruwen to protect himself, and he sorely needed that. If he wished to survive what was coming, he needed every advantage he could gain. He held out his wrist.

A viper coiled around a stalk of bamboo appeared on Padda's wrist, and then on Madda's. Unlike with Ky, who had made him repeat a whole litany of promises, Padda placed his wrist on Ruwen's and then removed it. A bamboo stalk appeared. Madda placed her wrist on Ruwen's and when she removed it a viper now coiled around the stalk.

A notification appeared with deep red script and like before his whole body felt tingly.

Thrum!
You have been offered a Soul Oath...
Learning to Crawl
A Bamboo Step Grandmaster and a Viper Step Grandmaster have deemed you worthy to bear the mark of the Bamboo Viper Clan, and have offered passage into the Clan's ranks as a Novice. You vow to never knowingly harm a Clan member unless your life is in danger.
Reward: *Novice Mark of the Bamboo Viper Clan*
Reward: *Ability to retain the first 10 Steps of each style*
Warning!

This is a soul binding and bridges death.

Accept or Decline

Ruwen selected *Accept,* and his whole body warmed like sunshine had enveloped him. The mark flared brightly on his wrist and then faded. He opened the new notification.

Ping!
You have learned the Ability Snake in the Grass
Ability: *Snake in the Grass*
Level: *1*
Class: *Any*
Effect: *Detect the presence of a member of the Bamboo Viper Clan.*
Type: *AoE*

Ruwen noticed new quests. They had the stacked appearance like Ky's Black Pyramid ones, but the symbol for these was the viper coiled on bamboo. Glancing through them it appeared there were quests for every Step learned for each style. He would look at them in more detail later.

"Welcome to our Clan, Ruwen, Champion of Uru," Padda said.

"May your Steps lead you to enlightenment," Madda said.

They each held their left fist out from their body and placed their open right hand on top of the fist. Ruwen mimicked them and bowed.

"You have honored me. I will do my best to learn," Ruwen said.

"Speaking of that," Padda said and faced Sift. "Adept."

Sift held out his fist and covered it with his hand. "Yes, Grandmaster."

Padda continued. "You will take charge of this Novice's training. His progress will weigh on the decision for your advancement to Master. Learning the Steps is difficult. Teaching them is harder. Do you accept?"

"I do," Sift said solemnly.

"May the Steps protect you both," Madda said. "I fear you will need it."

CHAPTER 26

*P*adda and Madda stood, but Sift remained seated. Both parents sat back down.

"What troubles you, Son?" Padda asked.

"I showed Ruwen a basic breathing exercise, and he immediately dropped into a deep meditation," Sift said.

"The sign of a tired mind," Madda said.

Sift glanced at Ruwen and then back at his parents. "They are getting deeper."

Sift spoke in another language, and *Hey You* translated one word. "Worried."

"Sift says you are excellent at meditation," Madda said.

Ruwen shrugged. "I just learned."

"How does it make you feel?" Padda asked.

"Rested," Ruwen said.

"How do you retain your focus?" Madda asked.

"I don't know. Everything kind of just goes black," Ruwen said.

"Maybe you could show them," Sift said.

The three of them stared at Ruwen, and it made his stomach turn in nervousness. He closed his eyes and imagined sitting in an empty room. Everything fell away: his aches, anxiety, fear, until nothing but the emptiness remained.

From a distance, he felt shaking and someone calling his name. Sharp pain on his cheek brought his thoughts back to the present, and he opened his eyes.

Madda had her hand raised to slap him again, but Padda stopped her.

"He's back," Padda said.

"Thank the balance," Madda said.

Sift's parents sat back down across from Ruwen, and he wondered what he'd done wrong. Why would Madda slap him for meditating? They had told him to do it.

Padda stared at Sift. "When did you teach him?"

"Last night," Sift said. "Did I do something wrong?"

"No, of course not. Meditation is valuable for all things," Madda said.

Padda and Madda spoke in a different language, and Sift's eyes grew wide. Ruwen immediately went to his Abilities tab and used his free ability point to increase *Hey You*. He wondered if the ability point he gained from the Observer branch could be used on a Worker ability and tried incrementing *Hey You* again. It worked.

He should have spent time considering the other abilities, but his curiosity demanded to know what these two were saying about him. The second level would take him from a five-year-old's vocabulary to a basic understanding of the language. The third level made him fluent. His concentrations had been so intense, he'd advanced both times without saying a prayer to Uru.

Ping!
You have advanced the Ability Hey You (Worker Level 2)
Ping!
You have advanced the Ability Hey You (Worker Level 3)

Sift's parent's conversation became understandable.

"...is bound to Uru. How can he even find his center?" Madda asked.

"I don't care. We vowed to never fight for those gods again. Why would we throw that away for this boy?" Padda asked.

"You witnessed it. Without guidance, you know the consequences," Madda said.

"We have taken him into our Clan. He will learn to protect himself. Anything more risks all our lives," Padda said.

"Have you become so fond of this life that you now fear death?" Madda asked.

Sift held up his hand. "Can I –"

Both Padda and Madda looked at Sift and spoke in unison. "No!"

Sift frowned but remained quiet.

Padda's voice rose. "All life is our concern, including our own. This play by Uru can only mean that war is imminent. We must not take part this time."

"We won't be. We are only keeping this boy from ruining his mind. We will set him on a path and let him crawl down it."

"You know Uru did this on purpose," Padda said.

"Of all of them, she is the purest," Madda said.

"That is irrelevant. Winning results in too much power for a single being to possess, even Uru. And by helping her Champion in this way, we are helping her. Just as she probably planned," Padda said.

"We have already helped by adding him to our family," Madda said.

"Don't make an equivalence. The difference between the Clan and what you propose is a raindrop to a thunderstorm," Padda said.

"I followed you here. You are my soul mate. But inaction is action itself. We cannot separate ourselves from this conflict." Madda held up her hand to stop Padda's argument. "I agree we will not be pawns in their game, but this is about saving this young man's life, not about the fate of the universe."

"It is connected," Padda said.

"Which is why I will not have my balance altered knowing we could have helped this boy and didn't," Madda said.

"We could forbid him to meditate," Padda said.

"Teenagers never listen, and what happens if it reaches for his active mind?" Madda asked.

"We are taking a step that might start an avalanche," Padda said.

"I created this problem," Sift said.

Sift's parents faced him.

"Don't blame yourself," Padda said.

Sift shook his head. "If I hadn't shown him how to meditate, we wouldn't be sitting here in a circle arguing."

"Don't carry baggage that isn't yours," Padda said. "He would have learned it from someone at some point."

"But he didn't. I taught him. This lands on my scales. If you don't help him, and something bad happens, it will weigh on us all."

Madda smiled at Sift. "He has his father's wisdom."

"Oh, that is not fair. Flattery and a lecture in the same sentence. I don't deserve you," Padda said.

"You do not," Madda said, still smiling. "But with effort, you might someday."

"Effort like showing Uru's Champion how to Cultivate?" Padda asked.

"We are only showing him the path, not guiding him to enlightenment," Madda said. "I will give him the standard geometry quests. By not revealing our personal Cultivation methods, we can't be accused of picking a side. It will take the boy decades to finish, and by the time he is ready to move into level two, the situation will be clearer."

Padda closed his eyes for a few seconds and then sighed. "Fine."

Madda switched back to Common. "Sorry about that, Ruwen. We were just discussing the best way to help you."

"Is something wrong?" Ruwen asked.

"Not wrong, just dangerous," Padda said.

Madda continued. "After the first few seconds, you aren't even meditating anymore. You're trying to do something called Cultivating."

"I've heard of that. It's the magic of the Unclassed and Godless," Ruwen said.

Padda's brow furrowed and Madda put a hand on his arm. "What you call magic is a manipulation of the energy that surrounds us. Everyone has access to it. When you bound yourself to Uru, she created shortcuts for your learning. Those who don't bind themselves to a deity can learn your abilities and spells, but it takes an immense amount of time and effort. That is why almost no one does that willingly. Before your gods, it was the only method."

"If Cultivation makes you more powerful, why doesn't everyone do it?" Ruwen asked.

Padda spoke up. "The problem is the process. It may take someone a hundred years of Cultivating to gather, understand, manipulate, and manifest the energy to create a small flame. It might only take a year after that to create and direct a ball of fire, but it's that first hundred years people are not willing to invest. Not when they can bind themselves to an entity that will just give them that power."

"Is Ruwen doing something wrong?" Sift asked.

Madda waved her hands. "No, nothing wrong. It's just he stumbled into his center, and without a little direction he could get stuck there."

"Oh," Sift said and looked down.

Madda reached over and squeezed Sift's shoulder. Ruwen wondered what had caused the sudden shift in Sift's mood.

Padda spoke. "People might spend their whole life looking for but not finding their center. There are many reasons for this. The most common being a blockage in too many of the twelve meridians. Without your center, you can't Cultivate energy from your surroundings. All you can do is sift through the energy that touches you or is directed at you."

A shard of light went through Ruwen's mind as his brain made a connection from what Padda had just said to earlier memories. Ruwen rubbed his temples as he remembered Sift saying it wasn't his name, it was what he did. And earlier, Sift had told Blapy his parents were trying to unblock him. Ruwen glanced at Sift and saw his friend still stared at the floor. Padda was describing Sift.

Madda continued the explanation. "Once bound to a deity, the chance of finding your center is almost zero. There is too much contamination of the lines of power in your body. It is like listening for a cricket in a thunderstorm. Possible, but unlikely."

"And you're saying that when I meditate, I'm going to my center?" Ruwen asked.

"More like you are being sucked into it," Padda said.

Madda leaned forward. "That is why we want to show you the basics. Your center is trying to Cultivate, but without direction or focus. When you meditate, your mind and its energy are freed from your body. Your center senses this unbound energy and starts to Cultivate it."

"I'm cannibalizing myself?" Ruwen asked.

"Yes, and without help, you will put yourself in a coma, and then die," Madda said.

Ruwen's mouth went dry. "I don't want that."

"Neither do we," Madda said as she looked at her husband.

Padda ignored his wife's stare. "Don't worry, the solution is simple. When you Cultivate, you pull energy from your surroundings and store that in a structure in your center. The most common form of energy is light, and the most basic structure is a point. All you need to do is focus your center outward, let it gather the light around you, and fill the point you created."

"Don't worry if your point never lights up," Madda said. "You aren't training to become a Cultivator, you're just trying to keep your center from destroying your mind."

"What happens if my point lights up?" Ruwen asked.

"You keep creating more advanced structures," Padda said. "A point becomes a line, a line a triangle, and then a square. You keep adding sides until you can create a circle. That completes level one and will probably take you a decade. Then you start again using three-dimensional shapes. A couple of decades later, if you work hard, you'll be able to form a sphere. That brings you to the cusp of level two, and then the hard work begins."

Madda held out her hand. "I know that was a lot of information. You have years to work through it all. And honestly, most Cultivators never finish level one. We are only doing this so you stop harming yourself."

"Show me, please," Ruwen said.

Madda moved to sit directly in front of Ruwen. He accepted the quest line she offered and saw them appear with his other quests. The Cultivation quest symbol was a green sphere.

Madda grabbed his hands and spoke. "There are as many methods as there are Cultivators when it comes to gathering. You can picture yourself at the bottom of a funnel or dozens of arms stuffing energy into your mouth or giant wings that scoop it into your body. The point is your focus needs to be outward, and those types of visualizations can help. Now, with your focus outward, close your eyes and imagine the tiniest point possible. So tiny you can barely see it. Do you have it?"

Ruwen nodded.

Madda's voice became a whisper. "When you start to meditate, and your mind begins to fall, bring this point with you. You will stay more aware of your surroundings since your center will no longer be feeding on your senses. Are you ready to try?"

Ruwen took a deep breath and nodded again.

He thought about what he should use to gather the energy around him. The dozen arms seemed too slow, and while the idea of wings sounded awesome, it still felt convoluted. From his laboratory classes, he knew the power of a vacuum. He'd gotten his hand stuck on the top of a flask after the liquid in it cooled faster than he'd expected. The vacuum it created made it impossible to pull his hand away, and he'd had to break the flask to free his hand.

So he pictured himself as an empty flask, void of anything, and then pulled his point of darkness down into this empty flask. The familiar calmness wrapped him like a blanket, and then his point exploded, and light filled his mind.

"I'm blind!" Sift screamed.

And just at the edge of his hearing, he heard Blapy's laughter and then her voice. "And so the avalanche begins."

CHAPTER 27

"*I* can't see," Sift said again.

"It will be okay, Sift," Padda said. "Ruwen has Cultivated all the light in the room. Your vision will return when the light does."

Ruwen heard this through the roaring sound of energy traveling into his body. It scared him, and he pulled away from the blazing white ball that surrounded him.

Madda's grip tightened. "Don't stop, Ruwen."

His heartbeat increased, and his breathing became more rapid.

"Release your fear," Padda said.

Ruwen didn't know how to do that. He pictured the fear outside himself, and to his surprise, the sphere immediately consumed it. His heartbeat slowed, and his breathing became more even.

"Good," Madda said. "Relax."

"It is getting cold," Sift said.

Padda spoke in a different language. "He is dipping into the lower energies."

"Should I move him somewhere safer?" Blapy asked.

"Yes, please," Madda said immediately. "Ruwen, stay in your center until the energy stops rushing toward you. Feed your fear or anything you don't want to keep, into the flow."

Why did they need to move him somewhere safer? Was he in danger? Did Cultivating make him vulnerable to some form of attack? The warmth of Madda's hands around his wrists disappeared. Was he alone now? He didn't think he could stay centered if he opened his eyes or talked. In fact, all his thinking made him feel unbalanced like he might start spinning. He focused on the rush of energy as it flowed into his growing ball of light and kept his mind clear.

Eventually, the flow of energy slowed to a trickle. A gigantic ball of energy now surrounded Ruwen's center. He felt like the pit of some enormous fruit. Wondering where he was, he opened his eyes.

Jumping to his feet, he turned in a circle. He stood on a footbridge at the edge of a vast ruined city. In the distance, at the city's center, a large pyramid stood like a needle piercing the sky. Outside the city, fog roiled and turned violently as if tornados were locked in battle. Fires burned around him, and all the vegetation had died. Looking down, he noticed his body steaming.

"What happened?" he whispered.

"Six hours of you," Blapy replied.

Ruwen jumped and turned to find Blapy sitting on the edge of the footbridge, her feet dangling over the edge.

"Me? What did I do?" Ruwen asked.

"What happens when you remove heat from the air?"

"It gets colder, water condenses..."

Blapy pointed toward the fog.

Ruwen laughed nervously. "Are you saying I did that?"

"Well, it was sunny when I put you out here."

Ruwen checked the time. It had been over six hours. His last clear memory was sitting with the Addas and Sift.

"Did I hurt anyone?" Ruwen asked.

"The sudden movement of energy caused some fires, and you killed all the vegetation, but this destruction happened long ago. Everyone in the Pyramid is safe."

Ruwen sat down. "I don't understand what happened."

"Me either. Your meridians should be blazing like suns and sitting here next to you, I can't even tell you're a Cultivator. How is she hiding that?"

Blapy pushed herself off the bridge and Ruwen lurched to try and grab her before she fell, almost falling off himself. Blapy stood in the air and pushed him back onto the ledge.

"You're the most incompetent Champion I have ever met, but your heart is pure terium. Your heart…"

Blapy tapped her teeth with a finger and then paced back and forth in front of him thirty feet off the ground. She suddenly stopped and faced Ruwen, her mouth open.

"Pull your shirt up," Blapy said.

"That is a really weird –"

"Do it now, or I'll surround you with centipedes. Starting in your pants."

Ruwen jerked his shirt up. Blapy looked at his chest, smiled, and held out her hand. A square piece of paper formed on it and she pressed it to his chest before he could react.

"What do your notifications say?" Blapy asked.

Ruwen opened his notifications only to find he had a stack of them. What had caused all these notifications? Terrified Blapy would stick a centipede on him, he closed the notifications and opened his log instead. He read the most recent entries.

Tring!
The Black Pyramid has rewarded you…
Name: *Fleeting Tattoo of Grotesqueness*
Quantity: *1*

Location: Torso
Quality: Rare
Durability: 1 of 1
Weight: 0.01 lbs.
Effect: Charisma -10.
Description: Place on your torso to activate effect. Effect valid until tattoo has faded. Please put a bag over your head.

The next notification confused him.

Only one torso tattoo may be active. Remove current tattoo and try again.

"It says only one tattoo can be active at a time," Ruwen said.

Blapy clapped her hands and ran around in a circle. Ruwen's body still steamed, and the tattoo had stuck to his chest. The thought of that tattoo activating made his stomach turn and he peeled it off. Blapy was jumping up and down talking to herself, so he stuck it in his Void Band.

Ruwen looked down at his chest. The only thing remotely odd on his torso was his birthmark. He triggered *Magnify* and studied it. The red lines came into focus, and Ruwen gasped. The birthmark was actually thousands of fine lines that formed multiple complex patterns. Looking at them gave him a headache, so he deactivated *Magnify* and rubbed his eyes.

That was definitely not a birthmark. Ruwen looked up to find Blapy right in front of him.

"She's a genius. And it doesn't break any of their rules." Blapy clenched her hands and squeezed her eyes shut. "The brilliance and craftsmanship of it defy comprehension."

"What is it?" Ruwen asked.

"At first, I thought it was just a concealment tattoo. Complicated to begin with, and never successfully used to hide a Cultivator. That would be fantastic enough. But it also hides your soul bond with Uru from your center. It's like a wall separating your center from your bond while masking your meridians from the outside world. It's why you can Cultivate even though you've Ascended and no one can see your Spirit."

"That's what my birthmark is?"

"An external and *internal* tattoo. It never even occurred to me to try internal."

"That sounds complicated."

"Impossible even for a god had I not seen it for myself."

Blapy grabbed his cheeks. Her black eyes were filled with small bright lights like he was looking at the night sky. She smelled like peppermint.

"Tell no one, absolutely no one, what that mark does. Uru's last three Champions disappeared. Almost three hundred years without a Champion made me wonder if she had faltered. The other gods think her weak. But this reaffirms everything I know about her. She is a true Navigator. Think about this. For you to bear that mark means you were chosen before you were born. Her ability to see the path is terrifying."

Ruwen swallowed hard. "No pressure or anything."

"THIS IS SO EXCITING!" Blapy shouted.

"Wait, the Addas said I'd kill myself if I meditated. What if I'd read a book on meditation a year ago and tried it? All this planning would have been for nothing."

"No, she wouldn't take a risk that large. If it were me, I would have blocked your ability to meditate or Cultivate, and then removed that blockage during Ascendancy when you reformed. Then I'd get you to a safe place to learn as quickly as possible."

Ruwen rubbed his birthmark. "Actually, it did look smaller after I Ascended. I actually wondered if Uru fixed people's blemishes sometimes. And I was here less than twelve hours after I Ascended."

"That is scary. I wonder how far back this planning goes.

There has never been anyone like you. Did she give you some way to quantify your power?"

Ruwen glanced at the corners of his interface and immediately noticed a change.

"I have a new bar called Spirit," Ruwen said.

Ruwen opened his Profile.

"I have a Cultivation level now, too. I'm level 19, and my Spirit points are –" Ruwen choked, and he forced himself to finish. "Three hundred and fifty-two thousand one hundred sixty-four."

"Interesting. Let me see if I can reverse that calculation. You were Cultivating for about six hours in the visible and thermal ranges. You affected everything in front of you for about a mile. That means the most likely solution is...you're gaining around 0.001 Spirit per foot Cultivated for light, and .002 Spirit per foot Cultivated for the red energy."

"That is some impressive math," Ruwen said. "Is that a lot of Spirit?"

Blapy shrugged. "I've seen higher."

Ruwen's shoulders slumped. He checked his other tabs, but his Abilities, Spells, and Skills, hadn't changed. Whatever his Spirit did, it didn't look like there was an easy way to spend it, and it sounded from Blapy like it wasn't that much anyway.

"Now what?" Ruwen asked.

"We need to make sure it's safe to take you back. Cultivate again and let's see what happens."

Ruwen closed his eyes and evened out his breathing. This time he didn't have to descend into his center, the white ball of energy already surrounded him. He imagined himself as the vacuum flask, and like before, he felt the energy flow to him. But this time, his center resisted the new energy. He concentrated on pushing the walls of his sphere outward to make more room, but after a great effort, he hadn't absorbed any of the energy around him. Cultivating now would be safe because he'd reached his capacity for his current level. He could now meditate while in his center without harming himself or those around him.

"Good," Blapy said.

Ruwen opened his eyes and stared at the maelstrom he'd created. He wouldn't put himself in a coma now. Instead, he had a terrifying ball of energy that he didn't understand, sitting like a bomb inside his body. None of that seemed good.

He focused on Blapy. "What do I tell the Addas?"

"That's complicated. Obviously, you can't mention the birthmark. They know you Cultivated, but they won't be able to sense it. This will confuse and worry them. They can't help you further anyway. Tell them a partial truth. That whatever happened seemed to have filled you up and that you can't Cultivate any more energy. That will allow them to sleep."

Ruwen remembered Uru asking him if he could swim in a sea of lies if it brought him to the shore of truth. It was easier to agree to that when you didn't have to lie to the people who just helped you. Plus, he had no idea what this new ability did for him. It seemed useless right now.

Ruwen took a deep breath and let it out. "I hate secrets, and they just keep piling up."

"Tell me about it," Blapy said, pointing at the Pyramid. "Look at what I had to build to hold mine."

Then she disappeared, and a portal opened on the footbridge.

Ruwen walked to the portal and wondered how many other things weren't what they appeared to be.

CHAPTER 28

The explanation to Padda and Madda was difficult, and Ruwen could tell they knew he was hiding details. But they congratulated him on his success and let him go without an interrogation.

Sift bounced with excitement as they left the rock garden, and he wanted every detail Ruwen could remember. Ruwen knew Sift was desperate to fix his own Cultivation issues, and Ruwen wanted to help his friend. But Ruwen didn't understand what had happened and didn't have anything to help Sift.

Ten minutes later Sift was still asking questions. They'd been climbing stairs the entire time, and Ruwen's curiosity forced him to interrupt Sift.

"Where are we going?" Ruwen asked.

"Since you wasted our whole afternoon, I'm doing what Ky told me to do."

Dread filled Ruwen. "What was that?"

"She wanted me to show you what the Blood Moss did."

Ruwen relaxed. He'd forgotten he'd taken that. That felt like weeks ago, but it really had been less than twenty-four hours here.

"This is probably high enough," Sift said.

Instead of continuing up the stairs, they took a hallway, and in less than a minute, they exited on to a walkway that wrapped around the Pyramid. A three-foot stone wall served as the only protection from falling to your death. Sift walked to the edge and leaned out. Ruwen shuffled to the wall and peeked over. The ruined city looked tiny from this height, and his stomach turned. He immediately stepped back.

"What's wrong?" Sift asked.

"I hate heights."

"I wish I could fly."

"Can't you? When you jumped to fight that Blind Nightmare, it looked like you were flying. It certainly wasn't natural."

"I know. Mom yells at me for the wasted Spirit. But I just can't help it. As soon as I've absorbed enough Energy, I use it to glide around for as long as I can."

"You used Spirit to do that?"

"It's a gigantic waste. I know I should be using it for internal things, and I do. But if I had my parent's power, I would jump off this ledge right now and fly."

"That fire roasted your brain. There is never a good reason to jump off a perfectly good balcony."

Sift looked wistfully out at the city for a few seconds and then focused back on Ruwen. "Anyway, let's talk about the Blood Moss. Blapy is pretty valuable because her loot goes all the way up to Legendary. Nobody knows how deep or far she goes. For all we know it might be this entire planet. She has levels that even challenge the gods. A city formed around her to trade with and prey on the people raiding the Pyramid. This created a lot of wealth. So, of course, someone else wanted it, and there was a gigantic war. As the city was about to fall, someone had the bright idea to launch their secret weapon into the invading army."

"The Blood Moss."

"Yep. It ate the entire advancing army. Then it ate all the survivors in the city."

"Blapy didn't stop it?"

"Not right away. I don't know if she was sick of all the people around her or if she just wanted to teach everyone a lesson, or who knows why?"

"That moss killed everyone?"

"Not just people. Over a million people, animals, insects, plants, everything."

"What stopped it?"

"Blapy pulled some sort of flammable gas from deep in the earth and then ignited it. This Pyramid is the center of a ten-mile circle of charred earth. If the Blood Moss missed anything, Blapy's fire didn't."

Ruwen really regretted taking the Blood Moss now. When he was on his way out, he would put it back. There was no way he wanted to carry such a destructive thing around.

"It's a plant, though. Doesn't it grow like an inch a week?" Ruwen asked.

Sift shook his head. "You have Blapy's mark, so you're protected. If you'd stepped into that room without it, it would have covered you like a living blanket before you'd taken two breaths. You can't outrun it."

They walked around the Pyramid. The sun was a fist from the horizon, and the heat of the day had dissipated. This high up a gentle breeze cooled the air, and Ruwen relaxed a little.

"Whoa, look at that," Sift said.

They had arrived on the east side of the Pyramid and columns of black clouds twisted at the distant city wall. Rain streaked the sky, and the ground looked white.

"I've never seen it hail here," Sift said. "I wonder what caused such a gigantic storm."

Ruwen had been a little vague on what had happened after

Blapy took him. He'd told Sift Blapy took him out into the city, but not about anything else. In fact, he still had a hard time believing he'd caused that storm.

"They probably happen a lot. You're just inside," Ruwen said.

"No, I come up here almost every night. It looks like Blapy is blocking the storm from passing into the city."

They felt a faint vibration as giant hailstones crashed into the ground just outside the city. Each one looked to be the size of a house.

"Wow, how long do you think those had to stay in the air to get that big?" Sift asked.

It had been twenty minutes since Blapy had opened the portal that brought him back. Lightning arced and thunder rumbled as the rain turned into a torrent.

"We should go," Ruwen said.

Sift reluctantly moved away from the edge of the walkway. "Okay. Are you hungry?"

Ruwen realized he wasn't hungry or tired. In fact, he felt fantastic. Was this some byproduct of the Cultivation?

"Not really," Ruwen said. "I kind of just want to go back to the room and work through everything that's happened today."

"Sounds good. I'm going to get something to eat. I'll see you later."

Sift held out his fist, and Ruwen stared at it.

"You put your hand on it, palm down. It's a Clan shortcut, so we don't always have to bow to each other," Sift said.

"What happens if we both put our fist out?" Ruwen asked.

"Look at the over-thinker at work. If that happens, the lower-ranked member changes to the palm. If they don't, that means they want to challenge you and try to advance in rank."

"Okay, so I'm basically always palm."

"Yes, probably for the rest of your life."

"Thanks."

Ruwen placed his open hand over Sift's fist.

Sift smiled and then touched the wall with his wrist. "Rec room."

A portal appeared in the stone.

"Hey, I'm glad you're coming back with us," Ruwen said.

Sift rubbed his hands together. "Oh, me too. I've never had my own Novice to torture before. This is going to be fun."

Ruwen couldn't tell if that was a joke, and Sift stepped through the portal before he could ask. A moment later, the portal vanished. Ruwen's Step lesson earlier today had gone terribly. Maybe joining a Clan hadn't been the best idea.

He touched his right wrist to the wall. "Sift's room."

A portal opened. Ruwen turned and looked at the storm again. Every few seconds, a giant piece of ice would strike the invisible barrier that Blapy had erected. The more he learned about himself, the more anxious he became. It felt like he was following a path Uru had made for him who knows how long ago, and it didn't feel good. He wanted to find his parents and then do great and marvelous things. But it didn't seem like his wants mattered. He was just being manipulated, marched down a predestined path. It felt terrible.

Turning away from the storm, he stepped through the portal and into the hallway in front of Sift's room.

"Thanks for the portal, Blapy," Ruwen said to the empty air.

Ruwen noticed the bins by the door had clean clothes, and he brought the clothes into the room with him. After placing his into his Void Band, he sat on Sift's bed and sorted Sift's clothes into two piles: stained and unstained.

Not wanting to ruin any of Sift's clothes, he decided to experiment on his own first. He sat on the floor cross-legged and pulled the hem of his pants away from his leg. He didn't know if he could channel *Scrub* into just one hand, so he decided to try that first. He thought of the icon, and his hands glowed. His Energy bar flashed a small one every second. He willed his left hand off, and the glow disappeared. The energy consumption stayed at one per second, though. Smiling, he grabbed the hem of his pants with his left hand and carefully brought his right hand near the cloth.

The dirt and mud that clung to the pants disappeared without any visible damage to the pants. When Ruwen's right hand neared his left, he felt a warm vibration that made his hand itchy. Satisfied, he grabbed Sift's pants with the bloody hem and set them on his lap. This time when he thought of the *Scrub* icon, he only willed it to his right hand. His left hand remained normal, and he picked up the pants.

It took him ten minutes to realize he could safely increase the channeled power level. Things went much faster after that, but it forced Ruwen to cast *Campfire* in the middle of the room. An hour later, he'd cleaned all the blood out of Sift's clothes. Ruwen didn't know how much of it was Sift's, but it demonstrated how dangerous Blapy was to anyone entering her halls.

As much as he'd looked down on Workers for these mundane tasks, there was a real pleasure in what he'd just done. It felt good to immediately see the result of your work, and Ruwen felt a small sense of accomplishment. It had also allowed him to let his brain rest without having to venture into his center and the blazing sun that waited for him there. He knew he was avoiding what had just happened to him, but he felt overwhelmed, and this needed to be done anyway.

But he couldn't put off going through his notifications any longer. When he'd opened them earlier, there had been too many to deal with, but now was a good time to sort through it all. He stretched out on his bed and opened the first one.

Ting!
You have completed the Quest – What's Your Point (Cultivation Stage 1).
You have received 100 experience.

The next one was the same. They were all from the chain quest Madda had given him.

Ting!
You have completed the Quest – Two Points Make a Line (Cultivation Stage 2).
You have received 150 experience.

In fact, the notifications were all completed Cultivation quests that increased in experience by fifty each time. It wasn't until after the Level nine quest, which was to form a circle in his center, that anything changed.

Ting!
You have completed the Quest – Going Around in Circles (Cultivation Stage 9).
You have received 500 experience.

Ting!
You have completed the Quest – Two Dimensions are for Novices
You have received 1000 experience.

He had moved from Novice to Initiate in Cultivation! But the next notification made him even happier.

Ding!
Uru's Blessings, Worker! You have reached level 4.
You have gained +1 to Strength!
You have gained +1 to Stamina!
You have 2 unassigned points.
Uru's Blessings, Root! You have reached level 4.
You have 2 unassigned points.
New Spells and Abilities are available to you. Choose wisely.

Ruwen's skin prickled when reading the notification. He had to fight the urge to open his Profile and start assigning attribute points. There would be time for that shortly. He took a deep breath and gave himself a moment to bask in his accomplishment. Then he resumed going through the remaining notifications.

They were still Cultivation quests. This time going through the three-dimensional geometric shapes. They started at six hundred experience, and each new one added another fifty experience. The last Cultivation quest Ruwen had completed required him to form a sphere in his center.

Ting!
You have completed the Quest – Sphere of Influence (Cultivation Stage 19).
You have received 1000 experience.

A different notification appeared.

Gong!
You have increased your Knowledge!
Level: 37
The intelligent know true power is held by knowledge. The wise know knowledge can be dangerous. Greatness is found between them.

The Knowledge increase must be from learning Cultivation. The final notification gave him the only remaining Cultivation quest.

Ting!
You have received the quest...
Pick One Side
As a Novice, you Cultivated into two dimensions and as an Initiate,

three. An Apprentice must embrace the whole, twisting their center to encompass both simultaneously.
Reward: *Cultivation Rank of Apprentice (Stage 20)*
Reward: *2,000 experience*

Well, that made zero sense. Ruwen shook his head and closed the notification. Immediately he opened his Profile and planned how to spend the four attribute points that he had control over. His Worker Class had already put a point into Strength and Stamina, bringing them both to twelve. Because they would both level as he did, he didn't want to waste any more points there.

Both his Dexterity and Wisdom were still 9. His weapon's modifiers had brought them high enough to get rid of his debuffs. But if he changed weapons, they would come back. Plus, he really wanted to get back to where he'd started before he'd taken a chaos blade to the eye and lost twelve attribute points.

He added a point to Dexterity and Wisdom, bringing them both back to his original ten again. That left two points. Many of the Observer Class spells and skills were based on Dexterity. That would be an excellent place to add points. Charisma was an option, but he already had a decent value of twelve, and a point there would benefit him the least. Wisdom was something he should seriously consider. He had made some poor decisions lately, and Wisdom would help with that. Finally, there was Intelligence. He had built most of his identity around this attribute because it had significantly shaped the last few years of his life. It also directly improved his ability to cast spells.

He thought about it for another minute and then added a point to Dexterity and one to Intelligence. Glancing through the other sections of his Profile, he noticed some changes. He had made good progress toward level five, and he now had a Cultivation Stage and a Cultivation Rank. Not only that, but his Cultivation Stage had affected some of his other attributes in a big way. His Resilience had increased dramatically, which had increased all his Resistances. Maybe even more significantly, his Perception ability had massively increased. He studied the items that had changed the most in his Profile.

Cultivation Stage: 19
Cultivation Rank: Initiate

Experience: 7,558/10,000

Strength: 12
Stamina: 12
Dexterity: 13
Intelligence: 18
Wisdom: 11
Charisma: 12

Knowledge: 37

Health: 145/145
Mana: 180/180
Energy: 247/247

Resilience %: 14.10%
Cleverness %: 39.70%
Perception %: 32.10%

His Resilience received half of his Cultivation Stage, and his Perception received all of it. With his Pacifist's Cloak bonus of 10%, it put his Perception over 30%! All his Resistances were now over 16% too, except for Dark and Chaos, which were just over 12%. It appeared that Cultivating had effects other than creating a terrifying ball of energy inside yourself. Those quests had also gotten him three-quarters of the way to level five. He closed his Profile and shut his eyes.

Another emotion overtook his happiness: fear. If he died here, before he could cross back over and synchronize with Uru, all this would be lost. He wouldn't even have memories of it. The thought of losing the last day terrified him. It felt like he'd packed an entire life of adventure and learning into his time here. In fact, the more he thought about it, the more scared he became. It paralyzed him.

"Hey," Sift said.

Ruwen screamed, his fear exploding like a bomb.

"Whoa," Sift said. "I didn't mean to scare you."

Ruwen's heart beat so quickly his chest hurt. He took a few deep breaths, and his heart rate slowed.

"It's okay," Ruwen said as he sat up.

Sift stood by his bed. He slowly reached down and picked up a pair of his pants. He rolled the hem, now free of Lylan's blood, between his fingers. After a few moments, he turned and looked at Ruwen, his eyes glistening in the light.

"Thank you," Sift whispered.

"Of course."

Sift sat on the bed, and tears fell silently down his cheeks.

"It's my fault Lylan died," Sift said. "Ky said to not blame myself, but I do."

"I assumed she was Ascended. Wouldn't she just be reborn?"

Sift wiped the tears away. "She was, but she lost all her memories of this place when it happened, and Ky wanted to wait before bringing her back."

"Did Lylan say where she came from?"

"Stone Harbor. That isn't too far from Deepwell if I remember right."

Ruwen nodded. "It's just a few days' ride east. All the way to the coast. Stone Harbor is way bigger than Deepwell." Ruwen thought for a few seconds. "If she accepted the Black Pyramid mark there, then she'd have memories of Ky and accepting it. So from Lylan's perspective, she stepped through the rock portal and then immediately woke up in the temple basement?"

"I guess. Ky didn't say why Lylan wasn't brought right back here."

"Poor Lylan. It's terrible enough to wake up from a death knowing how it happened. But to not remember it must be terrible."

Thoughts of the high priest's son flashed through Ruwen's mind. That is exactly what had happened to him and partly why Ruwen had been punished with his Worker Class. But whatever had happened in that distant valley, his parents hadn't killed anyone. His parents were good people.

Sift squeezed his eyes with his fingers. "That accident changed the trajectory of Lylan's whole life. She doesn't even remember me."

Ruwen finally understood. Sift had liked this girl, and her death had caused their relationship to be lost. It made him wonder if Sift had other reasons for wanting to cross to the other side. It also reinforced his own fears, which had just crystallized.

"I don't want to die," Ruwen blurted out.

"I don't want you to either. I couldn't bear to have that happen again."

They sat in silence for a minute, both lost in their own thoughts of death and loss.

"I have an idea," Sift said.

Ruwen looked up.

"You learned the cipher today, which gives you access to the lab. Let's go make some potions for tomorrow," Sift said.

"But I don't have many ingredients."

Sift set the pants down and waved a hand. "We can use the

quartermaster's stock. He just keeps nine of every ten things we make."

Ruwen liked working in the lab at school. He still needed to choose his level three spells, but he could do that later.

"That sounds fun, actually," Ruwen said.

Sift stood. "Let's go."

CHAPTER 29

They walked through the open double doors into a room almost as wide and long as the rec room. Rows of tables filled the room. Shelves that reached from floor to ceiling spanned the entire length of the room, covering the walls. They were filled with more jars, pots, and bottles than Ruwen had ever seen in one place.

There were four workbenches in each of the nine rows. A young man in dark clothes, a tan smock, and large glasses stared intently at a boiling flask. Other than Fluffy and the Addas, this was the first person Ruwen had seen here. The young man glanced up at them, and Ruwen waved.

"You see them?" Sift asked.

"Them? I see the guy in the tan smock and glasses."

"Well, that's progress."

"How many people are in here?"

"I see two and sense another two. But Ky's people are really good. That you saw anyone is amazing."

Ruwen's Cultivation had ramped up his Perception and it felt good to see the results of that. To be fair, the Shade had been highly focused on another task and probably wasn't concentrating on staying hidden, but it still felt satisfying.

Each table had a small fire pit on one end and a small fountain on the other. The space in between had a large work area, and flasks and beakers were lined up on a shelf that ran along the entire table. Under each table, there were additional glassware, metal bowls, and pots.

"Stop staring and come on," Sift said.

Ruwen followed Sift to a table right next to the door.

Sift removed a brown leather book from his belt, and Ruwen recognized it.

"That looks like the same book I got: *Five-Minute Fare to Die For*," Ruwen said.

Sift tilted it so Ruwen could read the cover, but the words were gibberish. It must be encoded in a higher-level cipher than Ruwen's level one.

"Mine's volume three," Sift said. "Get yours out."

Ruwen removed his book and set it on the table.

"Find a healing recipe you like," Sift said.

Ruwen opened his book and scanned at the table of contents. The contents were broken up into four main chapters: Contact, Injected, Inhaled, and Ingested. In each chapter, there were the following topics: Poison, Antidote, Recreational, and Healing.

The first healing recipe was in the Contact chapter.

Swab, Minor
Effect: Reduce Bleed damage by 1 HP/s for 10 seconds.
Effect: Heal 2 HP/s for 15 seconds.
Ingredients: 1 3x3 absorbent fabric, 1 Gintyl Leaf, 2 drops Felk Blood, 1 cup water, 1 pinch Pyramid Ash.
Recipe: 1) Add Ash to water 2) Bring water to boil, reduce heat 3) Add Felk Blood and simmer until dissolved 4) Crush Gintyl Leaf and add

to solution 5) Boil for three minutes 6) Remove from heat 7) Place fabric in solution and let cool.

"I found one for Minor Swab," Ruwen said.

Sift nodded. "That's a good one to start. Let me show you how to find the ingredients. Bring your book."

As they approached the closest wall, Ruwen marveled at the vast amount of ingredients. Sift pointed to the shelf under a large jar containing what looked like small river rocks.

"See the value under this jar?" Sift asked.

"L1709."

"Stare at the first ingredient in your recipe. What do you see?"

Ruwen stared at '3x3 absorbent fabric,' and after a second, a value appeared.

"Woah, the text disappeared and L3411 appeared," Ruwen said.

Sift turned to face the doors. "Pretend you're working at your bench." Sift stuck out his left arm. "Left side, that's what 'L' stands for. 'R' is for the other wall. The '3' is for the third row of tables. '4' means the fourth shelf up from the bottom. '11' means the eleventh item on the shelf."

"That is really clever."

"A huge book in the back lists all the ingredients and their locations. It makes finding things a breeze. But you don't need to fetch things yourself if you don't want to. There is an easier method."

Sift walked back to Ruwen's workbench, and Ruwen followed.

"Place the wrist with your Pyramid mark on the bench and say 'ten Minor Swabs,'" Sift said.

Ruwen placed his wrist on the table. "Ten Minor Swabs."

Ingredients rose out of the table. In moments, Ruwen's bench contained the ingredients to make ten Minor Swabs.

"That is amazing," Ruwen said.

"You can just leave all your things on the bench when you're done. Blapy will clean it all."

"What happens if I fail?" Ruwen asked.

"The recipes in your volume all have a 100% success rate. If you drop a beaker or something, the cost is reflected on Fluffy's ledger. The big book in the back will also tell you what everything costs."

Sift showed Ruwen how to adjust the heat and how to cool the water bath. "You good?"

"Safety stuff?" Ruwen asked.

Sift pulled out a drawer at the end of the table, and Ruwen put on the smock and glasses he found there. There were other items as well, but he didn't know their purpose, so he left them alone.

"Okay, I'm good," Ruwen said.

Sift walked to the next bench and flipped through his book. Ruwen looked at all his ingredients and wondered if any of them were dangerous. He turned to his book again and flipped to the back. As he suspected there was a glossary, and he skimmed down until he found Gintyl Leaf.

The entry listed the general uses for it and where it could be found, which to Ruwen's surprise, included more than one world. It also listed any safety concerns or if it needed special handling. Finally, it listed all the pages where it could be found in the book. Ruwen looked up all his ingredients, but none were dangerous. Satisfied he'd taken all the necessary precautions, he set up his table.

Ruwen loved working in the lab. Mixing ingredients together to create new things excited him. He completed the recipe from start to finish with a single beaker, noting how much time each part took. With this new knowledge, he determined he could make them in batches of ten and still be paying close enough attention that he didn't ruin anything.

He was on his sixth batch when Sift came over.

"I'm getting tired. You going to be much longer?" Sift asked.

Ruwen had utterly lost track of time. He really wanted to make a hundred of them, so he'd be able to keep ten for himself. And the truth was he wasn't tired at all. In fact, since waking up from his Cultivating, he hadn't felt tired at all. He felt amazing.

"If you don't mind, I'd like to get to one hundred," Ruwen said.

"No problem. You know how to get back."

Ruwen nodded and placed his palm over Sift's outstretched fist.

"See you later," Ruwen said.

He focused back on his task, and the world around him disappeared. The preciseness of the lab made his brain happy. When he finished the tenth batch, he almost started another but managed to stop himself. Blapy had absorbed nine of every ten swabs he made, but he now had a stack of ten himself. It was a nice round number, and if he kept going, his brain would make him go to fifteen. He placed the ten swabs in his Void Band and looked at the bench fondly. He wished he could take it with him so he could do it while away.

A thought occurred to him, and he placed his mark on the bench.

"Mobile Alchemy Lab," Ruwen said.

The benches next to Ruwen disappeared, and a box the size of a wagon appeared. Ruwen yelped and looked around. He couldn't see anyone, but that didn't mean much. Swallowing hard, he put his wrist back on the bench and tried again.

"Small Mobile Alchemy Lab," Ruwen whispered, terrified it might be bigger than the wagon. He really should have just walked back to the book and found what he wanted there.

The huge box sunk into the floor and the benches replaced it. Nothing else reappeared, and Ruwen's shoulders slumped. He turned back to his bench and found a wooden cube about two feet per side sitting there. Ruwen reached out and touched it.

Tring!
The Black Pyramid has loaned you...
Name: *Mobile Alchemy Laboratory, Small*
Quality: *Fine*
Durability: *100 of 100*
Weight: *30 lbs.*
Replacement Cost: *1,296 Black Pyramid Tokens*
Description: *Mobile lab for Alchemical creations. You break it, you buy it.*

The stained wood looked almost black, and Ruwen ran a hand over the top. A latch caught his finger, and he carefully pried it up. As soon as the latch released the box unfolded itself slowly, as if hidden gears and springs controlled it. The sides of the box spread outward and looked like two open arms. The top folded backward and formed a small pyramid with the rear of the box. Many of the same types of beakers, flasks, and glassware he'd just used were packed efficiently on the box's shelves.

"Blapy, you are so amazing," Ruwen said.

Ruwen carefully pushed the box back together and latched it. Wrapping his arms around the heavy box, he pulled until almost half of it hung off the bench. He opened his Void Band about three feet to fit the alchemy lab and tried not to panic at the flashing twenty on his Energy bar. He had two hundred and forty-seven Energy now, which gave him twelve seconds to get this done.

Holding his left wrist close to the table, he reshaped the Void Band until the alchemy box hung over a black hole. Praying this worked and he didn't destroy it, he pulled the top of the alchemy box downward. For a moment, it didn't budge, and then the entire box tilted forward and immediately slid off the table. Ruwen flinched, expecting there to be some sort of impact on his Void Band, but nothing happened. One moment the box had been teetering on edge and the next it had disappeared. Ruwen hadn't heard or felt a thing.

The same notification appeared that he'd seen after taking the Blood Moss. It had a timer, which had already started counting down from 10. Ruwen quickly read the notification to make sure it hadn't changed.

Notice: A living entity has entered your Void Band. Estimated energy consumption to sustain additional life: 0.25 energy per second. You are currently consuming 0.20 energy per second. You have 10 seconds to make one of the following choices:
Choice 1: Remove the entity.
Choice 2: Select Yes, incur the energy cost, and sustain the entity's life.
Choice 3: Select No, and the entity will perish

He selected *Yes*, and the notification disappeared. His Energy bar flashed yellow as he dropped under 25%. Ruwen realized he'd kept his Void Band open this entire time and immediately slammed it closed. His left wrist stung from the force, and he rubbed it. Reading that notification while his Void Band was open had almost killed him. He remembered Bliz telling him the ways he'd died being stupid and careless with the Void Band. Now, barely a day later, he'd almost had his own story.

The alchemy box must have some live ingredients in it. Since the cost had been so low, it must have been plants. Ruwen's constant energy drain between the Blood Moss and alchemy lab was 0.45 energy per second. His Regen was about 2.5 per second, so that gave him plenty of buffer.

He had other notifications that had remained minimized, and he opened them. They were all identical except for the level. He kept choosing *Accept* until he got to the last one.

Shing!
You have advanced a skill!
Skill: *Alchemy*
Level: *10*
Effect: *Alchemical creations gain a 5% increase in success and effectiveness.*

That was fantastic. It felt good to have his work result in tangible increases in his skills. Before Ascending, it felt like everything was a waste of time. But that wasn't true, the hours he'd spent in the lab at school had allowed him to advance more quickly now. Nothing was really ever wasted.

Glancing at his clock, he realized he'd spent the entire evening here. It was almost midnight, and he wasn't even remotely tired. In fact, since the Cultivation, he had been buzzing with energy. The truth was, the Cultivation situation scared him, and he knew part of his obsession in the alchemy lab was to avoid thinking about it.

He had very little idea what had actually happened, and Sift's parents had already made it clear they weren't going to do anything further. They had given him the first twenty standard quests that would get him to Apprentice, and they had expected that to take decades, not hours.

If he went back to his room now, he would lay in bed and think about the terrifying ball of energy in his body. He didn't want to think about that. Back home, he would have shelved books until he was too tired to stay awake.

Shelve books.

There was a library of sorts here, although it was a disaster. Sift said that the first level would be safe for weeks, so it wouldn't be dangerous to go down there. It had made him sad to see all those books scattered around the room.

He walked out of the alchemy lab and touched his mark to the wall.

"Library."

A portal opened, and he stepped through.

CHAPTER 30

*T*he library didn't look the same. Books still lay scattered everywhere, but the shelves along each wall had been repaired, and the tables and chairs were fixed as well. Brightly lit chandeliers hung every ten feet filling the room with light. He hadn't noticed the hanging lights earlier, but whether he'd missed them before or if they'd just been added, they were a welcome addition. It appeared Blapy had noticed his small attempt to organize one corner of the room and had taken steps to allow him to continue.

"Thanks, Blapy," Ruwen whispered.

"You're welcome," Blapy replied.

Ruwen jerked at the sound and then flushed. He had to stop thinking he was alone. No one was ever alone in the Black Pyramid. Blapy sat on a table to his right. She clutched her stuffed centipede in one hand and a book of animal drawings in her other.

"You're jumpy," Blapy said.

"I'm just not used to people appearing out of thin air."

"Shouldn't you be sleeping?"

"I'm not very tired."

"Why are you doing this?"

That question had a hundred answers. Most of which involved the new energy inside Ruwen, and he didn't want to talk about that. "Habit maybe? I help out in the library back home. Shelving is a great way to discover new books."

"You're looking for new books?"

"Kind of." He really didn't want to talk about himself, so he tried turning the conversation. "Where did all these books come from?"

"From the people who visit me. A momentary contact with a book or journal is all I need to duplicate it. For instance, I now have copies of all the textbooks you brought on Uru's Classes."

Ruwen remembered Blapy talking about the gods adventuring here. Is it possible that some of their writing might be here?

"That would make this an incredibly valuable library," Ruwen said.

"Everything about me is incredibly valuable."

"I believe that."

"The really interesting things are the esoteric writings in languages lost to mortals long ago. So book borrows are rare."

The word esoteric triggered a memory in Ruwen, but he set it aside for a moment. "Does that mean you let people borrow books from here?"

"If they have my mark, which very few do. You're the first person to touch a book in here in centuries."

"Then why do you bother copying all the material people bring?"

"The same reason you really came in here: knowledge."

Ruwen blushed. "I'm just trying to understand what's happening to me."

"Me too. You are like an island in the sea. What's visible is dwarfed by what pushed you to the surface. The fact that you are in this room, that you were drawn to it is a testament to that force."

"Uru?"

"Partly."

Ruwen rubbed his face. "That's part of the problem. Every decision I make feels like I'm performing some preordained plan. I'm starting to think I'm a puppet."

"It might feel that way, but only because of Uru's ability to navigate the most likely paths and plan for them. As time goes on, and more variables surround you, her touch will feel lighter. I'm having a blast watching you trigger traps that have been dormant, waiting for you, for centuries. I almost hope I don't kill you tomorrow."

Ruwen's stomach turned. "I've been thinking about that. Could I step back into my world for a few minutes? Just long enough to synch with Uru. The thought of losing everything that's happened here makes me sick."

"Ky controls access to your plane, and she's still gone. You could just stay in here, or in your room until she gets back."

"She said I needed to make it to level five if I had any chance of surviving when I return."

"That is a difficult situation."

"You couldn't just take it easy on me?"

"Sorry, when it comes to your kind, I have to operate by the gods' rules. One of which is 'no favorites.' One of my jobs is to try and kill anyone who ventures into my depths. No hard feelings. Although to be honest, I'm really hoping you die. I want a closer look at that birthmark, which I'll only get if I absorb you. Plus, with all the energy you just Cultivated, I could finish off my latest level. Honestly, you're lucky those rules exist. Otherwise, I'm not sure I could resist killing you right now."

Ruwen's mouth went dry. It was easy to forget when talking

with the cute little girl that Blapy was an ancient being who had spent eons perfecting ways to kill adventurers. Adventurers with far more skills than he had.

"Lucky me," Ruwen choked out.

Blapy grinned at him and hopped off the table. She gave her centipede a hug and then walked toward the doors. The doors opened as she approached, and she stopped and faced him.

"Do you know the only thing more powerful than knowledge?" Blapy asked.

Ruwen gave the question some thought. He had grown up thinking knowledge eventually beat every other source of power. With the right knowledge, you could overcome almost any obstacle.

"Nothing," Ruwen said.

"Knowledge is useless without the ability to comprehend it."

Ruwen nodded. "That's true. You need Intelligence and Wisdom."

"And something even more basic," Blapy said. "The ability to read it. I'll let you guess how many of the gods figured that one out and planned for it when constructing their Classes. See you in a few hours."

Blapy walked through the open doors and disappeared. Ruwen immediately took out his Worker textbook and flipped to the abilities section. He found *Hey You*, and read what each level offered.

He had remembered correctly. His level one ability gave him the vocabulary of a five-year-old, and level two gave him a firm grasp of the basics. At his current level of three, he was now fluent. When he took level four, he would understand technical and scientific items. The last level, five, he could understand and communicate on esoteric, arcane, and magical topics.

Esoteric. The same word Blapy had used to describe some of the books here. The desire to use the ability points he'd just earned for reaching level four to increase the level of *Hey You* to level five was almost unbearable. The thought of reading anything he wanted in this room, a room that might contain the writings of gods, made his head spin. What might he learn? Maybe something that would save his life. But, if he disobeyed Ky, there would be consequences, and that thought stopped him. He would just have to wait. Hopefully his current level would allow him to at least recognize what might be valuable to him right now.

Blapy's last comment about how the gods built their Classes made Ruwen wonder. He knew high-level Mages had spells to decipher text. Ruwen agreed with Blapy that the power to comprehend and communicate in a language was the foundation of knowledge. The more languages you could do that in, the more knowledge you gained. So, in a way, it did make it the most potent ability. And Uru had given this ability to her most basic Class. Literally half of her people had the potential to reap the benefits from this room or any foreign library. Even Mages didn't have that power, as their ability to read efficiently would be limited by their Mana pool and cooldowns. Once again, it made him view Workers in a different light.

He went to the corner where he and Sift had shelved books earlier, and slowly expanded from there. Ruwen glanced at every book he picked up. Most were readable and ran the gamut of a normal library: memoirs, adventure stories, illustrated and informational books, and manuals on everything from fishing to fighting. He had no idea the best way to shelve them, so, until he decided, he just focused on getting them off the floor and onto the shelves.

Four hours passed as he slowly filled two of the shelves. He stood in the corner and looked at the tiny area he'd managed to clear. It would take him months to finish, but he didn't mind. He hoped to come back to the library often. Looking at the two shelves with their neatly stacked books made him feel good.

The table nearest him had three books on it. All of them were almost entirely incomprehensible. He didn't know if that was because they were ciphered, the author was insane, or his *Hey You* Ability wasn't high enough.

The library reminded him of home, and he felt better. Reluctant to leave, he slowly walked around the room. Near the area furthest from the doors, many of the books looked older. Time had aged them, and a significant number had frayed edges. He would probably start here next time. As he turned to leave, the lights went out.

He stopped, paralyzed, his heart racing. The Jaga Wedding Band's 15% increase to ambient light turned the darkness into a murky grey fog. But he still couldn't see well.

"Really, Blapy?" Ruwen said in frustration. She probably had figured out he didn't like the dark.

"Limuno," Ruwen said.

The lights didn't come back on.

"Limuno!" Ruwen said, louder this time.

Still no lights. Maybe that only worked when you were on the top of the stairs. Or Blapy was trying to make him uncomfortable.

Blapy didn't respond. She might not have had anything to do with it. Maybe the lights went off automatically if, after so many hours, no one walked through the doors. Yes, that was probably it. That made him feel better. There was an easy way to test it. He just needed to make it to the door and see if it triggered the lights.

He activated his *Detect Temperature* to see if it would help him. His footsteps were visible, and anything he'd touched had a faint red glow. He could make out the far doors because the outer room was warmer and Ruwen could see the heat seeping into this room through the cracks around the frame.

He looked down to avoid walking on any books and gasped. Something bright red lay buried under a pile of books just to his left. Kneeling, he gently cleared the books away. The object was a book about the size of his two hands, but Ruwen couldn't make out the title. It felt warm, and he wondered what might cause that. Too late, he realized it might be a trap or some sort of bomb. He held it out, not sure what to do. After a few seconds, nothing happened, and he decided it was probably safe. Standing back up, he looked around the room but didn't see anything else giving off heat.

He took a step, and the lights came back on. No one had come through the door, and he remained alone in the room. It must have been Blapy controlling the lights. Had she turned them off on purpose to help him find this book? Why would she do that? He turned off *Detect Temperature* and looked at the book in his hands.

The book had a plain brown cover with two clasped hands. The book title, *A Worker's Guide to Harvesting*, made it sound like a book on farming. The clasped hands were the symbol for Uru's Worker Class, but that might be a coincidence. Why would such a nondescript book be warm? What would even cause a book to get warm?

He tried to open it, but the cover wouldn't budge. Turning the book, he looked at the edge, expecting to see decay or something that would cause the pages to be stuck together. But the page edges seemed clean. He used a little more pressure, scared of breaking the book, but wanting to at least try and open it. The book wouldn't budge.

Moving to the table with the other books he wanted to borrow, he set this one next to them.

"Blapy, I'd like to borrow these four books," Ruwen said.

Minimized notifications blinked, and he opened them.

Tring!
The Black Pyramid has loaned you...
Book Title: *<Unknown to Borrower>*

Topic: *<Unknown to Borrower>*
Author: *<Unknown to Borrower>*
Book Id: *459204*
Quality: *Rare*
Durability: *4 of 10*
Weight: *1.1 lbs.*
Loan Count: *4*
Restriction: *Black Pyramid mark required.*
Description: *Small red book with gold edges.*

The next two, a medium blue book and a small black one, were similar to the red book. The last notification listed the book he'd found with *Detect Temperature.*

Tring!
The Black Pyramid has loaned you...
Book Title: *A Worker's Guide to Harvesting*
Topic: *<Unknown to Borrower>*
Author: *<Unknown to Borrower>*
Book Id: *000003*
Quality: *Legendary*
Durability: *10 of 10*
Weight: *3.7 lbs.*
Loan Count: *1*
Restriction: *Black Pyramid mark required.*
Restriction: *Class, Deity's most common*
Restriction: *Harvesting Stage 10 (Minimum)*
Description: *Medium brown book with clasped hands. Warm to the touch.*

Ruwen's hand trembled as he reached out and touched the book again. He had dreamed of seeing a legendary item someday, perhaps even studying one at some point in his life. Actually holding one or, for that matter, taking it with him, had never entered his mind. They were so rare and powerful, King-doms had gone to war over them. They were items of immense power, and one had been laying on Blapy's first floor.

But unless you met all the requirements, you probably couldn't borrow it to see the item's information. Which meant no one probably even knew this precious book existed except for the author, Blapy, and now Ruwen. And Blapy had just told him she wanted to kill him. She had to be the one who had turned off the lights. She had effectively led him to this book. Did that mean it was dangerous and would kill him?

The other three books he'd borrowed all had identification numbers around five hundred thousand. This book had an ID of three. Did that mean it was the third book Blapy accepted? How old did that make it? And now he had a burning desire to find the books with an ID of one and two. Were they legendary as well?

The restriction referencing Harvesting confused him. If this was some powerful magic that helped you grow food, what did the "stage" reference mean? The only stage he had ever seen was the one that had recently appeared on his Profile. But it was for Cultivating.

He carefully put all the books in his Void Band and walked to the wall near the door. His curiosity demanded he spend more time trying to open that book. But he needed to focus on surviving. That meant not fiddling with something Blapy had led him to until after he'd synched with Uru, and improved himself however he could to survive Blapy's third level.

He'd already used both his level three ability points on *Hey You* when he wanted to understand Sift's parents. But he still had his level three spells to pick. He needed every advantage he could get so he wouldn't be Blapy's next meal.

"Sift's bedroom," Ruwen said as he touched his wrist to the wall.

A portal opened, and he gave the library one last look. The

real treasure Blapy held might not be buried deep underground. It might be in plain sight. It was just the kind of thing she would love. Adventurers walking over priceless artifacts on their way to likely death for lesser treasure. Yes, he needed to spend a lot more time in here.

CHAPTER 31

*R*uwen laid on his back, hands behind his head, trying to ignore Sift's snoring. For the tenth time, he studied the new spell choices available to him since leveling. He'd earned level four before he'd had a chance to allocate his level three spells, so now he could use those to pick a level four spell if he wanted and skip level three altogether.

He skimmed the level three and four Energy-based Worker spells again, ignoring the descriptions and casting information.

Spell: Kindling
Level: 3
Effect: Condense the air near your hand into a small blade.

Spell: Harden
Level: 3
Effect: Increase density.

Spell: Dash
Level: 4
Effect: Increase your top speed by 20%.

Spell: *Dig*
Level: *4*
Effect: *Remove material and place it nearby. The denser the material, or the faster the removal, the higher the energy cost.*

His Observer Energy-based spells made the decision even harder.

Spell: *Tight Rope*
Level: *3*
Effect: *Walk safely on any surface 2 inches or greater in width. Falls cause 10% less damage.*

Spell: *Street Fight*
Level: *3*
Effect: *Increase unarmed damage by 20% and Dexterity by 10%.*

Spell: *Obscure*
Level: *4*
Effect: *Decrease signs of passage by 20%.*

Spell: *Feather Feet*
Level: *4*
Effect: *Reduce the force of steps by 20%.*

One more time, he scanned the Mana-based Worker spells.

Spell: *Second Wind*
Level: *3*
Effect: *Reduce food, water, and sleep requirements by 10%.*

Spell: *Grasp Crate*
Level: *3*
Effect: *Increase the roughness of your hands by 10%.*

Spell: *Retrieve*
Level: *4*
Effect: *Retrieve items less than 10 lbs. that are within 30 ft. of your location.*

Spell: *Jump*
Level: *4*
Effect: *Increase the distance jumped by 20%.*

Finally, the four Mana-based Observer spells.

Spell: *Find Item*
Level: *3*
Effect: *Sense the location of an item when holding an associated item. The more closely related the two items, the better the outcome.*

Spell: *Charge Item*
Level: *3*
Effect: *Charge weapon with electricity, stunning the target for 1 to 3 seconds.*

Spell: *Pay Back*
Level: *4*
Effect: *Spring to your feet and quickly strike, stunning the target for 1 to 3 seconds.*

Spell: *Backstab*
Level: *4*
Effect: *Triple weapon damage when the target is struck from behind. Effect stacks with other modifiers.*

Level three was an odd level so he'd only gotten two spells, one for each Class. The four spells he'd gained for reaching level four he planned on saving because Ky had wanted him to wait.

So, with the two spells available, he could pick new ones, increase the spell level of earlier ones, or just save these two. There were just too many choices, and it overwhelmed him.

His focus was to survive today, closely followed by making it to level five. That meant anything he chose had to support those two goals. Looking through them all again, he decided *Backstab* was a clear choice. *Backstab* would stack with his *Bleed* spell and do six times the damage he would normally do. Since his damage output was so weak, this would allow him to contribute in a meaningful way. He looked at the details of the spell and cringed at the Mana cost of fifty. It took a second to cast, and the recovery was thirty seconds.

Even though the Mana cost seemed excessive, it did triple his damage, and the long recovery made sense for such a powerful spell. He focused on the icon for *Backstab*. Fittingly, it looked like a figure with its arms thrown backward as a dagger struck them from behind. He had already discovered praying wasn't necessary to advance an already learned ability, but he wondered if learning a new spell would be any different. Without any thought of Uru, he concentrated on the icon, and ten seconds later he felt the stab in his mind followed by the notification of his success.

He said a prayer of thanks to Uru, just in case. But he wondered what not having to pray meant. Did everyone have everything in their head already like Sift believed? Ruwen could see why you would want some information there. If someone left the area where their god could synch them, they would need to still be able to progress. He would have to think about that some more later.

For his last choice, a few spells would benefit him. He had started learning the Steps with Sift and *Street Fight* would make him more dangerous. He had just begun, though, and wasn't any good yet. Plus, he didn't want things getting that close to him.

His fear of heights would be manageable if he knew *Tight*

Rope. He wouldn't worry so much about falling. But again, he didn't plan on being anywhere high right now. The idea of digging holes to escape or for safety sounded awesome, but seemed very situational.

Really, it came down to two: *Pay Back* and *Retrieve.* Ruwen ended up on the ground a lot, and it would be nice to have a way to quickly regain his feet. Not only that, but it allowed him to attack and stun his opponent. The spell was very powerful.

Embarrassingly, the thing he seemed to do the most was drop his weapons. He knew it was his lack of fighting experience and that it would get better, but it didn't change the fact that his instinct seemed to be dropping whatever he held. A spell that allowed him to get his weapon back was a valid choice. Not having to leave his chair to grab a book from across the room didn't have any bearing. None.

He looked at the details of the *Retrieve* spell. Another expensive spell costing fifty Mana. It was instant cast though, which was nice. The one-minute cool down for the recovery sucked but was understandable. He double-checked the weight of his staff to make sure it wasn't over ten pounds and was relieved that it only weighed 4.2 pounds. He focused on the icon, which looked like a reaching hand, and, just like before, he learned a spell without following the normal process.

He sat up in bed and looked around the room. His Staff of Chimes leaned against the wall about ten feet from the end of his bed. He reached for it and pictured the icon for *Retrieve* in his mind. A fifty flashed on his Mana bar, and the staff flew toward him. He realized too late that where he focused on the staff mattered. Instead of looking at the middle of the weapon, he'd been looking toward the top, which now hurtled toward him like a spear.

He yelped and ducked as the staff flew past him. A crash sounded behind him, and he turned to find Sift standing in his underwear, crouched and ready to fight. Ruwen's staff stuck out of the wall where it had embedded itself into the stone.

Sift looked at the weapon stuck in the wall, the stone-dust falling to the floor, and then at Ruwen.

Ruwen winced. "Sorry."

"Even sleeping you throw your weapon." Sift sat on his bed and rubbed his face. "We might as well get an early start."

As guilty as Ruwen felt, he was anxious for the answer to a question that had bothered him. He removed the Worker textbook he'd gotten from Tremine and *A Worker's Guide to Harvesting* that he'd just borrowed from Blapy and held them up.

"Can you read these titles?" Ruwen asked.

Sift pointed to the textbook. "Worker Basics – Levels 1 through 9." He pointed to the other book. "I can't read that. I'll be right back. If I don't use the bathroom right now, I'm going to wet myself."

Ruwen put the books away. He had suspected his ability had allowed him to read the title, but he wasn't sure until now. That meant in addition to the book's stated restrictions, the reader needed to know the original language or have a method of translating it. Blapy had hinted as she'd left that only Uru had given her most common Class the ability to understand other languages. That meant the author of this book had likely written it specifically for one of Uru's Workers. Ruwen still didn't understand the 'Harvest' term. He started to look through the Worker spells for any that aided in harvesting crops.

Sift returned to the room.

"Have you ever heard of a Harvesting Stage?" Ruwen asked.

"No, but isn't that in the Fall?"

"Never mind, it was just something I read."

"Well, reading time is over. Let's start with some meditation…" Sift's voice trailed off, and he looked uncomfortable.

"It's okay. Blapy made me try it outside. I've reached some

sort of limit, and I can't Cultivate anymore. I'm full or something. So, meditating is safe."

Sift relaxed. "That's good." He pulled Ruwen's staff out of the wall and tossed it to him.

Ruwen needed to use both hands, but he caught the staff. He looked it over, but it appeared undamaged, so he set it on the bed. Sift had already walked to the center of the room and sat cross-legged on the floor. Ruwen sat across from him.

"You really scared my parents," Sift said.

"Really? They didn't want any details from me when Blapy brought me back. They just wanted to know if I was okay. They acted like nothing had happened."

"It's the first time I've ever seen them agitated."

"Do you think I did something wrong?"

"No, I think it's more what you mean for the future. They're worried what will happen because of you."

"Because of me? What am I going to do?" Ruwen pointed to the new hole above Sift's bed. "The only thing I pose a danger to are walls."

They both laughed.

"True. Maybe they'd be more relaxed if they'd seen you fight those chickens," Sift said.

"They were fast!"

Sift smiled and closed his eyes. Ruwen closed his as well and evened out his breathing. As soon as his mind cleared, the large, terrifying ball of energy appeared. His heart rate increased as he dropped into the energy on the way to his center. He could still hear Sift's breathing along with a hundred other small sounds. Leaving most of his focus at the surface of the ball, he brought a thread down with him to his center, like a lifeline to the surface. Sift's breathing became a distant thing, but still there if he needed to find a way out, and the world quieted again.

Other than his brief experiment with Blapy, he hadn't spent

any time here. It didn't take long before boredom caused him to start pushing and pulling on the energy surrounding him. One advantage of Cultivating his own mind had been the ease of focusing. Now, without being able to Cultivate and feed his center, he had nowhere to push his stray thoughts or fears. He wished Sift's parents would help him. Being stuck at this level for the rest of his life would ruin meditation for him.

He pulled at the energy around him to make a small ball, one that he could bounce around inside his mind. The energy around him responded, and he packed some energy into a ball. As soon as he did, he felt power trickling into him to fill the small hole left when the energy condensed. For a moment, he had Cultivated again.

"Did you just do something?" Sift asked.

Ruwen immediately let the condensed ball go, but it stayed the way it was. Did this mean if he wanted to continue to Cultivate he needed to compress the energy around him?

"Not sure, why?" Ruwen asked.

"It got cold for a second, but it's fine now. I'm probably just jumpy from before."

"I think I'm done. It's too hard to concentrate this morning," Ruwen said.

"Yeah, I feel it too. Ky will be back today, and we travel tonight."

Yes, assuming Ruwen didn't die first. Out of curiosity, he checked his Spirit, but it still stood at three hundred fifty-two thousand one hundred sixty-four. That made sense since Blapy's calculation had estimated 0.003 Spirit per foot per second. He had compressed such a tiny amount that his Cultivation to fill it wasn't measurable. But if he could figure out a better way to condense the energy, that would change.

They both stood, and Sift squatted down like he was sitting in the air.

"This is the first Step, which I always found funny because you don't actually move," Sift said.

Ruwen mirrored Sift. If this was what learning the Steps would be like, he'd be a master in no time. Squatting? He could do that.

Sift stood, walked over, and straightened Ruwen's back.

"You can rest your arms on your thighs for now. Eventually, we'll be practicing punches, blocks, and weapons like this."

"This seems kind of dumb," Ruwen said. Then quickly added, "I don't mean that in a bad way. It's just I don't see the purpose."

"It's okay. You're just ignorant."

Ruwen tensed at the insult, but he realized Sift hadn't meant it as one. It was just a fact. Ruwen forced himself to relax.

Sift slapped his thighs. "The reason it's important is that it's your foundation. It strengthens your legs and core. If your foundation is good, you can build your mastery on it. If not, your Steps will falter, and you will fail."

Sift pointed to Ruwen's feet. "Your feet are about shoulder length apart, which is good. But your left foot is angled inward and is slightly closer to your center. You are out of balance."

With his index finger Sift touched Ruwen's side, just under his ribs, and gently pushed. Ruwen immediately fell over. "Your foundation is weak."

Ruwen stood to regain his balance and squatted again, trying to mirror Sift exactly.

"Better," Sift said and then used his finger to topple Ruwen again.

Ruwen quickly realized how incredibly hard it was to just squat. It amazed him how many things could be out of alignment. After ten minutes, Sift stood.

"I don't want to overdo it today. Your legs need to be fresh for the third level," Sift said.

Ruwen's stomach twisted in anxiety.

Sift opened his bag and pulled out a lump of white wax. He twisted off a chunk and handed it to Ruwen.

"There will probably be Shriekers, so we'll use the wax to plug our ears. Do you have a scarf?" Sift asked, pulling out a Scarf of Freshness.

"Yes," Ruwen said.

"Also, make sure you're wearing tight underwear. You don't want them getting in your body down there."

"What?"

"Shriekers like holes."

"Can we skip this level?" Ruwen asked.

"You'll be okay. But I need to teach you some Shade Speak so we can communicate without having to hear. It will look like this."

Sift made three small gestures with his hand. *Stop. Danger. Forward.*

Without thinking, Ruwen responded. *Understand.*

Sift raised his eyebrows and quickly flashed. *You. Know. Speak.*

Ruwen had never tried to communicate nonverbally using his *Hey You* Ability. But the description had said communicate, not speak, so he guessed that included signed languages. He looked at his hand and then back up at Sift.

Know. Some Ruwen signaled back.

Sift smiled. *Good. Easier. Journey.*

Ruwen pulled another pair of underwear out of his Void Band and pulled them over the pair he was wearing. He was considering adding a third pair when Sift laughed.

"One pair is enough," Sift said and then grew serious. "The problem is when they get in your ears."

Ruwen knew Sift was thinking about Lylan and changed the subject.

"Can we get something to eat before heading down?" Ruwen asked.

Ruwen wasn't really that hungry and knew he was stalling, but he had a bad feeling about today. There was a lot to lose. Blapy had made it clear she hoped he died, and he was in no hurry to give her a chance.

CHAPTER 32

*T*hey walked down a tightly spiraling tunnel on the way to the third level. Ruwen had stuck so much wax in his ears they hurt from the pressure. He didn't care, though, he didn't want to end up like Sift's girlfriend. His Scarf of Freshness was tied securely across his nose and mouth, and his belt dug into his side from being drawn so tight. He glanced down at the hem of his black Shade pants. Sift had given him some string and Ruwen had tied the pants tightly to his ankle.

A notification pulsed in the bottom of his vision and he opened it.

Ting!
You have received the Black Pyramid quest...
Lend a Hand (Level 3)
Occupants will appreciate your helping hands as you find and destroy five Exploding Burrower nests.
Restriction: *Must complete in 120 minutes or less*
Reward: *15 Black Pyramid tokens*
Reward: *1,250 experience*
Accept or Decline

The quest text made it sound like people on this level needed assistance. It would be nice to have extra fighters when clearing the level. They just needed to find whoever wanted a hand and help them. Help would be especially welcome since this quest had a time restriction. He hoped two hours was enough.

He had cast *Bleed* and *Backstab* on both his staff and dagger as soon as he'd entered the dungeon. It had cost him one hundred and fifty Mana, almost completely draining his bar, but now, just over five minutes later, his bar was nearly full again. The full bars made some of his nervousness disappear.

Sift pulled two pairs of alchemical lab goggles from his belt and handed one to Ruwen. They put them on, and Sift touched the wax in his ears. He moved his hands in Shade Speak, tilting his hand to indicate a question. *Quest?*

Yes, Ruwen responded.

Good. Hope. Keep. Hands. Then gave the sign for laughter.

That was a weird thing to say, but maybe Ruwen had misinterpreted Sift's signs. The tunnel stopped spiraling and straightened for about ten feet before opening up into what looked like a jungle. Sift approached the edge slowly, and Ruwen followed.

The trees looked to be about sixty feet tall and had large oval-shaped leaves. Twenty feet up each trunk, branches grew and intertwined with the branches of nearby trees. In some places, they were so thick you couldn't see past them. Light filtered down from some invisible source. The air felt warm, and because of the scarf, he couldn't smell the dead leaves that littered the ground.

A tiny butterfly, only an inch long, landed on Ruwen's hand. The wings were iridescent, and they folded flat against the little bug's body, making it almost look like a worm. To his shock, as he focused on the creature, information appeared above its body.

Name: *Exploding Burrower Drone (Level 2)*

Health: 24
Mana: 0
Energy: 10
Spirit: 0

Even though he didn't know how to use his Spirit power, his Cultivation Stage had increased his Perception enough to see basic information. He wondered why it hadn't worked on any of the people he'd seen since his Cultivation incident. Then he realized everyone here at the Black Pyramid were experts at hiding, including their attributes. Still, this made him super happy. It showed that as painful as the last day had been, he had made some progress.

Sift's hands slapped together, crushing the beautiful little creature. Ruwen looked up at him in confusion. Sift made the exploding head motion. So these were what Sift called Shriekers. A timer had started in the upper-right side of his vision, just under the quest for this level. 119:54, 119:53, 119:52...

Another Burrower landed on Ruwen's arm. Pulling his scarf up, Sift spit in his hand and then quickly replaced the scarf over his mouth. He moved the hand near the Exploding Burrower that had landed on Ruwen. He watched as the little bug twisted its body toward the fluid. Even through the wax, he heard the little bug's scream and then it launched itself at Sift's hand. As soon as it touched the spit, it tried to burrow deeper, and then it exploded in size. The inch-long butterfly expanded into a ball a foot across.

Sift dropped his hand suddenly and then brought them together in a hard clap, smashing the now huge Burrower. Pieces of bug flew everywhere, and Ruwen wiped bug guts off his goggles. Both he and Sift were covered in grey slime like some giant had sneezed on them.

Sift cleaned his goggles as well and then signaled. *Sorry.*

Ruwen just shook his head. Now he understood why you

didn't want them in your body. Body fluids seemed to make them greatly expand. He needed to find five of their nests and destroy them, and he had less than two hours to do it now.

He activated *Detect Temperature,* and the flying Burrowers appeared like floating embers. They all had information now and varied between levels two and three. The Burrowers seemed to be coming from his left. He pointed that direction and Sift nodded. They moved slowly along the cavern wall, watching the jungle intently. They traced the line of Burrowers to a cocoon about the size of his arm. It hung from the lowest branch on a tree about thirty feet from the cavern wall.

Sift signaled. *Quest. Destroy. I. Locate. Next.*

Okay.

Sift continued down the wall and soon disappeared. Ruwen studied the trees and surrounding area. The quest made him think there might be helpful people here, and he didn't want to ruin that by accidentally attacking someone if they surprised him.

He slowly walked to the hive until he stood almost under it. It had the same grey-brown mucus color as the inside of the Burrower Sift had smashed. The hive hung by a stem about the thickness of Ruwen's wrist, and Burrowers fluttered around and on it. Ruwen couldn't see the entrance so he assumed it must be on top.

What would be the best way to do this? His dagger would be useless from down here. If he wanted to use it, he would have to climb the tree and cut the stem. Leaving the ground was always his last resort, so he thought of other ways to do this. His staff seemed like the logical choice. He could reach the hive from the ground, and the staff did a lot of damage. The issue though was what happened after that. He assumed the Burrowers would be upset and fly around. Striking them in the air with his staff would be ten times harder than hitting chickens, and that had taken him ten minutes.

Ruwen looked down at his Baton of a Thousand Uses for a few seconds and then removed it. It took him three tries to find the correct bump that magically pulled out into a shovel. It seemed ludicrous to start a fight with a shovel, but the surface area would give him a massive advantage when trying to hit the tiny flying creatures. It just felt wrong, somehow, to be in a dungeon fighting this way. To be fair, the Rod Spiders had been mostly desperation. But this time it was deliberate.

"Oh well, you don't get experience for style," Ruwen said.

He took a few practice swings with the shovel and then studied the hive again. It didn't seem worth it to spend Mana on *Bleed* or *Backstab*. This seemed pretty simple. Knock it down. Smash it. The few Burrowers that survived shouldn't take long to finish off.

Taking two more practice swings, he let himself relax. This would be easy. Taking careful aim, he swung his shovel at the hive.

The stem attached to the tree was stronger than Ruwen thought. Instead of the hive falling nicely to the ground, it exploded. He stared in shock as thirty Burrowers shot into the air from the force of his blow. Screeching made it through his earplugs, and he turned to see all the Burrowers that had left the hive come flying back. All of them headed directly at him.

He swung his shovel around in a panic and managed to kill a few. But it didn't take long for almost fifty Burrowers to be crawling all over his body. He smashed them against his body, but there were too many he couldn't reach. The feeling of them crawling on his skin made him panic. His heartbeat thundered in his ears, and he did the only thing he could think of. He dropped to the ground and rolled around, trying to smash them into the ground.

Ruwen didn't know how long he'd been rolling and smashing when he caught sight of Sift above him. It was enough to calm Ruwen's mind, and he stood up. About ten

Burrowers crawled on Sift, and another twenty or so were still on Ruwen.

Sift signaled. *Serious. What. Wrong. You.*

What?

You. Hopeless. Sift flicked a Burrower that had crawled on to his nose. *I. Demonstrate. Before.*

Thought. Plan. Work.

You. Think. Extra.

Ruwen guessed Sift meant he overthought things. Something Ky had told him as well.

Sift pulled a water-skin from his belt, pulled the stopper, and quickly spit in the top. He tucked the scarf back down, placed his thumb on the top, and shook the water-skin. He walked to the tree and dumped a little of the water down the trunk. He pulled a Burrower off his arm and stuck it on the wet area of the trunk. It started shrieking, expanded, and then fell to the ground. At the sound of the shriek, all the Burrowers had raced for the tree. In moments, all the remaining Burrowers were a foot big and nestled like giant seeds around the bottom of the tree.

Shaking his head, Sift stoppered the water-skin and handed it to Ruwen. He took it and placed it in his Void Band. His cheeks burning, he picked up his shovel, and in less than a minute all the Burrowers were dead. His timer read ninety-seven minutes. Now that he knew the trick to killing them, the others should go much faster. Ninety-seven minutes should be plenty of time.

Just to make sure this wasn't all for nothing, he opened his quest. It now had a counter that read one of five complete. Closing the quest, he wondered if Sift and Ky were right. Did he overthink? His plans had mostly been disastrous here, but a lot of that was because he had never fought before. He still had trouble controlling his fear, and it made him do dumb things like drop his weapons or roll around.

The problem might be he wasn't leaning into his one advantage, Intelligence, enough. He hadn't taken the first plan that came to his mind, but he also wasn't thinking things through or getting more information before acting. That might still happen, as many things happened too quickly to think about. But if he did have time, he needed to think more, not less, if he wanted to survive. The more information he had, the better the plan he could execute. Intelligence was his real advantage, and for the most part, he'd been ignoring it.

Sift tapped Ruwen's forehead, and Ruwen focused on Sift.

Ready? Sift signaled.

Ruwen nodded and followed his friend.

Using Sift's water-skin, the next three hives went much faster. When they had finished the fourth one, Ruwen still had forty-two minutes on his countdown clock.

Sift signaled. *Danger. Soon. Hands.*

Ruwen didn't understand what Sift meant, but the quest referenced hands as well. It said 'Occupants will appreciate your helping hands…' so it must almost be time to offer someone a hand. It would all be clear soon. As they began walking deeper into the jungle, Ruwen thought about the abilities and spells he'd learned and tried to think of smart ways to use them. When Sift slowed and dropped to his stomach, Ruwen decided he also needed to stay focused on the present, or he might get killed.

Sift crawled forward and Ruwen followed. Half a minute later the trees started to thin. They moved forward another twenty feet and stopped as a large clearing, at least three hundred feet across, appeared. Near the center, two humanoid creatures sat next to a fire. A single tree stood near the pair, an Exploding Burrower hive hanging above them.

The sitting pair had green skin with brown ridges on their hairless scalps. Something seemed odd about them, and when the big one stretched, Ruwen saw they each had four arms. The smaller of the two had a stick in each hand. Fire shot from one of the sticks directly into the fire and Ruwen realized they were wands. The Mage pointed another wand at the base of the fire, and it suddenly blazed higher as air was forced onto the coals. Ruwen guessed the other two wands were water and earth, making the little one an Elemental Mage.

The big one clapped his hands together in some complicated pattern. Ruwen couldn't hear it, but the Mage bobbed up and down to the beat. Ruwen named the big one Clapper.

Their mouths looked too big for their heads, and sharp yellow teeth protruded like daggers. They each wore a necklace made from bloody hands. Most of which were not green. Ruwen shook his head and reread the quest description.

Occupants will appreciate your helping hands as you find and destroy five Exploding Burrower nests.

"Damn you, Blapy," Ruwen whispered.

He focused on Clapper and the Mage. At first, just their type appeared: Clapping Brawlers. As he continued to study them, more information appeared.

Name: *Clapping Brawler, Mage (Level 5)*
Health: *62*
Mana: *136*
Energy: *50*
Spirit: *0*

Name: *Clapping Brawler, Chief (Level 7)*
Health: *238*
Mana: *0*
Energy: *190*
Spirit: *0*

Sift pointed to each side of the clearing. Ruwen's *Detect*

Temperature identified the outline of another four-armed creature on each side. He couldn't see them as well, and the information he garnered was limited. He studied the one on the left first, and then the right.

Clapping Brawler, Fighter (Level 6)

Clapping Brawler, Fighter (Level 4)

Something bothered him about the tree in the clearing, and he studied it. The branches had a lot of foliage, as much as the trees directly above him, but that tree didn't have others to intertwine with it. That meant someone had added those leaves.

Ruwen activated *Magnify*, and the tree grew large in his vision. He slowly moved his eyes across the tree until he caught a sliver of red, mostly hidden behind the trunk and leaves. He stared at the area, and after about ten seconds he was rewarded with some information: *Clapping Brawler, Assassin (Level 5)*

He turned off Magnify and signed to Sift. *Assassin. Tree. Above.*

Sift concentrated on the tree, nodded at Ruwen, and then turned and crawled back the way they'd come.

When they could no longer see the clearing, Sift stopped.

Make. Fire. Please. Sift signed.

Here?

Sift nodded.

Ruwen cleared an area with his foot and then focused on the *Campfire* icon. Five seconds later, his Mana bar dropped from one hundred eighty to thirty. It flashed yellow in warning as he fell below 25% capacity. He seemed to do that a lot.

Sift signed, *Thanks*, took off his shoes and stuck his feet, hands, and arms directly in the fire.

Ruwen managed to swallow his gasp. Sift, just like when the Roasting Lizard had set him on fire, was unfazed by the heat.

Because of his recent Cultivating experience, Ruwen had finally put enough pieces together to understand what was happening. Sift couldn't pull energy toward himself, he needed it to touch him so he could 'sift' through it and make it useable. Once again, they were on opposite sides of a problem. Ruwen had absorbed an immense amount of energy and had no clue what to do with it. Sift had skills but was forced to charge himself up by sitting in a fire.

Extra. Enemy. Need. Plan. Sift signed.

They sat in silence, and Ruwen's Mana bar had completely refilled before he signed back.

I. Have. Plan.

CHAPTER 33

*R*uwen stopped walking when the level four Fighter became visible with Ruwen's *Detect Temperature*. He turned it off, and after a few seconds of searching with his normal vision, he found the green skinned Fighter.

The plan was simple. Ruwen would use his *Distract* spell on the far part of the clearing. When the Brawlers were distracted by the spell, Ruwen would kill the lowest level Fighter, and Sift would take out the level six Fighter on the left side of the clearing. When Ruwen finished his opponent, he would crawl to the edge of the clearing and wait for Sift to kill the Assassin. Then Ruwen would create an even louder distraction at the far end of the clearing, run out and destroy the hive, and then help Sift if he needed it.

Originally, Ruwen had wanted to kill the Mage first. Sift had signaled that the Mage's magic would provide Sift energy while the Assassin's blades were the real danger. Ruwen had wanted to know how Sift would make it to the tree undetected, and Sift had pointed at himself. Ruwen didn't know if that was Sift bragging or if Ruwen had just misunderstood. It didn't matter; Sift was capable of handling himself, and while

Ruwen couldn't see his level, he knew it was higher than any of these Brawlers'. The only person in danger here was Ruwen.

He focused on the Fighter again, and more information appeared now that he could see the Brawler better.

Name: *Clapping Brawler, Fighter (Level 4)*
Health: *124*
Mana: *0*
Energy: *98*
Spirit: *0*

As Ruwen snuck up on the Fighter, he debated between using his dagger or staff. The problem with the knife was he had to get closer, and it did less damage. The problem with the staff was he needed room to swing it, and if the chimes sounded when he did, it would give him away. Now that he was closer, he could see there was room to swing the staff.

The dagger did four to eight damage, but the staff did six to twelve. He wasn't strong enough to get any bonuses, and his chance for a critical strike was just over 2%, so he couldn't count on that. But with both *Bleed* and *Backstab* active, he could do up to seventy-two points of damage in one blow with the staff. Over half of the fighter's Health. He wouldn't swing the weapon until necessary, though, because he couldn't count on the staff's chimes triggering the *Distraction* effect.

The counter on his quest was down to four minutes. They were really cutting this close. He didn't have any more time to waste. He took a deep breath and let it out slowly.

Ruwen crept to within ten feet of the level four Clapping Brawler and noticed the Fighter's small size. Ruwen nicknamed him Tiny and felt a little bad about ambushing him. Ruwen carefully raised his staff over his head, preparing to strike Tiny. Focusing on the area behind all the Brawlers in the clearing, he brought the *Distract* icon into his mind along with the desire for a medium-loud sound.

A dull boom made it through the wax stuffed in his ears. Tiny tensed and took a step toward the clearing. Ruwen sprinted at Tiny, the 20% force reduction on his Feather Boots of Grasping helping to make his steps quiet.

As Ruwen brought the Staff of Chimes down, Tiny turned, probably hearing the chimes. The staff smashed into the hollow of Tiny's shoulder and neck and caused him to stumble to the left. Both the *Bleed* and *Backstab* icons appeared above Tiny's head, and his Health dropped by thirty-five. Another two points disappeared every second as the *Bleed* effect took hold.

Ruwen brought the staff down again before Tiny could react, and his Health dropped another ten points. Tiny fell to the ground, and Ruwen knew he'd won. It had been much more straightforward than he'd thought, too. He raised his staff to smash Tiny again but discovered the Fighter aiming three blow-pipes at Ruwen's face.

A dart struck Ruwen's goggles, the needle cracking the glass and making it hard to see. He felt a sharp pinch on his forehead and then his neck. The Poisoned debuff flashed under his bars. He felt a little dizzy, but the heightened resistances from his Cultivation Stage tempered the worst of the poison.

A two flashed every second on Ruwen's Health bar as the poison tried to kill him. Another dart struck his goggles, cracking it even more, and he could no longer see out the right side. Sharp pain in each thigh meant two more darts had found a home. The damage from the poison rose to four per second, and Ruwen staggered a little.

Tiny had a blowpipe in three of his hands and used the fourth to reload darts. That didn't seem fair. Not wanting to get struck again, Ruwen swung his staff at the two-foot blowpipes. He connected with two of them, and they flew out of Tiny's hands.

Tiny brought both feet up and struck Ruwen in the stomach. It only did two points of damage, but it took his wind. He staggered back, gasping through his Scarf of Freshness. Tiny jumped to his feet and pulled a dagger and a whip from his belt.

Ruwen regained most of his breath and faced the Fighter. Tiny brought the blowpipe to his lips, between the jagged yellow teeth, and shot another dart. Ruwen tried to dodge it, but it struck him in the shoulder. He raised his staff to strike Tiny, but before Ruwen could attack, the Fighter flicked his whip up into the trees and used his two free hands to climb. In a blink, Tiny had disappeared into the trees, taking the whip with him.

Activating *Detect Temperature*, Ruwen scanned the trees but didn't see Tiny. Ruwen had lost thirty-seven Health points and had nothing to show for it. He felt a pinch on the back of his neck and pulled a bone needle out of his skin. The Poisoned debuff flashed again, and Ruwen realized Tiny's strategy. The Fighter planned to harass Ruwen from above, slowly poisoning him to death.

Ruwen moved behind a trunk and scanned the tree branches again. He only had two minutes left on his timer, and Sift was probably waiting for Ruwen to start the next phase. A long delay here could jeopardize Sift's safety. He looked out into the clearing, searching for Sift, and gasped.

A crouching man-sized form moved slowly across the far side of the clearing toward the three Brawlers in the middle. Was there another creature here besides the Clapping Brawlers? Whatever it was gave off a lot of heat. Ruwen turned off his *Detect Temperature*, and his normal vision saw nothing but an empty field. When he turned it back on, the red form appeared. It looked to be the same size as Sift. Could that be Sift? If so, how was he doing that?

Then like a puzzle, the pieces fell in place. Sift 'sifted' through the energy that touched him, which included light. Ruwen had assumed Sift absorbed all this energy to power his abilities, but he didn't need to. He could sift through the available energy and let some of it pass through him, unabsorbed. Ruwen's normal vision couldn't see Sift because Sift let the light that touched him pass through his body. Nothing was reflected back to be seen by an observer. But his clothes would still reflect light. Which led to the logical conclusion that once again, Sift had abandoned all or most of his clothes.

Sharp pain on Ruwen's hand made him jerk. He removed another bone needle as the familiar Poisoned debuff appeared, and moved around the tree to put Tiny behind him. Glancing around the trunk, Ruwen searched the branches but couldn't see anyone. Another dart struck his goggles, and they shattered. Small pieces of glass hit his eye, and a five flashed on his Health bar.

Ruwen crouched behind the trunk and removed the goggles. His eyes stung and watered, but after a few seconds, his vision cleared. Looking back into the clearing, he noticed Sift had already climbed the tree containing the Assassin.

The timer on Ruwen's quest read fifty-nine seconds. There was no way he would find Tiny in the trees above him and make it out to destroy that hive in less than a minute. Not finishing this quest meant he might not have enough experience to level, and he didn't know if there would be time to gain more. He doubted his level was high enough to survive Blapy's level four. That left one option. Proceed with the attack on the three Brawlers in the center and come back for Tiny later.

With fifty-five seconds remaining, Ruwen confirmed Sift had made it near the Assassin in the tree. Concentrating on the back of the clearing, Ruwen created another *Distraction*, this one louder than before. All the Clapping Brawlers turned in that direction. Ruwen dashed out of the trees and sprinted toward the group, and the Exploding Burrower Hive hanging from the tree above them.

Ruwen had made it halfway to the tree when the Mage, and

the Chief they'd named Clapper, looked up. Sift and the Assassin battled in the branches. The Mage pointed upward, and a stream of fire surged into the tree. Clapper slapped the Mage and yelled at him. A moment later, the Mage pointed a different wand upward, and ice shot into the tree.

A tiny cloak flashed at the top of his vision, and four areas turned red on the ground between him and the tree. Ruwen slowed to a jog as he processed this new information. They were all roughly square-shaped, and they seemed to be staggered outward from the tree. He realized his Pacifist's Cloak's *Detect Trap* passive ability had triggered, and he slowed to a stop. There were traps all over the clearing.

Ruwen immediately channeled his *Detect Traps* spell. His Energy bar barely moved at the two Energy per second cost. It gave him an extra 10% chance to detect a trap for every minute he studied. He didn't have a minute, but he wanted to take a few seconds to try and find any additional ones. The last thing he needed was to get trapped.

Another two red areas appeared on the ground. The tree was only forty feet away, but there were traps everywhere, and Ruwen's quest counter was down to thirty-five seconds.

A dart struck Ruwen's neck, quickly followed by one to the back of his head. He'd lost almost half his Health to that irritating dart blower. The Mage and Clapper faced Ruwen, and he guessed that Tiny had alerted them to Ruwen's presence. Ruwen wished his ears weren't plugged. Losing his hearing wasn't making this fight any easier. Neither the Mage or Clapper moved toward Ruwen, but the Mage pointed a wand in Ruwen's direction.

The ground vibrated, and Ruwen didn't wait to see what would happen. Channeling *Leap*, he jumped as hard as he could toward the tree. The earth exploded behind him at the same time, helping to propel him forward. He needed to destroy that hive. As he approached the ground, his *Detect Traps* found another trap, right where he would land.

Ruwen struck the ground and immediately fell into a covered hole. His staff flew from his hands as intense pain flared around his right ankle. A twenty flashed on his Health bar as it dropped. The severe pain caused his eyes to water, and he screamed. The pit swallowed him up to the waist, and something had snapped tight around his ankle. He was scared of moving his left foot in case there were more traps in the pit. His quest counter ticked down to twenty-eight seconds.

Clapper and the Mage were staring up at the tree again where Sift and the Assassin still fought. The Mage's earth explosion had aided Ruwen's jump and had put him within twenty feet of the hive. He could see it there, just out of reach. An Exploding Burrower landed on the ground in front of him. It looked up at Ruwen, and he realized he no longer had his goggles on. If that thing made it to his eyes it would dig right into his brain and then explode. The last two days and all his work would be for nothing. The Burrower walked toward him, and his quest counter reached twenty-three seconds. Three more Burrowers flew toward him. Nothing had gone to plan. This had all been a disaster. Worse even than the chickens.

The thought of the chickens from level two and their exploding eggs triggered a burst of activity in Ruwen's head. It felt like his mind had turned to ice as ideas flicked impossibly fast through his thoughts. He latched on to two of them and ripped open his Void Band.

Three Booming Eggs dropped onto the ground in front of Ruwen. He'd only wanted two but didn't have enough control yet to manage that. Thankfully, none of them exploded when they struck the ground. The Exploding Burrower had jumped onto his hand and started crawling up his arm. He tried to ignore his impending death as three Floating Clasper Suckers fell on the Booming Eggs. One landed in the dirt but the other two each stuck to an Egg.

He held his Void Band over one of the Eggs that had a sucker, and Sift's water skin fell on it. Ruwen picked up the waterskin, Clasper Sucker, and Booming Egg sandwich he'd made to see if it would hold together. As the Exploding Burrower reached his shoulder and the quest timer ticked to nineteen seconds, Ruwen threw the waterskin at the tree. He prayed it would be enough to draw the Burrowers away from him and save his life.

The waterskin struck the tree skin first and the Egg didn't explode. Ruwen brushed the Exploding Burrower off his shoulder, but he knew it was over. It would be back in a few seconds, along with the three Burrowers flying toward him.

The waterskin bounced off the tree, fell to the ground, and exploded. Spit water covered the entire area under the tree and much of the trunk. A moment later, screeching made it through the wax in his ears as the Burrowers all flew toward the spit-soaked tree. In seconds, expanded Burrowers covered the entire area beneath the tree. The Mage and Clapper kicked them in frustration.

The quest timer reached fourteen seconds.

Ruwen held his Void Band over the dirt, and the jar of Fire Mucus dropped out. He stuck the Fire Mucus to the Egg with the Clasper Sucker and then threw it as hard as he could at the tree.

The quest timer reached ten seconds.

He hadn't aimed directly at the hive because his Dexterity was far too low to hit it even from this distance. Instead, he had aimed for the branches above it. A second later, the egg exploded, and Fire Mucus sprayed over everything around the tree.

The quest timer reached eight seconds. Unfortunately, it would take five seconds for the Fire Mucus to ignite, leaving only three seconds to destroy the hive. He didn't think that would be enough.

The Mage and Clapper were wiping the Fire Mucus off their faces and glaring at him. The Mage lifted a wand, pointed it at Ruwen, and grinned as fire erupted toward Ruwen. The entire area exploded in flames.

The quest timer reached six seconds.

Ruwen started to open his quest log to see if he'd completed the quest in time when his Energy bar flashed red. Ruwen slammed the Void Band closed. He had to pay closer attention to that. Once again, he had almost killed himself, and now he didn't have much Energy left.

Keen Senses triggered, making his skin prickle, and he twisted his head to see Tiny ten feet away. The Fighter had recovered his blowpipes, but all three were hooked to his belt. Tiny raised two hands above his head and clapped; another hand held a dagger, and the fourth stroked the necklace of hands around its neck.

Tiny stared at him and then laughed. Ruwen assumed that was what the hacking sound meant. Tiny stopped clapping, one hand pointing at Ruwen while the other swung up and down like it was beating the ground.

Tiny spoke, and while Ruwen couldn't hear it, his *Hey You* ability allowed him to read Tiny's lips, or gnashing teeth, in this case.

"You funny. Pretty hands. Look soft," Tiny said as he stepped toward Ruwen.

Ruwen had no idea what the odd behavior meant or why Tiny thought Ruwen funny. Had there been something funny about their fight? He pushed the question to the side and concentrated on surviving.

Trapped as Ruwen was, his options for fighting were limited. A plan occurred to him, but he needed a couple of seconds to set it up. Unfortunately, it required him to be facing Tiny. Ruwen shuffled his left foot around as he turned his body in the pit. When he had almost completely turned around, his left foot triggered another trap, and he groaned in pain. His Health dropped eighteen points.

Still needing to delay Tiny another couple of seconds, Ruwen forced the pain away and focused on communicating with Tiny.

"Fire. Chief need Fighter," Ruwen said.

It didn't come out like he'd formed it in his mind, but that was probably because he thought in his own language, not Tiny's.

Tiny froze and stared at him. "How you speak Clap?"

That was all the delay Ruwen had needed, as he retrieved the Fastidious Dagger from his belt. He raised the blade above his head and gently threw it over the Fighter. Tiny watched as it arced over his head and landed behind him.

Tiny turned back to Ruwen. "You worst fighter ever come."

"Me know. Me working on it," Ruwen said.

Tiny moved toward him again, and Ruwen waited until only a few feet separated them. Then he raised his hand until it was chest high on Tiny, focused on the Fastidious Dagger, and pictured the icon for *Retrieve*.

Tiny smiled, clapped two of his hands, and took a step forward. The Fastidious Dagger struck him in the back, triggering *Bleed* and *Backstab* as it tore through Tiny's body on its way back to Ruwen. Tiny's Health dropped by forty-one, and he collapsed forward in pain.

The vibrating dagger flew toward Ruwen's hand. He tried catching it, but his low Dexterity made that almost impossible. Instead of snatching it from the air, it impaled his outstretched hand. He screamed as his Health dropped twelve points. Making it worse, the dagger, coated in Tiny's and Ruwen's blood, vibrated at an alarming rate as it tried to clean itself.

Ruwen pulled the dagger from his hand and immediately

cast *Bleed* and *Backstab* on it. It took two seconds and seventy-five Mana. Ruwen hoped he'd been quick enough.

Tiny had collapsed in shock from the blade ripping through his body, and only had twenty-five Health points left. Ruwen, trapped in the pit, couldn't do the *Retrieve* trick again because of the minute cooldown. That meant he had to quickly end this.

Ruwen tried to pick up the dagger with his uninjured hand, but its frantic vibrations made it impossible to hold. Using both hands, he gripped the blade and quickly slammed it into Tiny's back. Ruwen left the dagger there, vibrating madly, and leaned back. The information above Tiny's head turned grey, and all the values fell to zero.

Ruwen tried to turn himself around, but with both ankles trapped, he couldn't move. He twisted his neck around to see how Sift was doing. The tree had caught fire, and he could feel the heat from it on his face. He immediately turned off *Detect Temperature* as it hurt to look at such a massive blaze with it on. With his normal vision returned, he gasped at how far the fire had spread. Almost the entire clearing behind him burned.

The Mage lay on the ground, a wand in each ear and in both eyes. His information was grey. A body hung from the branches, completely engulfed in flames. The fire made it impossible to read the Assassin's stats, but since his whole body was on fire, Ruwen put him in the dead category as well.

Clapper still had one hundred and nineteen Health points but seemed more interested in getting out of the fire than fighting Sift. But Sift, most of his body on fire, kept Clapper under the tree. The Chief had lost his weapons and fought with his hands. Sift didn't seem to mind that his opponent had four arms. Clapper spent fifteen seconds throwing everything he had at Sift, but the young man moved between the punches like water over a rock. Only once did Sift have to use his hand to redirect a blow.

Sift signaled to him. *Done?*

Surprised that Sift could talk while fighting, Ruwen signed back. *Yes.*

Sift stepped forward and snapped Clapper's neck. The Chief Clapping Brawler went limp, and his information turned grey.

Sift signed. *Remove. Wax.*

Safe?

Sift gestured at the gigantic fire. Ruwen pulled the wax out of his ears and pulled the scarf off his nose and mouth.

Flames covered most of Sift's body, and Ruwen had to squint to look at him.

"You could have helped me this entire time and didn't?" Ruwen yelled.

"You have to significantly participate in the level to get any experience. Blapy doesn't like power leveling, and killing Shriekers doesn't count. When I saw the little Fighter was still alive, I couldn't risk intervening. If I had, Blapy might have materialized something really dangerous in here to teach me a lesson. And in case you forgot, I don't get a second chance."

Ruwen hadn't forgotten, and it made him feel bad for accusing Sift. It didn't surprise him that Blapy didn't like power leveling. Dungeons were supposed to be dangerous, and everyone needed to be at risk.

Ruwen opened his Void Band and then grabbed the sole remaining Floating Clasper Sucker by its edge and removed the grass. He dropped it in the Void Band, carefully added the Booming Egg, and then closed his Void Band.

A pair of underwear appeared on the ground between them, followed by a mound of gold coins, and then a spear with a black shaft and a tip that looked like glowing quartz.

"Great, your fire must have burned my clothes. How does she always know when I'm out of underwear?" Sift asked.

"You're naked under those flames? You have a real problem."

"Listen, I can't be invisible with them on. What would you

do if you saw a floating pair of underwear? That's hard to ignore."

Ruwen didn't answer. Instead, he pulled a pair of underwear from his Void Band, balled them up, and threw them at Sift.

"Thanks!" Sift said, holding them away from his burning legs and chest.

"Wash those before you give them back."

A leather bag appeared next to the gold mound of Sift's treasure.

"Well, it looks like she thought you did enough," Sift said. "Hey, did you complete that quest in time?"

The quest. Had he completed the quest? His stomach turned with anxiety as he opened his notifications.

CHAPTER 34

*T*he first notification was for his staff skill increasing.

Shing!
You have advanced a skill!
***Skill:** Staff*
***Level:** 4*
***Effect:** Increase damage by 2.0%.*

The next one was for his dagger skill.

Shing!
You have advanced a skill!
***Skill:** Dagger*
***Level:** 2*
***Effect:** Increase damage by 1.0%.*

His anxiety growing, he opened the next one.

Ting!

You have completed the Black Pyramid Quest – Lend a Hand
(Level 3).
You have received 15 Black Pyramid tokens
You have received 1,250 experience.

Relief flooded through him. With a grin, he opened the final notification.

Ding!
Uru's Blessings, Worker! You have reached level 5.
You have gained +1 to Strength!
You have gained +1 to Stamina!
You have 2 unassigned points.
Uru's Blessings, Root! You have reached level 5.
You have 2 unassigned points.
New Spells and Abilities are available to you. Choose wisely.

He'd done it. The fear of failure drained out of him, and his hands shook.

"Are you okay?" Sift asked as he knelt in front of the pit.

"I made it. I'm level five."

"Gratz, my friend. You really know how to cut it close."

"I don't do it on purpose, believe me."

"Let's get you out of that trap."

Ruwen held up two fingers. "Traps. There's one on each ankle."

Sift shook his head and started clearing the top of the trap away. Ruwen couldn't help because it hurt to move, so he opened his log to see how much experience he'd gained.

The Exploding Burrowers were each worth around 79 experience. But he was only getting 17 of that because of Sift took 78% of it. Between the five hives though, he had killed 137 of them, and that added up. But he'd gotten the experience all at once, right after the last hive had been destroyed. Each Exploding Burrower death was in his log, but the experience said 'Deferred' and that the hives were part of a 'Nest.' In fact, it looked like if he hadn't destroyed the last hive, he wouldn't have gotten any experience at all. Thankfully, the fifth hive had granted him two thousand three hundred twenty-nine experience and put him at nine thousand eight hundred eighty-seven of ten thousand. The quest had added another one thousand two hundred fifty and leveled him.

The last part of the log had more of the deferred verbiage.

A Clapping Brawler, Fighter (Level 6) has died!
You have gained 175 (795*(22% level modifier)) experience!
<Deferred>
< Clapping Brawler, Fighter (Level 6) is a member of a War Party (1 of 5)>

The Assassin and the Mage had similar entries. He found where he'd killed the Fighter.

You have killed a Clapping Brawler, Fighter (Level 4)!
You have gained 39 (176*(22% level modifier)) experience! <Deferred>
< Clapping Brawler, Fighter (Level 4) is a member of a War Party (4 of 5)>
A Clapping Brawler, Chief (Level 7) has died!
You have gained 234 (1,063*(22% level modifier)) experience!
<Deferred>
< Clapping Brawler, Chief (Level 7) is a member of a War Party (5 of 5)>
A War Party has been destroyed!
You have gained 555 (2,524 *(22% level modifier)) deferred experience!

It appeared that the five Clapping Brawlers were part of a group, and you only got experience if you killed them all.

That disappointed him. He had thought about farming the Exploding Burrowers for the experience. Most people who came to fight in Blapy were high enough level that the two thousand three hundred experience on level three wasn't worth the two hours. For him though, especially if he could do it himself and avoid the power-level penalty, that experience would catapult him in levels. But if the last hive was always above the Clappers, which he suspected would be the case, he couldn't do it by himself.

It did explain why he hadn't gotten experience from killing Naktos's servant in the park in Deepwell. The Mage must have been part of the larger group trying to kill him. It didn't explain why the deferred message didn't appear in his log though. Maybe parties made from people differed from those of monsters. He'd ask Ky about it.

Ruwen closed the log.

Sift had cleared the area around Ruwen, and he looked down at what had latched onto his feet. Sharpened branches from the trees around them had been fashioned into traps resembling open mouths, and he had stepped into two of them.

"Why didn't you tell me about the traps?" Ruwen asked.

"They're new and so was the Assassin. Blapy must have really wanted us dead. Or she is warning us about our level difference."

"I'm going with dead."

"That Assassin was especially nasty. This area is too big for me to sift well, and that Assassin would have ambushed me. I'm too relaxed in these early levels. Good job spotting him."

Sift's offhand praise made Ruwen feel good. He belonged in a library, not fighting dungeon monsters, and being barely helpful in these levels was hard for him. It also said a lot about Sift that he admitted to missing the Assassin's presence.

Sift walked over and picked up the Staff of Chimes where it had landed when Ruwen fell into the trap. He spun the weapon in a fast circle, and the chimes sounded as if they were in a howling wind.

"You do understand weapons work better when you hold them," Sift asked.

Ruwen glared at him.

Sift spun the staff behind his back. "Because you are either dropping them or purposefully missing enemies with them."

"Hey! That was planned."

Sift walked back to Ruwen. "Another thing. Your plans are terrible."

"It worked!"

"My favorite part was when you caught your dagger."

Ruwen's cheeks grew warm. "Well, that part could have gone better."

Sift smiled. "It was actually really clever. Except for stabbing yourself."

"Thanks."

"So were your bombs. Overkill to use the entire jar of Spitter snot, but I'm guessing you didn't know how powerful it was."

"And I didn't have much time."

Sift stabbed the staff down into the pit and triggered each of the remaining traps. Once they were all sprung, he jumped down and pried open the traps that held Ruwen.

Ruwen pulled himself out of the hole and rubbed his ankles. Sift handed him back his staff.

"Since you leveled, we'll spend the rest of the day doing Step work," Sift said.

Ruwen nodded, stood, and put the staff back in its harness. He walked over to the leather bag, knelt, and dumped it out. A ring, a green shirt, and a pair of green pants tumbled out. The ring's silver band had tiny Exploding Burrowers surrounding it, each of their wings colored an iridescent pink. He picked it up and opened up the notification.

Tring!
The Black Pyramid has rewarded you...
Name: *Ring of Exploding Regeneration*
Quality: *Fine*
Durability: *18 of 18*
Weight: *0.1 lbs.*
Effect (Passive): *+1 to Health, Mana, and Energy every second.*
Description: *The power of the hive has burrowed into your Regeneration pools. Don't let your tiny pools keep you down. It's not the size of your pools that matter, it's how you use them.*

His Rock Serpent Ring of Health was on his right hand, so he slipped this ring on his left next to the Jaga Wedding Band. Just like before, the ring shrunk until it fit snuggly on his finger.

He opened his Profile and looked at the Regeneration section.

Health Regen: *1.31*
Mana Regen: *1.45*
Energy Regen: *3.60*

The +1 made a gigantic impact on his Regeneration rates. Even with the Health ring, his Health pool was the smallest of the three, and it received the largest benefit from this new ring. With a 1.31 per second Regen rate, he would go from empty to full in just under two minutes! Before it would have taken eight minutes. This benefit would taper off as he gained more levels, but right now, it made a huge difference.

He closed the Profile and looked down at the bright green long-sleeved shirt. It had four handprints, shaped like a flower, in the middle of the chest. The softness of the cloth surprised him.

Tring!
The Black Pyramid has rewarded you...
Name: *Clapper Skin Undershirt*
Armor Class: *25*
Quality: *Uncommon*
Durability: *50 of 50*
Weight: *2 lbs.*
Effect (Passive): *Repel Exploding Burrowers.*
Effect (Triggered): *Shirt will halve bleed effects up to 4 times per day.*
Description: *Will apply direct pressure on a bleeding wound. Perfect for those who could use a helping hand. You need four.*

He whistled when he saw the AC of the shirt. Then he realized what he'd done and looked up at Sift. Sift glared at him.

"Sorry," Ruwen said.

"What was so good?" Sift asked.

"The AC on this shirt is twenty-five. That's a lot of protection for underwear. I scanned the Worker abilities, and it doesn't look like they get any proficiencies in Armor. Not even leather."

"What about your Observer ones?"

"There was a leather one there. But I'm supposed to be a Worker. I really can't be seen wearing leather without causing suspicion."

"That makes sense. Once you get some Cultivation training, you won't need armor."

Ruwen's stomach turned at the mention of the mysterious power inside him. "Well, I don't see that happening any time soon."

He picked up the pants. They were called Clapper Skin Long Underwear and had the same bright green color as the shirt. They didn't have the hand-flower imprint and lacked the triggered effect to halve bleeding. They still resisted Exploding Burrowers and had the same excellent AC of twenty-five.

The two items tripled his Armor Class, but that was mostly because he only had two pieces with AC to begin with. His boots had five and his cloak ten. This would provide some sorely needed protection.

"Do you think they're really made from Clapper skin? That's kind of gross," Ruwen said.

Sift rubbed his hand over the shirt. "But softer than I'd imagined."

"Yeah, it does feel comfortable."

"Well, they wouldn't think twice about wearing your hands as a necklace. Shade's first rule: you die how you live."

"So you'll die naked," Ruwen said as he stood.

Sift punched Ruwen in the shoulder. "It's never my fault!"

They laughed as Sift led them to his charred clothing. He retrieved his Traveler's Belt and removed Io. Io must have made fun of Sift's lack of clothes because Sift explained again how it wasn't his fault. The tree still burned, but the grass had already turned to ash, and they made it to the exit safely. When Ruwen entered the tunnel, his wrist turned cold just like before. He looked down to see the Black Pyramid mark with a three under it.

Ruwen touched his wrist to the rock wall. "Naked's room."

A smoky grey rectangle appeared.

Sift shook his head. "That is so dangerous. That portal could go anywhere." Sift's eyes widened. "What if you walked in on a naked Fluffy. Oh, I dare you to walk through it."

Ruwen hadn't thought a door would appear. He'd just been making a joke. The thought of a naked Fluffy terrified him.

Sift narrowed his eyes. "If you stand there much longer, you're going to lay an egg."

"Are you calling me a chicken?"

"Shade's first rule –"

Ruwen held up his hands. "Stop!"

Ruwen took a deep breath and then another. *Please for the*

love of Uru don't let there be a naked Fluffy on the other side of this portal.

Sift put his hands in his armpits and flapped his arms.

Ruwen stepped through the portal.

CHAPTER 35

uwen stepped into the hallway in front of Sift's room, and relief flooded him. A moment later, Sift appeared out of another portal and looked disappointed when he saw Ruwen.

Ruwen grinned. "See, even Blapy knows."

Sift shook his head. "It's never my fault."

Laughing, they walked into their room.

Ruwen spent the next three hours alternating between cramping muscles and frustration. Sift was supposed to be teaching him Steps, but instead, Ruwen just squatted in place and did a simple block and punch over and over again. At first, he wondered if Sift was upset with Ruwen's joking and was punishing him. But it only took a moment of thought to realize Sift wasn't that type of person.

"Isn't this called *Step* training?" Ruwen asked.

Sift squatted across from Ruwen, doing the same block and punch. "Infants must learn to crawl before they can take their first step." Sift smiled. "And imagine how hard it will be for a fish."

Ruwen narrowed his eyes. "Are you calling me a fish?"

"No, probably more like a snail. It matches your speed."

"Hey!"

Sift laughed. "You're doing fine. It took me –"

Sift suddenly stopped talking. A heartbeat later, Sift leaned forward while kicking backward with his right leg. Ky appeared out of thin air, stepped to the side, and grabbed Sift's leg, twisting it. Sift turned his body to keep his leg from snapping and aimed his left foot at Ky's head.

Ky let go of Sift's leg and crouched, letting the kick go over her head. She punched at Sift's exposed back, but the young man continued his twist and did a half cartwheel to end up on his feet.

"Glad you're back, Mistress," Sift said.

"You let me get too close," Ky said.

"I know."

Ky lashed out with a right jab to Sift's chest. Sift trapped her hand against his chest and used his other hand to grab her elbow. Ky quickly stepped forward and swept Sift's feet. Sift released Ky and used his free hands to break his fall and maneuver away from Ky.

Ruwen had been on the losing side of a few fights and watched many others. The fighters usually had their hands up to protect their face. Ky and Sift stood a few feet apart from each other with their arms at their sides. They both looked relaxed.

"Why did it take you so long to sense me?" Ky asked.

"I guess because I was focused on Ruwen, and I felt safe in here," Sift said.

"You know better. Shade's first rule: there is no safety."

"I know. I will do better," Sift said.

"We cross the Blood Gate in a couple of hours. You're better prepared than most for the dangers there, but we can't treat this like a vacation," Ky said and then looked at Ruwen. "Hey, kid. How was the dungeon?"

Sift took Ky's shift in attention as an opportunity to step forward and reach for Ky's neck. Ky slapped his hand away and punched at Sift's face. Sift stepped to the side to avoid the blow and brought his hand down on Ky's arm, quickly twisting and then bending forward. Ky flew forward, but instead of landing on her face, she tucked into a ball and did a somersault. In a few heartbeats, the two stood facing each other again. Ruwen couldn't believe how fast everything happened.

"Your parents brought him into the Clan," Ky said. "You are his Sisen?"

"Yes, as a condition for my advancement," Sift said.

"I'm relieved. I didn't know how they'd react to him. Especially after hearing of our deal and the danger he poses." Ky looked at Ruwen again. "Your odds of surviving just increased dramatically. Maybe even to 10%," she said with a smile.

Ruwen's stomach turned. "That's a joke, right?"

"I wish you could have seen him fighting the chickens on two," Sift said.

"I did. Blapy gave me the memory as soon as I returned. It's a Pyramid favorite. She said the chickens have been really strutting around with all the attention."

Ruwen's brow furrowed. "Wait, what? What is a Pyramid favorite?"

Ky bowed to Sift, and he returned it. She held out her fist, and Sift placed his hand on top.

Ky turned to Ruwen. "This is Blapy's kingdom. When you kill something, she brings it back, and they keep their memories. She keeps a library of all the best memories the monsters can replay whenever they want. It's entertainment for them. Usually, the popular memories are of adventurers dying gruesomely."

"The monsters are watching my fights?" Ruwen asked.

Ruwen remembered the odd behavior of Tiny as he approached Ruwen in the pit. It hadn't made sense at the time, but now it was crystal clear. Tiny had been making fun of Ruwen's attempt to kill the chickens. Ruwen's cheeks grew hot.

"Can Blapy share that with others? I'd love to show my parents," Sift said.

"Hey!" Ruwen cried.

Ky looked thoughtful. "I'm not sure. I've never asked her. I wonder if she could display them somehow in the rec rooms?"

"Let me see," Blapy said.

Ruwen jumped at the new voice. Blapy sat on his bed, her stuffed centipede resting on his pillow. A round crystal the size of his arm appeared in the middle of the room. It floated and pulsed with different colors of light.

"Hmm, that's not working. I'll keep at it in my research lab while I finish up here," Blapy said.

The cute little girl made him forget that Blapy was actually an immensely powerful being. As she talked to them, she would be doing a hundred other things at the same time. Opening portals, rebuilding levels, making new levels, handling the alchemy lab, managing the thousands of monsters here, and creating a tool to display his not-so-proud moments. Ruwen's shoulders slumped.

"Why so glum?" Blapy asked Ruwen.

"I'm just embarrassed," Ruwen said.

Blapy nodded. "Well, you should be. But you should also feel good. The early levels are rarely cleared. Even Sift ignores the chickens. It's been over a thousand years since those chickens have put anyone in danger. Your lengthy...battle...has reminded them of their purpose, and that as small as their contributions are, they matter."

Blapy's comments were eerily close to the worthlessness Ruwen had felt when fighting next to Sift. How perceptive was Blapy?

"Are you calling me a chicken?" Ruwen asked.

Blapy smiled at him and then turned to Sift. "I want you to

know I was this close," Blapy held her thumb and finger together, "to porting him into Fluffy's shower. He was even in it at the time."

Sift groaned. "You should have! That would have been hilarious!"

Blapy nodded. "Three thousand years ago...maybe, but maturity has made me value good working relationships. Fluffy would blame me, not you two idiots, and I like our quartermaster's efficiency. I'd hate to lose him."

"Agreed. Fluffy is more valuable than both of you nitwits," Ky said.

Blapy hopped off the bed, walked to Sift, and looked up at him. "Ky told me you're going on a trip."

Sift nodded and tried not to grin. "She's taking me through the Blood Gate."

"I've enjoyed trying to kill you, and wanted to give you a going away present," Blapy said.

Sift narrowed his eyes. "Will this mean you win?"

Blapy stomped her foot. "No. This is a gift, not loot."

Blapy pointed to the bed, and a long shirt, loose pants, underwear, and soft shoes appeared there. They were light brown and looked thin.

"Those look like Step clothes," Sift said.

Ky cleared her throat. "I asked her to find a solution to your naked problem. You can't run around naked over there."

Sift's cheeks turned red. "It's not like I want to be naked. Blapy is always trying to kill me, and my clothes get in the way."

"Exactly," Ky said. "Blapy is gifting you with something you'd need to go a hundred levels deeper to earn yourself. She is doing this on her own, as there are simpler solutions."

Sift looked down at Blapy. "Really?"

Blapy nodded. "I want you both to come back. You two could be incredibly powerful, more than you realize, and I want the chance to kill you. The lower levels are almost as bad as the upper ones, and my monsters are bored."

"That is almost sweet," Sift said, walking over to the clothes. He picked up the shirt, and his eyes unfocused as he read the notification. He looked at Blapy. "What does Harvester mean?"

Ruwen perked up at the question. The book he'd found in the library had used that word.

Ky answered. "It is an older term. People call them Cultivators now."

"Their name, like their mindset, keeps them caged and weak," Blapy said.

"But I can't Cultivate," Sift said.

The shirt burst into flame, engulfing Sift's hands. Sift held the blaze away from himself to keep from burning his clothes. After a few seconds, the flames disappeared. The shirt looked untouched. Ice formed on Sift's hands, and the air grew cold in the room. Sift moved the shirt, and it seemed completely unaffected by the frigid temperature.

"How?" Sift asked.

Blapy sighed. "It makes me sad how far the world has fallen."

"Some believe leaving rampant chaos and unending war in the past is progress," Ky said.

"Nonsense. Nothing interesting ever comes from peace," Blapy said.

"The shirt?" Sift asked again.

Blapy pointed to the shirt. "Harvesters would gather so much energy they would make the area around their body unstable. They needed clothes that would survive that, and not impede the energy's absorption by their body. Your needs are similar."

"It's the opposite of armor," Ky said. "It lets everything pass through it. Hammer blows, fire, chaos bolts, punches, all of it will transfer directly to your body. It is useless or priceless, depending on the owner."

Blapy nodded. "Ky is right. I'll just add that these reflect a tiny portion of the light spectrum to give them color and provide some privacy. You can change the color with a thought once you're wearing it."

Sift's eyes glistened. "Thanks, Blapy. This is the best gift ever."

"I'm doing it for the people of the universe. None of them should be subjected to your nakedness," Blapy said with a smile.

"One other thing," Ky said. "I asked Blapy to make a chest tattoo for you. We are going to be traveling with a large group, and you'll stand out if you aren't Ascended."

Blapy held up a small paper with a black snake on it. "This tattoo will make you appear as one of Uru's Ascended Fighters. It should mask your true nature from most people."

"Why didn't I just do that instead of almost dying multiple times in here?" Ruwen asked.

"This will only work because Sift isn't Ascended. Not even Blapy can mask your nature once you're Ascended," Ky said.

Blapy locked eyes with Ruwen. "Yes, hiding something like that would truly take divine power."

Ruwen rubbed his stomach and the birthmark there. "I see."

"How long will it last?" Sift asked.

"I'll remove it when you get back," Blapy said.

Sift removed his shirt, and Ky handed him the tattoo. He pressed it to his chest and then gasped.

A thick snake with indigo scales wrapped around Sift's torso. The head appeared on his right shoulder, mouth wide, ivory fangs glistening with venom. It looked so real Ruwen took a step backward.

"I thought you wanted him to keep his clothes on. He'll never put a shirt on now," Ruwen said.

"Is it awesome? Show me, please," Sift bounced on his feet.

A full-length mirror appeared in front of Sift. He took a step toward it and ran a hand over the snake's head. He traced the coil as it wrapped the front of his body.

"Blapy...this is...I mean...you really," Sift was quiet for a few seconds. "I love it."

Ruwen saw Ky give Blapy a wink.

"Well, I'm glad it's okay. It's just something I made last minute. Nothing like the thought I put in the tattoos you leave uncollected in my dungeon."

Sift's eyes grew wide, and Blapy grinned.

Sift's name floated above his head now, and Ruwen focused on him to see what else appeared.

Name: *Sift Whistler*
Age: *17*
Class: *Fighter*
Sub Class: *Unarmed*
Class Rank: *Initiate*
Level: *10*
Health: *210*
Mana: *120*
Energy: *453*

Sift's attributes were listed as well, but Ruwen skimmed them since he knew they were fake. He chuckled at the last name. Blapy just couldn't resist poking people. The little girl, as if knowing he had thought her name, faced him.

"Your turn," Blapy said.

"Me? You didn't need to get me anything," Ruwen said.

"I know," Blapy said, and then pointed to Ruwen's bed. His cloak lay across it, and he noticed the hole had been fixed.

"Thanks for mending my cloak," Ruwen said.

Blapy nodded. "I gave it a hood, so you have something to protect the rocks in your head, and added a couple other things as well."

"That is awesome," Ruwen said as he walked over and picked it up.

Tring!
The Black Pyramid has gifted you...
Name: *Hooded Pacifist's Cloak of Wandering*
AC: *25*
Quality: *Special*
Durability: *50 of 50*
Weight: *1.0 lbs.*
Effect (Passive): *10% Perception, 10% Detect Traps.*
Effect (Passive): *Everything within 50 feet is immune to Location magic.*
Effect (Passive): *Hood enhances all senses by 10%.*
Effect (Triggered): *Once per day can harden into a 150 hit point shield.*
Restriction: *Weapons of any kind are prohibited.*
Description: *Why can't we all just get along?*

The cloak had been great before, but now it was fantastic. The problem with hoods is they blocked your vision and impaired your hearing. But this cloak actually enhanced them. And, as the number of people who wanted to kill him increased, not being able to locate him with magic would be a real plus. The increase to Armor Class and the shield were welcome as well. This was indeed a special cloak.

"Hey! There's a sheath built into these pants. Is that for Io?" Sift asked.

"You shouldn't indulge him," Ky said to Blapy.

Blapy shrugged. "It makes them both happy. Call me sentimental."

Ky faced Ruwen and sighed. "So, against my better judgment, I've agreed to Blapy's other gift. We will need to discuss the rules before you use it, but Blapy has a compelling argument for you having it."

Ruwen turned back to Blapy, who held a black rock about the size and shape of his finger. It looked very similar to the one Ky had used to draw the door that brought them here. His hand shook as he took the rock from Blapy. He immediately opened the notification.

Tring!
The Black Pyramid has gifted you...
Name: *Portal Chalk of Blood*
Quality: *Epic*
Durability: *5 of 5*
Weight: *0.5 lbs.*
Effect: *(Active): Create a connection with the Blood Gate.*
Restriction: *User must bear the mark of the Black Pyramid.*
Description: *Not every door should be entered.*

Ruwen gasped. This gave him the ability to come back here.

"Thank you," Ruwen said.

"Ky will show you how it works," Blapy said.

Blapy glanced over at Ky and Sift. Sift was showing her how Io fit perfectly in the sheath.

"Sift has spent his whole life here, and more time in the dungeon than almost anyone. I'd be sad if someone other than me killed him. You understand?" Blapy asked.

Ruwen didn't, but he nodded.

"Good, because I'll blame you if something happens to him," Blapy said and then in a louder voice, "I did it."

"Did what?" Sift asked.

A grey portal appeared on the wall, but instead of being shaped like a door, it looked like a window. The grey faded, and colors emerged.

"Oh, no," Ruwen said.

Sift and Ky laughed as the window portal showed Ruwen chasing the chickens around swinging his staff, but it only lasted a few seconds before a very young-looking Ky appeared.

"Oh, no," Ky said.

The young Ky lifted her dagger and prepared to attack a large grey mushroom. As she moved to strike, she tripped on a rock and landed face first behind the fungus. Sift burst out laughing, and Ruwen couldn't hide a smile.

The pictures changed again, and this time Sift came into focus.

"Oh, no," Sift said.

In a quickly moving montage, Sift battled different monsters but always ended up covered in something destructive: fire, acid, lightning, more fire, some kind of whirling bladed tree, and more fire. In every instance, Sift ended up naked.

Blapy looked pleased with herself.

Ky shook her head and muttered. "Shade's first rule: karma is an echo, and it speaks your name."

CHAPTER 36

*R*uwen followed Ky and Sift as they walked toward the Blood Gate. Blapy didn't allow portals to that area for security reasons. They'd eaten dinner with Sift's parents, but most of the discussion had centered on Sift and travel advice. No one brought up Ruwen's Cultivation incident.

He asked Ky something he'd wondered since coming here. "Why does Blapy need you?"

Ky looked at him and raised an eyebrow.

Ruwen flushed. "Sorry, that came out wrong. I just don't understand the relationship."

Ky nodded. "Adventurers from all over our world want to come here. Blapy has the best loot, hardest challenges, and gives the most experience of any dungeon. The issue is getting here. That's where I come in."

"Blapy can't get them herself?" Ruwen asked.

"Blapy can't leave here. Trapped isn't the right word...more like bound. So, I'm like her face in our world. I feed the beast."

"You bring people here?" Ruwen asked.

"Yes, many. There are over twenty parties in Blapy's depths right now," Ky said.

"But I never saw anyone," Ruwen said.

Ky shook her head. "The top levels are mine, and you need my mark. Those parties can't come up. They can only go down or exit."

"How does that benefit you?" Ruwen asked.

"That is a good question, my young Spy," Ky said. "Blapy obviously gets entertainment and new items to clone. I have the most secure hideout in the world, and the price for entry into Blapy is usually information. Blapy and I both love what we shouldn't have. It cements our relationship, I think. But there are powerful items in the world that people know how to keep from us. Blapy and I both want them. Shade's first rule: goals are like air."

"That's another thing, why are all the rules number one?" Ruwen asked.

Ky smiled. "Shade's first rule: there's no second rule."

Ruwen waited a few seconds. "Okay, that didn't help."

"It means all the rules are important. Ignoring any of them might cause disaster," Sift said.

Ky nodded at Sift.

They walked in silence for a few steps and then Ruwen opened his mouth to ask another question.

"Stop!" Ky said. "You *are* worse than Tremine. You're like some kind of information sponge. Let's finalize your build before we cross over. How much did you leave unspent?"

"I have four attribute points from reaching level five, and I still have my spell and ability points from levels four and five," Ruwen said.

"An odd and an even level is three spells for each Class, which means you have six spell points and four ability points to allocate?" Ky asked.

"Yes."

"Good. For your attributes, increase your Dexterity at least once per level. Preferably twice. Are there any abilities you desperately want?" Ky asked.

Ruwen immediately thought of the last two levels of *Hey You*. He knew that wasn't critical though, so he just shook his head.

"Excellent. My recommendation is two points in *Fade* and two in *Fabricate*. For *Fabricate* make yourself appear to be a level two Worker. That is so close to the truth that it will fool everyone. As you advance in levels, you'll need to increase the level of *Fabricate* to keep the illusion. *Fade* is probably good at level two. If that gets too high even your friends forget you."

"Do me a favor and stick them all in *Fade*," Sift said.

Ruwen punched him in the shoulder and Sift laughed.

Sift wore his new Harvester outfit, and he'd changed the color to black. His Dimensional Belt was wrapped around his waist, and Io fit snugly in the hidden sheath on Sift's right hip. Sift hadn't stopped smiling since he'd left dinner. Ruwen wore his new protective underwear beneath his Worker garb along with his improved cloak. The staff he'd placed in his Void Band. The weapon would be too hard to explain. The Fastidious Blade, however, sat on his right hip, opposite his Worker's Baton.

Ky continued. "I don't have any advice yet on your spells. Once I have enough information about where Big D is taking us, and who else has arrived to kill you, I might have some thoughts."

"Wait, how many people want to kill me?" Ruwen asked.

"Naktos's servants already tried and at least two are still around. All the excitement in Deepwell will not go unnoticed by the other deities. The gods that border us will for sure send some spies to investigate. More distant gods will too. You mustn't draw attention to yourself."

Ruwen's throat constricted, making it hard to swallow. "Okay."

"So, keep a couple of spell points just in case. We need to

keep leveling you, too, or you won't survive long. We can talk about that after we're on our way," Ky said.

"You're coming with us?" Sift asked.

Ky shrugged. "I'll be watching for others who are watching. Don't depend on me for help. At this point, it's safer for you to die again than for me to reveal myself by aiding you."

Ruwen's stomach clenched.

Ky looked at Sift. "Same goes for you."

"I can protect myself," Sift said.

"You two are both idiots," Ky said. "I meant don't help Ruwen if he's attacked. Follow his killers back to their nest. That way, we get them all."

"What if it's the blue beam thing from the Naktos Mage?" Ruwen asked. "Tremine said that would have trapped me, not killed me."

"You got attacked by a Naktos Soul Mage?" Sift asked.

"You know what that is?" Ruwen asked.

"Both of you shut up. You can swap stories and do your hair later. But that is a valid point about the binding magic." Ky faced Sift. "If it looks like anyone is channeling a spell on Ruwen, it's okay to kill them."

Ruwen had felt better about his trip with Big D knowing Ky and Sift would be there. But most of that optimism had just disappeared. They wanted to find everyone trying to kill him, not just a single Assassin, which made him happy. The cost, however, might be his life, which didn't. His shoulders slumped.

"Did you dump all your Spirit?" Ky asked.

Ruwen opened his mouth to respond when he realized Ky had been talking to Sift.

"Yes," Sift said.

"Remember to get rid of any Energy you sift right away. You're not trained to mask it, and you'll look like a beacon to anyone with Cultivation training. The last thing we want is attention." Ky said.

Sift nodded.

Ky didn't look at Ruwen, but he wondered if she'd been talking to him as well. Like Sift, Ruwen didn't know how to mask his Spirit. If something happened to his birthmark-tattoo, he might be in trouble.

They entered the cavern where Sift had poisoned Ruwen. That felt like weeks ago, but it had been less than two days. Ruwen opened up his Profile and added two of his four attribute points to Dexterity. His Wisdom, with the Staff of Chimes bonus, was still only eleven. If he died, he would wake up with the *Foolish* debuff again. He didn't want that, so he added one more to Wisdom.

That left one point. Ruwen knew the right thing to do was place it in Dexterity, but he'd already added two there. Leveling twice and not putting anything in Intelligence hurt. His Intelligence had been part of his identity for a long time, and seeing it lose ground to all the things he never cared about, like Strength and Stamina, made him sad. He just hadn't come to grips with his new Class yet. Dreaming for years of becoming a Mage didn't disappear overnight, so he added the last point to Intelligence.

The attribute points distributed, he looked through his Profile to see how far he'd come in the two days he'd been here.

General

Name: *Ruwen Starfield*
Race: *Human*
Age: *16*
Class: *Worker*
Hidden Class: *Root (Observer)*
Level: *5*
Class Rank: *Novice*
Cultivation Stage: *19*
Cultivation Rank: *Initiate*

Deaths: 2
Deity: Goddess Uru
Experience: 1,692/15,000

Marks
Black Pyramid: Novice
Bamboo Viper Clan: Novice

Pools
Health: 155/155
Mana: 190/190
Energy: 273/273
Spirit: 352,164

Attributes
Strength: 13
Stamina: 13
Dexterity: 15
Intelligence: 19
Wisdom: 12
Charisma: 12

Ratings
Knowledge: 37
Armor Class: 82
Max Encumbrance: 195
Critical Chance %: 2.50%
Power Strike %: 2.60%
Haste %: 3.00%
Dodge %: 5.00%
Persuasion %: 6.90%
Resilience %: 14.50%
Endurance %: 2.60%
Cleverness %: 39.90%

Perception %: 32.40%

Resistances
Elemental Resistance %: *16.50%*
Poison Resistance %: *16.50%*
Acid Resistance %: *16.50%*
Mind Resistance %: *16.50%*
Order Resistance %: *16.50%*
Chaos Resistance %: *12.50%*
Disease Resistance %: *16.50%*
Light Resistance %: *16.50%*
Dark Resistance %: *14.50%*

Regeneration
Health Regeneration per second: *1.31*
Mana Regeneration per second: *1.48*
Energy Regeneration per second: *3.73*

He closed his Profile, happy with the progress he'd made. Removing the Observer textbook from his Void Band, he looked up the symbols for *Fade* and *Fabricate*. He memorized the symbols and then put the book away.

They turned down a familiar dim hallway, and Ruwen concentrated on the symbol for *Fade*, which was an eye that slowly faded until a third of it was barely visible. It took over ten seconds to feel a tension in his mind and then what felt like a pop. He opened his mouth wide to relieve the pressure on his ears and maximized the new notification.

Ping!
You have learned the Ability Fade
Ability: *Fade*
Level: *1*
Class: *Observer*

Effect: *Lower the perception of anyone viewing you by 20%, making it difficult for them to remember you.*

Type: *AoE*

He repeated the process and incremented *Fade* to level two, which was easier, just like *Hey You* had been. He read the new notification and saw Fade now lowered the perception of others by 40%. Ruwen moved on to *Fabricate*. The symbol for *Fabricate* was all six Class symbols arranged in a circle. A minute later, his *Fabricate* was also level two. He looked at the final notification.

Ping!
You have learned the Ability Fabricate
Ability: *Fabricate*
Level: *2*
Class: *Observer*
Effect: *Alter the Name, Class, Subclass, and Attributes displayed to others.*
Type: *AoE*

Knowing this Ability needed more input, he opened his Ability tab and focused on *Fabricate*. The six Class symbols appeared, and he concentrated on the clasped hands of the Worker. More options appeared, and he filled them in with a few thoughts.

At his current level of *Fabricate*, he could only pick a Class and Subclass. He would need *Fabricate* level three to choose a Specialization. When Ruwen finished, he looked like he should for one day after Ascendancy, a level two Worker.

They reached the end of the hallway, which was nothing but a flat wall, and Ky turned to Ruwen.

"We'll use your chalk," Ky said.

Ruwen removed the Portal Chalk from his Void Band.

"The rules are simple. Draw the correct five gate runes, or

you'll likely die. If you leave a portal behind, always double check the runes before using it to make sure it hasn't been tampered with. Do you remember the sequence I drew in the library?"

Ruwen nodded.

"Good. Those gate runes will always bring you to the Blood Gate. Blapy will destroy this connection once we've passed. Go ahead."

Ky stepped away, and Ruwen quickly drew a rectangle. Carefully, he drew the five runes he'd memorized when Ky had drawn them in the library, and then put his Portal Chalk away.

Ky studied them and then nodded. "Good."

Sift shifted from foot to foot. "This seems like an unnecessary risk. Blapy opens a door for me when I'm feeding the Blood Moss. Wouldn't that be safer?"

"Shade's first rule: there is no safety," Ky said.

"Shade's first rule: risk is death's currency," Sift responded.

Ky nodded her head and placed a hand on Sift's shoulder. "That is an excellent rule." Then she shoved Sift hard, and the young man disappeared through the door.

"After you, kid," Ky said.

Ruwen took a deep breath and stepped through the stone. As he exited the portal, he tripped over Sift, who lay sprawled in front of the door. The Blood Moss cushioned his fall and crept up his body. His wrist with the mark grew cold, and the Blood Moss retreated. Ky came through and carefully stepped over the two of them.

Ky spoke as the two of them got to their feet. "Portals are complicated. Do you remember the one we came through?"

Ruwen looked around and realized the doors were no longer in the same order. It took him half a minute to find the door with the gate runes he'd memorized just after he'd arrived. He pointed at it.

"Good. Now if someone discovered our library portal and

destroyed it, the connection still exists, but the exit is now a little more...fluid," Ky said.

"What does that mean?" Ruwen asked.

"It means we should come out near the original portal, but not always. I once stepped through a portal into the ocean a mile from shore. Which is why I now hate sharks," Ky said.

Sift looked like he might be sick. "I can't swim."

Ruwen's stomach turned. "I can't either." Other terrible scenarios occurred to him. "What if they move your door somehow?"

"That happens more than you'd think." Ky started to count on her fingers. "I've stepped through into a prison cell, a blazing furnace, ambushes, a cliff face, a –"

Sift held up his hand. "I'm having second thoughts."

"The portals are a powerful tool, and that means they carry risk. Just be prepared," Ky said.

Ruwen remembered the six doors he'd found that were safe in the Blood Gate when he first arrived. "How many portals do you have open in here?"

"Excellent question. I use this room as a hub to travel quickly all over the continent," Ky said.

Which didn't answer Ruwen's question. A thought occurred to him, and he opened his map. The room appeared along with its three hundred plus doors. Now, however, around thirty of them had labels. When he concentrated on the door to the library, which read *Deepwell, Uru*, the label expanded and gave him five gate runes and the description "library basement, west conference room."

Powerful Mages could portal to different locations, but portals were rare, and their creation was time-consuming and expensive. To have a room like this was an incredible asset, and the list he'd been given had portals covering the entire continent. The thought of nearly instant travel to distant places was so mind-blowing that for a few seconds Ruwen couldn't do anything but stare at his map.

Ky flicked him on the forehead. "Stop that."

Ruwen stepped backward and rubbed his forehead. Behind Ky, he could see one of the blank doors.

"What are the doors without gate runes for?" Ruwen asked.

Ky rubbed her temples and did a poor job of keeping the irritation off her face. "They're to handle new connections, like when we created one from the library. Also, some places are so dangerous you don't want to risk a constant link. You'd use one of the blank doors to create a temporary portal. Blapy always keeps a few blank ones available."

"Hundreds of doors in here lead to instant death, and you're saying there are even more dangerous places?" Ruwen asked.

Ky nodded.

"Like where?" Ruwen asked.

She looked at the ceiling, muttered something about a muzzle, and then faced him. "Like one of the deities' realms."

"You can actually travel to a god's home?" Ruwen asked.

"No, mortals can't go there," Ky said and then looked down at Sift's waist where Io was sheathed. "Okay, once, but we were so quick it hardly counts. No, you can't tell them. I swear between you, Tremine, and the kid, I'm going to swallow a hisser and end it."

Ruwen started to ask another question, but Ky pointed a finger at him, her lips pressed together, and he snapped his mouth shut.

Something about the blank doors had caused his brain to itch. There was a connection he wasn't seeing. He unfocused his eyes and let his brain go blank, allowing it to sort through his memories. The itching was replaced by a swirling cold and –

"Hey!" Ky said as she clapped her hands.

Ruwen jumped and then focused on Ky, his thoughts scattering. "Sorry."

She lowered her hands. "You ready?" Ky asked, looking at Ruwen and then Sift.

Sift looked terrible and wiped the sweat off his forehead. "Maybe I should stay. Who is going to feed the Blood Moss or sweep the early levels? Blapy needs me."

Ruwen didn't know if Ky's portal horror stories had gotten into Sift's head or if the fear of leaving everything Sift had known had finally hit him. Either way, Ruwen felt sorry for his friend. Ruwen had only been here two days and already had mixed feelings about leaving. But to find his parents, he needed to return, and he wanted to make sure Hamma was okay.

"Hey, this is going to be fun. On the other side of that door is adventure and freedom and probably a warm welcome. It's going to be okay," Ruwen said.

"Probably not, actually," Ky said.

Ruwen looked at Ky. "You're not helping."

Ky looked up at the ceiling for a second. "Fine." She turned to Sift. "There is something you should know about Lylan..."

Then without finishing, she stepped through the portal to the library and was gone.

"What?" Sift almost screamed and jumped after Ky.

In the space of a heartbeat, Ruwen was alone.

"Hey," Blapy said.

Ruwen yelped and jumped to the side.

"Wow, you are nervous," Blapy said.

"You could really use some sort of announcement, like a gong or something."

Blapy tilted her head. "That is not such a bad idea." A gong sounded, and Ruwen covered his ears. The sound echoed in the room for a few seconds and then disappeared. His hearing still rang.

"A little loud," Ruwen said.

"I'll work on it. Anyway, my portal windows that replay memories got me to thinking."

"That can't be good."

"Depends on your perspective. But I made this," Blapy said and held up a thin silver ring with a grey pearl.

"What is it?" Ruwen asked.

"An experiment."

"Again, that doesn't sound good."

Blapy shrugged. "It will either work or it won't. But it shouldn't harm her."

"Harm who?" Ruwen said as he took the ring.

"Lylan," Blapy said and then disappeared.

Ruwen opened his notification and read the description.

Tring!
The Black Pyramid has gifted you...
Name: *Moonstone Ring of Remembrance*
Quality: *Epic*
Durability: *8 of 8*
Weight: *0.12 lbs.*
Effect (Passive): *+2 Charisma*
Effect (Triggered): *When worn by Shade Lylan of the Black Pyramid, memories of her time there will be restored.*
Restriction: *User must bear the mark of the Black Pyramid*
Description: *Some memories are worth keeping.*

Ruwen carefully placed the ring in his Void Band and then stepped through the stone portal.

CHAPTER 37

*R*uwen stepped into the back of the tapestry, which he pushed to the side. His clock read 5:17 in the morning. He'd been gone only about ten hours. Glancing around the room, he didn't see Hamma, and his shoulders slumped.

Sift stood to the side of Ruwen with a big grin.

"Lylan is coming," Sift said.

"What?" Ruwen asked.

"Ky sent for her. She'll be here in a few days," Sift said excitedly.

"You probably won't even see her. Also, she doesn't remember you, so don't do anything dumb," Ky said.

"That is great, Sift," Ruwen said, thinking about the ring in his inventory.

Ky faced the two of them. "If anyone asks, you slept at an inn near the east gate. Sift is your cousin from a mountain village, he's new to Deepwell, and working as a servant. The less talking you do, the better. Keep stories simple, vague, and provide one specific detail to make it seem real. Ask me where I was last night."

Ruwen and Sift looked at each other and then Ruwen spoke up. "Where were you last night?"

Ky spoke in a friendly voice that shocked Ruwen. "Oh, it was some dreadful place near East gate, and I barely slept a wink. The mattress must have been stuffed with rocks. Did you sleep well?"

Ruwen opened his mouth, realized he hadn't slept since his Cultivation incident, and his simple lie evaporated. Instead, he wondered if maybe he'd broken his brain Cultivating and he would soon die of sleep deprivation. He felt fine, though. Although –

Ky flicked Ruwen in the forehead. "Ugh, what did I do to deserve you two?"

"You only have yourself to bla..." Sift said and then trailed off as Ky glared at him.

Ky rubbed her face. "Always end with a question to force the focus away from yourself. Shade's first rule: the best lies are unspoken. Understand?"

Ruwen and Sift nodded.

Ky continued. "Deepwell has been alive all night. The Council tried to reject Big D's outing because of the attack yesterday. They claimed it wasn't safe. She argued there were no exemptions for safety in the original agreement and that if they didn't enforce the law, she would organize a recall based on the Council not doing its job."

"Who is Big D?" Sift asked.

"A formidable woman and not one we should cross lightly. Big D wants a better life for her Workers, and this trip is a way to destabilize the current power structure," Ky said.

"At my expense," Ruwen whispered.

"Everything is always at someone else's expense. Big D's point is that's usually a Worker," Ky said.

Which only made Ruwen feel worse. Guilt for looking down

at Workers his whole life swirled with his depression at being one. His chest tightened, and his throat constricted.

Ky flicked him in the forehead again. "Feel sorry for yourself later, this dagger has left the sheath. It actually might work in our favor. You'll be in plain sight, but also the lynchpin for hundreds of people. We can use you as bait to find those trying to kill you."

"Wait, what do you mean hundreds of people? The last two months couldn't have had more than a hundred people Ascend," Ruwen said.

Ky nodded. "Because of the attack, all the Academies are sending extra instructors to protect their students. The Council is making the best of a bad situation and sending at least fifty Enforcement Soldiers along as a show of how much they care. Then you have all the rich kids who will have extra protection in addition to their normal servants. It will be a circus."

"I agree with Ruwen. I don't understand why all this is necessary," Sift said.

"If you wanted to change my direction, which would be easier? Chasing Crickets or Gentle Rain?" Ky asked.

Sift replied immediately. "Chasing Crickets."

"Why?" Ky asked.

"Because you're already moving," Sift said.

"Exactly. That is what Big D is doing. She is getting things moving to make a change later easier."

Ruwen's map pulsed.

"Both of you open your maps," Ky said.

Ruwen opened his map and saw a new marker had appeared. It was an address not too far from the Workers' Lodge.

"Hamma is there," Ky said. "I don't want to leave her in Deepwell when you depart, so I've arranged for her to be part of the Order Class contingent. It was mostly Enforcement Officers, but they needed a few Priests in case anyone got injured. I made sure her name was included."

Ruwen's heart beat faster, and his cheeks flushed. "Thanks, Ky. That was nice of you."

"Nothing nice about it, kid. If we left her here, she'd be easier to capture and used as leverage against us. I don't want to risk it."

"Oh, well, I'm glad she's coming," Ruwen said.

"Really? You hide it so well," Ky said.

Sift laughed, and Ruwen glared at him.

"Pick her up on your way to meet Big D," Ky said.

"You're not coming with us?" Ruwen asked, unable to keep the fear out of his voice.

"I'm still working on mobilizing my people, and you'll be safe anyway. Guardians are still circling above the town. Naktos's followers will keep their distance until things settle back down. If we're lucky, they won't even realize you left, and you'll have a relaxing camping trip," Ky said.

"I'm excited to try camping," Sift said.

"You're sure it's safe?" Ruwen asked and then held up his hands. "I know there is no safety. But do you think we'll be fine on our own?"

"You are enabling all this, and plenty of people want you dead. But none of them know what you look like and they can't locate you by name anymore. By the time people discover those things, you'll be too surrounded for them to kill you. Can you think of anyone from Deepwell that wants to kill you?" Ky asked.

"No," Ruwen said.

"Then you shouldn't worry," Ky said. "Fade will protect you unless someone already knows you and is specifically searching for you."

Tremine walked into the room and smiled at Ruwen. "You survived!"

Ruwen returned the smile. "Barely."

But that reminded Ruwen that he'd reentered Uru's Protection area and his progress would have synched to the goddess now. Relief flooded him.

"Who's your friend?" Tremine asked.

"Servant," Ruwen said.

"Cousin," Sift said at the same time.

Ruwen and Sift looked at each other and then turned back to Tremine.

"Cousin from a village," Ruwen said.

"I'm a servant," Sift said at the same time.

Ruwen and Sift looked at each other again.

"Hopeless," Ky said, shaking her head. "This is Padda and Madda's boy. He calls himself Sift."

Tremine bowed to Sift. "It is an honor to meet you, Sift. My name is Tremine, and I'm the librarian here. Your parents are special people."

"You know my parents?" Sift asked.

"Yes, we worked together in my younger days. What a special day to meet their son," Tremine said.

"Enough jabbering, Tremine. At your age, you don't have much time left. You ready?" Ky asked.

Tremine bowed to Ky. "I am at your disposal, Mistress."

"You two idiots know what to do?" Ky asked.

"Pick up Hamma on our way to meet Big D at the Lodge," Ruwen said.

Ky nodded and then turned to Tremine. "Let's go old man."

Tremine waved at them as he and Ky left.

"I can't believe I'm actually here," Sift said.

Ruwen smiled, and some of his worries disappeared.

They left the library and headed toward Hamma. Sunrise was over an hour away, and they kept to the main roads where there was more light. The streets weren't busy, but there were far more people awake than usual. Occasionally, Ruwen heard the sound of a Guardian passing above them. It took them almost an hour, but they arrived at the address Ky had given them.

Ruwen knocked softly on the door, not wanting to wake up anyone in the neighboring houses. He was about to knock again when the door opened a crack, and Hamma peeked through. The door flew open, and Hamma stepped forward.

"I'm so glad –" Ruwen started.

Hamma slapped him.

"You can't just disappear!" Hamma shouted. "Do you know how worried I was? I came back, and everyone was gone. I thought you'd died!"

Ruwen stood speechless as his cheek burned. Hamma hugged him, but before he could hug her back, she stepped away.

"Is this what you meant by a warm welcome?" Sift asked.

Hamma put her hands on her hips and glared at Sift. "Who are you?"

"My cousin," Ruwen said.

"A servant," Sift said at the same time.

Ruwen and Sift looked at each other.

Hamma raised her eyebrows. "You two better work on that."

Hamma stepped out of the house and closed the door. She wore boots, pants, and the long white shirt of the Order Class priestess.

"Ky said to be ready to go," Hamma said. "Nice haircut by the way. You should try a barber who can see next time."

Ruwen's cheeks warmed, and he ran a hand over the hair he'd cut himself. He couldn't tell her about the Rod Spiders and their blood that turned hard as a rock. "I know."

Hamma smiled. "It's kind of cute."

Ruwen thought his face might burst into flames. He checked his map and marked the Workers' Lodge. It would be a fifteen-minute walk. That would put them there around 6:45, fifteen minutes earlier than Big D had told him. They started toward the Lodge, with Hamma between Ruwen and Sift.

"I'm sorry you thought I'd died," Ruwen said. "I would have told you sooner if I'd been able."

"Well, why didn't you? Ky had to do it," Hamma said.

Ruwen bit his lip. "Ky kind of stuck me in a safe house, too. I couldn't get out."

"Well, I guess that makes sense. I was just worried, and I hate being worried," Hamma said.

"It's good to see you," Ruwen said. "I'm glad you're coming along."

While many lights were on in the houses around them, there were very few people on the street. They encountered a young kid who immediately ran off when they saw him and a drunk looking for his house. In the distance, they could hear the activity at the Workers' Lodge, and the city grew brighter in that direction.

They were five minutes from the Workers' Lodge when Ruwen's *Keen Senses* triggered. He stopped his two friends. They were still in a residential area, and the street was decently lit, but the small courtyards and alleys around them provided plenty of darkness to hide.

"Something's wrong," Ruwen said.

"It is hard to sift in the open like this," Sift said.

"What's wrong?" Hamma asked.

Half a figure emerged from an alley thirty feet down the street. Ruwen activated *Magnify* and saw a grey vest on a light blue dress. He couldn't see the woman's face, but she raised her arm and pointed directly at Ruwen. She had a ring on every finger, each with a small glass bulb. Ruwen could see movement in the glass, and his stomach clenched.

Ruwen turned off *Magnify* and faced Sift. "We should turn around."

They all turned around but found three people pointing

crossbows at them. Their faces, as well as their names, were hidden, but Ruwen's perception worked well enough to get the basics. They were all Fighters, with levels ranging from fourteen to eighteen. There was no way they could survive a fight with them.

They turned back around. The woman in the dress was gone, but three more Fighters stood in her place, crossbows raised. They had their faces covered as well. The one in front was level twenty and held a black crossbow. Ruwen assumed it was the leader.

The leader spoke. "It isn't personal, son. It's just now isn't a safe time to leave the city. It would be better for everyone if you took a nap at the temple."

Hamma stepped forward and shouted. "I command you, in the name of Uru, and by the power invested in me as a servant of Order, to put down your weapons."

"Lower your voice, girl. We're only here for the Worker. There's no reason for anyone else to meet any harm. Just step away from him," the leader said.

"Sift, I'm going to deafen them, you get Hamma out of here," Ruwen whispered.

"I'm not going anywhere," Hamma said.

Hamma pointed to the sky and a beam of light shot from her finger. It reached a hundred feet into the air before arcing back down like a gigantic weeping willow. The entire area became brightly lit.

"She signaled Enforcement!" yelled a Fighter from behind them.

"Now," the leader shouted.

Three quick thuds struck Ruwen in the back, pushing him forward and making him stumble. His cloak's shield had triggered and blocked the bolts' damage. The three Fighters in front of him had fired as well, and before Ruwen could even react, Sift had dived in front of him.

Sift and Ruwen hit the ground together, and Ruwen looked down to see blood covering his chest. But it wasn't his. Sift had three crossbow bolts sticking out his chest. Ruwen got to his knees and laid Sift flat on the ground.

"We need to work on your reflexes. You are terribly slow," Sift mumbled.

"We will, we will," Ruwen said.

Hamma knelt across from Ruwen and laid her hands on Sift.

"How bad is it?" Ruwen asked.

Ruwen looked around, but the street was empty. The Fighters must have assumed him dead when he collapsed. Hamma's signal didn't give them the chance to confirm it.

Sift looked at Ruwen. "Tell Lylan I...even though...doesn't... remember"

Hamma looked up. "Something's not right. He has far more Health than his stats show. But it still won't be enough."

Ruwen didn't want to explain that right now. "Is it bad?"

Hamma nodded. "I just spent all my Mana healing him, but the bleeding will still kill him. I think those bolts were poisoned. He'll be in the temple basement soon."

But Sift wouldn't go to the temple basement to be reformed and given life again. He would be dead. Forever.

The End of Divine Apostasy Book 1

EPILOGUE

Uru sat in the grass, listening to the waves crash against the rocks below. Dark clouds ripped themselves from the horizon's grasp, and she wondered if it might rain. An emotion she hadn't felt in over a thousand years crawled through her chest.

Worry.

A loud gong sounded, but Uru remained focused on the distant storm.

Footsteps approached from behind her.

"That's new," Uru said without turning.

Blapy sat down next to Uru and crisscrossed her legs, resting the stuffed centipede in her lap.

"The gong? A suggestion I liked from a new acquaintance," Blapy said.

Uru smiled. "Anyone I know?"

Blapy laughed.

They were quiet as they watched the grey clouds roil and climb into the sky.

"Are you here on business? Did I break any rules?" Uru asked.

Blapy placed her hands on the ground behind her and leaned back. "Not business. You kept the letter, if not the spirit, of all the rules."

"Good. The time for breaking them is fast approaching, but I must not be the first."

"So, this is it?" Blapy asked.

Uru sighed. "Yes."

"I tried to kill him. Despite his terrible skills, he survived."

"He's special. More than anyone knows."

Blapy leaned forward and brushed the dirt from her hands. "I never really believed you. But now, seeing how long you've planned. You were telling the truth."

Uru nodded.

"I'm sorry. It's not like your kind to be honest," Blapy said.

"I know. Which is why all of this is necessary."

They looked out at the ocean for a while. The clouds had formed a massive storm, and it raged above the horizon. Lightning arced across the sky, and a few seconds later, the thunder reached them.

"I love this view," Blapy said.

"It's worth dying for," Uru whispered with a small smile.

Blapy hugged her centipede. "They are worried. He came to see me."

For the first time, Uru looked at Blapy. "Already?"

Blapy nodded. "They know your Champion entered the Pyramid, and they've all been watching me. The boy's Harvesting prompted the visit. I tried to keep it contained, but he was too strong. His reach escaped my influence, and Izac noticed. I feel a little bad lying to the boy about his terrifying strength. Thankfully I'd pointed him in a direction without cities, and no one died."

Uru placed a hand on Blapy's knee. "Thank you, Mira, that would have broken my heart."

"Of course, neither of us wants the innocent to suffer."

Uru nodded. "I should have anticipated that. There is always another detail."

The sea below turned from blue to grey as the clouds strangled the light.

"Does he know it was the boy?" Uru asked, her voice concerned.

"I don't think so. Everyone knows Harvesting is impossible for the Bonded. I told Izac I couldn't explain what happened, which is the truth."

Uru tilted her head. "What if they ask you about the lights?"

"What lights?" Blapy asked innocently.

"When they look through your logs, they'll see the anomaly in the library."

"No, not an anomaly, just a beginning. I turn off the lights, every night, at the exact same time now."

Uru raised her eyebrows.

"I need energy for my newest level. Lights are a waste," Blapy said.

Uru smiled. "But you don't play favorites."

"Certainly not. I hate you all, actually. Just some I hate a little less."

Uru nodded. "Well, it's good to know you're still following the rules. I'll know things are serious when you break them."

"I'll never break them," Blapy said.

Uru just nodded.

They sat in silence as the storm moved toward the shore. The wind whipped the grass, and the tree behind them creaked.

"It is good he found the book. I miscalculated his initial strength, and he'll need guidance sooner than I thought," Uru said.

"It will be chaos when they discover what you've accomplished."

"Worse, it will unite them against me. Izac will be nearly unstoppable."

"Nearly?" Blapy asked.

Uru smiled at the little girl. "Let's hope he's ready."

"Did you see the chickens?"

They both laughed, and the thunder above them echoed their amusement.

Uru wiped her eyes. "Well, he still has a little time."

Go to www.afkauthor.com to stay up-to-date on the Divine Apostasy.

APPENDIX

Item Quality/Inventory Color
Common/White
Uncommon/Brown
Fine/Green
Rare/Yellow
Special/Orange
Epic/Blue
Legendary/Purple

Metals
Bronze
Iron
Steel
Titanium
Obsidian
Terium

Class/Symbol/Color
Worker/Hands/Brown
Mage/Brain/Black

Observer/Eyes/Green
Order/Heart/White
Fighter/Body/Blue
Merchant/Mouth/Red

Money

Copper
Silver (100 Copper)
Gold (100 Silver)
Platinum (100 Gold)
Terium (100 Platinum)

Rank/Level

Novice/1-9
Initiate/10-19
Apprentice/20-29
Journeyman/30-39
Acolyte/40-49
Disciple/50-59
Expert/60-69
Adept/70-84
Master/85-99
Grand Master/100

Level Start/Experience/Level End

1/1000/2
2/3,000/3
3/6,000/4
4/10,000/5
5/15,000/6
6/21,000/7
7/28,000/8
8/36,000/9
9/45,000/10

10/55,000/11
11/66,000/12
12/78,000/13
13/91,000/14
14/105,000/15
15/120,000/16
16/136,000/17
17/153,000/18
18/171,000/19
19/190,000/20
20/210,000/21

.

.

.

97/4,753,000/98
98/4,851,000/99
99/4,950,000/100
100/5,050,000/101

ACKNOWLEDGMENTS

First, and most importantly, I want to thank **you**. Without someone to enjoy the story, much of the fun disappears. I understand some of the demands life places on your time, and I'm so thankful that you chose to spend some of it with this story. Truly and sincerely, thank you.

To follow my dreams, others made sacrifices, and my family bore the brunt of them. Thank you, Megan, for answering all my grammar questions and for sharing your own creative works, which inspire me. Zachary, my reluctant reader, thank you for spending hours talking through ideas with me. Our conversations always resulted in a better story. Nicole, my first and best reader. Your support has been unwavering and allowed me to push through hard times. I don't know where I'd be today if not for your steadfast belief in me. Thank you. Now all three of you, go clean your rooms!

Erika, time together can sometimes be hard to find, and it means the world to me that you never made me feel guilty for wanting to write. Some of my favorite writing memories are sitting with you in a coffee shop as you read a book, making my writing process a little less lonely. Thank you.

Jason, you have been with me since the start. You have always encouraged me and listened patiently to my problems (about writing and life!). You are my best friend and make me want to be a better person. Your instinct for story is always spot on. As a friend and a writer, I am truly blessed to know you. Thank you.

Coral and Samantha, I am so thankful to have you in my life. You both act as touchstones and enrich my life with your amazing writing and personalities. Thank you both so much for all the extra drafts you've read and advice you've given. I am a better writer and person for knowing you both. Go, Trinity!

My critique group has made a huge difference in my writing. I resisted joining one for too long. Kellye, Lisa, and Oz, you are all such fantastic writers and provide me each month with insightful feedback. Joining your group was one of the best decisions I made. Thank you for all your help.

Bret, I wish I could see you more. Your productivity and eclectic creativity is an inspiration to me. Your students are so blessed to have you in their lives. You are genuinely terrific, and people like you are so rare. Thank you for being part of my life and being a great example to me.

Samuel, you were a surprise addition to the beta team. But your enthusiasm and insightful comments made this project better. Thank you for your help.

Mom, my first clear memory of positive feedback about my writing came from you. I might not remember what I had for breakfast, but that moment is scorched into my brain. It was the beginning of a dream that didn't come into focus for decades, but like so much in my life, none of it would have been possible without you. Thank you.

Dad, thanks for being an example, good and bad. You helped shape me into what I am today. I am a better Father and Husband because of you. You wouldn't have understood this book, but you would have supported me. I miss you.

AUTHOR'S NOTE

Four years ago, I signed with a literary agent, and I thought my dreams had come true. Instead, I learned new ways to hate my writing and smother my creativity. Calling those years a mistake would be untrue, but they clearly halted my progress as an author. Earlier this year, we parted ways, and this book is the result. A work of pure love. As much happiness as this book brings me, it makes me sad that it took so long to be born. I can hear Kysandra in my head right now, *Shade's First Rule: dreams should be chased, never caught.*

In a sense, I feel like I've finally Ascended, crawling my way out of Hamma's temple vat. I've taken a hit to my stats, but I've been given a second chance. I hope you like what I've done with it. This story is epic, but it's only worth telling if others join me on the journey.

Sincerely and truly, I appreciate you taking the time to read this story.

Shade's First Rule: move fast alone, travel far together.

Let's go far.

LITRPG LINKS

Join these great LitRPG groups to discuss your favorite books with other readers and learn about new releases and promotions.

LitRPG Society
www.facebook.com/groups/LitRPGsociety

LitRPG Books
www.facebook.com/groups/LitRPG.books

LitRPG Forum
www.facebook.com/groups/litrpgforum

LitRPG Releases
www.facebook.com/groups/LitRPGReleases

LITRPG FACEBOOK GROUP

To learn more about LitRPG, talk to authors including myself, and just have an awesome time, please join the LitRPG Group.

Made in United States
Troutdale, OR
04/11/2024

19095618R00268